Praise for John Brady's
MATT MINOGUE series:

Islandbridge GLOBE AND MAIL TOP 100

SHORTLISTED FOR THE 2006 DASHIEL HAMMETT PRIZE
A GLOBE AND MAIL BEST BOOK OF THE YEAR

"Particularly powerful stuff...genius." – TORONTO STAR

Wonderland GLOBE AND MAIL TOP 100

"IF THERE ARE AUTHORS BETTER THAN JOHN BRADY at
chronicling the events of modern Ireland, I HAVEN'T YET READ
THEM . . . Brady's best so far." – GLOBE AND MAIL

"ANOTHER SUPERB NOVEL BY A WRITER OF INTERNATIONAL
STATURE." – TORONTO STAR

"BRADY'S BEST: informed, subtle and intelligent, with Minogue
revealing a hitherto unseen depth of soul, humour and emotion."
– THE TIMES UK

A Carra King GLOBE AND MAIL TOP 100

"DENSE AND MULTILAYERED . . . a treasure of a crime novel."
– TORONTO STAR

"Brady has a great eye for the telling detail . . . and a lovely slow pace
of storytelling. There's much talk and thought about events and you
can't read this book at warp speed. Instead, save it to savour."
– GLOBE AND MAIL

All Souls

"As lyrical and elegantly styled as the last three . . . A FIRST-RATE
STORY WITH MARVELLOUS CHARACTERS . . . Another masterful
tale from a superior author." – GLOBE AND MAIL

"Nothing gets in the way of pace, narrative thrust or intricate
story-telling." – IRISH TIMES

"A KNOCKOUT." – KIRKUS REVIEWS

Kaddish in Dublin

"MATT MINOGUE, THE MAGNETIC CENTRE OF THIS SUPERB SERIES . . . and Brady's tone of battered lyricism are the music which keep drawing us back to this haunting series." – NEW YORK TIMES

"Culchie Colombo with a liberal and urbane heart . . . like all the best detective stories it casts its net widely over its setting . . . [Minogue is] a character who should run and run." – IRISH TIMES

Unholy Ground

"RIVETING . . . The suspense builds to barely bearable intensity . . . crackles with pungent Irish idiom and its vignettes of the country's everyday life." – TORONTO STAR

"Excellent Sergeant Matt Minogue . . . MARVELLOUS DIALOGUE, as nearly surreal as a Magritte postcard the sergeant likes, and a twisting treacherous tale." – SUNDAY TIMES

A Stone of the Heart

"Towers above the mystery category as AN ELOQUENT, COMPELLING NOVEL . . . a tragic drama involving many characters, each so skillfully realized that one virtually sees and hears them in this extraordinary novel . . ." – PUBLISHERS WEEKLY

"A MASTERFULLY CRAFTED WORK of plot, atmosphere and especially characterization . . . Minogue, thoughtful, clear-eyed and perhaps too sensitive . . . is a full-blooded character built for the long haul of a series . . ." – MACLEAN'S

The Good Life

"Brilliant Craftsmanship." – LIBRARY JOURNAL

"Brady's dead-on ear for dialogue and his knack for creating instantly engaging characters keep the pages flipping...one line of prose leads inexorably, compulsively to the next..." – QUILL & QUIRE

"Brady, like Chandler, has a poet's eye for place...(he) is emerging as one of the supreme storytellers of Canadian crime fictions." – GLOBE AND MAIL

Published in Canada in 2008 by
McArthur & Company
322 King Street West, Suite 402
Toronto, ON M5V 1J2

Library and Archives Canada Cataloguing in Publication

Brady, John, 1955-
The Going Rate / John Brady.

ISBN 978-1-55278-739-7

I. Title.

PS8553.R245G59 2008   C813'.54   C2008-903476-7

Cover, Image & Composition by *Mad Dog Design*
Printed in Canada by Webcom

The publisher would like to acknowledge the financial support of the
Government of Canada through the Book Publishing Industry
Development Program (BPIDP) and the Canada Council for our publishing
activities. The publisher further wishes to acknowledge the financial
support of the Ontario Arts Council for our publishing program.

10 9 8 7 6 5 4 3 2 1

JOHN BRADY

The Going Rate

A MATT MINOGUE MYSTERY

McArthur & Company
Toronto

Nel mezzo del cammin di nostra vita
mi ritrovai per una selva oscura
ché la via diritta era smarrita
— DANTE

For Hanna,
Strength and love; trust and patience.

Chapter 1

Darren Mulhall's last day would be short.

THE DAYLIGHT PART BEGAN with his awakening to the sound of a door chime. Pieces soon began to fall into place. He was in Martin's house, in Martin's bed. Martin's wife Bernie was no longer beside him, however.

He remembered vodka, and lager, and a bit of hash that Bernie had found in one of Martin's toolboxes after his arrest. It was gone three o'clock when he had finished with Bernie. They had done pretty well everything. He remembered her complaining she didn't want to do it anymore. Well, that only egged him on, and sore or not, she looked happy enough with the proceedings. Of course she could have been faking it. Big surprise, there. It wouldn't be the first time, would it, and she was a bit afraid of him, after all. He didn't mind that one bit.

His mouth was cracked and furry, and his eyes felt like they had been shoved back hard into his head. He rubbed the hardened goop from the edges of his eyes, and he tried to swallow. There was light on the curtains. He found the alarm: nearly ten o'clock? Jesus. He lay still, listening. There were footsteps coming up the stairs now. He kicked away the sheet and the eiderdown. The chill air washed over him, and he rolled sideways to reach under the bed for the pistol. He was on his feet when Bernadette came in the door. She was breathing hard. She wasn't even trying to hold her dressing gown closed. Her mouth hung open and for several moments she stood still, her chest

1

heaving so much the shadow between her breasts seemed to have a life of its own.

"I don't know," she whispered. "Gas company? On a Good Friday?"

He kept up his stare, waiting for a giveaway sign.

"What're you looking at me like that for? I didn't call them, did I."

The redness around her mouth and neck from last night seemed to be getting even deeper.

The doorbell's ring was ten times louder this time.

"Gas company," came a Dublin accent. "Anybody home here?"

Mulhall picked up his underpants and jeans on his way to the window. He got his second leg in as he inched the curtain away from the wall. The white van out on the road was open, and there were tools and pipes on the bed of it. An average looking joe in overalls was setting up a workmate by the curb.

"I don't know anything about this, Darren–"

"Shut up a minute, will you."

He realized that he was shaking, and that she could see it.

"They look okay," she said. "Don't they?"

"I'll decide that," he said.

He put the pistol on the bed, and leaned his back against the wall while he pulled on his jeans. A cool head, and a dry pants, he thought. Overreacting was the worst thing to do.

"Give me me Nikes there. No – no socks."

His T-shirt was on the chest of drawers.

"Me phone," he said. "Were you using it?"

She shook her head, but her eyes stayed on the pistol.

"No, no. I don't think I did."

"Go back downstairs. Tell him you're coming."

She seemed paralyzed. Her eyes moved from the pistol and back to him. He swore and shoved her toward the door. He tried to keep in step with her as she descended the stairs, whispering.

"Tell him you're coming, I said."

She pulled at the belt of her dressing gown, losing one end. He laid his arm on her shoulder, with the pistol pointed at the hall door. He felt her start when she saw it.

"Jesus, Darren, what's the need of that?"

Her voice was strained with the panic.

"Just keep going, will you."

He looked down the hallway. Martin had set up an escape route when they moved in here three or four years ago, and one night last summer he had shown Mulhall the setup, his master plan of getting out in a hurry. Three steps out the door to the garage – Martin had never used it as a garage but as a workshop, where he kept all his tools in perfect nick – and a couple of steps to the workbench. Then, up to the window he had put in three-quarters the way up the wall and Bob's your uncle: you were in the neighbour's. He had even timed himself taking a few gos at it, he had told Mulhall with pride.

Mulhall had been careful not to scoff at Martin's meticulousness. Martin was such an iijit. His whole Mission Impossible type of approach made the others slag him mercilessly. Even Murph, who took the gold for being the most complete iijit in the known world, knew that Martin was an iijit. But everyone had still depended on Martin for the welding and the locksmithing.

Even if Martin was no mastermind, he'd had a good run. He was always careful and modest in his work. It was only bad luck that a cop car was passing that petrol station that night. Though Martin would never admit it, Mulhall was certain that he had only started into his own line of robbing because of Bernie, with her shopping and her holidays and her decorating shite.

Mulhall's tact had earned him Martin's trust. It was to Mulhall that the same Martin had turned after his sentencing. Could Mulhall look in on things while he was inside, could he keep an eye on things? Murph could barely look after himself, not to mind someone else. Bernie needed minding sometimes, Martin told him. She wasn't always on the ball: she didn't have much confidence. He should make himself at home, naturally. Did that include drinking Martin's vodka, Mulhall had wondered daily since he had come here last week to lay low. And did the make-yourself-at-home bit cover riding Bernadette twice a day until they were pouring sweat and aching?

Mulhall tiptoed around her as she took the last step down, and he turned toward the kitchen. He heard the man at the door whistling softly to himself, his blue overalls visible even through the frosted glass of the hall door. He kept Bernadette in front of him, ignoring the shudders that had begun to seize at her.

"Stand there," he whispered. "Right there, where he can see you're there."

"Why are you doing this? Christ, stop pushing me, will you."

He tugged on her shoulder.

"Here," he hissed. "Count up to ten– No! In your head!"

He pulled the collapsed back of his Air Max up over his heel, swore at the sharp pain as his finger was squeezed, and then he opened the door out to the garage. His nostrils filled with the comforting smell of oil and old grass from the lawn-mower. The door swung shut silently behind him: Martin's work again, he was sure.

Sure enough, in three steps, Mulhall was on the bench, stooped, and pulling the bar release from the window. The neighbours' garden wasn't a garden at all: it was more of a dump. Maybe it had started as storage, all the lengths of warped timber and the pieces of ruined particleboard, the cement blocks, and three or four disemboweled lawnmowers. But like Martin had pointed out, the neighbours had let the fence fall apart just like everything else of theirs, and there was a clear run to the lane. Lifting the window, he rolled into the opening. He dropped onto a soggy patch of last year's leaves that were already almost covered by new grass.

He stayed in a crouch, staring at a deflated soccer ball, and listened. There was nothing out of the ordinary. A face appeared at the kitchen window, an unshaven man, drawing on a ciga-rette. It was Martin's neighbour, Mr. Depressed, Mr. Alco. Mulhall gave him the nod, and then he skipped toward the stack of cement blocks. He threw his leg over the wall, gasping as he felt it tear through the denim at his skin. He straddled the wall carefully for several moments before swinging the other leg behind it.

The laneway was graffiti world of course, with all the usual half-arsed, jerry-built cement block sheds and old corrugated iron, and plenty of barbed wire. Dear Old Dublin. Again he listened. The scrapes on his thighs began to burn. The cold morning air had made his hangover vanish. Movement to his right broke his gaze from the glints of light that the broken glass in the laneway. A pudgy man was stepping away from the wall of the laneway ahead, his green safety vest and yellow hard hat almost glowing now in the spring light.

Mulhall teetered between annoyance and relief: so it was the gas company, after all.

"Howiya," he called out, warily. He was frowning now, his eyes straying to the pistol in Mulhall's hand.

A bit late to be trying to hide it now, Mulhall decided. He waited for fleeting eye contact, and then the man quickly looked down at his feet.

"Howiya yourself," Mulhall said. "Get to work, why don't you, you fat gobshite. And not be annoying people this early in the day."

Well that was settled, then. More relieved than he was sore, or even angry, Mulhall strode down the lane, mapping out in his mind the entry of the laneway onto Ossory Road. He'd cross there, and head somewhere where he could lie low. The dumpsters behind the shops there would do for a short while, or even an old garden shed in one of the houses there. Then, back to Bernie, get some stuff and clear off. Mr. Gas Man down the lane was hardly going to keep his trap shut about seeing a fella with a gun, was he. Mulhall could hardly blame him.

The weight of the pistol dragging on his arm with each stride came to his attention. The laneway was covered in damp patches, with clumps of mashed cardboard every now and then. It felt greasy underfoot. God, but he must look totally stupid, he thought, like a schoolkid holding his mickey and going up to the teacher to get permission to go to the toilet.

He thought for a moment of Bernie, and suspicion flashed across his mind. It didn't last. Bernie, if it were possible, was even thicker than Martin. He slowed, and the anger returned. This was what he was reduced to, hanging with the likes of Murph, and Martin, and Martin's retarded missus? Something had to give here, he murmured. Maybe it was time to do the thing, make his move.

He had saved the copper's number in his mobile under the name "Paddy," and he had added two digits to each number in case anyone ever snooped through his numbers there. Molloy – no: Tommy Malone. It was Murph told him about Malone, warned him about him. Malone was a Dub, and he was smart. He knew the score in Dublin nowadays, with everyone paranoid and jumpy, and looking for a place to hide, or an escape hatch from this dump of a city. Malone was doing what coppers always did, putting out feelers, trying to get fellas to grass on the higher-ups.

But according to Murph, Malone talked serious money. He hinted that he could even deliver the whole package, even a new identity. According to Murph anyway: as far as that went. He didn't believe Murph on the last part, but money could sort a lot of issues.

This was the end of the lane ahead. He slowed, his chest pumping in the cold air and his own hot, rank breath coming back over his face. It was definitely the lie-low-and-wait option.

There was a car up ahead, not moving. Green, older Jap car: a Corolla? Someone was standing behind its half-opened driver's door, a man in a leather jacket. He had noticed Mulhall too. He did not seem in the least bit put-out to be seeing a man in a T-shirt on a cold spring morning, holding something the shape of a gun.

Mulhall stopped, undecided. There was a faint smell of aftershave, or cologne or something expensive. In this laneway, here in this kip, on a lousy damp cold Dublin morning? Hallucinating, that's what it must be surely.

But it was too quiet here. It'd have to be back the other way, he decided, over the walls and off through the gardens. He picked a cement block wall a half-dozen houses away and headed for it at a jog.

Then there was a door opening into the alley to his right, a figure emerging as he ran by. He did not slow, but he took the pistol out, and broke into a sprint instead, weaving from side to side. There were other footsteps running behind him now, almost matching his own. Turning to cast a quick glance over his shoulder he saw flashes, and he felt himself being punched over against a wall.

He was able to squeeze the trigger once but then his arm fell as did everything else, sideways and buckling. He heard his own knees hit the cement, and the skin tearing as his momentum carried him scraping along the laneway.

He came to a stop, and felt his chest rising and falling on the slimy, cold cement. This new sideways world was way too bright. He'd need to lie here a few moments only, until he could figure out if he had broken something. Slowly, he flexed his fingers. The pistol was gone somewhere.

There were footsteps on the cement nearby, soft shoes at a walk.

Mulhall wanted to shout, but the voice that came out was a whisper.

"Hey," it said.

He wasn't sure if he had actually spoken the words.

"Why did you do that?"

It was his own voice. His chin and his cheeks were scraping the cement.

"Who are you?"

Someone was breathing hard nearby.

"Ma?" Mulhall said then. "Jesus, Ma. I'm having a terrible dream."

There was a ticklish movement around his cheek, and something red flowed by his chin. A car started nearby but the noise soon died away. This is a concussion, he decided. He must have slipped or something.

"Going to wake up now," he said, or thought.

He was being rolled over. The sky was blinding him.

He couldn't focus his eyes. A shape moved dimly not far above him. He heard the strained breathing again, breathing out the nose. A black spot appeared between him and the shape above, wavering slightly, and Mulhall had a moment to conclude that it was the barrel of a gun.

Chapter 2

GOOD FRIDAY CAME AND WENT, and in its wake the Easter. A freakishly warm holiday Monday drew Minogue into the garden, and there he worked fitfully at rehabilitating the rockery. It was a yearly ritual now. That was how he missed the phone call with the news that the Commissioner's wife had died.

He replayed the message twice to be sure he had the funeral details right. When Kathleen came home, he waited until she was settled before telling her the news. She was more upset than he had expected. After a while, he brought out two kitchen chairs, and then two tumblers of Jamesons to the patch of grass that was now home to a dozen or more large, marooned rocks.

The sun made an unexpected appearance, taking the edge off the cool air, and turning the scruffy spring growth a bright green while it incited more noise from the birds gadding about unseen in the undergrowth.

The whiskey was quickly downed. Kathleen and he sat together for the better part of a half-hour, adrift in the smells of torn earth, the stirring leaves and grass, and the birds' unceasing bustle. Every now and then Kathleen recounted things that Rachel Tynan, artist and teacher, had done in the recent past.

Minogue did not tell her that it had been only a fortnight ago that he had spotted Rachel Tynan and her husband on Dunlaoghaire Pier. She had been pale and thin, and she moved haltingly along arm-in-arm beside him. Minogue had not wanted them to see him, and a gap in the sea wall let him escape. His excuses – it was dusk and they wouldn't have spotted him, they needed no interruptions – had crumbled long before he had gotten home, but the shame of his evasion stayed with him.

Wednesday was a long time coming, but by nine o' clock that morning, Minogue was backing out of the garage in his new Peugeot, listening for squeaks from the chassis as it rolled down to the gate. He was trying not to be impatient, but he was losing. The collar on his new shirt chafed. He just couldn't find a decent driving position in his new car, and he was bewildered as to how he had missed this on the test drive. And now, Kilmartin, the very one who had guilted him into taking him along to the funeral, was late.

At least he had time for a re-read of the file he had been hurriedly handed yesterday afternoon.

Tadeusz Klos, a twenty-three-year-old Polish national, had arrived in Ireland five days before the assault that ended in his death. Klos had been beaten and stomped into a coma a stone's throw from the Custom House, in the centre of the city. The considerable amount of blood that he had left on the footpath behind him was quickly determined by the State Pathologist to have been cranial in origin. The report did not mention that it would have been thickly mixed with that night's rain into something that Minogue knew would be as greasy as it would be acidic from the roadway to where it had flowed. Klos was resuscitated twice in the ambulance. He died about a mile short of the hospital entrance.

The briefing file contained a copy of a passport photo and four photos taken in the hospital. Three of the four haunted Minogue much of the evening and early morning. It took a lot to crush a man's skull with kicks.

The matter was being handled by a crew from Fitzgibbon Street Garda station, and they were going full tilt at it. Already there were copies of emails in Polish, complete with literal, often clumsy, translations. The inventory of effects from Klos' room at the hostel offered little. His wallet was missing, but no one had tried to use his bankcard since the assault.

There were no arrests as of last night. Nor were there suspects.

Mr. Klos had a mother, but no siblings. His parents had separated when he was a child. His father had minor convictions from a decade back. He had not had a close relationship with his son, or his former wife. There was a matter of alcohol abuse in the father's history.

Klos had what looked like a post-secondary certificate of some kind to do with tourism. He smoked roll-your-owns. There were no indications of drugs on his person or in his belongings. In his pockets were clippings from a Polish newspaper published in Dublin. Along with those items were scribbled notes including phone numbers of restaurants and hotels and an immigrant aid office on Church Street, and several Dublin City bus tickets. There were remnants of potato chips in his pockets, foil from bars of chocolate, matches. An optimist apparently, Mr. Klos also carried three condoms.

An iPod type of thing was found at the scene, in several pieces. A note from the Technical Bureau declared that its flash memory could not be read, as it had been trodden on. Minogue surmised that this deed would have been close to the moments when Klos' white earphone wire had been pulled up through his jacket and lodged in his zipper, peeling the plastic back to the bare wire.

The file made no mention of friends and associates, Polish or otherwise, in Dublin. Klos' mobile phone, an unlocked Nokia he'd brought with him from Poland, with an Irish SIM card, had not been found. There was one page to the mobile phone records. He had made two brief calls to his mother, seven to the hostel where he was staying, four to restaurants. Two restaurant managers deposed that Klos' English was spotty. One thought he "had issues." Meaning? "Wouldn't look me in the eye... shifty impression..."

Minogue had already read the copies of statements from people in the hostel several times, in full. One mentioned the Internet café where Klos had visited, and a reference to Skype, an MSN account, Hotmail. No-one knew Klos' passwords. A search of the routine online jungle – MySpace, Bebo and FaceBook – came up dry. Googling Klos' name returned four hits, all relating to Polish sites and sources, but only one relating to him, or rather his email address.

This was Minogue's fourth re-read of the files on Klos. In spite of their efforts, the team was getting nowhere. His gaze slid from the pages and over the dashboard to the passenger seat. The bit of sun yesterday had really awakened the new-car smell again. Kathleen had told him that the new-car smell was very toxic. She didn't mean to take the good out of it, she reminded him.

Peter Igoe, the Chief Super for Minogue's department, had floated into the office yesterday afternoon with this file under his arm, and a tight smile that Minogue knew right away meant trouble.

Igoe wasn't above flattery. While going over what was needed of Minogue in this afternoon's meeting concerning Klos, he made much of Minogue's past expertise in the Murder Squad. The Poles needed to leave that meeting knowing that the Gardai were putting everything they had into the investigation.

Naturally, Minogue wouldn't be called upon to give any detailed answers specific to the case. The case detectives would do that, with the Technical Bureau to back them up. The optics needed to be sharp, Igoe had said. Telephone calls had been made between governments. Minogue already knew that the newspapers in Poland had fairly leaped on the matter.

PR, in other words, Minogue muttered that evening when Kathleen asked why he seemed so cross-grained. He should be flattered to be invited, was her retort; another feather in his cap et cetera.

Minogue had to let that go by. Since his posting to the International Liaison Unit at HQ in the Phoenix Park, his wife's proud conviction had been unshakeable: her husband finally had a proper nine-to-five. He should be delighted to be out of the pressure-cooker that had been Jim Kilmartin's fabled Murder Squad, now decorously disbanded two years ago.

So now with the guidance of the Aspergian Sergeant Áine Collins in the Europol National Unit, Minogue was learning how to process Analytic Work Files. He worked with coppers from London and Spain, and another from Austria, a gateway for Eastern European crime. The dubious excitement of a month on the Offshore Financial Centres section awaited. He had taken to making up his own acronyms from those initials for the OFC.

So far on his way through the unit, Minogue's training had taken in matters that Kathleen believed were very exciting. There were counterfeit designer goods coming in from China to figure out. A Croatian immigrant making good money as a window-washer had three passports. The case of three Nigerian brothers who preyed on West African refugees with a mixture of witchcraft, intimidation, and extortion was still dragging through the system. The twenty-first century...?

Minogue powered down the window, pausing and reversing it twice to test it. It was quicker than he liked, but there was no slack. He looked down to the files again. He might as well practise pronouncing names. Klos, like close. Tad-eh-oosh.

Another name he had to know was that of the middling bigwig from the Polish Embassy, an attaché named Juraksaitis, who would be accompanying Mrs. Klos. Juraksaitis was to be pronounced like You're Excited.

A diesel clanking announced Kilmartin's arrival. Minogue watched him in the mirror as he reversed a battered and sagging farm Jetta he had borrowed from his brother, to the curb behind. There was some difficulty to locking the door. Kilmartin put his overcoat on the back seat next to Minogue's funeral gabardine and he sat in.

Chapter 3

DERMOT FANNING'S BIKE had a puncture. It was the same wheel as last week's. It might even be the same puncture.

He leaned the bike back against the wall and he resolved to be calm about it. There were basically two possibilities: a) a fresh puncture, b) he hadn't mended the last one right. It was likely b), he decided. It was all too easy to pinch the tube during a repair, enough to cause a slow puncture.

But the truth was, there was a c). He could have bought a new tube and a new tire as well. This he had refused to do, citing to Bríd the outrageous prices of same. This wasn't news, of course.

Bríd, his wife, needed the car: a teacher couldn't be late. Their daughter Aisling had still said that she liked going to the child-minder's on Dadda's bike anyway. That had changed lately, when she had become very clingy with Bríd in the mornings. Tears, haste, annoyance, guilt. Repeated several times daily. Were there Terrible Three And A Halve's?

Fanning didn't like to think that Aisling had picked up on something between himself and Bríd. He felt sure that Bríd had been on the brink of asking him why exactly Aisling had to go to a child-minder's all day. It was understood that he needed time to himself for his writing and the freedom to think – or not think.

He checked the windows around the house again. Then he

set the alarm, pulled the door behind him, and he locked it. It was only a quarter to ten, so he had plenty of time yet to get into town, and up to that restaurant in Smithfield. Even if he were a few minutes late, it wouldn't be the end of the world to keep Breen, Colm Breen, Irish film's mover and shaker, waiting for once. And whether Breen liked to be reminded or not, he and Dermot Fanning went back a long, long way. Breen had been the gawky newcomer in the Film Society then, and Fanning the third-year student running the meetings.

Breen had become master of the schmooze, his country accent massaged to mid-Atlantic over the intervening years. To be fair, he had always made time for Fanning, and as much as it had angered Fanning over the years, Breen's praise had also buoyed him.

But it was no time to think of the past now. This was business, networking, something he had neglected for far too long, and realized its costs only lately.

Some things were working his way, Fanning saw then, as the 62 bus appeared at the bend. He stayed downstairs after he got on, at the back of the bus, and took out his notebook. He thought about the points he wanted to leave Breen with, the three key things he'd remember. It took only a few moments of this for Fanning's mind to turn to what was coming up later after the schmooze with Breen, however. The field trip – he had described it to Bríd. He had fudged it for her benefit though. A dog fight would horrify her, freak her out completely. Her husband attending one would be even worse.

As the bus carved its way through the lighter post–rush-hour traffic, Fanning's spirits lifted. He was raring to go on this script, and he was so close now. Nobody had yet treated Dublin crime the way it should be treated, as social commentary, as critique – as family drama. Breen would get it, probably. But if he didn't, well there were others outside of Ireland. The Sopranos would look like summer school compared to what he would be coming up with. He'd have a draft by the summer for sure. Then it'd be summer holidays for Bríd, and they'd have the summer of their lives, the three of them.

The bus shuddered to a sudden halt by a zebra crossing. A black woman waited uncertainly by the curb, her hands on a buggy laden with at least two children that Fanning could see. A car horn sounded somewhere, then another. People were so impatient, Fanning reflected. He heard the driver say something that had an exasperated tone to it. Then he too hit the horn. With a stricken smile, the woman pulled the buggy back, and shook her head.

Fanning's thoughts went to Aisling. After dinner he'd bring her out in the buggy. Bríd could decompress, have her bath, a cup of tea on her own. Actually, he might even take Aisling over to Bríd's Ma and Da in the car. Ah, no. What was he thinking? It was not casual anymore. Danny, the Da, was okay, but the Ma was a different kettle of fish. Maybe it was just her age, but she was definitely going over to the dark side this last while.

Time was she was almost fawning over him. He'd heard she talked about him as her son-in-law, very well respected as a writer, you know. Fanning could see her trying not to be annoyed at him this past while, however. It was the little things gave her away. A look, a pause, the way she spoke slowly; the subjects she avoided, and the ones she went to too often. Her favourite in that area was loaded, of course: "God the changes we've seen in our own lifetime! My oh my, all the jobs and the opportunities out there nowadays."

Fanning was first off the bus. He legged it up the quays smartly, not at all displeased with the dank, colder air coming at him over the parapet of the River Liffey. His Dublin had always been shabby and smelly, and real. That Dublin was still there if you knew where to look. Fanning had never had time for any nostalgia about Good Old Dublin. The new restaurants and apartments being steadily inserted into parts of the city centre areas that had been no-go areas were welcome. Sometimes, though, their sudden arrivals gave Fanning a feeling of bafflement, and even dismay. Still, he was careful not to fall in range of the running joke in Dublin for at least a decade now: "When did that place go up?"

Fanning was entering Smithfield sooner than he had expected, and within minutes of leaving the quays he was turning the corner in sight of the restaurant. There was Breen in the window, and as per caricature, he was on his mobile. Fanning stepped back, and he took up a spot next to a delivery van. No way would he be caught sitting meekly and waiting for Breen's phone conversation to end. He'd watch the performance instead.

He could have predicted Breen's smiles and shrugs, and the fake, rolling laugh that he retailed. Scene Two would roll out just as predictably. That was when Breen would wear that that put-upon look, the smile of regret that he excelled in. It would be followed up with an apology for being "so busy."

The hardest bit to take would be Breen's attempt to be the common man, a hapless beleaguered gobshite, sighing that he was "running around like a fart in a bottle," or he "didn't know whether he was coming or going." Then, Breen's twinkling eyes would almost disappear when he put out his fake smile. Fanning wondered if anyone had ever told Breen how fat he was getting these past few years, how … fulsome was the word, Fanning thought then, the exact word. He was pleased the word came to him so easily.

Fanning didn't mind Breen's act itself as a piece, say, of theatre. After all, Breen the impressario was a character study in his own right. He would soon find his way into a Dermot Fanning script soon enough. But the sting in it all was that Breen assumed that Dermot Fanning was stupid enough to be taken in by it all.

Fanning felt the injustice glow stronger in his chest, and so he distracted himself by beginning a careful, neutral study of the buildings around him. More than their lines or even shapes, he observed their textures and shadows and tones, all the things that escaped day-to-day notice. Behind the crane swivelling slowly overhead somewhere near Capel Street were light-grey clouds, like a cannonade from some long-ago naval battle. The sky to the south was parchment – no: pearl.

The cobblestone lane was new. The old one had been torn up last year and had been meticulously replaced. Brickwork had been re-pointed, pipes proudly exposed. Copies of recently dis-covered daguerrotypes of Dublin from the 1840s and 1850s had been placed in salient windows of the restaurant.

Sa Bhaile – My Place. Staff would speak Gaelic if requested, was the boast, or the "brand," but diners could expect a savvy, cool dining experience in what had been a livery, a storehouse, a bicycle factory, and then lain abandoned for decades, and was now a backdrop for celebrity snapshots. The lettering on the restaurant sign was harsh modern, doubtless intended as a statement to that effect.

But he really should be thinking about his pitch, the three points, and no more. Three was a natural number for people to remember, a trinity, just like the old Irish proverbs. Breen sure as hell wasn't one to take notes. He didn't have to. The higher up in the firmament you were, the more causal things seemed to be. A whim, a mood, a coincidence, pure luck: they were the reigning deities in the world of film. The true talent had never been the actual writing.

Fanning had been to book launches here. No-one he had met those times seemed to be interested in the fact that ten years ago this area was where you'd come to fence stuff, to rent a gun, to buy heroin.

Oh oh: Breen had spotted him. He held up his hand, his fingers spread, and then detached the mobile slightly from his ear. He issued the smile and the eye-roll that Fanning had pre-dicted, and went back to his call. Fanning had mustered a smile, and he slowly nodded his understanding.

His chest felt overfilled. He took a few steps toward the door of the restaurant, and made a last effort to get his thoughts in order. With Breen you basically had one minute, and it had to be clear and simple, the less said the better. Breen wouldn't admit to calling it a pitch, of course. It was always "a chat," or a "bring me up to date." He wanted to just gossip, or tell a joke, or drop names and tell anecdotes.

Fanning let his breath out slowly and drew in another just the same. He was conscious of his smile, and maintaining it. Smiling alone, the act of it, made one relax, he had read.

Breen knew what the business wanted, network or studio. For one thing, poverty in Ireland didn't sell anymore. As a matter of fact, Ireland didn't sell anymore. Anyway, as Fanning well knew, the whole business was full to the gills with talent and writers. A few of the younger ones were smart enough to latch on the foreigner thing, like that Mira's Story, about the divorcee who emigrates to the wilds of Galway. Light, merry, conflict-of-cultures stuff. Throw in a woman's empowerment, craggy Irish faces, bleak and rain-swollen bog, and the search-for-home stuff. It wasn't hard, when you thought about it.

Fanning strolled to the window display of a new decorative ironworks. A slideshow was projected onto a piece of glass just behind the window of the shop. He'd seen the stuff before, but it was still eye-catching. Pictures and movies seemed to float in the air, like holograms. Celtic designs twirled and shrank, and were morphed into door-knockers. Old photos of Victorian gaslamps dissolved into replicas in front of homes that looked Dublin-ish, or at least the U.K. A hotel balcony from a photo of Joycean Dublin gave way to an exact copy, mounted on a French window of a home with Killiney Bay in the background: "For your Juliet balcony."

The show began to loop yet again. Just before Fanning turned away, a logo caught his eye, and he stared more intently as it appeared and grew. It was the Magritte all right, Memory: the bloodied head, the stone. Sure enough, he saw it was Mick Lally's outfit – doublin.com. Talk about coincidence.

He hadn't spoken to Lally in five years. Mick Lally, the great Bohemian, slagger and friend all through university and beyond, had gone into multimedia. Every time that Fanning had seen mention of Lally's company, he was reminded of their endless arguments about Fassbinder or Antonioni and Foucault – everything and anything, for God's sake. It was Lally who had been his partner in the first screenplay he'd ever done, made in pubs and flats, often stoned and more often half-drunk too.

He turned away. Breen was standing in the window, waving, with that hang-dog look. He made a big issue of powering off his mobile, and winked. Fanning took in the shirt collar opened the regulation two buttons, the straining belt turning down on his hips. As he made his way over to the restaurant door, he tried harder to smile in return.

Chapter 4

Traffic on the N11 was sluggish, with a lot of odd, clumsy driving. To Minogue, it seemed as if every driver driving this main road south out of the city was clumsy or distracted today.

Kilmartin eyed a Porsche passing another car with a few feet only to spare, and then racing toward the next back bumper.

"That goddamned recession can't come soon enough," he said, mildly.

Red lights dogged them past Foxrock. Things only got worse by Cabinteely, with traffic lights on the blink, and a flustered-looking Guard on point duty directing stop-and-go traffic. Gámóg, Minogue heard his friend whisper almost fondly when they got by at last.

Kilmartin craned his neck to look up through the steeply raked windshield at the sky over South County Dublin.

"A drop or two on the way," he said. "A day for the old umbrella."

This made no sense to Minogue. All an umbrella would do for a man up on Calary Bog on a day like today would be to pitch him airborne, and to fling him to hell back down to the coast.

They got a good stretch of open road, and were soon in sight of the roundabout at Shankill. Minogue drove hard through the curve. The Peugeot settled back on itself with ease on the far side.

"A fair bit of go in it," said Kilmartin. "For such a dainty little car."

He tried the radio then, but seemed to have little appetite for figuring out the buttons or the sophisticated display. He turned it off almost after a few moments.

"It's always that one on anyway," he said. "She drives me up the walls with that voice of hers. A real bitch. Like a teacher I had back in the Primary."

Minogue eased up at seventy, and listened to the faint whirr of the tires and the wind rushing by. He pretended to check traffic in the mirror so he could steal an occasional glance at his passenger, the new James Aloysious Kilmartin, this familiar stranger with a beard, a suit, and an odd stillness about him. Minogue wanted to believe that any return of Kilmartin's mocking ways was good news.

Kilmartin had gone quiet since his suspension back in October. Persuaded to talk about anything in the news, he usually spoke in a tone of gentle contempt. Minogue missed Kilmartin the exultant cynic more than he would ever admit, even to himself.

Kilmartin had lost weight – maybe too much. Could he have even shrunk a little? He seemed to be using air-quotes a lot, as though nothing was to be taken at face value anymore, and more than a few times, Minogue suspected that Kilmartin had a wandering head.

There were too many topics of conversation out of the blue. Did Minogue know that Irish sailors had given Columbus the know-how to get across the Atlantic? Had he noticed the word scenario cropping up everywhere? Did he notice that no-one spoke in sentences any more? And what did Minogue know about the Culdees, the old Irish Christians who ignored Rome? Global warming, WiFi networks, the vomeronasal organ, J. Edgar Hoover's belief that De Valera was a secret Jew?

He and Kilmartin still went on the walks each week. They were on varying days: one up at Carrickologan, the other at

Dunlaoghaire Pier, or Killiney Beach. The walks had begun as a gesture but they had passed quickly through routine, into habit, and they ended up as duty. Minogue was less than thrilled about his. His real walks – as distinct from strolls with Kathleen – had been in the spirit of Augustine, solitary and self-escaping. James Kilmartin was a ruiner of walks.

But to his credit, Kilmartin had never been first to bring up mention of his travails. It had been Minogue who had worked up the nerve to ask him about Maura in the weeks and months after she had tried to kill herself. He had been met with an uneasy silence. The topic was a no-go area.

Kilmartin didn't join in the mischief and slagging at get-togethers in Clancy's pub with the other veterans of the Murder Squad. Tommy Malone, their colleague from Murder Squad glory days didn't give up trying, however. He offered Kilmartin openings galore, with talk of culchies and cowshite and country music, all delivered in the disdainful nasal Dublin drawl that Kilmartin had tried to mimic. But these sterling efforts had done little to animate this new James Kilmartin who had emerged from the shambles of that night when everything had gone up in smoke on him: wife, job – Kilmartin's whole life, pretty well.

He seemed to have settled on renouncing things. The house that he and Maura had been so proud of was up for sale. His Audi was sold. No cigars. He took only the occasional drink, and rarely ate a meal in a restaurant. Though he now rented a boxy apartment near Thomas Street, he actually spent a lot of time on the family farm in Mayo. That was where his older brother Sean, gone very bad with the arthritis, was avoiding making decisions about the future, Kilmartin told Minogue. None of his brood wanted to make a go of the farm, apparently.

Kilmartin's time there in boggy, wild and wet Mayo were more in the nature of dude ranching, he told Minogue. Bringing in the cows, driving the tractor; fixing drainage in the same boggy fields he had worked decades before; repairing sheds, the barn. Biding his time.

One evening, he listed his foods for Minogue. It was as

though they were a guide to the New James Kilmartin: cabbage for the dinner – spuds of course; porridge every day; fish on Friday. Evenings on the farm meant sitting by the fire, reading the paper or the odd bit of television. No satellite tolerated, no sirree. A game of cards with the neighbours, or he'd try reading books he wished he had read years ago. A bit of yoga too, imagine that. He was trying to improve himself, he told Minogue, filling in gaps, so to speak.

Kathleen Minogue had spotted Kilmartin early in the New Year, looking through the self-help section in a Dublin bookshop. She swore that she had seen earphones and the tell-tale white wire of an iPod on him too. Minogue felt a strange embarrassment and even pity when he had heard this.

For Minogue's part, he kept track of the progress of the internal investigation into the shennigans at the Kilmartins' house that night. The Ombudsman's Office had been up and running nearly two years now, but it was still the Commissioner who had the final say in discipline.

Minogue had now been interviewed three times about that night at Kilmartin's – or as Plate Glass Sheehy had whispered in his ear one evening at Clancy's pub, in a parody of a come-all-ye that Kilmartin would have appreciated in better times, "The Night Before Jimmy Was Stretched." Well, nearly stretched.

The interviews had been low-key, and terribly polite all the way. Two of the "chats" had been with that reed-thin sergeant, Feeney; Feeney of the strangely white teeth and peppermint breath, Feeney with the skin tight over his forehead, a man who seemed to be perpetually straining, or holding back some great revelation, or fury.

The same Feeney had a soft manner that Minogue didn't trust one iota. There had been a civil servant there at the second meeting, a woman from Justice who liaised with the Director of Public Prosecutions. Minogue remembered she wore those small and severe oblong glasses that were the style everywhere now. The suspicion, maybe even the assumption, that a friend of Jim Kilmartin's like Minogue had to have been privy to Kilmartin's doings sat like another party in the room. It was hardly news that Coopers looked after one another, was it.

Several fragments of the conversation had lodged in Minogue's mind, and he had replayed them over and over again since.

"You and Superintendent Kilmartin are friends for some time."

"That we are."

"Working together for many years, I believe."

"A good long while, yes."

And on it had gone, with Feeney making observations more than asking questions. All very mild and civil, like a chess game. Minogue knew that a lot of it was for the benefit of the civil servant. She'd had to report to her department and minister, and so he had resolved not to react strongly to anything Feeney might say or insinuate. He had nevertheless prepared an aggressive statement, and he often itched to pull the pin on it.

Even at the time, he was glad that his chance never came, and more pleased yet when he got out of the meeting. He was nevertheless dismayed that he had been unable to divine: whether anyone clearly believed a) Kilmartin had been dirty, or b) had been in cahoots with his wife when she was having her odd phone conversations – very, very odd indeed – with the head of a Dublin crime family.

It wasn't so much a shunning of Kilmartin that Minogue had observed since that night. It was noticing how few of Kilmartin's contacts in the Guards had made a point of meeting Kilmartin face-to-face, or showing up at any of the sessions in Clancy's.

Well who could blame them, Kilmartin had quietly explained to Minogue. They probably thought he was gone off the deep end. Or maybe being seen with him might affect their careers. Kilmartin had chuckled to himself then, Minogue recalled. Career, Kilmartin had mused wryly later on, and raised a smile. He had turned the word from a noun back into a verb, hadn't he?

The point was, Kilmartin was owed, and that was that. Minogue wasn't going to budge on that. It had been James

Kilmartin who had set up the shaky Matthew Minogue in his Murder Squad years ago, when Minogue himself was damaged goods. Jittery, inert, and numbed by his own near-miss with death, Minogue was soon a probationer with Kilmartin's Squad, and the years that followed had been Minogue's best, working with Kilmartin, close to the dead.

A few cars passed faster now as the city traffic fell away. Minogue again pretended to check his far mirror. He saw that Kilmartin had fallen asleep.

Chapter 5

COLM BREEN DID A LOT of his trademark slow nodding while Fanning talked. He kept his spoon going, carefully turning it on the tablecloth in a series of quarter rotations clockwise, stopping every now and then to rotate it back. Fanning refused to be distracted, or irritated, by it.

Fanning was aware that he was nearing the end of his time.

"It's so intense," he said. "Dublin, the real Dublin. No U2 concerts, no trendy apartments by the Liffey stuff. Life in the raw."

"Gritty, Dermot. That's the key."

"Gritty doesn't go near it. Think of it as a medieval city all over again."

Breen nodded again.

"What I'm trying to get across," Fanning went on, "is something beyond any genre, you know. That's the thing about it being a medieval city."

"Right," said Breen. "Not a lot of people would see that."

"Dublin itself is the story – now I know that sounds corny."

"No way. You're not one of those fellas trying to rewrite Ulysses. Thank God."

"There's the nobility, if you want to call them that, behind their railings and burglar alarms. Then there's the ones with nothing, nothing to lose, I mean."

"'Two Irelands,'" said Breen. "'Two Dublins'?"

"Exactly. It's its own world, unto itself. But universal, like a city is a city."

"Well, they say it's worse than we think it is. Worse than the Guards let on."

Fanning had expected this. He had his sombre tone ready.

"That it definitely is, without a doubt. A senior Guard has told me exactly that."

He felt sure that this quiet affirmation had had an effect on Breen.

"The underworld," Breen murmured thoughtfully. He looked out the window.

"Tell you something else," said Fanning. "Going around with the guy I'm with, it's pretty scary. It's like a completely foreign city. And I know Dublin."

"Your guide to the underworld," said Breen, another wry smile creeping into his fleshy face. "This Orpheus, let's call him. Is he a big thing, what they say, 'connected'?"

"Well he talks a lot. Watches too many gangster flicks probably."

"Scarface? Tony Soprano?"

"Pretty much."

"Living the dream, is he."

"We could talk about the semiotics of it."

Breen actually smiled.

"Jesus, Dermot. Spare me. Remember all that crap?"

It was another test, but Fanning had a lot of ground to give. He smiled, and he shrugged. Breen uncrossed his legs and sat up.

"So what's the going rate for this, em, tour of the underworld?"

"The usual thirty pieces of silver."

Breen seemed to enjoy that.

"But he gets me places," Fanning went on. "Even if he is a name-dropper."

"Names?"

"Not any big scandal, well not yet. 'You'd be amazed who buys heroin in this city,' he says. Things like that. And he talks about his sources in the Guards."

"Bent ones?"

"Hasn't said outright. He has a contact in the Drug Squad, the Central one."

Breen's face became fixed in an expression of kind interest.

"'The Wire' you're talking about, maybe?"

Fanning knew he had to be careful.

"Possibly, sure. Why not. Let's say it's a starting point, but better."

"Take the bad guys' side then? The O'Sopranos, maybe?"

He almost forgot to acknowledge Breen's quip.

"It could go that way," he said. "I mean it could be done. But the real star of the story? The real star is Dublin. Local. Vernacular. Right in your face."

Immediately, Fanning wished he hadn't uttered those words.

"I'm not saying it right, Colm – but you know what I mean. The Dublin we know, or at least we think we know. But in fact we don't?"

Breen's brow creased.

"But Dublin's a destination now," Fanning said. "We're on the map, right? Boomtown, the Celtic Tiger, all that. I know it's jaded by now – for us, like. But the U.S. viewers? No, they're behind, obviously."

"No more colleens and shamrock, thank you very much. The Quiet Man done gone."

"Listen. Have you ever stopped on any street here and just listened?"

"Listened?"

"I mean the languages. Arabic, I heard the other day. Polish, lots obviously – but I mean, it's kind of like we missed out on some stage. Like we went straight from the past, and we woke up in the future, and found the place is full of foreign – immigrants, I mean. New faces, is what I mean, I suppose."

"Well you can certainly hear them when you buy a cup of coffee, or a pint."

"Absolutely," said Fanning. "You're right there."

He wondered when Colm Breen had last walked into an ordinary pub and bought an ordinary pint to drink with ordinary people. Decades.

"Let me just fire a few images your way," he said to Breen. "Then I'll be off. You know me, I've been around. But this place today – no-one, I mean no-one has this. Ready?"

Breen smiled, and nodded.

"Everyone who can get their hands on one carries a gun."

"Really," said Breen.

"Broad daylight, I swear. People I'm seeing are not just thieves, or B and E go-boys. These are serious people. You can feel the voltage off them. It's nothing for them to go to Amsterdam and do deals, or Bangkok – anywhere."

"I heard that."

"The cops don't want people to know the situation. Oh sure, they make statements and they talk about the new seizure laws and all the rest of it. What they don't say, is that they're not on top of this at all."

"Scary."

"You're telling me. The hair stands up on the back of my neck. It's life or death stuff. There are no laws for these people, no rules. Psychopaths."

"Russians, I heard? Eastern Europe stuff?"

"You're reading my mind! That's in the story too. When the old guard, the Dubs let's call them, decide to settle with all these fellas coming into the country and starting their own gigs."

Breen leaned in over the table.

"Is that what's going on at the moment, these shootings the past while?"

"'Spring cleaning,' Murph calls it."

"Murph."

"My contact, takes me around and about. My tour guide. Told me that the guy killed the other night was a friend of his.

The name of Mulhall, I think."

"Really," said Breen. "Isn't that kind of, well, too close for comfort? Pardon the cliché and all that."

"Well Murph doesn't seem to think so. 'It's only messers and two-timers need to worry,' says he."

"And this character was a friend of his," said Breen. "What does he say about his enemies, I wonder."

Fanning couldn't be sure if Breen was ahead of him here in the irony stakes. He thought again of their early days together as students, when Breen was an awkward gobshite that he had taken under his wing in the Film Society.

"Murph's not the fastest bunny in the forest, I have to say," he said.

"You trust him?"

"As much as I trust any skanger, I suppose."

Breen smiled.

"Plus he keeps telling me how well-in he is. Mr. Untouchable."

Breen's smile faded into a dreamy look.

"'Spring cleaning,'" he said. "'The Rites of Spring.' Plenty grotesque."

He rearranged himself in his chair. His eyes slipped out of focus for several moments, and then snapped back to Fanning's.

"Tell you what, Dermot Fanning: you've got the makings of a damn good documentary here. A damned good one."

The anger detonated into Fanning's chest. He tried to match Breen's grin.

"We need the whole ball of wax," he said. "Inside out. The full emotional whack: characters, levels, conflict. Family, feuds. Revenge. The voices, the faces. You won't be able to take your eyes off them."

"It sounds huge."

"There's a series in this, for sure. I'm telling you, I started out with the usual, you know: a knockout pilot, and eight episodes ready. But that won't be enough, it just won't. There's so much."

Breen smiled again.

"You are the real McCoy, Dermot. By Jesus. You've got the fire in you."

"I hope that's a good thing?"

"Of course it is, don't be silly. Of course it is."

"'Stories tell the higher truth.'"

"I was waiting for that one," said Breen. Fanning didn't want to notice that a tail of Breen's shirt had become dislodged, and now hung over his belt.

"We're talking The One," he said. "Look, I know I'm just rabbiting on here. But have a look over the summary, the first chapter. I know you're a busy man."

"No sweat, Dermot. Never a problem. It's the story, the writing, in the final analysis – always. And by God I know you have it in you."

Fanning watched Breen's hand resting on the folder, as though to guard it. He knew he should leave it at that, but he couldn't resist.

"Ask me where I'm going right after," he said. "Ask me."

"Okay. Where are you off to?"

"A dog fight."

Breen sat up.

"You mean dogs fighting?"

"Exactly. Murph has an in, and he's bringing me."

"Where are you going to see this?"

"About two miles from where we're sitting."

Fanning waited a few moments. He was pleased with Breen's reaction.

"I don't know the address," he went on, "But it's the real thing. And a lot of the big shots show up."

"The bad guys."

"Yep. It's a kind of neutral place, where they might bump into one another but no-one starts throwing shapes. Business gets discussed, and all that. But it's for betting. Been going on for years."

Fanning finally felt he was getting through to Breen. He stared at him.

"Oh. And they go for blood-lust, I'd have to say. That

medieval thing, it keeps on coming back, you see."

Breen's blank expression gave way a little. He gave Fanning a rueful look.

"Savage," he said. "Incredible. But are you going to be able to handle it?"

"I'll have to, won't I."

"Christ, I hope, you know..."

"I'll be okay. But you can see where this could go."

Breen nodded. Then something slid into his thoughts and his face changed.

"Absolutely, yes. Okay. Let me know. Okay?"

Fanning had chosen his words carefully for this moment.

"I wanted you to know first," he said.

Breen's schmoozing smile appeared He leaned on toward Fanning.

"Thanks, Dermot. That means a lot to me to hear you say that. A lot."

"This is the one. I'm sure of it."

"If anyone can get this – I mean really get it – it's you, Dermot. We'll talk?"

Chapter 6

THE MOTORWAY BEGAN ITS LONG, banked curve inland, and Sugar Loaf mountain slid into view over the trees. Minogue eyed the low clouds shrouding its peak. The rain would surely have started up on Calary Bog and its Protestant church where they were headed.

"What?" Kilmartin asked, with the urgency of the suddenly awoken.

"You were asleep."

"I am not. What did you say before that?"

"I didn't say anything."

"Well you cursed. Under your breath. That I know."

"I must have been thinking of someone else."

A heavily loaded lorry overtook them, swaying a little as it returned to its lane. There were left-hand drive cars coming toward Dublin from the Rosslare ferry now. Many towed caravans, French a lot of them.

Kilmartin sat up, and turned in his seat.

"Oh oh," he said. "Thought I heard something. Action stations."

The blue lights of the Garda car came up fast in Minogue's mirror. He checked the speed, and felt for his wallet. The squad car went by at ninety. He got a quick look at the two Guards inside. They were in traffic gear. The passenger with a mobile to his ear looked to be about twenty.

"Bigger rogues than us to be chasing. What speed were you doing?"

"Seventy something," Minogue said. "Eighty, maybe."

He was already anticipating the route from the turn-off at Kilmacanogue, along the Roundwood Road that climbed up to Calary Bog.

It had been months since he had been up here. The houses would peter out within a half mile of the motorway, he recalled, and then more and more rock would surface in the scruffy, marginal fields. A mile or so in, the kingdom of brambles, ferns, and furze would take over. He half-remembered views of Glencree, with whitethorn hedges and the yellow, spring-flowering gorse leaning in over the road.

"Super-cops," Kilmartin murmured.

The squad car had taken the ramp up the overpass toward the start of the Roundwood Road. It was long gone by the time Minogue drew up to the stop sign. Descending then toward the junction, he spotted an old man, ruddy-faced and gaunt, standing in the car park of the pub. Beside him was an old Land Rover. A Wicklow collie sat in the passenger seat, apparently following its master's lead in watching Minogue and Kilmartin. The old man's long face had something of a horse about it, Minogue decided, especially with the breezes tossing the tufts of snowy hair that swelled out from under his tweed hat.

Kilmartin had spotted him too.

"I don't care what anyone says," he said. "There's a look to them."

Political correctness was still alien to Kilmartin, but Minogue had to admit that his friend was probably right. This was borderland after all, the edge of the Pale in former times, raider's country. Rachel Tynan's family name had been Weekes, a name with a distinctly Cromwellian sound to it, to Minogue's ear.

He had often forgotten that the Tynans' mixed marriage meant something to other people, especially because Tynan had spent a few years as a Jesuit seminarian. He had once heard a whispered superstition concerning why their marriage had remained childless.

"They're very organized," said Kilmartin. "That's all I'm saying. I mean there he is, making sure that iijits like us find their way up to this church."

The turn off the motorway seemed to have awoken Kilmartin.

"She planned it all, I heard," he said, warming to his topic. "Mrs. Tynan, I'm talking about. Rachel, I should call her now, I suppose. She planned this place here, the event even."

Recent years had drawn her back, Minogue had heard, and especially as her illness advanced, here to where she had spent her childhood. Those visits had resulted in a series of paintings of the bog with a grandeur of space and skies that Minogue had believed that no-one but himself had marvelled at.

He felt the tires bite loose gravel by the verge of the road.

"'A celebration,'" Kilmartin went on. "None of this, what's the word? None of this... lugubrious stuff. A lot to admire in that, I must say. Yourself?"

As earnest as Kilmartin seemed, his words were unconvincing to Minogue. It was long an open secret that funerals still put Irish people in quiet good humour.

Minogue said, "Couldn't agree with you more."

"Why's that? – Oh I see now. You're getting your Irish ready for the mass above. What am I saying, 'mass.' Christ. The ceremony, I mean. The service – the celebration. Whatever."

Minogue had half-forgotten that the service was to be in Irish. There would be paintings, he had learned, hers and her students,' displayed in the small church. Music was to be a big part of the event also.

The rain had come though here not so long ago. Wet ditches and half-dried roadway now ushered Minogue and Kilmartin up the narrowing road toward Calary, the Peugeot jiggling as it followed the shape of the road, leaning and swaying to its rises and dips – its very camber even, altered as it was yearly by the boggy soil beneath. Minogue struggled to detect which of the puddles might be potholes. It was no use. At least there was no oncoming traffic.

They were almost by a quarry when the bend abruptly

revealed cars stopped in the road ahead. Minogue didn't like the faint squeak from the brake pedal.

There were people out on the road.

"Oh Christ crippled on a crooked crutch," Kilmartin said with little feeling. "And His Blessed Mother of course. Is that who I think it is, standing on the ditch there? 'Ill Be Hooves'?"

"Could be him, all right."

"It is," Kilmartin added. "And what's-his-face there. The sidekick. On a mobile, Delahunty. That hoor. Pinky and Perky, the pair of them. Christ."

Minogue recognized Deputy Commissioner Eoin Burke, sleek in a well-cut navy-blue coat. It was Burke's MBA-style talk and his fondness for press conferences, more than the suspect touch of dandyism, that had drawn the name on himself. A testy exchange on Meet the Press, a current affairs free-for-all that encouraged what were called stakeholders to vent about anything, had been the occasion of Burke's folly.

Unwisely, Burke had thought himself equal to all comers, but under pressure early, he lapsed into chiding a rabid whinger, a self-styled citizen's rights maniac who was widely hated by rank-and-file Guards, the very people on whose behalf Burke believed he was sallying forth: "It ill behooves Mr. X here to be criticizing hard-working Gardai who..." And that was enough.

Minogue recalled Delahunty from a seminar on something to do with Biometrics. Much like Burke, Superintendent Delahunty worked at being approachable. That only made things worse. Both men were being groomed for something new, however, something very high-tech.

There were a half-dozen cars, a lorry, people standing around. Minogue put down the windows. Engines had been turned off. The wind was uncertain here, but it seemed to be picking up. Radio traffic filtered through the hedges, along with a more subdued but steady racket from the bickering, warbling birds of County Wicklow.

He pulled on the handbrake. Tight, maybe too tight. He couldn't ignore the squeak from the chassis as the Peugeot tried to roll back against the brake.

"I'll see what the story is ahead," he said to Kilmartin. "Are you coming?"

"I'm not," Kilmartin replied. "I'm grand here. In your nice new French car."

Minogue climbed out of the car, lit a cigarette, and began to stroll toward the other Guards. The first lungfuls of smoke invigorated him as much as made him dizzy.

There was a mocker's gleam in Burke's eyes. He shook Minogue's hands a bit too heartily.

"Matt. Never knew you smoked."

"Eoin, how's things with you and yours."

"Top form, and thanking you. Is that himself inside in the car with you?"

"None other."

"The funeral, I take it? Or what are we calling it, the memorial service?"

"I'm not sure of the official title. To pay our respects."

Burke squinted at the shiny windscreen of the Peugeot, mischief flickering around his mouth. Minogue half-remembered Kilmartin grumbling about Burke's self-promotion some years back: was it a wall-eyed bastard he had called him?

"You frisked Jim, I hope."

Minogue prepared to give him the eye, and to verify if Burke's eyes did indeed merit Kilmartin's jibe, but a gust of wind took Burke's hair and drew it straight up. Minogue glanced up to the rioting comb-over instead. He hoped Kilmartin was watching.

"What do we have up the road?" he asked Burke.

"Crash," said Burke. "Fifteen, twenty minutes ago. The ambulance came already. Hardly worth your while to find another road now. Not that there are any up here."

Delahunty closed his phone and issued Minogue a nod.

"They'll give us the go-ahead in a minute," he said. His modulated Cork accent couldn't quite shed that nasal uplift at the end, and robbed of its melody, it came across to Minogue as strained, and even querulous.

The wind was now prancing about in uncertain bursts,

tugging and then releasing Minogue's coat. He looked at the drooping brambles that swayed and jerked over the roadway, and the new rushes bowing in the breeze.

He caught Burke glancing back at his new Peugeot.

"Wild enough, here," said Burke, stifling a yawn. "Nice all the same," Minogue said.

"I suppose," said Burke, suspecting contrariness. "But if it's wild we want, we should go back to Dublin, hah?"

Minogue made no reply. He had long ago given up trying to find a subtle way to advertise that he, a countryman like most of his fellow Gardai, was not therefore a reflexive slagger of Ireland's capital city.

"Baker's dozen the other day," said Delahunty. "Including that Mulhall fella."

Minogue didn't like the light-heartedness in his tone.

"Canoodling with his mate's wife, I heard," Delahunty added. "'Lying low?'"

"How many's that for the week now?" Burke asked.

"Eight in the last ten days," Delahunty said. "Spring cleaning is what they're saying. And a fine Hundred Thousand Welcomes to our friends from across the water."

Quite the pair, Minogue thought. He drew on his cigarette, and realized he had no idea what Delahunty meant.

"Welcome to Ireland," said Burke. "'We have enough of our own bad guys and gougers thanks very much. So bang bang, and pip-pip. Home in a box.'"

Delahunty turned to Minogue with renewed interest.

"But sure you'd be the man of the hour on that," he said. "Wouldn't you? Liaison keeping tabs on the flotsam and jetsam washing up here from wherever?"

"Hardly," said Minogue. "I'm only a runner-in there. Learning the ropes."

Neither man believed him, Minogue was sure. The subject was gone after a brief lull. It was Minogue's chance to disengage.

Burke had read his mind apparently. He demanded to know what Minogue thought of the big upset at the Munster Finals last year. Minogue mustered his own staged indignation.

"I'm always upset by Cork hurlers," he declared. "Especially the one or two good ones they seem to be able to muster."

"Oh the diehard Clare fan," said Burke. "Go away with you, and the rest of the Clare crowd. Department of Lost Causes."

Minogue managed to make his way back down the road, alternately eyeing the saturated mash of dirt and humus by the ditches, and the mountain slopes in the distance.

He elected to finish his cigarette standing by the passenger side of his Peugeot.

Kilmartin stepped out presently.

"Stretch me legs," he said. "And just so's you know, I won't be hiding in a car from the likes of Burke. Ill Be Hooves himself. He'll have to find someone else's grave to dance on."

"Sounds like you're setting yourself up to having a go at him."

"I would if I wanted to," said Kilmartin, mildly. "No better man, I tell you."

Minogue was suddenly uneasy. Kilmartin might be unpredictable, already moved off into the territory where nothing much mattered any more, and where he had nothing to lose. He exchanged a glance with him.

"Look at you," said Kilmartin, with a wry expression. "Expecting the worst."

"Behave yourself," Minogue said. "You Mayo bullock, you."

Kilmartin looked through the dense thicket of hedge.

"I saw them eyeing me," he said. "Those two feckers. What'd they say?"

"They asked to be remembered to you."

"You lying whore's ghost. I could tell by Burke's face."

Kilmartin buttoned his overcoat. Minogue noted how loosely it fit him.

"You should have the sense to give up the fags now," said Kilmartin. "I'm going up here a bit and see what the commotion is."

Minogue took a last, long drag of his cigarette while he watched Kilmartin's progress up the road. In time, he set out after him. He kept his distance following him nonetheless, all the while taking in the forward cant, that assertive flat-footed gait, and the weary swagger that still hinted at a man who had been limber and strong, and once purposeful.

Chapter 7

THEY LEFT MURPH'S CAR PARKED at the side of the warehouse. Fanning made a quick survey of the half-dozen sagging and rusted transport trailers huddled on the broken asphalt alongside the building, slowly sinking in amongst the weeds. A smell of engine oil hung in the air, pierced every now and then by a brackish, industrial tang. He heard the hush of traffic on the bypass a half-mile away.

"Any more news on your friend," Fanning said. "Mulhall?"

"News?" said Murph. "What do you mean news exactly?"

"Like, what happened?"

"He got offed, didn't he. That's the news."

"I just thought you might have heard something since. Being as you're in a position to hear things."

"Meaning?"

"Well he was a friend of yours, you said."

Murph made a flick of his head.

"There's friends, and there's friends," he said.

Two men were waiting by a metal-clad door propped open at the side of the warehouse. They didn't seem interested in Fanning's or Murph's arrival. While Murph stopped to light another cigarette, Fanning counted seven parked cars, and two vans.

"Hey," Murph said. "Stop gawking! That scrutinizing.

I seen that before."

Fanning said nothing. The excitement he had felt on the drive here was gone, and in its place was a restlessness that was making him more uneasy as the minutes passed. He was used to Murph's oscillations between bluster and sly charm.

"So cut it out," Murph added. "People'll think you're a copper."

"Which reminds me," said Fanning. "What did he say, your copper, Malone?"

Murph turned on him, blocking his path.

"What? Are you out of your mind? You're asking me here?"

"Just asking. What's wrong with that?"

"Don't even think about stuff like that here. Do you know what'd happen if anyone here heard you? Have you any idea? Jesus!"

"Okay. I get it. "

"You've got to start using your head, man. Anyone here got wind of that stuff, they wouldn't even ask me about it. They don't care, you know?"

"I said I get it. Sorry."

"Sorry? Like that's going to help? Listen, this isn't a story here, I keep telling you. Stuff happens in this world, you know. It's not on a page, or has special effects, or anything like that. The real world, you understand?"

Fanning saw that Murph's chest was not heaving so much now.

"Like, we're talking people with no morals or anything," Murph went on. He leaned in.

"Mental issues, you know? Nutters. I mean a lot of these people got hard going when they were kids. Abuse and all that? So, like, now, well I mean to say – would you turn out normal after that? You know?"

These people, Fanning thought. If anything crystallized Murph, with his delusions, that had to be it right there.

"Am I getting through to you at all?"

"Oh sure. I forgot, I suppose. I get it."

Murph's straining and bloodshot eyes still bored into his.

"So did he?" he murmured. "Malone...?"

For a moment he thought Murph would actually hit him.

"No he didn't," said Murph between clenched teeth. "And he told me to stop annoying him with it. He doesn't want anything to do with it."

Fanning took a step back but Murph's sour breath seemed to have stuck on him. He spoke in a low voice.

"I don't know if I want to go in there with you. I mean, what'll you come up with next?"

"It's okay. I know, now."

"But do you? Really, do you?"

"Let's just go in. Look, I spoke out of turn. Bad timing. Okay?"

"But you're the fella with the degrees and the books and everything. And what am I? Kicked out of the school. Haven't read a book for years – but at least I know reality from fake, from, from fantasy."

"I hear you. Can we go in now?"

"If you make a promise to keep your trap shut, maybe, just maybe."

"I promise."

He watched Murph search his face for any sign of irony.

"Remember me telling you, my turf, my rules?"

"I remember."

"You better. You don't ask anybody anything in here. Not even 'what day is it.' None of that, you know, what do you call..."

"Small talk."

"That's right! No chit chat. This is a business here. The people that come to this don't come here for the scenery, I can tell you. They want to relax a bit, sure. But they're betting. And they take it serious. They're not there to talk to you, and they don't want to be wondering who you are, or what you're doing here. All they know is, you're with me. So that's good enough for them. They'll leave it at that."

"What if one of them starts talking to me?"

"Not going to happen," Murph said quickly. "I'll do the talking, if there's any. I set this up, with Jacko – that's him at the door there, in the red, the butty little fella."

Fanning watched Murph draw hard on the cigarette and begin to smoothen out a patch of broken bitumen with slow, rhythmical side-to-side movements of his foot. Then Murph jerked his head up.

"And none of that jotting down notes effort," he said. "Like you were doing in the pub the other– Hey: you carrying that recorder thing I seen you using before?"

"No."

"Oh. And give me your phone."

"It's off," Fanning said. He had to clear his throat. "I'm not using it."

Murph squinted at him, and he grimaced. Fanning tried not to notice that his yellowing teeth had a shade of green near the gums.

"My turf, my rules," Murph said. "Phones are cameras, remember."

Fanning got his thumbnail under the catch, took off the lid, and slid the SIM card into his wallet.

A Fiat van arrived. Instead of parking with the others, it made its way wallowing and swaying over the asphalt toward the back of the warehouse. Fanning caught a quick glimpse of the driver, a late middleaged man with a greying seventies moustache, and a stud in his ear. One of the two men who had been standing by the door, a skinny twentysomething-looking one in a hoodie, walked after the van. From around the corner of the warehouse, Fanning heard a door being pulled up.

"That was Tony," said Murph. "In the van. Pretty well top of the heap. Goes all over the country with them dogs of his. There's a story about him I can't tell you."

"I won't be using names," Fanning said.

Murph chuckled.

"Okay," he said. "Let me just ask you something then. What would you do, if you were breeding a fighting dog and it turned on you, the dog?"

"I don't know. I'd get it put down, I suppose."

Murph tugged at his nose. The rash on his nostrils became a brighter red.

"'Put down? There is no putter-downer for a dog like this. What would you use, I'm saying."

Then he winked at Fanning, and he took a last, hurried drag of his cigarette before flicking it into the weeds.

Jacko was flabby but sort of well tended in a wholly unoriginal way, with the stock Beckham stubble and cropped hair, and a plain silver chain showing by the zipper of his jacket. Turning his head for a moment, revealed a small Bluetooth earpiece that Fanning had not noticed before. His empty gaze settled again on Fanning as he followed Murph to the door.

"We're here and gone, Jacko," Murph said. "Just a sampler, is all."

Jacko flicked a look from Fanning to Murph and back.

"Yous are here to play or not?" he asked.

"Course we are," Murph said. "Been looking forward to it."

"Where are you coming from," Jacko said to Fanning. "Who do you know?"

"Jacko, man, come on," Murph said. "He's with me, he's sound."

"Doesn't mean anything to me."

"Jacko, we already talked about this. You know me, you know the score."

"Well the score's nil-nil right now. Far as I can see."

"Look," said Murph. "Phone me, later on. I might have something for you."

"Stuff. What sort of stuff."

"This and that. Situations. Transportation business. Stuff like that."

"Really. I'll talk to my parole officer about it."

Three more men appeared from where the cars were parked.

"Step aside for these men here," said Jacko.

"How come they don't get hassled?" Murph asked.

"They paid the admission fee. That's how."

"Ha ha," Murph said. "Nice one, Jacko. There's no such thing."

Jacko shifted on his feet.

"There is now, brother. So step aside."

Chapter 8

"WHAT'S YOUR HURRY," Minogue called out after Kilmartin.

As Kilmartin drew closer to their car, Burke and Delahunty seemed to feel the time was right to retire to its interior. Kilmartin gave them a short, ecclesiastical stare before he conceded a nod in, and passed on. Minogue ignored a wink from Burke as he passed them himself.

He recognized several Guards biding their time in the cars ahead, a Deputy Comm from Cork, a few more Superintendents. He passed two ancient priests sprawled in the back of an old Passat, some of Tynan's former Jesuit mentors from his seminary days, he was willing to bet. A fat, frustrated-looking man sat in the champagne-coloured Lexus ahead of them, talking into his mobile and making elaborate gestures, all the while glancing at papers on the passenger seat. Beyond the Lexus was a bread van, with its driver leaning on the door of a lorry that preceded him, talking with little enthusiasm to whoever was in the cab.

A dozen or so metres farther on was the back end of a squad car, the Primera that had sped by Minogue on the motorway. Kilmartin slowed and then stopped, and moved his head about to get a better view of something.

"You can see some of the goings-on from here," he said.

"Not sure I want to."

"The van went off the road. Looks like it rolled too, down that bank. Look, you can just see a bit of it."

There was a car on its side in the ditch, and beyond that an ambulance. The fire brigade must have come down from Roundwood, the ambulance too. As though on cue, a Guard came skipping back from the road and waving.

"Ambulance," he called out. "Make way, now. Pull in tight. Ambulance."

Minogue and Kilmartin found a spot close into the ditch. Kilmartin squinted as he looked back over the cars toward Minogue's Peugeot. Other cars had drawn up behind it.

"I left room," Minogue said to him.

They watched the ambulance nose by, and then pick up some speed. A man with a white dressing held to his head appeared on the road in its wake. The blood that had run down the side of his face and onto his shirt was a brighter red than Minogue expected. It was the overcast day, he decided. The white shirt that made it stand out.

The man's dark growth of beard ran right up almost to his eyes. He was talking fast, his eyes glittering and darting about. He was soon shouting. Nobody calmed him.

"What the hell's that fella saying," Kilmartin said under his breath.

"Okay," he said after a few moments. "Let me guess. Romanian."

A Garda stepped over to the man and took him by the upper arm. The man looked confused, then cowed, and then angry.

"Aisy there now," Kilmartin declared. "That man's in shock."

Another Guard came over hurriedly. The man seemed to get the idea.

"Do they have their own language, those people?"

Minogue spotted bloodstained paper towels in the ditch. There was movement amongst a group that had gathered behind the squad car.

"There's your problem right there," Kilmartin said. "Shouldn't be on the roads here. Shouldn't be let near a car, even."

A hatless grey-haired Garda sergeant approached the group, and said something to them. They answered a question with a vigorous nod. The sergeant made a flourish with his hand in the direction of Calary. The group turned almost as one, and headed back toward the line of cars. Minogue turned too. Kilmartin was already on his way.

Back in the the car, Kilmartin became almost expansive.

"They tried everything, I heard," he said as Minogue turned down the lane toward the church. "Lourdes, even."

The place reminded Minogue of an oasis, with small, hilly fields hard-won from the bog, and clumps of trees. Cars had been parked tight into the banks that lined the lane. Minogue had to wait for people to walk ahead of his car before he could follow the directions toward a parking place.

"A great turn-out," said Kilmartin.

Though the church itself nestled amongst a stand of mature trees, the banks and the small, hilly fields seemed to form a funnel for the wind.

Kilmartin suddenly unhitched his seat belt.

"What are you at?"

"I can't," said Kilmartin. He pulled at the door release. "Sorry. I just can't."

"Christ almighty Jim, don't jump out. At least let me stop the car."

"I'm sorry, Matt, I am."

The wind tore the door from Kilmartin's hand, and Minogue felt it bounce back hard on its hinge. Papers erupted behind Minogue with a loud flapping sound. Two, then three pages, were whipped out the open door, one bouncing off a hedge before soaring and twisting in the wind.

"Close the door at least, can't you!"

His belt held him back. He pulled up the handbrake and released his belt, and dove across the passenger seat to get at the door handle. Another page hit the top of the door, curled, cracked, and flew out. Another was flattened against the front window. Minogue lunged at it, and crumpled it just in time to have another nick him in the cheek as it went by.

He cursed again. Kilmartin, hunch-shouldered and indifferent to anything but his own hurried strides along the muddy lane, did not look back.

Pages hurtled over car roofs, one slapping a windscreen of a Nissan. It was one of the hospital pictures, the full-on one of the man's swollen face streaked with blood. One of the laser-printed photos was inching its way up his window. It flapped once and then took off, higher than any of the others.

Cars were waiting behind. Minogue let off the handbrake and headed toward a gap in the high bank by a bend, where a man was waiting to direct him.

The farmyard was half-full of cars already. He turned off the ignition and leaned back to get the folder from the back seat. There were only two pages left in it. He heard paper rustle when he moved his feet by the pedals. There was another page half under the seat. Ten pages missing, fifteen?

He took out his mobile and he waited, his thumb over the Send, trying to compose a sensible question: Eilís, thank God you got a transfer over to Liaison, you know how thick I am, so you won't mind asking for copies of that file...?

A man rose up from a crouch in Minogue's side vision, holding up one of his pages. Minogue closed his phone.

Kilmartin's face had changed completely. The page flapped enough to tear as he held it up to eye level. He tugged on the door handle, and holding the door against the wind, slid into the passenger seat with a sigh.

"Mother of God, Jim. What the hell was all that about?"

Kilmartin didn't look up when he spoke.

"It's hard to explain."

"There's three-quarters of my briefing notes flying around Wicklow – scene photos, personal information!"

"No need to be roaring at me. I couldn't help it."

Minogue looked around the farmyard for any of the pages.

"A savage bit of wind," said Kilmartin, quietly. "Always like this up here?"

"It's March," Minogue declared. "That's what it is."

"Fierce bleak too. Bog, bog, and more bog."

Minogue threw another glare at Kilmartin. Sure enough, he had that faraway look again.

Within a few moments Kilmartin started out of his thoughts, and ran his hand along the armrest.

"It was a panic attack," he said.

"A panic attack."

Kilmartin nodded.

"No warning?"

Kilmartin shook his head.

"It has to do with the other business," he murmured. "You know."

Minogue waited.

"I get these, well…," Kilmartin went on, his voice dropping even more, "…images, I suppose you'd call them. Sometimes I get them in dreams."

He looked up suddenly at Minogue and smiled bleakly.

"'The Half-Three Devils,' I call them," he said. "They kind of crowd in all of a sudden. And you don't know whether you're awake, or whether you're asleep. Ever have them, back when, you know, the, em, episode?"

The bombing he meant, Minogue knew.

"I suppose I did," he heard himself reply.

This seemed to release Kilmartin from something. His voice took on its customary assurance again, and he sat back.

"Funerals," he said. "Churches. Graveyards even. It keeps coming back, that I could be going to Maura's. Sort of a flash-forward, not a flash-back. You see?"

Minogue nodded. Somehow, his patience had returned.

"I remember you talking to me years ago about your little lad," said Kilmartin. "Éamonn. How you'd see him at different times. And you couldn't go into the bedroom for fear you might see him again, and you knew you couldn't get to him in time."

The waving new growth on the banks all about suddenly faded for Minogue.

"Am I out of order in bringing it up?" Kilmartin asked.

Minogue shook his head.

"For me, it comes down to this," Kilmartin went on. "With Maura, I couldn't protect her, I couldn't save her. And that's the crux of the matter. Where the shite hit the fan for me. Simple enough to say, but..."

The seconds ticked by. Minogue listened to the wind hissing around the car, trying to see if there was a melody in it. "The Wind That Shakes the Barley" skittered through his mind, his father's favourite tune. Or was it "The Pigeon on the Gate"?

"So what's that word again," Kilmartin was saying. "Lugubrious, is it?"

"Listen to you," Minogue said. "You and your Half-Three Divils."

"You can laugh. Hey, you're allergic to churches, as I recall."

"I don't be leaping out of cars when I get near one, do I."

"Each to his own, but."

Kilmartin let out a long breath through pursed lips. Then he held up the page he had grabbed on the laneway.

"Well, here's one of your bits of paper," he said. Makes no sense to me."

"It's Polish."

"Good. I thought I was after having a stroke or some-thing."

"Half the County Wicklow will think the same thing, when they read it."

Kilmartin reached inside his jacket and took out another sheet.

"Well this belongs to you too then."

"Any more you're hiding on me?"

"As if I would. But what're you doing with scene photos? You're not in the game anymore, remember?"

Minogue gave him the eye.

"What," Kilmartin said. "I'm only making conversation."

His gaze returned to the muddy tire tracks in the yard alongside.

Minogue jammed the remaining pages between his seat

and the console. He recalled Kilmartin's talk about being power-less to protect his wife, and the panic attacks he got. Maybe Kilmartin had really gone over the edge that night, and there would be no coming back – at least to his job as a Garda.

Someday he'd ask him if he had really believed that Rynn or one of his gunmen had been out there in the garden that night, coming to kill him and Maura. Things you remember, but things the mind decides to hide under the bed. But the body remembers things. At times, Minogue himself could feel the broken china and glass under his elbows that night in the Kilmartins' shattered kitchen, scrabbling and grappling for Kilmartin's arm – or rather the police-issued automatic at the end of that arm – then the blinding floodlights, and the shout-ing.

Betrayed was an odd word. It had an old-fashioned sound to it. It was plain that Kilmartin loved his wife. Minogue knew that because he had sat with Kilmartin for two nights at the hospital after Maura Kilmartin had overdosed. It had been exactly one week after the fiasco at their home. The whole thing had been his fault, not hers, Kilmartin had said several times. After all, what kind of a detective was he, that he'd miss something right under his nose for years?

Wind buffeted the car once, twice.

"I'm going in," Minogue said finally. "Come on in your-self, sure."

Kilmartin pretended to think about it.

Chapter 9

"JACKO'S A PSYCHO," Murph said. "Only you're here, I'd tell him what's what."

Murph had insisted that Fanning give him the two fifties. He would do the business with Jacko. His role, he had called it. Fanning eyed three more men arriving from the parking area. With their darker, wind-burned faces and their country accents plain in the sparing words, he was sure they were tinkers.

"Extortion is what it is," said Murph. "I'll sort him out later. Come on."

Fanning watched Murph hand over the money.

"Behave yourselves," Jacko said. "And bet lots."

Murph pulled the handle on the galvanized door, and Fanning followed him into the dimness beyond. A short passageway led to a room the size of a school gymnasium, a storey-and-a-half high. Small groups stood around, men all of them, and they talked in low voices under small, slow clouds of cigarette smoke. There was some kind of half-disassembled industrial shelving at one end of the room, and discarded pieces of engine parts in a heap to the side.

Fanning's first thought when he saw the chain-link was that it was a mistake. A chain-link cage simply belonged outdoors, not indoors. The strangeness of it continued to rub at his mind until the astringent smells pressed in sharply on him, cleaning fluids and fresh sawdust scattered in the enclosure. The chain link had to be six feet high, at least. A yard brush leaned against the outside of the cage, and beside it a shovel. The bright blue heads of masonry nails stood out from the bases of the sockets that anchored posts to the cement floor.

Fanning stood next to Murph, and avoided any eye contact with the groups of men. He studied the walls instead, the windows that had been filled in, the two painted-over skylights. One man from a group had detached himself and had begun strolling toward the far end of the room, slowly rubbing his face up and down like a comedian pulling faces while talking on his mobile.

"How come he gets to keep his phone?" he whispered to Murph.

"None of our business."

A squat, bearded man walked smartly in from the hallway. His beard had the same blue-black tinge as his hair. The groups of men had noticed him, and they shuffled and turned to face him.

"I'll take bets before," he called out.

He had the same torn and gravelly voice as one of the Dubliners, the folk group that Fanning's father had liked, and whose LPs he had later regretted discarding after the funeral. The bearded man coughed, and rubbed his hands.

"No bets during. For those of you here the–."

He held up his arm then, and he fumbled in the pocket of his wind-cheater. He turned away then and spoke into his phone.

"We'll see the talent in a minute," Murph murmured to Fanning. "No rush."

The smell of disinfectant was stinging Fanning's nose now. He noticed darker patches on the cement floor next to the wire. The bearded man closed his phone, and whistled.

"A squad car taking its sweet time out on the Ballygall Road," he said.

The shuffling stopped, and most of the men looked away. Low talk resumed. The man with the beard strolled toward where Murph and Fanning sat.

"Do I know you," he said to Fanning.

"No way," said Murph, smiling. "A mate of mine. Sound, so he is."

"Is he not able to talk?"

Murph's laugh was forced.

"Ah no, he's not. He's a dummy. Aren't you?"

Fanning said nothing.

"There's a pair of you then," the bearded man said. "If and he's in your line of caper, Murph."

"Comedy club we're in here, is it."

"I'm not trying to make a joke."

He turned back to Fanning, who concentrated on putting on his most neutral, attentive expression.

"Been here before?"

Fanning shook his head.

"He's just trying it out," said Murph. "See if he can make a few bob. I got the okay from Jacko."

The bearded man's eyes drifted slowly away from Fanning's.

"You have him gambling for his fix, do you," he said to Murph.

"Christ," said Murph, and shook his head. "What a thing to say."

"Why's that? Business these days. Oh. Tell him if he pukes he'll be cleaning it up himself."

His eyes darted back to Fanning.

"No hard feelings there, head-the-ball."

"Ah no," said Fanning. "You're grand."

Something that was almost a smile came to the man's face, but his stare remained flat and empty.

"He says I'm grand. Did you hear that. 'You're grand' says he."

"He only means he gets it," said Murph. "He understands, like. Not as thick as he looks."

The bearded man's attention went to the hallway then, and he turned away. Murph elbowed Fanning.

"What did I tell you? Didn't I tell you to keep your trap shut? Didn't I?"

"He asked me a question."

"No he didn't. He gave you notice, that's what he done."

"Notice, what notice."

"You're on his radar, is what. Don't be telling people 'You're grand.' Especially him. He runs the thing."

"I know who he is, you know."

"It doesn't matter who he is. This is just something he does. On his own."

Fanning stretched slowly, to put distance between himself and Murph's breath. Turning, he saw the bearded man in profile. He was talking quietly to a man with a deeply furrowed forehead and bloodshot eyes.

"He's one of the Delaneys," Fanning said, unwinding his stretch.

Murph gave him a scathing look.

"Their pictures are in the papers," Fanning said. "Newspapers, that is."

Murph spoke in a low voice, barely moving his lips.

"Christ's sake. We have serious talking to do after this, I'm telling you."

Goading Murph had given Fanning a small portion of satisfaction. While Murph took out his cigarettes, Fanning stole another glance at the man Delaney was talking to. He was clean-shaven, in his late twenties Fanning calculated, wearing a newish leather jacket. The furrows on his forehead suggested that listening to Delaney took all his concentration, or patience. He gave curt answers to Delaney, pausing to yawn once. Fanning heard him say something about an Eddsie. It was an odd accent, not quite Dublin-sounding.

Delaney asked him another question. The man answered. Delaney's head went back, and a look of distaste came to his face. "West Ham?" Fanning heard him say. "What kind of a name is that?"

Smoke from Murph's freshly lit cigarette washed over Fanning's face then. As he batted it away, a smell of aftershave came to him in its wake. Who the hell would douse themselves with it, and then show up here?

Delaney and this man were now joined by another man, also in his early twenties. There was a sleepy, morose look to him. His hands hung in the pockets of a plain, zippered jacket. His eyelids slid open and shut to reveal a flat, unfocused gaze. The bored teenager look about a decade later than it should be, Fanning wondered. Probably just stoned. Delaney was staring at him, but the man seemed to be making a point of avoiding eye contact. Delaney glanced at the maroon T-Shirt showing above the zipper, and a sliver of some crest visible, and he turned away.

Murphy's elbow was sharper than it needed to be.

"Cut the gawking."

"What colour's the West Ham jersey?"

"The what? West Ham what?"

"The football team."

"Christ, I don't know, do I."

Another volley of cigarette smoke came his way from Murph.

"Well, who is that guy?" Fanning asked.

"What guy? I don't know. And quit asking."

"He said something about Eddsie."

"Who did?"

Fanning saw that he had Murph's interest now.

"That guy, the leather jacket there. And his mate, the dopey-looking one. Who's Eddsie?"

Murph stepped in close and glared at him.

"When we get out of here…"

He waited for Fanning to meet his eyes, and jabbed him in the chest.

"This can't be going on, you hear? You're going to get us into trouble if you can't keep that mouth of yours shut."

"It's just a question. After all I'm paying, right?"

"It's not about the money. This is my call here. I told you already."

The man said something into his mobile and handed it to

Delaney. Delaney held it to his ear, and listened. He nodded slowly several times, said something and handed it back. He looked uncertainly at the two men again and then ushered them by with an open palm. Then he walked back to face the groups, and he waited. Fanning saw him glance several times at the two men, now settling themselves into the small crowd.

"Ready when yous are," Delaney called out then.

Fanning studied the group of men congregating at the far end of the cage. He saw corners and sections of banknotes in several hands. The men shuffled again and the talk subsided.

"Them tinkers have plenty of money, I tell you," Murphy said.

"Get yourselves in order," said Delaney. "'When the cage is set, that's it as regards to bets. Rules is rules."

Fanning had no idea what breed of dog was now walking by the gate of the enclosure. The dog – mastiff, bulldog – jerked its head constantly as if it were having fits, straining and lurching clumsily at the end of its leash. Tony didn't glance up from the dog once.

The dog stopped pulling then, and it lifted a leg. Murph nudged Fanning.

"Marking the place," he said. "That's what that is."

Fanning watched the dog being led back to the hallway.

"Territorial, that's what that was. Did you know that?"

Fanning noticed that Delaney was again eyeing the two men he had spoken to earlier. The second of the two had taken out a flask. He took a drink from it, and passed it to the other. As he let back his head, the man stared back at Delaney. It was Delaney who looked away first.

"Can anyone come to this?" Fanning asked Murph.

"Are you joking me," Murph replied with a sneer. "You know what I had to do to get you in here? This is strictly invitation only."

Fanning looked over at the mismatched pair again. The one in the suit kept his gaze on the cage, but Fanning was certain that he had everything he wanted to notice in his peripheral vision.

"Invitation only," he repeated back to Murph.

"Didn't I just say that? You can't just walk in. No way."

"People come a long way for this," he said to Murph. "Do they?"

"I suppose."

"England, maybe?"

Murph had been rooting in his pocket for something. He stopped.

"England? Why are you asking me that?"

Fanning nodded toward the two men.

"You are so fu– so nosy, you'll get us both– Look, here's Tony's."

As quickly as Murph had turned angry, his expression had changed.

"Tony's not a man to bet against," he murmured.

Something in Murph's tone made Fanning look over. A blank expression had taken over Murph's face now, Fanning noticed. Mister Expert himself couldn't hide his own nervous anticipation of the fight to come.

The second dog looked like a terrier of some kind. It had no ears. It walked with a more jerky intensity than the first, growling low in its throat, and straining to get to the small pool of piss. The man pulling it back kept talking to it. Definitely a tinker, Fanning concluded.

"Wouldn't be here if there wasn't something to him," Murph said.

"But he's been hurt," said Fanning. "Look at his mouth."

"No he's not. Don't be stupid."

"That's blood there."

"So?"

"He had another fight earlier?"

"Listen," said Murph, dipping his head close. The scorn had returned to his voice. "Question for you. Where do you live again? Dundrum, someplace?"

"Near enough. Why?"

"Any pets missing there?"

"Pets? I don't know. Why?"

Murph let smoke out the corner of his mouth.

"Cute, cuddly little pets? Kittens, like?"

Fanning stared at him until Murph looked up.

"Now, are you happy?"

Something shrank in Fanning's stomach, and he looked away. Everything was crowding in on him now, the smells, the faces, the slow movements of the men, all under the milky overhead light that cast soft shadows and a pale, dun cast over everything and everybody here.

He half-heard Murph say something about jaws, and teeth, and stamina.

"A hundred, I said."

"What?"

"Give me two fifties, is what. We're going to do a bet."

"Go ahead, yourself. I'm here for research. Not gambling."

"Yeah, well research me the money or we're leaving."

Fanning gave him the eye. Well, at least he had tried. Slowly, he reached into his jacket.

"Fifty for me, fifty for you," Murph said. "Winner splits anyway."

"Bets!" Delaney yelled. "Your bets!"

Chapter 10

After the service, Minogue found himself making his way to the churchyard wall. From there, he had a view of the mourners coming out after him, and a place to smoke on the sly. The wind cut into his coat, but he welcomed it, as he did the patches of sunlight that had appeared on the sides of the hills behind the church.

"Very creative," said Kilmartin, sidling up. "Very unique. Is that normal for a Protestant thing nowadays, I wonder."

"I'm hardly the one to ask."

"Bet you liked it all the same," Kilmartin said. "Right up your alley. That sort of pagan aspect. Unless you want to try telling me it was a hundred percent Christian."

Minogue made a quick study of Kilmartin's face for signs of mischief.

"It wasn't bad, I suppose," he said. "Pity you weren't up to coming in."

"Anyway. What was that plant she was talking about again, in the bogs?"

Minogue knew that Kilmartin had hung around the door to the church. He would have heard plenty from the speakers. Three women who had met outside the door to the church began to laugh like seagulls.

Kilmartin eyed Minogue.

"'Celebration of life,'" he said. "Right?"

Minogue was reasonably sure now that Kilmartin missed the traditional, lugubrious funeral service he had hoped for.

"Ash–, As– Ash something, what was said in the service," said Kilmartin then. "I must Google it."

"Asphodel."

"It's a plant?"

"Bog Asphodel."

"Grows on the bogs? Funny I never knew the names of the things you'd find growing in a bog. All the years I spent mul-locking about in or near bogs too. Ironic, or what. And some legend? What was that about?"

"Persephone."

"I've heard of her. Okay. But who was the other one? Dam, Dem...?"

"Demeter. Her mother looking for her every year, and she in the Underworld – Persephone, I mean. The seasons. All that class of stuff."

"The Underworld."

"That asphodel is Persephone's flower."

"That's nice, I suppose."

Minogue had had years of practice returning Jim Kilmartin's goads with his own.

"It'd be a sacred flower too, then. Obviously."

"Oh obviously. Very nice entirely."

Minogue felt for his car keys. A bird scolded from a hidden place nearby. Was it the same one, he wondered, he had half-believed was calling to him in the middle of that old Irish hymn, Be thou my vision. For a moment, he took it to be a cry of grief and anger from the birds who themselves would miss Rachel Tynan, painter and worshipper in their domain.

"But why all the pagan stuff in a church? I'm only saying."

"It had to do with resurrection," Minogue replied. "I sup-pose."

"Right," said Kilmartin, thoughtfully. "Easter and all that. But you'd have to know poetry or that, mythology, to get that. Bit over my head. Other people too."

Minogue did not agree. That disagreement was not sufficient to prompt him to discuss the matter further. Kilmartin shifted his feet so he was looking over Minogue's shoulder into wilder Wicklow.

"Never in all my life did I think I'd hear people singing in Irish in a Protestant church," he said. "It was Irish, wasn't it? But fierce old Irish...?"

Minogue was suddenly weary of Kilmartin's archaic approach. Maybe Jim Kilmartin would be wondering next why the hesitant fiddle playing of the nine-year-old girl for the hymn had brought everyone to tears.

"I want to ask you something now," Kilmartin said, clearing his throat. "And of course it goes without saying, I understand your position."

Minogue waited.

"Any word on whether Tynan is going to call you in?"

"Why would he call me in?"

"You know what I mean. A straight answer is all I'm asking."

"He's busy," Minogue said. "As you can see."

This drew a scowl.

"The whole Garda doesn't just shut down if Tynan's out of the picture, does it? All I want to find out is one simple thing: how long is he going to leave me hanging. He's the man with final say. Something's got to give here."

Minogue spotted Sergeant Brendan O Leary emerging from the church. He was talking to a short, older man with a hearing aid. O Leary took his leave of the man, and he began to thread his way toward Minogue and Kilmartin.

"What more does he want," Kilmartin went on. "Listen, Tynan has had all the documentation for what, three months now? What's stopping him?"

Minogue pulled his coat tighter around his chest.

"Well," he said, "if he calls me, in I go. I suppose."

"Of course you do – but not without an AGSI go-ahead, right?"

Minogue had already had two calls from the Association of Garda Sergeants and Inspectors on the matter. He had not told Kilmartin.

"Maybe you should give me your script and I'll just memo-
rize it."

Kilmartin took a step back.

"Kick a man when he's down. Very nice, I'm sure."

Minogue watched the Commissioner's aide, Sergeant
Brendan O Leary, talking to a grey-haired, fiftyish man in a
navy-blue Loden overcoat. O Leary eyed Minogue, and the man
looked over too, squinting against the unexpected patches of
sunlight. He began to make his way toward Minogue.

"Barry," he said to Minogue. "Barry Conlon, Foreign
Affairs."

Kilmartin had already made himself scarce.

Conlon's vigorous handshake was rendered uncongenial
because of his bony hands and long, skeletal fingers. Minogue
had dropped his cigarette behind, and now attempted to locate
the smouldering butt with his heel. He noted that in contrast
with the out-of-date cosmopolitanism in his overcoat, Conlon's
shoes were a generation too ambitious, going on forever to that
narrow, squared-off tips that curled upward.

"I'm glad I was able to reach you," said Conlon, his eyes
blinking rapidly under thick iron-coloured hair, trimmed tight.
Impatience showed only around his mouth.

"We wanted to be sure you were on track concerning this
man Klos."

"Yes."

Conlon raised his eyebrows.

"Didn't want to leave anyone out of the loop."

Minogue waited several moments for the slurs to subside
within.

"Well I know where I'm going anyhow," he said. "And
why."

Conlon nodded, as though a weighty issue had been settled.

"We don't want to step on one another's toes, now. Last
thing we need."

Minogue hadn't a clue who or what Conlon meant.

"True for you," he said.

He could no longer see Kilmartin. For a moment, he imagined him sprinting in panic through the fields and across the vast bog to the southwest.

"And it goes without saying," said Barry, "that it will be comfort to them, the man's mother, I mean, to know of your background."

"Grand, so."

"As long as it's brought up with, you know, with sensitivity to the situation we find ourselves in."

We find ourselves in: the phrase ran back in Minogue's mind a few times.

Conlon seemed to be waiting for his reaction. Minogue thought he saw Kilmartin disappear around a bend in the laneway

"Your former work?" Conlon said.

"Oh, the Murder Squad, you're referring to," said Minogue, caught between embarrassment and annoyance that he had missed the hint.

"That sort of expertise, yes."

"Well, I'm – the team on this case, the people at Fitzgibbon Street station – they would... Well they would be the people who would..."

"We'll touch base then," said Conlon.

"We'll talk anon, em, Barry. Yes."

"Feel free to phone – me, or the department. Any time."

"Well, thanks very much now."

He took Conlon's card, and set out to find Kilmartin.

He and Kilmartin had a free run all the way back to the city. Minogue considered parking, and going into the shopping centre for a cup of coffee, but Kilmartin would keep him there for hours, yapping.

"Thanks," said Kilmartin, pulling open the passenger door. "Glad I went."

He paused and looked over.

"But that was funny," he said, and winked. "You have to admit, those papers blowing around like that."

Minogue waited until Kilmartin had started his relic of a

Jetta, and as the sooty cloud from the exhaust settled over the street, he gave Kilmartin a salute and headed into town. The Dublin area had fared even better than Wicklow with clearing skies. Except for the usual curse-of-God Donnybrook village and the Mercedes cluttering up the kip there while their owners shopped for courgettes and sun-dried tomatoes, mid-day traffic was obliging.

The Garda at the barrier in Harcourt Terrace was unfamiliar to Minogue. He looked up from the HQ parking sticker that Minogue had slid down the dashboard.

"Doesn't work here," the Guard declared.

"They usually make an allowance here in the visitors' section."

"They put in bike racks there last month," said the Guard.

"But sure I'm only coming from the funeral."

The Guard's expression didn't change.

"So I imagine that there's at least one spot that won't be used today."

The Guard gave no sign that he had gotten the hint.

"Well try your best with the visitors' spots," he said, and turned away.

Minogue pulled in to the Commissioner's spot, wrote his mobile number down on a piece of paper and placed it on the dashboard. He checked the file again and decided that there were indeed five pages missing at most. Locking the car and taking in the Dublin-filtered spring air about him, he imagined his missing pages fluttering against a hedge, and then being suddenly whisked into the air again higher up into the Wicklow Mountains.

He was waved by the desk by Moo, the near-to-retirement Garda Mooney, a man with a fearsome memory for hurling games, teams, errors, players, catastrophes, and tactics back at least thirty years. Minogue recognized several of the faces that he passed on the stairs, and he returned the nods and one "How's the man." Two flights above him he heard two men with heavy Midland accents, laughing. "What odds says I," one man said quickly between guffaws. "Isn't that what we have car insurance for?"

A short hallway opened out into a room sectioned off by a half-dozen cubicles. Newish dividers covered in grey cloth and lateral filing cabinets filled in the spaces. Beyond it was an open area where desks and tables faced one another. Minogue remembered that there were two conference rooms at the far end of the open area.

There were only two people he could see in the whole room. One, a woman, was on the phone and smiling, the other, a detective who looked or at least dressed and coiffed like a rowdy film star.

"How are you. I'm looking for a meeting...?"

The detective put down his sandwich.

"The Polish man? In 207 there. People there ahead of you."

He gave Minogue the eye and he tapped his nose.

"Thanks."

The door was half ajar. Minogue passed and glanced in. The two women there turned toward him. No Detective Hughes. He smiled sympathetically at the two and headed for a man's voice.

Kevin Hughes was on his mobile by a window. He raised his eyebrows at Minogue and he shifted his feet.

"We're starting now," he said. "I'll be off."

But before he closed the phone, Hughes listened, and his eager look, with Viking blue unfocused eyes resting on the view across Harcourt Street. The brace of fat pigeons on a parapet seemed to make him half grin. His lower jaw moved from side to side.

"No," he said finally, with a smile. He closed the phone, pocketed it, and extended a hand toward Minogue.

"Kevin Hughes, Fitzgibbon Street."

"Matt Minogue. I'm up in the Park. Next to the Zoo, as they say."

Hughes smiled. Minogue saw that his front teeth crossed slightly.

"With International Liaison," Minogue said. "I had better say."

Hughes stooped to pick up a slim leather briefcase. Late thirties, Minogue decided, thinning a bit up top, and filling out his jacket with little enough room to spare. Hughes rummaged in his briefcase and then he looked up.

"How's the weather in there?" Minogue asked.

"Not bad at all," said Hughes. "Stoic, is the word. The mother was prepared for it, so she was."

"So, no changes? We go ahead with this meeting?"

"Information session, we're calling it. Yes. You had a look at the file we sent over yesterday evening?"

"I did, Kevin. Yes."

"You don't read or write Polish, anymore than I do, I take it."

"True for you. Has the mother any English at all?"

"Little or nothing. The one from their embassy will be helping. I have her name here, starts with a D. See if I can say it."

"Danutay?"

"Danute Juraksaitis."

"You do speak Polish," said Hughes.

Minogue waited for the humour to do its work.

"What do you see then, er, Kevin?"

Hughes hesitated. Then he spoke carefully.

"Well what we're seeing is this man, Mr. Klos, and he's in the wrong place at the wrong time. Basically. The old story, I know."

He looked to Minogue for some approval.

"Here's a man doesn't know his way around Dublin," he said. "A newcomer. He's had a few jars – but he's not drunk. He's nowhere near his place, the hostel. Is he lost, wandering about? Or is he tagging along with somebody? Was he told to go down there off the quays? Was he lured?"

Minogue's inner eye moved through the streets and lanes that led back from the Liffey quays.

"Then," Hughes went on, "they – there were two different sets of shoes – start to kick the shite out of him. It's a sudden attack. Full speed right from the start. And down he goes. Pretty soon he's defenceless. His hands and his nails tell us nothing, except that he didn't put up much of a fight. Didn't get the chance to put up a fight? He had marks – ruptures, bruises – all along the small of his back. It looks like there were people taking penalty shots at his head."

Minogue winced.

"Swarmed?" said Hughes, with a sigh. "I'd say yes. A gang, some savage initiation thing? Don't know. Onlookers, kickers, I'm thinking – or I'm hoping, I should say. It's the ones who looked on will grass the others. How many's a swarm? Was he with someone, someone offering him something? Don't know."

"Substance abuse issues with him?"

"Not known."

"What's top of the list for pending? Closed circuit? Door to door? Site material?"

Hughes sighed and stroked his Adam's apple again.

"The post-mortem?"

Hughes stopped stroking.

"Say he's dropped there," he said to Minogue. "Afterwards, like."

"Bouncers at some club, or a pub, and they went too far? Dropped him there?"

"Yes," said Hughes. "That's open. We're working on it."

"What have they given you from the lab so far?"

"There's dust and things on his clothes. He was dragged, or he was falling around, or being thrown around. Roll-up papers. Tiny traces of dope. Marijuana, I mean."

"And all you have from the pathology so far for cause is on the file that I got? The brain hemorrhage, the fractures?"

"Skull fractured. Eye sockets broken, broken nose. Teeth out. A dozen and more serious soft tissue injuries. Several fractured ribs, fingers broken."

"Toxicology, how long are they telling you for that?"

"Monday. Hopefully."

Something scattered the pigeons from the roof opposite. Minogue followed the movement of a crane as it slid across the rooftops.

"It was wet that night," Hughes said. "So what we got at the site isn't clear. I don't know if it will ever be clear. We pegged it all out, lasered it."

"Footprints, shoe markings?"

"Yep. Incomplete, the lot of them. Mixed and mucked up with the rain."

"You tapped into the station for local info."

"First thing, yes. There's plenty of lowlife roving about the area. In spite of the fancy, what d'you call it, rehabilitation?"

"Gentrification, I believe they call it."

"Yes," said Hughes. "A lot of people passing through the area. Not just the office people during the day. Dealers, we know them, most of them. There's sex trade. Low key. It's a zone for a particular group, or shall we say family."

"Let me guess. Egans?"

"Fair play to you. We have it – via some Guards in that area – that the Egans have nothing to do with this though. Legit."

Minogue had checked area stats twice on the computer, but the GIS plotted only three years back. He had clicked through each year watching the lanes and buildings appear as the map changed. The whole area had been transformed in a very short time indeed.

"So he's off the map a lot that evening?"

"So far, the only times we can place him are leaving the hostel. A Slovenian – where exactly is Slovenia anyway? I forgot to find out."

"I'm not sure. Across the water, anyway."

"A Slovenian fella said he had a few words with him. Like, the Polish lad asking if he wanted to go out on the town a bit."

"'A bit.' What's a bit?"

"Fella says he had the impression that it was whatever he could find – pubs, clubs. That's just before eight. But there might be something from a shop there in Abbey Street. Maybe bought some papers, like roll-ups. The girl's not sure."

"What's the story at the hostel? Any talk of him there, pals? His effects?"

"Well, Slovenian boy alluded – is that the right word? …
Well he says that they'd be doing a little pot at the hostel – no
not inside, obviously. Everyone does, says he. He had – the
Polish lad now – he had a suitcase back at the hostel, and a
rucksack. Clothes, toiletries, magazines, some johnnies. Some
class of foreign booze, Polish writing on it. Biscuits – local.
Gum, matches. A few bits of paper with writing on them,
turned out to be names of organizations and things here to do
with Polish living here now. I got it all handy from people down
there at St. Michan's. That's their church now, you know, the
Poles."

"No grudges or bad feeling with people in the hostel? A
row at all?"

Hughes shook his head.

"No-one checked out in a mad hurry either. We got ahold
of every one of them who was there that day. Only two we had
to go foraging for, one girl went to Cork on the train. Another
fella, a Swedish lad, was doing his biking around Ireland thing.
We found him down in Waterford."

Minogue remembered then that all of Hughes' information
had been gathered in only two days.

"That's a hell of a lot done since the murder there, Kevin. I
just realized."

Hughes shrugged, and tried not to show his pleasure at the
comment. He winced then, and took a breath.

"Are you all right?"

"Grand. I've been getting these little I-don't-knows in me
belly since yesterday. No more curry for a while, says I."

Minogue took in the rueful grin.

"So, no sign of the man's phone at all," Minogue resumed.
"Passport?"

"Ah. It was locked in a safe they keep for the people staying there. So he had a head on his shoulders, you might say."

The crane began to swivel again, its hopper of cement
emptied.

"All bagged," Hughes said. "All gone to the lab."

"'Hurry up and wait,' is it."

Hughes shrugged.

"They're inundated, I hear," he said. "As usual."

"Okay," said Minogue, and looked at his watch. "Thanks for all that. Now. Have we a notion of how we're going to present this to the family inside?"

"I have a plan I suppose, yes."

"Spare her the details I'm thinking?"

"I'm with you there."

"Unless she insists, which is unlikely."

"We'll be talking through the embassy one anyway. The language issue."

"So: 'wrong place, wrong time' etc.?"

"That's about it."

The image of a man being mobbed, and taken down had come to Minogue several times today already. It brought to his mind something from a nature series on the telly. Hyenas, jackals, ravening, tearing at an animal they had cornered.

"Really not looking forward to this," said Hughes.

"No easy way, Kevin. No easy way here."

Chapter 11

Fanning was surprised that he had forgotten about the stink now.

There was hardly any movement in the small crowd of men now. He did a rough count: thirty something, maybe upward of forty in the crowd here. He had been to enough race meetings to know the steady, building charge of anticipation before a race, the burble of talk and the last shouts before the race began. This was different. The quiet seemed to deepen, making way for the sound of traffic in the distance. Then he heard footsteps and scratching close by, and then a low, intermittent sound that he did not like to think was a dog growling.

Fanning felt that he couldn't draw a proper breath, and was suddenly seized by the urge to be out in the open air. He pushed back at it, distracting himself by watching Murph wait his turn to hand the bet to Delaney. Then he pretended to yawn, and as he stretched, he took in the faces through his almost closed eyelids. There were thoughtful expressions on many now, and a quiet expectancy that on one or two faces that looked like the beginnings of a smile.

It was vital that he remember details like that. Just had to find a way to convey this sense of something primeval in this ritual. With his mind falling into the habit of searching for words and phrases, Fanning felt his breathing begin to ease.

A blue haze of cigarette smoke had gathered by the sky-lights. The man in the leather jacket was edging his way by some of the men, extending his arm to hand over a bet to Delaney. Something about his expression – distraction or detachment, Fanning couldn't decide – and the way he waited while the others milled around Delaney, kept him watching.

He wasn't quick enough turning his gaze away. Their eyes met for a moment. Fanning felt the man's eyes on him for several moments after.

"What's that face for," said Murph. "Are you going to puke?"

"Two hundred, in the space of five minutes? You could have told me."

Murph shrugged, drew out a cigarette, and lighted it from his finished one.

"That's the going rate," he said. "A hundred's nothing here."

"Not to you, it's not."

"Don't be fussing. You'll get it back with Tony's beast."

"What about the other one? The 'wouldn't be here for no reason' one?"

Murph blew out more smoke.

"The tinker's dog? Another time, maybe."

"What are the odds?"

"They don't do odds here. Jacko and them, they get their cut, for holding the thing. Then the owners get a quarter of the pot each. The rest of it, the losing bets pay for the winning ones."

"Who'd waste their money with these odds?"

Murph coughed, and gave him a disbelieving look.

"It's not just bets," he said. "It's the whole vibe. The scene. Get it?"

Yet another sour reminder of Murph's B.O. came to Fanning, and he shifted and turned away. When he glanced around at the faces again, it was the man in the leather jacket, the one with the peculiar accent, who looked away.

There was fervour on some of the faces now. Strange

sounds came from one of the dogs behind the plywood divider.
It sounded like a hum or a small whirring engine. Delaney
wrote something on a yellow stickie note he had been attaching
to the money, and then pocketed it. He looked around the room.

The light seemed dimmer now. Murph's face had grown
more pale, and the bags under his eyes even darker. Fanning's
neck and scalp began to prickle. His chest had tightened again.
He tried to breathe deeper. It wouldn't take long, he thought.
And these were animals, not people. He didn't have to look
directly at it when it happened.

"Scratch," Delaney said. "...And let them go!"

The Tinker's dog, the terrier-cross, was the first to reach
up in the air, its back claws scratching violently for a grip on
the floor. A cry of surprise, something between a whine and a
growl, erupted from one of the dogs. The men holding the dogs
crouched low, their leashes cutting into their hands. Tony's dog
was half-crouched, its back legs locked even as he pulled it back
to the line.

"Come on," he heard Murphy say, and then yell. "Let's
go!"

Fanning heard his own breath whistling out of his nose in
short bursts. Again he scanned the faces, taking in the narrow-
eyed scowls, the frowns caught between glee and cruelty. The
West Ham character was taking another swipe from the flask,
wiping his mouth.

There was a shout, and both dogs shot from their handlers'
grip. Teeth flashing, they launched themselves into the space
between one another. They hit together in a frenzy of violence,
and above the snarling, Fanning heard a clap of bone on bone.
Twisting and spinning still, their back legs dug in when they hit
the floor again. The terrier-cross twisted away from the bulldog's lunge.

Something flew through the air, a line or filament of something. Steady again for several moments, the terrier-cross reared
and then dived, his teeth looking for a leg. He missed by inches.
The bulldog took the opening, and sank his teeth into its shoulder. The terrier-cross jigged and arched, its back legs tightening

and then trembling with the effort of pushing them both sideways. He had the bulldog off balance almost right away, but its
jaws stayed clamped on his neck.

Someone bellowed. Fanning instinctively lifted his hands
toward his ears. More men were yelling now. He leaned in
toward Murph.

"When do they stop it?"

"What? Stop what?"

"When will they stop the fight, like when is there a clear
winner?"

Murphy turned to him, a raptuous scorn on his face.

"Are you joking me? With the money that's on this?"

The man in the leather jacket was on his tiptoes now. The
West Ham character seemed to have woken up a little, and now
began to punch the air in a slow, rhythmical duet of fists, his
jacket rising to his belt each time. Fanning saw the gun lodged
in the small of his back.

"Christ," he said to Murphy. "Look."

The terrier-cross was up again, he threw his head back,
twisted his body and whirled back. Both dogs hit the floor hard
churning their legs at one another.

"Not the neck!" Murphy shouted. "The belly! Tear his
nuts off!"

Fanning grabbed Murphy's arm. Murphy turned to him,
wild-eyed, and Fanning leaned in close

"He has a gun," he said. "That guy there–"

Murphy grabbed a lapel on Fanning's jacket and twisted it.
There were more shouts now.

"Shut your mouth," Murph growled, his eyes glittering with
anger. Somewhere Fanning felt pleased to have provoked him so.

"Let go of me," he said.

Murph loosened his grip, but didn't move back.

"Where do you think you are? This isn't a joke, you know.
It isn't one of your film things. This is the real thing here, isn't
it. And these are very serious people."

Somebody roared nearby. Murphy stepped back and turned
back to the fight again.

Blood whipped into the air in long strings that broke before falling to the floor. The terrier-cross was being heaved side to side but Fanning saw that it was the terrier-cross that had a grip on the bulldog's head.

The bulldog thrashed and reared, and then dove to the floor as though burrowing into it.

"No way," Murphy said. "He's got him, he's got his eye out. Did you see it?"

The bulldog pulled his head up, tossing blood, and got one paw over the terrier-cross's neck, but his head was pulled back down to the floor again. The terrier-cross began to pull harder. Together the two lurched across the floor until they hit the side of the cage again. That was when the bulldog pulled at the terrier-cross's leg, clamping it and pulling back. Their frantic twisting slowed.

"He won't let go of the head," Murphy said. "Even if the other one..."

The crack of bone breaking brought groans from several of the men. The terrier-cross leaned in as his leg snapped but he kept his grip. Fanning shuddered and turned away, but the noise and the smells rushed in on him again. He glanced over at someone who was beginning a chant. It was that dopey-looking sidekick of the man in the leather jacket. The booze, or whatever he was on, was working now. His eyes were shining and he beat his arms in the air to keep time with the chant.

"Finish it! Finish it!"

Definitely English, Fanning was sure now. The zipper had slid down. Sure enough, it was a football shirt. The crest was blue, with two hammers crossed on a shield. Other voices began to join in. Light-headed now, he heard Murph's yell as though from a distance.

"He did it, he did it! Jesus, he did it! Unbelievable!"

The bulldog's fur was wet halfway down its back, and the side of its face was a mass of gaping flesh. His upper and lower teeth showed plainly, fixed on the cross-terrier's throat. A weak fountain of blood spouted near where he worked at the throat. The terrier-cross's feet slowed even more until one came to rest on the bulldog's foreleg.

"Choked the frigging life out of him," said Murphy. "Absolutely unbelievable!"

Tony was walking slowly into the arena, talking. The Tinker stepped in too and took an awkward step to avoid a gout of blood.

The bulldog was still gnawing on the terrier-cross's throat. Every few moments, it gave a hard, tearing twist. The terrier-cross's legs moved again.

Tony entered the cage after the Tinker, both holding basins and dripping sponges. Tony went down on one knee, talking to his dog. The bulldog's head turned a little but his jaws stayed shut. The Tinker bent over and looked at his terrier-cross and frowned. Tony said something to him but the Tinker didn't answer. Instead he stepped around to get a different view. There was blood spreading beneath the terrier-cross now.

Murph's voice seemed to come from faraway.

"You look like shite. Better sit down."

Fanning realized that the shouting had stopped.

"I've got to get out of here."

Murphy blocked him.

"Whoa, there. You can't just walk out. We have a bet to collect."

"You get it. I've got to go."

"Wait," Murph grunted, grabbing Fanning's arm. "People are looking at you! Look, look – this is the finish. You've got to see this, you've got to."

Fanning saw the Tinker shake his head once and look away. Tony glanced at the spectators, and at Delaney, and then he reached into his jacket.

Fanning had seen pistols on sets before, those replicas on the set for Terrible Beauty last year, the heavy Parabellums used back in the early 1900s.

Tony's pistol was small enough to cover with a spread hand. That was what he did at first and then he passed it to his other hand. In a second it was inches from the terrier-cross's head, and Tony's thumb was on the hammer. He seemed to search for a spot where the dog's neck met his skull. The dog made a feeble twist, and when it stopped, Tony pulled the trigger.

"Jesus Christ," Fanning said.

There were starbursts in front of his eyes now. He turned, lunged, pushing away Murph's arm. Murphy grabbed at him again, but he had pulled away. He aimed for the doorway, tensed for another shot. The door was cool on his palms, and he shoved at it hard.

There was cigar smoke here. The door to the laneway was closed. Jacko turned to him.

"I need my mobile back, I'm going."

"Hold your horses," Jacko said.

He didn't want to look at Jacko's face.

"The Nokia one there, yes, that one."

Jacko took his time sliding a bolt and pulling the door open a little. "Wait, I said," Jacko told him. "Are you deaf or what?"

Fanning pulled the closing door and yanked on it, knocking Jacko off balance. He stepped into the yard and began a fast walk toward the cars. The door was closed hard behind him.

The damp air felt almost greasy, but Fanning took in deep, hungry breaths. He remembered the turns that Murph had taken, the bus stop, the passing traffic. He'd even phone a taxi.

"Hey, hey, hey!"

He didn't need to turn to know it was Murphy's running footsteps.

"Hey! Stop! Stop right there! You don't just do that!"

Murphy skipped in front of him and began walking sideways, his chest heaving.

"What the hell are you doing?"

"I'm doing what I need to do. Right now I want to be on my own."

"No, no, no! We're a team here, pal. Remember? You go with me, you get what you want, I bring you to the next gig."

They passed the parked cars. A lorry drove by on the road outside.

"There is no next gig," said Fanning.

Murphy got in front of him.

"What are you talking about?"

"What I said. There's no more gigs."

He tried to get around Murph, but his feints were matched. He stopped.

"We have a week's worth of places to do yet!"

Murph began counting on his fingers.

"The pool club yesterday, Alfie's. There's the Big O in Clondalkin, you see them fencing stuff, remember? Then Mickser, the garage? The piranhas, the one-hour jobs?"

"We can talk later, I have to go."

"Hop in the car, we'll talk on the way then."

"I need to be on my own."

"What 'on my own'? Look, I worked on this thing here."

"I know. I know."

"You don't know, you know? Do you know how much I had to do to get us in there? You have no clue. No way you'd get near any of this if it wasn't for me."

"Tomorrow."

"Screw tomorrow. I have it set up, and we're going. We have to go."

"Aren't you forgetting something? I'm the one decides. I'm the one paying."

"Stop right here! Just stop!"

Fanning felt the ache in his shoulders stiffen toward a cramp. He looked up at an overcast, immobile sky, the classic Irish mass of grey and tan cloud that somehow managed to look soiled as well as glowing. The last thing he wanted to see was another episode of Murph working himself up, full of that indignation and what he thought was his charm or smarts, into another stupid soliloquy about real life in Dublin. look soiled as well as glowing.

"No speech," he said to Murph. "Okay? Just give me time."

"Time?" said Murphy. "Time? Do you know how many looks you got back there? How many you got on me, and me trying to calm you down while you're having your spaz? The way they were looking when you done a bunk like that?"

"Okay. I admit it. It was too much for me. Shouldn't have gone."

"A bit late to be telling me that! You done damage here, serious damage."

"What damage?"

"There's your problem right there! You don't know what you're doing. You don't even see what's going on. That's exactly why you haven't a clue, exactly why you'll go dead wrong in this film of yours."

"It's a script."

"Whatever! You want to get it dead-on, right? 'The real thing,' says you. You wanted an entry, so here we are. But it's costing me, costing me big-time."

"Like what? What's it costing you? Nothing – that's what."

Murphy took a step back and he waved his finger like a windscreen wiper.

"Don't go there. Don't."

"I'm the one paying," Fanning said.

"Just 'cause you can't handle it. That's what it is. You want, what's it again, gritty? I gave it to you. The real thing. Now you don't like it?"

"I didn't expect someone to pull out a gun and kill a dog."

"That's what you got to do sometimes. That's how these things work!

Get real here, or you'll never get anywhere. Everyone has guns, everyone who's anyone. And another thing–"

Murphy stopped. His eyes were fixed on the warehouse behind, and the opening doorway. Fanning looked around.

"Shite," Murph said. He shoved keys at Fanning. "In the car. I'll handle it."

Fanning saw Murphy swallow hard, and then straighten up. Then, clearing his throat, he rolled his shoulders and he walked back toward the man in the leather jacket who had come out.

Chapter 12

Mrs. Klos – Anya Klos – was very, very shaky. Her hands trembled when she took out a pencil to place beside a pad of paper on the table. She was trying too hard to keep her head from trembling too. Minogue wrote the name of his section, a telephone number, and his email on the pad after the introductions.

Danute Juraksaitis' narrow black-framed glasses said something to him: economist, doctor, lawyer. Something serious, thoughtful, exact. She made only the briefest of smiles at the exchange of cards. Then she took a small notebook from another bag by her feet.

Mrs. Klos blinked a lot. She seemed to be holding her breath.

Hughes began with condolences. He spoke slowly, and with a simple eloquence that impressed Minogue. The real Ireland still existed, he began to believe again. Hughes looked from one woman to the other, pausing often, and nodding for emphases. Did they understand what he was saying? Would they like anything repeated? Did they know that they could interrupt him at any time?

Danute Juraksaitis spoke to Mrs. Klos in Polish. A look that Minogue read as ironic crossed her features briefly, and she glanced at Hughes.

"Mrs. Klos has some of words in English," she said. "The

rest is up to me."

Hughes made a sympathetic smile. Then he began with the times, the log of events that had preceded the arrival of the squad car to the laneway where Tadeusz Klos lay. He paused at the end of each sentence and waited for the translation, and a nod from Mrs. Klos.

"Ambulance?" Danute Juraksaitis said.

"The one phone call does ambulance and Guards," said Hughes.

"They think he was alive then?" she asked. "That is why the ambulance?"

"Well that wasn't clear," Hughes replied. "That wasn't what the two Guards believed."

As Hughes' reply was translated for her, Minogue studied the changing expression on Mrs. Klos' face

"But the ambulance?"

Mrs. Klos' face twisted up, and she quickly put her hands over her face. She shook her head and she turned away. Danute Juraksaitis put her notebook face-down on the table and stood up slowly, her hands clasped awkwardly. Then she placed a hand on Mrs. Klos' shoulder. Sharp intakes of breath brought Mrs. Klos' shoulders up, and they sagged again as the sobs seized her.

"Tea is needed here," Minogue said. "Coffee. Something. Anything."

He didn't wait for a comment, but got up and headed for the door.

He took his time getting to the canteen. He was aware he was trying to remember that perfume. Those glasses on that woman were actually severe, in a way. The thought of her brought a mild confusion to him, and a twinge of something unfamiliar.

The coffee he found waiting for him had been sitting in the pot since Adam was a boy. He opted instead for two teapots of boiling water and four bags of Lyons' Tea. The milk would be a problem, but it was a chance for a detour down to the cafeteria.

"I'll bring the jugs back so I will," he said to the cashier.

"How do they know you won't rob them," asked the sergeant in line beside him. Had he met him a few years back?

"The crime of the century," he said to the sergeant, hiding his irritation. "All my plans ruined now."

The Guard laughed as he counted out his own coins.

"I'll vouch for this fella," he said to the cashier. "One of Kilmartin's crew."

"And how is the bold Jim anyhow?" the sergeant whispered

"As ever."

"Really? Well tell him I was asking for him, there's a good man. Tell him 'The old dog for the long road,' will you?"

"'The pup for the path'?"

"Exactly. Good man!"

Minogue trudged up the steps balancing the tray loosely. Was every Guard in Ireland going to be asking about Kilmartin? His thoughts returned to Tadeusz Klos, and his mother. She didn't look Polish, he thought. But what did Poles look like, then? A Slavic or Russian look?

He was careful opening the doors from the stairs. He stepped into the hallway, and he paused, listening to the cylinder at the top of the door hiss softer as the door came closer to rest. There were voices from the open area beyond the conference rooms. Someone had recently had an egg sandwich. But unless his mind was playing tricks on him, there was the faintest trace of that same perfume again. Hardly possible, his mind declared, but there it was.

Hughes had a map of Dublin spread out on the table. He was pointing out where the hostel was.

"The city centre here is very walkable," he said, and waited. Minogue saw him wince and move his hand reflexively to his lower ribs.

Mrs. Klos did not seem much interested in the map. Minogue laid down the tray. Danute Juraksaitis had finished noting something. Her gaze turned to the teapots and then met Minogue's eyes for an instant.

"Ah," said Mrs. Klos. Then she said something in Polish.

"You are so kind," said Danute Juraksaitis. "Mrs. Klos said."

Minogue looked at Mrs. Klos. Her eyes were red and there were blotches on her face from crying.

"Nothing stronger I'm sorry to say," he said. Mrs. Klos waited for a translation. Hughes cleared his throat and continued while they waited for the tea to draw.

"The clubs serve drink," he was saying. "Alcohol?"

He cleared his throat again, excusing himself as he did. A pallor had settled on his features, and Minogue thought he spotted beads of sweat near his hairline. He hadn't realized that Hughes had been that nervous.

"Pretty well every night of the week is party night now," Hughes went on. "Dublin is very busy. Very modern."

Minogue could not understand one word that Danute Juraksaitis translated of this. Mrs. Klos nodded.

"It is the same in Poland Mrs. Klos said," said Danute Juraksaitis. "The young they want… life. Fun. This is freedom."

A rough translation, Minogue decided.

Hughes turned to Danute Juraksaitis, and cleared his throat yet again.

"So, in the light of what has happened since," he said, tentatively. "What's in the briefing here…"

Mrs. Klos leaned in slightly toward Danute Juraksaitis.

"Did Mrs. Klos need help understanding it maybe?" Hughes asked.

No, was Mrs. Klos' translated response.

"It was forwarded to her by our federal police," said Danute Juraksaitis.

Then she said something to Mrs. Klos. It was answered with a nodding of the head. Minogue saw now that Mrs. Klos' head had begun to shake, and her face had taken on that slack, stricken look he had seen too often over the years. He looked to see where she might fall, if she was indeed to keel over in a faint.

"It was explained to her," she added.

Minogue busied himself pouring the tea while he eyed Mrs. Klos' state surreptitiously. Hughes' voice was tight when he spoke now.

"I could move on then and tell you what we know so far. What the investigation has come up with?"

He took his cup while he waited for the translation.

"Or maybe Mrs. Klos would prefer to ask questions right away?"

With Hughes' question translated, Mrs. Klos shook her head gently, twice. Hughes nodded slowly. After several moments Minogue realized that everyone was staring at the teapot. It looked like nobody was keen to resume the conversation.

The scent of the tea took over Minogue's senses, along with the tings, slurps, and the stirrings of spoon against the cups. Mrs. Klos used three sugar bags, and blew on her tea. Danute Juraksaitis didn't touch hers. The room felt smaller now. More small beads had formed on Hughes' forehead.

Supposedly moody, passionate, the Poles, Minogue wondered – but where had he picked up that stereotype? There was surely some common thing between the Poles and the Irish. It couldn't just be the Catholicism. A rough history too maybe, with their own overbearing neighbours, and their own wide scattering to America.

Mrs. Klos shifted in her seat. She said a few words in a flat tone. Minogue noticed that Danute Juraksaitis had half-moons on her fingernails, that her hands moved slowly and deliberately when she translated, pivoting at the wrists as though she were doing tai-chi.

The silence in the room turned to awkwardness.

"I wouldn't risk the coffee here," Minogue said.

"True for you," said Hughes.

Mrs. Klos smiled thinly when the translation had finished. She said something in Polish, with the word Guinness in it.

Danute Juraksaitis turned to the policemen.

"She said she has tried Guinness."

Minogue pretended to be shocked. Mrs. Klos made a so-so

gesture with her free hand. The smiles faded as quickly as they had arrived.

"Mrs. Klos," Hughes began then. "I'd like to begin?"

Mrs. Klos tilted her head to listen to the translation, but her empty stare lingered on the map.

"And I'll be asking you for information."

That was enough to break her stare when the translation came to her.

"...Things about your son that you might not like to say..."

With the awkwardness thickening the atmosphere even more, Minogue released part of his mind out onto the coast of his native Clare, to the waves crashing on the Flaggy Shore. He wondered all the while if Danute Juraksaitis would balk, and suggest legal counsel.

"...For example, his friends, or troubles..." he heard Hughes continue. "Such as problems with the law back in Poland..."

Mrs. Klos bit her lip and her eyes went out of focus.

"She says she will help," said Danute Juraksaitis.

"Only to help us see if there is any connection to here, perhaps another Pole, I mean, Polish person he knew...?"

Mrs. Klos listened carefully, and looked from Hughes to Minogue and back.

"It's okay, she says. Tadeusz – her son – was not an angel always."

Hughes seemed to be waiting for an okay from Mrs. Klos. Danute Juraksaitis murmured something to Mrs. Klos, who nodded.

"I'll ask her a few questions then?"

Danute Juraksaitis nodded. Minogue saw her Biro waver as she held it over her notebook. He looked again at the half-moons on her nails, the sinews that ran to her knuckles, her wrist bone. She wrote slowly and sparingly as she listened to Hughes. When he stopped to await her translation, she turned the Biro on its head and let it tap on the notebook as she spoke to Mrs. Klos. Minogue found himself wondering if she was always so grave and so poised.

Mrs. Klos had only vague answers for Hughes, and Minogue was reasonably certain that everyone in the room was aware that he was merely going through the motions, asking the questions that they expected a policeman to ask. Who really knew their children, he heard himself say within.

Chapter 13

Bríd had picked up a pizza from Superquinn on the way home from the child minder's. Aisling was clinging to her, and her cheeks were red. She'd been crying. Fanning was at the door first.

"Go to Daddy," said Bríd, trying to pick up her schoolbag along with the shopping bags.

Fanning put his hand on his daughter's back. She clung tighter to Bríd.

"Let's see if your dolly talks to us today," he tried. She sniffed and buried her face in Bríd's collar.

"Sit down why don't you," he said to Bríd.

"I can't," she said. "Take the bags will you?"

It was the hardest time of the day. Bríd in from school, tired after the day with those hellions. The blood-sugar low, Aisling cranky and fighting one bug or another since before the Christmas. If it wasn't a sore throat it was teeth, or a cold, or diarrhea. The kettle popped.

"Cup of tea? Or something decent?"

Bríd's frown eased a little.

"Have we something to celebrate?" she asked.

He smiled.

"Well this gorgeous woman just walked in the door, an angel in her arms."

"You're such a ham."

She sniffed the air.

"You've had a little something already, have you?"

"Pretend we're living in Paris," he said. "Just for this evening."

"And you're Johnny Depp?"

He knew she was searching around this hour of no man's land for something easy, something innocent to say. Still his irritation was building. He needed a knife to get a start on stripping the wrap off the pizza.

"Pepp-er-only," he sang to Aisling. "Pepp-er-only and geese, Aisling. Won't that be the bee's knees? The cat's pyjamas?"

Aisling made no move. He closed the oven door and tickled her ankle. She didn't react. Bríd frowned at him.

"You're in fine fettle," she said. "Things went well for you today?"

"Pepp-er-only?" he said to Aisling. "Geese too?"

"It's not geese," she said still buried in her mother's neck. "It's cheese, Daddy. Don't be silly."

"Breakthrough Day?" Bríd asked him.

It was a code word he wished she'd forget, something from long ago when they'd talk together for hours about what he had written that day.

"Well, I talked to Breen."

Bríd made a face.

"He liked it," Fanning went on. "Very positive."

Bríd closed her eyes and sighed. Aisling let herself be picked up. Fanning loved the weight of his daughter. The ease and trust she expressed with her whole body when she draped herself over his shoulder. Her cheeks were raw from crying.

"Are your toothies hurting you, love?"

She shook her head.

The smell of her hair, even the staleness of her clothes. But most of all the feel of her baby fat cheeks on his neck.

Bríd yawned and draped her coat over the couch.

"He always 'likes it,'" she said. "But he does nothing about it."

Fanning felt Aisling grow alert in his arms. She must sense

his anger.

"We'll get there," he managed to say.

"I thought you had another one of your field trip things today."

Fanning's anger vanished when he saw again the arm raised, the thumb cocking the hammer, the barrel inches from the bloodied dog's head.

Aisling twisted around awkwardly, and leaned back against his arms.

"Daddy, you're wivering."

"Shivering," Bríd said quickly. "Shivering, Aisling. Don't use Daddy's make-up words any more."

Fanning's arms were turning to water. A sour taste filled his mouth, and an image of the men yelling to finish the fight flared in his mind again.

"Are you okay," Bríd asked. "Have you the flu or some-thing?"

Aisling was playing with his shirt buttons.

"I'm okay," he said.

"Well I'm wasted," Bríd said.

She sat down heavily on the couch and began drawing out notebooks from her bag. Fanning heard the gunshot again, felt how his ears had rung.

"Staff meetings," she murmured. "The tenth circle of hell."

The dog would have been thrown into a pit or something, its torn lifeless body there to rot and be forgotten about. They'd find others, train others.

"And it's a marking night too," Bríd said. "Jesus."

Aisling seemed to have calmed down. His strength was coming back. He began to dandle her a little, bobbing and weav-ing gently.

"That can wait," he said.

"It can't," she said without looking up.

"If people only knew," he said, "how much work teachers actually do."

She glanced up with that curious smile that had so aroused him in the past. Then her expression changed, and her eyes lost focus

"Breen," she murmured. "I'd like his job. If that's what you could call it."

Fanning poured soup into bowls. He put an ice cube into Aisling's and tested it with his little finger. She was crying again, and Bríd was trying to humour her.

Bríd found time on the weekends to make the soups for the week. It was something she liked doing, she said, because she knew that Aisling would be getting at least one solid part of her day's food homemade and organic too.

Fanning admitted he was hopeless about food. He enjoyed a meal, and the more variety the better, but something happened to his brain when it came to organizing and cooking a serious meal. He'd liked to make Bríd laugh back in their early days, about cavemen multitasking, cooking with fires and so forth.

Time had gone strange somewhere in the past few years. The clock ruled now, with things that had to be done, and by a certain time. Awkward bills came in the post, and everything cost so much. They'd had a few heart-to-hearts about it, the money / house / career – monster. It didn't help really.

He and Bríd had been together since third year – except for the summers when he had gone to London and Copenhagen, that is. They had just carried on after they got their degrees, even staying in the same flat. Both of them were vehemently for staying in Dublin while so many had left. There was not even a hint of any boom back then. He had always regarded himself as being on the ball, alert to social change, to the zeitgeist, no matter how small the signs. Being alert was his strength, he felt, noticing things, especially things that everyone else seemed to ignore.

He licked the soup off his finger and he took out a bib for Aisling. It was the only one she'd allow now, the one with the elephants. There was something sticky on the floor underfoot. A door closed hard in the adjoining flat, where the Spanish kids had arrived before Christmas, and he heard their television go on.

Aisling had stopped crying. He heard Bríd's footsteps in the hall. Aisling was asleep on her shoulder, her cheek almost flagred now. Bríd hadn't even had a chance to get out of her school clothes. Gingerly, she edged onto the seat. Teeth, she mouthed at Fanning. He turned to the cooker and checked on the pizza. He glanced back at Bríd to offer her a smile. It was a small way of saying thanks for all that she did. But her eyes were closed too now. Already her breathing had slowed. He wondered why she hadn't put Aisling down if the child was so sleepy or aching with baby teeth? Even lie beside her a few minutes like at bedtime.

Was this what they called the terrible twos? Bríd wondered if it was some separation anxiety thing and she felt guilty, especially at the babysitter's. But even during their worst arguments she had never come out straight and told him that she wanted him to take over the breadwinning thing and let her stay at home with Aisling.

He pushed the edges of the hardening yolks as they began to flap. He'd lost count of the number of times Bríd had fallen asleep with Aisling at bedtime only to wake up with a start herself and start marking student stuff until well after eleven. All the while he'd had his notebooks out pretending to work, or revising, or editing.

"I was having a dream," she murmured. A small wistful smile appeared, and she opened her eyes.

"You'll never guess," she said, and yawned. "This guy knocks at the door. He wants to buy your script off you. 'Any price,' he says and he wants to make it. And we have to go with him to Hollywood so we can coach him getting the Irish accent right..."

She opened her eyes wide and stared at him.

"Brad Pitt auditioned" she whispered, "I'm ashamed to say."

A surge of irritation swept through Fanning. He felt he was losing control of the muscles in his face and neck. He tried to hold a smile, but he had to turn away.

"It must be a good omen," she murmured. He knew she

was still smiling.

"Well," he began to say, his throat almost too tight to let the words through. He stopped when the phone went.

Chapter 14

HUGHES LED THE TWO WOMEN DOWN TO THE FOYER. Minogue followed. In the lift, Hughes was at pains to repeat something he had spent considerable time on earlier.

"I hope that Mrs. Klos leaves here certain that..."

Mrs. Klos nodded with the translation.

"Certain that we'll do our best. We'll treat this as we treat any murder."

Hughes glanced at Minogue as Danute Juraksaitis translated this.

Mrs. Klos made a bleak, momentary smile and resumed her stare at the worn symbol on the Door Close button. There was awkwardness at the door out of the building.

"Mrs. Klos has a place to stay, I suppose," Hughes said. "May I ask?"

"In Fairview," Danute Juraksaitis said. "Bed-and-breakfast."

"She has people here?" Minogue asked.

Danute Juraksaitis asked Mrs. Klos something.

"Yes. There is a priest. He is Polish. And she knows the Polish newspaper and shops."

"And to contact Mrs. Klos it's best I should...?"

"It is better you phone me first."

Hughes took out her card and turned it over.

"Mobile. It is on always."

No-one knew what to say or do then.

"Sure we can't give you a lift?" Hughes asked.

"My car is parked a hundred metres down this street."

There were no handshakes. The two women prepared to head out into Harcourt Street. Hughes said "God bless," something Minogue could not remember hearing for many a year. He heard what sounded like the word "Christ" in the translation. A ruined smile came to Mrs. Klos' face.

"Thank you, thank you. Yes, thank you."

Both he and Hughes watched the women gain the footpath and soon disappear from view. It was nearly one o'clock.

"Jeeee——sus," Hughes whispered then and let out a big breath. "Glad that's over with."

He turned to Minogue.

"So how do you think it went?"

"As good as it could, I suppose."

"The language thing though – that's a killer. Like, I don't want her coming back at us, you know, 'they didn't explain this, they didn't explain that.' You know?"

"I daresay we'll be okay on that one."

Hughes cocked an eye at him.

"Not the mother. I mean the other one. Ms. Juraksaitis."

Hughes' tartly precise enunciation caused Minogue to turn from his covert survey of three detectives waiting on the lift.

"Well she didn't exactly give off the best vibes," Hughes said. "Did she."

Minogue remembered her glasses, how she turned her hands when she translated.

"Well it was great you were there," Hughes said then. "So thanks."

Minogue tried to remember if Danute Juraksaitis had a Polish accent or not. It puzzled him that he had not noticed.

"Mind me asking a question?" Hughes asked. "Now, I'm sure you've been asked a thousand times."

"Fire away."

"Do you miss it, the Squad?

Minogue had had plenty of practice in prevaricating.

"Oh I don't know," he said, easily. "All the high tech and training nowadays? It was time to decentralize, I suppose."

Hughes raised an eyebrow. Minogue felt the return of the hunger he had been ignoring during the interview.

"Does Mrs. Klos know what's coming up?" he asked Hughes. "The arrangements, the release of the body?"

"I told the embassy one, Miss Juraksaitis. The body could be released within a few days if the toxicology's done and clear. Then I suppose she'd bring him back home – the mother, I mean. And that's another thing."

"What is, Kevin?"

"Ah, that one, Juraksaitis. I asked her if the mother'd get help, making the arrangements. 'Arrangements will be made,' says she. Just like that. And changes the subject right away. Like it's not my place to be asking."

"It could be a language thing."

"Hah. She speaks better English than I do. No, I have a feeling about that one. I say that she's not that thrilled to be involved. I mean this Klos man is, uh, was not top shelf, strictly speaking. And she knew he had been done for petty crime, sure. Maybe diplomats turn up their noses at this type of work."

Hughes made a fluttering motion with his fingers. Minogue thought of the missing pages from the file fluttering higher up the more desolate slopes.

"Or just doesn't like having to deal with coppers," Hughes added.

Hughes stretched, and spoke in a faux-Polish accent.

"'Arrangements will be made.'"

Minogue tapped his file folder, and silently cursed the slow lift here.

"I wonder," Hughes said then, shaking off a yawn at the same time. "What it costs anyway. You know, 'the arrange-ments'?"

"No idea."

"'Cargo' and so forth," Hughes murmured. "Cost a fair whack, I'm sure. Whatever the going rate is for–"

Minogue looked over at Hughes' abrupt pause. Hughes

grimaced and said something under his breath. Great, Minogue thought: he'd be taking Hughes' flu, or whatever he had, soon enough himself now.

"Funny phrase," Hughes said, letting his breath slowly out his nose. "That 'going rate.'" I suppose things stick in your head, like that."

"'Young people of Ireland...'" said Minogue.

Hughes smiled.

"The Pope," he said, quickly. "The old pope, I mean. John Paul. The Polish pope."

"I thought it might be a bit far back for you," Minogue said.

"No way. My family went to that big mass, above in the Phoenix Park. And me dragged along with them."

"You and the rest of the million people."

"You too?"

"Ah no," said Minogue. "I was out of the country. Unfortunately."

"But you're right," said Hughes. "How a phrase sticks in your mind. You see, I was on to a certain party yesterday, beating the bushes for any info on street crime there around where the poor man was beat up. Murdered I should say. Something in the drugs and street crime line, I was angling for, pointers, like. This fella I was talking to is the man to go to, I hear. Drugs Central, but runs his own thing."

"Ah."

"So, I'm talking to him, you know, see if he or any of the other cowboys – sorry, Drug Squad – will put out feelers about Klos. 'Up to our necks,' he says. Tells me about the shootings, you know, the gang stuff and all."

"It's always that way in Drugs, I hear."

"I know that," said Hughes. "But it would mean a lot to us, I says to him, you know. 'Okay,' says he, and I think I'm getting somewhere. 'How much would it mean,' says he. 'I don't get it,' says I. 'What's the going rate?' says he."

"Quid pro quo," said Minogue.

The lift bell rang at last. Three detectives went in first.

"Well what have I got, I could give him? More like a 'get lost' to me."

"Tommy is sound," Minogue tried. "Lot of pressure on the job there."

"You know who I'm talking about?"

For a moment, Minogue believed that he was well and truly had, that Hughes was setting him up.

"Tommy Malone. Yes, I do."

"Well small world," said Hughes, following Minogue into the lift. His tone seemed genuine to Minogue now. They stood next to the doors.

Minogue could almost sense Hughes thoughts turning over.

"I wonder," Hughes began, hesitating over his words. "If it'd be out of order asking you, if you could maybe, you know…?"

Minogue thought of Mrs. Klos, her hands that wouldn't stop shaking. Bed-and-breakfast, Fairview. A stranger in a strange land.

Chapter 15

MALONE WAS IN A CAR SOMEWHERE WHEN MINOGUE CALLED. He was more than a bit surly.

"Hughes is being taken care of," he told Minogue. "Tell him to get his hearing checked."

"He believes that I have an in with you," Minogue said.

"Really. Well I believe Posh Spice is my half-sister."

"It's working its way through, I'll tell him then?"

"Tell him what you like."

"Did I tell you it's murder, that the man is dead?"

"Twice already. Is it your case?"

"I sat in, that's all. He's a Foreign National. But the man's mother is here. An only son. The father is a ne'er-do-well, not involved at all. The mother's on her own here, well except for someone from the consulate."

"Sounds to me like Hughes is after guilting you. So now he can jump the queue here and get the glory."

"He doesn't want the glory, Tommy."

"Wait a minute, will you, hold on, I think I see Santa Claus here, oh look, it's the Tooth Fairy as well."

"Did you hit the sack at all over the past few days?"

"Oh, I know where this is going. 'You sound contrary.'"

Minogue had to smile at Malone's effort at a country accent. A pang of nostalgia arced in his chest when he thought of the sessions back in the Squad, with Kilmartin and Malone going at it. There was no going back.

"Look. Hughes is not being bollicky. He knows how busy you are."

"Busy? Nice of him. Tell him we're in the middle of a war here. Mulhall, the other day? I was working him, trying to work him, you know. Wouldn't listen to me. I told him he wouldn't last. I told him…"

"All hands on deck then, is it."

"You're telling me. It's like last year's big thing never happened. Oak and Anvil…? Might as well be ancient history."

Minogue recalled the haul displayed on the television and in the papers. Over five hundred kilos of cocaine was on show, close to a million Euro, an assortment of pistols, submachine guns, and two assault rifles. He never found out who had called it Operation Oak and Anvil in the first place.

"Okay," he said to Malone. "I'll relay that. Sin sin."

"What shin?"

"Sin sin. 'That's that.' You should have taken Irish lessons."

"There's a thick idea. A dead language, for culchies."

"How's the Cantonese then?"

There was a pause.

"I'm jealous," said Minogue. "That's all."

"I'll bet. Tell you what. Stick to your fecking French lesson things. French is a joke compared to what Cantonese is doing to my head."

"You'll have a lifetime of peace from the in-laws. Respect too, of course."

"My arse, I will. Her ma's grand, but that oul lad of hers will never change. Sweet and sour I call them now. I leave it up to you to figure out which is which. You're the Detective Inspector, after all."

Someone asked Malone a question then. Minogue waited for the hand to be taken off the mouthpiece. He couldn't make out the words but he was reasonably sure that Malone swore twice.

Whoever was in the car with Malone was using the radio. Malone's hand came off his mobile.

"Leave it for now," the Guard said. "Wait 'til he comes out."

"Look," said Malone then. "I'm on the job here, I have to go. I'll see you Monday. The usual."

He meant the get-togethers, Minogue knew. The Club Mad had moved location to Clancy's on the North Strand. It was the only pub that remained locked in the 1970s, reliably dreary and down-at-heel, and all due to a long-running dispute between two brothers over a will. The mixture of heavy daytime drinkers from the corporation flats nearby, the few greying Bohemians, and a changing set of petty criminals half-pleased Minogue. Neither Plate Glass Sheehy nor Jesus Farrell – not even the tee-totaller Shea Hoey – had complained about the place. Kilmartin had nevertheless pronounced Clancy's a dump, but still attended.

"Monday's a long way away, Tommy. Can't you do better?"

Malone didn't answer.

"Hughes has done fantastic work here," Minogue said. "More in two days than we'd have done in a week, I have to say."

"Good for him."

"But he's run ragged, Tommy, spinning his wheels."

"Happens to the best of us."

"The mother, come on – you can imagine, hardly a word of English. An only child."

"Everyone has a mother," Malone was saying. "You never know that?"

"You're a hard man, Tommy. A real desperado, these days, I tell you."

"Ah don't start that crap."

"Just give Hughes a start."

"What do I have?"

"One of your touts."

"I don't believe you actually said that. I don't."

"Just someone who's not in this big war thing you're in the middle of."

"I can't believe you'd ask me for the loan of a source. Jesus."

"Anybody. This Klos man is showing up with cocaine in his system."

"Who doesn't, these days? Any club now, you see people snorting."

"Be that as it may. Give the mother something to hope for, and she taking him home."

"You are frigging piling it on, so you are."

"You know I'll be above board with whoever you give me."

"What do I tell him? What's in it for him?"

Minogue thought about it for a moment.

"'Assisting the Guards.'"

"Don't be an iijit."

"Is he coming to trial, sentencing maybe? Paste it into a plea for him?"

"Uh-uh. Anyone worth anything isn't going to be in any position."

"What, then?"

"M-O-N-E-Y. That works nicely."

"You pay them?"

"Damned right we do. It gets results."

"Really. Okay then. What's the going rate?"

Chapter 16

MINOGUE ATE AT HIS DESK. He was glad of the Pepsi to push the taste of the so-called brioche with its cargo of dry ham and chalky cheese, and its too-sharp crust that gouged his gums. There was nothing left worth reading in the newspaper. Still he searched. Someone had spray-painted the wall of the Muslim school in Clonskeagh. A road rage thing that led to fines of over a thousand Euro. An Aran islander who spoke no English had just died at the age of 105. The forecast said changeable, but to be on the lookout for showers coming in from the West. He almost missed the ping from his mobile. Don't screw up, Malone had texted. The name he offered was for someone Murph. He was to wait until Malone had gotten in touch with this Murph character. No address of course. In caps then the following: NOPRESSUREONHIM.

The low-hanging slabs of clouds that had formed the sky over the funeral this morning had now given way to masses of torn and running clouds. They lost their shapes quickly, but they occasionally revealed patches of blue. Minogue composed a rare text reply of six letters and one space: TA ASAP.

Eilís was trying to get a printer to work.

"What's up?"

"It looks like the damned thing is broken. Do you know anything about...?"

"I'd do more harm than good, Eilís."

"Well, horseman, pass by, so."

He heard her cursing quietly in his wake. He wondered if every Irish speaker knew so many curse words.

On his way back from the bathroom, there were two messages in his box, proof of the mysterious dispensation of fate that timed phone calls for when he entered a bathroom.

Eilís was shoving the paper tray hard into the bottom of the printer. She spoke without looking up.

"Peter Igoe," she said. "Wants to talk to you."

Odd, Minogue thought, and unwelcome. His head of section loathed meetings, preferring to network at a distance.

"A matter of some urgency," she murmured.

"Concerning?"

Eilís grunted as she pushed the tray home yet again.

"Didn't say."

Igoe asked Minogue to wait a moment so he could step out of the meeting to take the call. Minogue heard a door closing.

"Thanks, Matt. You got to that meeting there, the Polish matter."

"I did."

"Fair play to you. A good send-off for Mrs. Tynan this morning?"

"It's how she wanted it, I believe."

"Sad. Now listen, before I pass on the news to you, remind me what you're at. Current casework, I mean."

"The papers from the raid on the building sites in Cork and Waterford."

"Right, right. How goes it there?"

"I sent off scans of them to The Hague yesterday. I'm going through the lists of contractors now for more."

"Good, good. Listen to me, now, and brace yourself, I suppose."

"Is it going to involve brown trousers, Peter?"

"Ah, no. Okay. I just got off the phone from the Deputy Comm. You were with a Garda Hughes? Kevin Hughes, case lead on the murder?"

"This very day – is he all right?"

"As a matter of fact he's not. But he will be. He has appendicitis. Apparently he had to go to hospital."

"I'm sorry to hear that. Nice fella, a workhorse entirely, by God."

Her arms folded, Eilís was standing by the printer now. There was a faraway look in her eyes and her bottom lip was working its way slowly over her upper teeth. No one in the section had yet dared ask her if she was still off the cigarettes.

"Howandever. Now. I've been requested to free you up, so you can stand in for Hughes."

"Requested, Peter."

"You know the score, now."

"I have the impression there are a lot of people expecting CSI here, all wrapped up in forth-five minutes before bedtime?"

"Hard to argue with you there," Igoe agreed. "A lot of publicity, over in Poland and here. Yes."

Minogue knew Igoe long enough to recognize what his tone meant.

"But the point is," Igoe said, "this case has moved right up the ramp. So you have the whip hand, as they say. Ask for anything, and it's yours. You have only to ask."

Minogue kicked back the slurs forming in his thoughts.

"Up the ramp," he heard himself say.

"That's right, Matt. Right to number one."

This time when he phoned, Malone was somewhere quieter.

"Didn't we just talk about this?" Malone said. "Alzheimer's now?"

"Ancient history now, Tommy. The whole thing just got a kick, a big kick from on high. Here's the short version: I'm on the job, the Polish man's murder."

"April Fool's."

"I'm not joking. The case lead detective is in hospital."

"Well whatever you said to him, or did to him..."

"Acute appendicitis. So it's me now."

Several moments passed.

"Well best of luck to you," said Malone. "Let me know how it goes."

"Full steam ahead, is how it's going. I was given the keys to the kingdom."

"Everybody says that. Then they sober up."

"Seriously, Tommy. I hit a bump in the road, I pick up a phone: it's fixed."

Malone had nothing to say.

"So let me get to this Murph, Tommy. If you please."

"I told you," said Malone. "I haven't been able to get ahold of him."

"Sooner the better, and phone right away? It'd be much appreciated."

"Are you pushing rank my way?"

"Would that help if I did?"

"Like a hole in the head. I told you I have enough to do. Look, there's not much I can do until I get hold of this guy."

"How about I send you an email with lots of smileys? Would that do you?"

"You can shove your smileys. And since when do you use email?"

"Where are you?"

"I am in a car."

"Where?"

"In the back seat."

"So you're operational."

"I'm trying to be. But everyone's hiding under their beds."

"Your clients."

"Yeah, my 'clients.' Forget the global warming stuff. I'm already dealing with an endangered species here."

"You're environment is under pressure, it seems."

"Yeah. We call it the Mulhall effect. Lead poisoning."

It wasn't like Tommy Malone to be flip about murders, even when criminals were doing one another in. Minogue wondered if it was a signal that Malone was ready to give up.

"Let me guess where you are: Capel Street area?"

"Not bad. Near enough."

Over the top of his cubicle, Minogue now saw that rain was landing in streaks on the window beyond Eilís. The sky was bright behind.

"That coffee place up by Smithfield Market," he said to Malone.

"Beanz," said Malone. "What about it?"

"Ten minutes."

"That's kind of pushy."

"I'm buying."

"Do I have to salute when I show up?"

There were few umbrellas showing here on Capel Street. Minogue drove past a half-dozen secondary-school students who stood clumped around the entrance to a kabob restaurant. In the stop-and-go traffic he had landed in since turning off Parnell Street, Minogue's thoughts had slipped the leash again. He eyed two slight Indian-looking men walking past, flinching from the rain. He wondered what their home streets and towns looked like. Full of people, no doubt, but sunny and hot and colourful.

Some honking started far ahead. A woman crossed through the stopped traffic, her head and shoulders hidden by her umbrella. What did Juraksaitis mean? Minogue imagined her at work listening, noting, drinking tea, walking through rooms. His unease grew. The van ahead of him lurched forward. He got the Peugeot into second gear.

He spotted the parked Octavia with a man behind the wheel just after the junction of Little Mary Street. He slowed, looking for any space at all to pull in. There was someone in the passenger seat, just the tip of his nose showing from the reclining seat. He pulled in behind a delivery lorry not far ahead, and slid his sign down on the dashboard. The Garda radio antenna on the Octavia was the new black one that looked like a claw. A silhouette moved beside the driver as Minogue approached.

Malone stepped out awkwardly. He held the door open and said something to the driver, a balding man in a Nike jacket with a mobile in his lap. The driver shrugged and gave Minogue a nod. Malone, unshaven and looking generally creased, pale,

and irritated, closed the door. From the slight shrug he gave as
he stepped forward Minogue knew that he was wearing a ballis-
tic vest.

"Thanks," he said to Malone.

"I haven't given you anything yet."

"Am I interrupting anything?"

He held open the door of the restaurant for Malone. The
smell of ground coffee that met him livened Minogue consider-
ably.

Malone's eyes wandered the restaurant. Minogue ordered
an au lait, and Malone's usual black. The man who took the
order sounded Spanish. He would bring them over. They were to
relax, he said.

A teenager with very black hair, and her boyfriend, were
the only others here. They looked far beyond even glum. The
girl stared at the street while the boy played with a twisted-up
sugar packet. A difficult age.

Minogue settled himself ceremoniously at a table.

"You've got that look about you," said Malone. "On the
mooch."

"You're a victim of your own success. Legendary."

"Success," said Malone and scratched at his stubble. "You
think, huh."

Minogue waited a moment.

"Your film career," he said. "Any day now?"

Malone wrinkled his nose.

"What's his name again?"

"Fanning," said Malone. "But he's a complete iijit."

"Not working out for you?"

Malone flicked his head.

"Just what we need," he said. "Some wannabe like him
glamorizing the whole thing."

"Has he given up phoning you then?"

"I wish," said Malone, his voice rising. "He keeps on
trying to get a foot in."

"What exactly did he want, again?"

Malone sighed.

"What didn't he want, you should be asking. I don't know anymore. First, it's can we talk. I give him the brush-off, but nice enough, right? You know me."

Minogue almost smiled.

"Maybe he's deaf, I thought," Malone continued. "When he gets a 'no' for the chat thing, bejases if he doesn't ask for something more instead! Sit-down interviews, he wanted next, big long Q and A sessions. Listen, says I, write what you like, but stay away from me. Not in so many words, now."

"Any of the words start with an F?"

Malone ignored the jibe.

"He got bolshie on me then, like, 'I want to give the Guards the opportunity to tell things from their side,' says he. Like, make me an offer or I'll make the Guards look like iijits in this."

"Ah. He must have known you like a bit of extortion."

Malone's glare seemed cool enough, but a slight pursing of his lips told Minogue enough.

"What was your response to that one?" Minogue asked.

"The exact words?"

"The gist, if you please."

"'There is only one side. Get on it. But leave me alone.'"

"Loud and clear, I'd have thought, Tommy."

"Oh. I called him an interfering bollocks. Forgot that."

"How did he take to that?"

"Got on his high horse. Something about art and life? Gave me a headache thinking about it. Put down the phone on him."

"End of story, then?"

"Uh-uh. He tries to get to me though one of my... guess who?"

"No idea."

"Sure you do. Or you will, when you meet him. Murph."

"Big city, small town, Dublin," said Minogue.

"Fanning's decided that Murph, my fella, is the man, and he's getting toured around by him. You know, sights and sounds of the Dublin crime scene."

"He'll wake up in hospital if he's not careful," said Minogue.

"Do you see me worrying about it?"

"You coulda been a contenda, Tommy. Movie stah."

Malone shifted in his seat.

"Yeah yeah yeah. But you know what really got under my skin about this whole thing? There's this guy, Fanning, and he's the first one to slag the Guards. Kind of fella with plenty of edumacation and, I don't know, can tell you lots about all the fine wines of France or somewhere. Never went a day without his cappuccino kind of guy. Now he thinks all the scumbags of Dublin are worth making a film about. Okay, I says to him the first time he phoned, if you can guarantee me that the good guys are the heroes in this thing, maybe we'll talk."

"Your fame will have to wait then."

"Watch me care. There, did you see that? But this guy's persistent. He gets Murph to annoy me about it some more. Keeps on asking me. 'Your man' – Fanning, like – 'wants to show you a plot, see if you like it.'"

"Be a consultant then. Keep your day job and all."

Malone gave Minogue a scathing look.

"Don't go there. Seriously. I made a promise, remember. After Terry...?"

Minogue had underestimated how hot under the collar Malone had become. It was another sign of the stress he was under. The anniversary was around this time of year too. Malone's twin brother was gone four years now. The post mortem could not reveal if Tommy Malone's suspicions were true, that his brother had overdosed on heroin that was intentionally spiked.

"Anyway," said Malone after several moments. "There's a gang war going on. Some gobshite wants to hang out with me on the job, so he can make a movie out of it. And now you want to poach on my sources."

"You couldn't make this stuff up. Right?"

Malone darted a glare his way: the goading was working too well.

"Okay," Minogue said. "You win."

"Win? Me bollicks. With you, a fella never wins. A sneaky fecker, is what you are."

"Am I still invited to the wedding?"

"Don't start, I'm telling you. That on top of all this? What else could there be?"

"I could pass on Jimmy boy's musings on Irish life and society, a bit about the funeral there."

Malone's face turned sombre.

"You know, I would have gone. Really I would have. After seeing what she did with those kids there in Ronanstown, and the art classes? But I tell you, I'm living in a car the past few days, waiting to see who gets it next. Trying to get a step ahead."

"And are you?"

Malone's face now took on the mask of the mordantly skeptical Dubliner.

"Just between you and me," he muttered. "N. O. www.wedon'tknow whatthehellishappening.ie. Or .com. Whatever. Ever been to that site?"

"Well I won't tell you how often, will I."

"Rumours, that's the best we can do. And that's from all the millions and millions thrown into the, er War on Drugs, bejases. Rumours. Hearsay. 'A fella told me that a fella told him that...'"

Malone rolled his eyes, and then rubbed hard at them. He opened his eyes abruptly and eyed Minogue.

"The latest one is that someone brought in people from the outside, some hit men. 'Pros.' Paying them for results. 'A clean sweep' is the story. 'Things was getting' out of hand...'"

"Things are always out of hand, Tommy."

Malone looked away, testing his vision.

"Yeah, well it doesn't take much, does it. The rats are all under the bed now. Can't get any info at all. Phones not answered, stools empty in the pubs, nothing stirring."

He turned abruptly to Minogue then.

"Jesus, but you're getting me all depressed now, thinking

about it. Sidetracking me there. Get back on track, I say."

"On the double."

"Well what's the story with you here?"

"Let me give you some names of places," Minogue said. "For starters. North wall. Sherriff Street. Custom House Quay. Do they figure in your line of work?"

"Is the Pope Catholic?"

"Castleforbes Road?"

"Plenty going on there too, all right. That's where they found your man, I take it. The Polish fella?"

Minogue nodded. Behind him, the barista began clearing the filter holder from the espresso machine. Malone tensed.

"Headache, have you?"

"Not yet. That banging your man is at there, it sounded like something else."

A man entered then, smiled broadly and called out in Spanish to the man making the coffee.

Something had made Malone grin.

"What's the joke?"

"Nothing," said Malone. He shook his head, sat back, and chortled softly. Minogue couldn't remember the last time he'd seen him laugh.

"I'd like to try some of that 'nuttin' of yours so," Minogue said.

"Okay. You ready? Has Hughes tried to figure out if there is a Polish Underworld here in Dublin, then?"

"That's funny, I suppose. Or maybe you're overdue a holiday."

Malone sighed and sat up. "Why not," he said. "Everyone else's gangsters are here."

The coffee arrived.

"It is good to be happy," said the waiter, beaming. "Everyone must be happy, no?"

Minogue looked up at him. "It's true for you," he said. He turned to Malone again.

"What goes on in that area at night?"

"What doesn't. Do you mean a concert at The Point? You

get the same people showing up here you get at any event. Push, pedal, pimp. Car thieves, pickpockets, junkies, pushers. Gobshites, gangs, gougers."

"There was nothing going on that night, at the Point."

"The Point? When's the last time you were there?"

"Years."

Minogue tested his coffee. Promising – but way too hot. He put it back on the saucer.

"Kathleen does be there a bit, the job, she's in apartments, that class of thing. Rentals and sales. It's the coming area."

Malone nodded, as if that were something he wished to know before. Across from them the boy began talking to the girl, but she remained listless and indifferent. Bright light flooded the street, but the rain had still not stopped. Malone stopped stirring his coffee. Just as Minogue was concluding that he had been transfixed by the spoon, or by his own thumbnail, he looked up.

"Okay," he said. "I'll check in what I was at here. We'll head over in your car?"

"I don't want to take you away from your thing here."

"Yeah, yeah, yeah. Look, tell you the truth, my fella's not going to show. It'll be a while before they're back on their perches, this crowd. All the goings on has them hiding under their beds."

The barista and his newly arrived friend were having a great laugh. A middleaged woman with a sun-bed tan came in, smiled at the barista, took a table, and opened her phone. Minogue stole a quick look at her shoes. Malone winked and made a small nod in her direction. Minogue feigned disbelief. A knocking-shop here? Malone nodded again twice, a twitch of amusement playing about his mouth.

The coffee was decent.

Minogue asked Malone about the plans for the honey-moon. Sonya was too excited, Malone related. She couldn't believe he had agreed to a week in Paris. Malone couldn't either. Minogue asked him if he had heard of Kilmartin's remark about a slow boat to China. Sooner China than frigging Mayo, was

Malone's take on that. He asked Minogue for some phrases in French: You're the waiter, I'm the customer, so stop acting like a snobby bastard or I'll knock your head off, you poof. Brief was best, Minogue tried to explain, and Con was the word to use, if you wanted a scap. Malone asked about hand signals then. The talk passed on to places to visit in Paris.

The girl was crying as they left. The barista was talking to the tanned woman. The footpaths outside were greasy and shining.

They stopped by the Octavia.

"Leave it, Ger," Malone said in the window to the driver. "They're gone to ground for sure."

The driver looked annoyed, and relieved. Malone turned back to Minogue.

"I'll do what I can in the matter," he said.

Minogue was not sure if it was mock formality at all. He saw Malone dip his head, and look up under his eyebrows at him.

"All that's reasonably possible."

Chapter 17

FANNING STEERED THE CAR AROUND the parked cars cluttering up the estate, and up toward Bird Avenue and the Goatstown Road beyond. He did not look back. If he did, he believed he'd have seen Bríd at the window, watching him leave. She had tried to pretend she wasn't annoyed, convincing herself perhaps. Certainly not him. He had to go see Murph, he told her; an opportunity he shouldn't miss. He'd be home in an hour, an hour and a half.

What he didn't tell Bríd was that he was more than glad of an excuse to get out for a pint. For some reason, he wanted more than a few pints this evening. Maybe it had something to do with wanting to wash away the confusion he had brought home with him after that dog fight.

He stared into the red traffic light as the car came to a stop, and fell to speculating again when he'd ask Bríd to go away with him for a night at least. It'd be a proper date: babysitter for Aisling, a dinner reservation, meet up with friends, if that's what Bríd wanted. It was too important to postpone.

They could talk about anything and everything that way, no holds barred, and most importantly where they were headed – as a couple, as parents, in their work. He'd bring up the unthinkable, getting out of Dublin to try the continent again: Berlin, Copenhagen. Amsterdam. The South of France even. They needed to remember that they were not just another set of suburban clones, doing the family thing and the 9 to 5. Well, her 9 to 5, anyway.

Maybe that was it, he thought then: farmers versus cowboys. Simple enough really. Bríd wanted a real home, and she wanted more kids before it was too late. She wanted a provider. She couldn't admit these things to herself. Even if she could, she wouldn't want to tell him that because she knew he would unsettle him. And on the other side of the equation, he wanted...?

The lights changed.

The interior of the car had warmed up, and Fanning became more aware of the flowery scent of baby powder that was always in the car, and how it blended with the stale rankness of milk spills that were already baked into the upholstery. Stains on the dashboard, dust. Soon he was in sight of Ranelagh village.

Galloping Hogan's was one of the newer pub makeovers here. He saw no sign of Murphy's pimp-mobile white BMW. He let Murph's words play back in his thoughts again: "He wants to meet you, he who can help with your project."

"Help you with your project."

Well that was scripted, for sure. Murphy didn't talk like that. He probably didn't even think like that. But Murph wouldn't answer any of his questions during the phone call. When Fanning had told him he was needed at home with his family, Murphy had pounced on him. He had to come, he just had to. The opportunity of a lifetime. Fanning let himself believe that the tension in Murph's voice was from anticipation of some coup.

A Range Rover was leaving, with two men in suits laughing about something. Fanning took their spot.

Galloping Hogan's was doing good business for this time of evening. The big screen was on Sky, but it wasn't loud. Iraq again.

Murphy was suddenly beside him.

"Okay," he said, "about time."

Fanning tried to settle on what was different about

Murphy's features. He looked older, tireder? Maybe it was the light.

"So where's this fella, this exciting pal of yours?"

"He's not actually a pal. He'll be here in a minute."

"Is he someone I'd know?"

"I doubt it."

Murph's eyes moved around the room. Fanning saw he was biting his lip.

"I'm not sitting around, waiting for anyone," he said.

"Just listen to what he has to say, okay?"

"Get him to email me."

"Don't try to be funny about it."

"You're telling me what to say now?"

"Shut up," said Murph suddenly. "Just shut up, will you. For once?"

A threshold crossed, Fanning knew. Murphy wouldn't meet his stare.

"Okay," Murphy said then, and straightened up.

Fanning followed his stare. The man wore the same leather jacket, and even the same expression that Fanning had seen at the dog fight. He was light on his feet, loping gently more than walking. As he came closer Fanning saw that there were bags under his eyes and the beginnings of five o'clock shadow.

"Quit staring," Murphy hissed.

Fanning watched the expression on Murphy's face turn into a manic smile. A waft of cologne came to him, and he almost sniggered. Hadn't everyone gone through that when he was fifteen or something?

"Cully, man" Murphy said, clearing his throat. "Great to see you."

The man seemed to look to both sides of them. He drew to a stop, gave Fanning a quick look and nodded.

"Okay," said Fanning. "Sure – yeah, thanks. Okay?"

Cully said nothing, but waited for Murph to go. Then he turned to Fanning.

"You're Dermot Fanning? Michael Cullen. Cully, people say."

No handshake was offered. Fanning gave him a howiya.

"Buy you a drink there, Dermot?"

The lack of eye contact irked Fanning.

"Well I don't know," he said. "I'm thinking of heading home."

Cully nodded several times

"It'd help you in your work, you know."

Fanning couldn't place the accent at all yet. Cully gave him a glance, but quickly returned to his study of the mirrors behind the lines of bottles.

Maybe he was just painfully shy, Fanning thought. Shy more than crazy.

"Better than what you have now," Cully added.

There was definitely a Dublin accent buried in there somewhere, Fanning decided.

The barman placed beer mats in front of them. Cully ordered a brandy and soda. Fanning shrugged, asked for a pint of Budweiser. Cully leaned his forearm on the counter, and turned to him.

"You're working on a project I hear."

"It's at the research stage, yes."

"Research stage," said Cully, as if it pleased him. He scratched at his palm with his baby finger.

"Might come to nothing of course," Fanning said. "But that's the way."

Cully looked sideways at him.

"You put a proposal, don't you? A pitch?"

It was a Dublin accent all right, Fanning was sure.

"Or you get someone to do it for you. A connection in the business helps."

"And then they...?"

"Well they see if it could have legs. They could shop it around for me."

Cully nodded slowly. He looked down onto the counter where the barman was now placing Fanning's glass. Fanning took a long swallow.

"That business earlier on today," Fanning said afterwards.

"Yes. Something else. What do you think?"

Wotcha, Fanning heard. He shrugged, and exchanged a look with Cully. There was an indifference in his expression, almost a blurriness, that seemed to echo the montone in his way of speaking. It didn't come across as sarcasm, or even irony.

Impressions collided in Fanning's mind: well dressed, maybe even fastidious, and yet there was something careless and unfinished about the guy too. There was an air about him that suggested to Fanning that he didn't much enjoy, or even want, to be here.

"That was part of the research," he said to Cully. "The visit to that place."

"Right. Murph brought you."

"He did. He's my 'guide.'"

"He says you pay him. Like you employ him."

Fanning bit back his irritation again.

"That's research for you," he said. "I'd probably never get near the likes of that unless I know someone. And I don't."

"First time? The dogs, I mean."

"First, and last. Never again."

"Bit rough, isn't it."

Innit: Estuary English popping up clearly now. Fanning couldn't decide if Cully's tone carried some derision too.

"Left in a bit of a hurry, didn't you."

"And you stayed for more?"

Cully didn't seem to take the remark as cheeky.

"Maybe I'm more used to it."

"How does a person get used to it, to something like that?"

Fanning took a quick mouthful of beer. Cully had no answer to that one, apparently. He took his first sip of brandy.

"Now, I had a suggestion for Murph. What did you call him again, your..."

"Guide," said Fanning. "I don't really mean that. I don't know what else to call it. Working for you isn't Murph's only line of work, you know. Obviously."

Fanning nodded. It occurred to him then that Cully might well be high. He'd find a way to get a look at Cully's pupils.

"A good idea," Cully said, pausing to take a sip. "To get someone proper?"

"Well I don't know about that," Fanning said. "I'll think about it."

"He's nothing but trouble," Cully said. "Really."

"But you don't mean that in a bad way, I suppose."

The sarcasm went by him, it seemed.

"Why do you hire people like Murph? Can't you just make up a story?"

"That's not what I do."

"Everyone else does."

"That's why they're crap then."

"Ah."

"I would think you'd agree with me."

Cully shrugged. "Tell me, what do you care about this stuff. This crime stuff."

"It's not crime for its own sake. It's like a window on life, generally."

"I think I get that. Society, like? That kind of thing?"

"Yes. But I'm not out to give a message. No moralizing. I just want to show what goes on. Be objective."

"Very interesting. Yes, very interesting."

"You think so?"

"I do. But tell me something to think about. This the kind of research you do? You know, whatever you pick up could be very valuable to some people."

"You mean the Guards."

Cully didn't react to the bluntness.

"They'd be the ones I was thinking of," he said. "Yes."

"I'm not telling the Guards anything. Why would I?"

Cully stretched his neck a little, and began to rub at it.

"That's what Murph says. 'Why would he do that?'"

"Well, what can I tell you."

Cully stopped massaging his neck.

"You could tell me a lot, I think."

"For instance?"

"Well, for instance this. Is there going to be a film here?"

Fanning let his gaze roam the pub with a calculated vagueness.

"If you're actually paying to do this research," he heard Cully continue. "And this film thing you want done so badly, this film goes belly-up...?"

Fanning had decided. He'd finish his pint, no hurry, tuck the stool under the counter and leave. No retorts, no arguments.

"I'll burn that bridge when I get to it."

"I don't get that. That bridge thing."

"I'll deal with it," said Fanning.

"Murph's a floater," said Cully then. "You know what a floater is? A shaper. A dickhead. Hasn't a clue. So you're wasting your money on him."

"So what I need," Fanning said, "is real expertise, I suppose you're going to tell me. The opposite of a dickhead. That should be easy enough."

Cully seemed to savour this particular sip of brandy.

"But by definition," he said, "that person won't go near you."

"Well I won't take that personally."

Cully was still immune to the sarcasm.

"The thing is, this crime business, as they say in the news, this crime business is like an iceberg. Not a good comparison, but you get the idea."

"An iceberg."

"Such a person," Cully went on, "they could tell you, for example, that the cops are way behind, the Guards. That they only get lucky now and then."

"You can back that statement up of course."

For the first time Cully seemed to focus his attention on Fanning.

"Such a person," Cully said, slowly, "would have no reason to talk to you, no need to. You see? I mean if your work is to fade into the background, the fly on the wall routine, you don't go having a fit like we saw back at the, the event."

"I couldn't take it. It was too much."

"Ah."

"Is that a character defect or something, in your opinion?"

"I'm only making observations," said Cully. "Offering a bit of advice."

"It's only losers need lots of advice I suppose."

"Now there's another thing with you."

"What is?"

"Sarcasm. I didn't come here to call you a loser, or run you down."

"Fooled me."

"Back to the point here. Giving Murph the heave-ho is proper order."

"I haven't given him any heave-ho."

"Well do you see him here?"

"What does that mean?"

"He doesn't do it anymore. He got out of the research business."

"Says...?"

"He'd wreck your project. He talks, and he talks. It's all he does."

"I'm okay with that. The talking."

"Except when he's smoking crack."

"Who told you that?"

"Come on now. How much of what he told you is bullshit, would you say?"

"Some days ninety percent," said Fanning. "Other days, maybe ten."

"You'll never know, will you."

"Well it's like you said, I can make it up then, can't I?"

Cully pushed away slowly from the bar. He shoved his hands into his trouser pockets, and looked down at his shoes for several moments.

"There's a man over there," Fanning said. "A man who was at the, the event, earlier. Friend of yours."

Cully raised his eyebrows.

"Is that a coincidence he's here?" Fanning asked.

Cully turned, picked up his glass.

"A mate of yours. Right?"

"In a manner of speaking," said Cully.

Fanning waited until Cully had finished his brandy.

"Likes a certain football club. Reputation for crazy fans?"

"Pretty observant bloke," said Cully.

"Well thank you. Just so's I'm clear on this before I go."

Cully nodded.

"You wanted to meet me to...?"

"Advice. Like I said."

"And to tell me Murph is a useless iijit. To give him the sack."

"Right. Better off without him."

"And that this project will go nowhere."

"Did I say that?"

Cully reached into his jacket pocket, and flipped open his mobile.

"Remember what I said about people who know," he said

"Sort of. I suppose. What did you say?"

"They're the ones who wouldn't want anything to do with your research."

"Very encouraging."

"Unless," said Cully, eyeing the display. "Unless it's something they want."

"I don't get this. What am I missing, again?"

"Say you had this," said Cully. He held the mobile toward Fanning.

The sound on the video was little better than static. The camera had moved unsteadily when it panned. But there was Murph on his tiptoes, staring at the fight, and Dermot Fanning. He heard the yelping of the dog in the static.

"People notice things," Cully said. "I mean I did, didn't I?"

"Do they know you did that?"

Cully shrugged.

"They had no problem with you doing this."

"Here look, wait: that's you again. Can you see it? Crap

screen, I know."

"Nobody tried to stop you. I find that interesting."

"...that's when he had him, he got under his jaw but he kept him rock steady. And over he goes..."

Fanning wasn't watching. Instead he took in details. Cully's hairline, a small scar by his ear.

Cully held the phone up closer to Fanning's face.

"And now look."

It was a still image when Fanning first looked. Then Cully pushed with his thumb and the clip began. Fanning saw Delaney, the bearded man, close his eyes and then flinch. In the blocky, shadowed movements behind, a man's figure shook when the gun went off.

"I missed it," said Cully. "But you know the rest."

He folded the phone and let it drop into his jacket pocket.

"Came with its own script," he said. "You just had to press Record."

Fanning picked up his glass. His back was tightening up, and he was suddenly aching. The noises in the pub around him seemed different now, sharper, somehow personal.

Chapter 18

MINOGUE SPOTTED EILÍS IN THE CAR PARK, standing by her new Mini. The cold breeze had reddened her eyes. She was smoking. He was disappointed for her, but relieved too. He parked and, skirting the grey, mossy wall that separated the Liaison office from the hulking headquarters and its sprawl of offices built in the 1970s, he made his way toward her.

She was indeed humming. It could be a Buddhist prayer for all Minogue knew. Sparing with words, this widely read and travelled Irish-speaker loner might well be proof positive of reincarnation. She was taking night courses, she told him last month. Spanish, for Peru. Eilís seems to have been serially "disappointed in love" for all the years he had known her.

"Dia dhuit, a stór."

"God be with you, too, Your Honour," she replied in Irish. "All well with you and yours."

"Not bad at all. Considering the times we're living in."

There were piled-up grey-brown clouds looming over the trees. He spotted the trailing wires from an iPod hanging from her bag.

"April will be doing us no favours, Eilís, I'm thinking."

She flicked her head for an answer and she drew on her cigarette. Kilmartin had first hired Eilís for the Murder Squad nigh on twenty years ago. She had applied for an opening in

Liaison, telling Minogue later that it had sounded glamorous. Kilmartin had recently admitted to Minogue that he was half-afraid of her yet. He had also asked him if he, Minogue, had ever wondered if Eilís was one of them. Minogue baited him with it, goading Kilmartin to say "lesbian."

She held out her pack of Gitanes.

"No thank you. Later, when there's no one looking, maybe."

"No later for you today, Your Honour. You got marching orders I hear. Someone hors de combat on a case. The Polish matter."

"Just as you say."

Eilís' Munster Irish had revealed to Minogue exquisite nuances of sarcasm and irony that had escaped him before. Kilmartin had always been suspicious of her use of the state's other official language. He had made irresolute efforts to match her using his own lumpen schoolboy Irish. It had never once been anything but a massacre, of course, and Kilmartin had learned to desist.

"As we go forward, it becomes necessary to go backward also."

He turned his back to the breeze. Mischief rising in him suddenly

"God almighty, Eilís. That's a bit dark. If you don't mind me saying so."

"I don't mind at all."

She drew on her cigarette, ground it underfoot, and then fell into step beside him. She always had an athlete's easy, ranging walk, Minogue remembered. That observation alone had been enough for him to like her, from the moment they had begun working together so long ago. It, and her unceasing restlessness, signalled to him a kinship, another who might also wonder how and why one was so often an apparent stranger to so much about them.

"Taking a turn at the old job should brighten things up," she said to him.

Peter Igoe spotted him on the way in.

"So you're off, Matt," Igoe said. "'At the pleasure of the Commissioner.'"

"God help me so."

Igoe raised an eyebrow. Minogue had heard that Igoe's success in golf was attributed to his ability to provoke and to distract.

"You're right, of course. It's Tuohy you answer to. Technically."

Assistant Commissioner Tuohy had come on strong the past few years as Commissioner Tynan's chosen one.

"'No big to-do,' says Tuohy," Igoe said. "'Matt'll hit the ground running.'"

Minogue let his gaze drift across the notice board. Dance and Social for the AGSI; training courses in Britain, deadlines highlighted in yellow. The newish daily circulars reminder, the "Have You Seen?" that every Guard in every corner of Ireland was to eyeball daily now.

"All the joys of Fitzgibbon Street," said Igoe. "El Paso. But it's different than when I knew it. I shouldn't be talking."

For several moments, Minogue's mind roved the night streets around the quays, that lone figure walking from light to light.

"And wrap it up quick" Igoe called out.

"As if," he said.

He took his time getting to Fitzgibbon Street Garda Station. He crossed over the River Liffey by the Custom House, ignoring the honks when he slowed to peer down the quays where Tadeusz Klos had passed. Soon enough, he was turning around Mountjoy Square.

It was part of the city he had never liked. He could not get by what he had known of the area when he had first come up to Dublin, with its scarred blocks of flats and its hard-faced inhabitants. Several flowing robes and more brown faces at the corner of North Earl Street drew Minogue's eye. He was careful not to stare, or, more precisely, not to be seen to be staring. Gardiner Street began its slow ascent and Minogue turned his attention

to the budding trees that crowned the summit of the street,
behind the railings of the Square.

He steered into one of the spaces reserved for Garda cars
almost directly in front of the station. He checked twice that he
had left nothing valuable on show, and then locked the face-
plate for the stereo in the boot. Casting a last gaze at the
reflections of the clouds running across the gleaming panels, he
pressed the remote. He wasn't much reassured by the wirps
from it, and so did it twice again. His new car still looked very
vulnerable.

A poorly cleaned Garda squad car slid in quickly beside
him.

"Shift it, boss," said a Guard from the passenger seat.
"Garda cars only."

A lifer, Minogue could see, with sunken cheeks and wavy
grey hair. The driver leaned down to see Minogue under the
edge of the roof.

"Wait a minute, you're what's his name."

"That's me, all right," said Minogue.

The driver eased himself out from behind the wheel. He
winked at Minogue.

"Long as you're not a social worker–type or something,"
he said.

A shot across the bows from two hard chaws like this
wasn't so much cheek, Minogue knew, or even challenge. It was
merely the talk that got Guards through their shifts here in the
inner city.

The driver was still waiting for a reaction. There was
something about him that put Minogue in mind of the white
pudding that the Minogues had taken off the breakfast menu a
decade and more past. Tightly held together, fleshy.

"Jehovah's Witness," Minogue said finally. "How'd you
make me so quick?"

"Nice wheels. New?"

"It is. And thanks."

"You're Kilmartin, aren't you? Or wait – you're the other
one?"

"I'm the other one."

The driver was out on the street now. He hitched up his belt.

"It's the Polish man, am I right?"

"You're in the right job," said Minogue.

"Nothing to it. I heard Hughsie got himself taken to the hospital all of a sudden. Appendicitis or something?"

"Could be," said Minogue.

"We did some of the door-to-doors on it. Round one of them, anyway."

The driver introduced himself as Dan Ward. There was a cantankerous edge to him, Minogue decided, another copper poisoned by his work, maybe.

"Enda Callinan," said the other, shaking Minogue's hand.

"'Enda the world,'" said Ward.

"Long here at the station, are ye?"

"At Skanger Central here...?"

Minogue gave Callinan the eye.

"Seven year," said Ward quickly, as though to be first with a reply.

"Me, four and a bit," said Callinan. "Hoping for early parole."

Callinan thumbed his way through menus on his mobile.

"It's that good here is it," Minogue said.

A radio transmission came through Ward's walkie talkie. He turned his lapel to get at the mouthpiece

"We are," he said. "He flew the coop yesterday, she says."

He waited for Dispatch to respond.

"Fella has a go at his missus yesterday morning," he said to Minogue. "But she only phones in this morning. What do you think about that?"

Minogue shrugged.

"Could hardly understand a word she said," Ward said, his thumb wavering over the button. "They do speak English in Nigeria though, don't they?"

"Ten-four Badger One," Dispatch said. "We'll just log it, so."

"So there," said Callinan. "Something new every day, they say."

"Except it's not new," said Ward

Minogue realized he had little chance with this twosome.

"So you did door-to-door," Minogue said, instead. "How did that turn out?"

"Useless. Am I allowed to say that? Anyway, they're in the case files, er."

"Matt."

"'The Book,' they call it, right? When it turns to murder?"

"That it is."

"We weren't the only ones," said Ward, "there were upwards of a dozen out the first day."

"They'll have to broaden it out no doubt," said Ward. He spoke as though it had been a serious, unwarranted imposition. "The zones business of theirs."

"Unfortunate poor divil," said Callinan. "Whatever possessed him to wander up here?"

"More than enough head cases there," Ward added, almost placidly. "Any day of the week. Day or night. You name it, it's here."

"Is that a fact."

"Not so much the numbers," said Callinan. "It's the types."

"All comes down to drugs," said Ward. "Take a stroll over there, down the lane, and it's all there: needles, bits of pipes, johnnies..."

Callinan had slid his mobile into the breast pocket of his tunic and he was giving his partner the eye to go.

"Social work," Ward said. He yawned as he shifted the Kevlar vest under his tunic. "That's the line nowadays, isn't it."

Minogue stood by the duty sergeant's desk waiting for someone to fetch him. It was quiet enough. A man with his arm in a sling, and bloodshot eyes, was watching him from a seat. He half-heard a Garda trying to explain that a barring order had to be renewed.

"Psychosomatic," said the Sergeant and looked up.

"No doubt," said Minogue, for lack of any clue.

"Hughsie, I mean. The stress of it all. Did he tell you?"

The Sergeant looked like he'd been a runner some years back. "Maybe I wasn't listening properly."

"The wedding. That's what tipped him over, I reckon."

Minogue inspected the Sergeant's sombre expression. It was hardly laziness that stopped him shaving the errant hairs high up on his cheekbones.

"A cry for help maybe," said the Sergeant.

"Ah now I see," said Minogue. "Men have feelings now, I hear."

The Sergeant beckoned him closer.

"Hughsie worked like a demon," he murmured. "Night and day, on this."

"Well it certainly shows."

"And a top-notch crew above there too, let me tell you."

Was the whole station full of comedians, opinionators?

"And a direct line to the Man Above too," the Sergeant added. "But don't let on I said that. Might be offended. But he wouldn't let on, fair dues to him."

"To whom, now?"

"Wall. A detective above. Very strong on the old religion. Shocking nice fella, don't get me wrong. But just so's you know, the cursing and that?"

"I shouldn't curse? Well there won't be much getting done so."

The Segreant smiled thinly.

"The Holy Name," he said. "You can eff and blind good-oh."

He nodded at a younger Garda standing in the doorway beside a photocopier. Minogue followed the Garda up the stairs.

"Incident room," said the Guard, stopping by a door with a glass panel that had been covered from the inside. "Or command centre. Call it what you like."

Detective Garda Kevin Wall turned in his chair, a squeaky swivel from where he had been consulting something on a computer screen while he conversed on the telephone.

He slid his hand down the receiver, freeing the other to shake Minogue's hand and introduce himself.

"Mossie's on his way," he said. "Tomás, that is."

Trim, and with a face that said teacher – or maybe priest – sooner than Guard, Wall pointed Minogue to the table where he had placed the casebook, along with two file folders. Behind the table was a monitor with a slowly moving screensaver picture of Zidane headbutting the Italian player.

"Look around," he said to Minogue. "I'll be done here in a minute."

Chapter 19

Bríd had a half cup of coffee in front of her. She didn't look up but kept writing, her head sideways on her palm.

"Still at it," he said. She nodded.

"Is Aisling asleep?"

Bríd's writing slowed, and she wagged the pen from side to side. She seemed to be trying to think what way to phrase something.

"The usual marathon," she murmured. "I must have conked out with her."

Fanning looked at the sinews that stood out on the back of her hand as her pen sped up again. The sleeve of her T-shirt had rolled up over her upper arm. He saw the outline of her bra strap. Caravaggio, he thought, and Rembrandt, the shadow on the light from the table lamp she preferred to work by. Her T-shirt had shrunk and he saw the small of her back, the channel of her spine pushing against her skin. He stepped closer and began to massage the muscle that stood out over her collarbone.

She put the pen down slowly and lifted her head and turned to him.

"Well," she said.

"I might be on to something," he said.

She narrowed her eyes as though to assess him more exactly.

"The crime story," he said. "The script."

"Your research," she said.

Resentment crushed his stirring lust.

"Yes, a character. Well, a guy who seems to have an inside..."

"Insight, did you say?"

"Inside."

"You have one already don't you?"

"He wasn't my first choice. I knew he was a gobshite."

He tried to read her comments on the paper she was marking. The Irish Monastic System.

"Well we're not short on iijits in Dublin."

"Well this seems to be more of what I need."

"Really."

"I think he's different."

"How so."

"It's hard to describe. He sets a tone. Scary guy, perhaps."

He saw that now.

"Perhaps?"

"Who knows," he said. Her T-shirt had slid up at the front too.

"You like that."

She didn't look up, or even pause, when she said it.

"It's not exactly 'like,'" he said. "Come on."

"Come on yourself," she retorted, almost kindly. "You get a kick out of meeting people like him. The more dangerous, the better. A thrill."

"No, actually. I am not 'thrilled' to meet him."

She smiled briefly.

"It's nothing to be guilty about."

"Did I say I felt guilty?"

"He's a criminal though, isn't he."

"Well that's a funny thing, isn't it. I actually don't know."

"Hit a tender spot there, did I."

The warmth was gone from her voice, he realized.

"Whatever. The thing is, there's something about him that you catch on to right away. If you're careful, I mean. He strikes me as smart. Disciplined or something."

"Well that's a nice change."

"He's not a slob. A careful sort of guy, I think. A planner."
She looked down at the papers in front of her.

"You're getting a crush on him, are you."

"Well maybe I will then."

"Is he your run-of-the-mill Dublin gangsta?"

"I haven't quite figured out," he said.

"How hard could it be? Dis dat dese and dose. Gimme dis, givis dat."

"A few times he sounded English, actually. 'Innit?' 'Roight.'"

"Man of mystery then."

She'd go on, he knew, until he'd react.

"He could deliver on bits that are weak now. The way he talks even."

"Grit."

Perhaps she wasn't taking subtle digs at him, he thought.

"Not that, more weight, sort of. A bit of gravitas, I was going to say, but that would be stupid. I mean, face it, it's probably criminal, whatever it is."

"Your Mista Gangsta."

"Okay, I get it. Loud and clear. Thanks."

She folded her arms. He imagined her breasts held there just as they would be when she'd lie on him.

"We're close," he said then. "With this story, I know it. It's not science. But you know it when it shows up."

"Aren't you getting that in with the Guards? You know, go around in a squad car or sit in a session with some of them?"

"It's not about them, the Guards. Principally, I mean."

Bríd craned her neck and became very still. Fanning listened too. It was people in the other flat.

Bríd slumped back in the chair. She drew her hair back with both hands. "Aisling was soooo wound up," she said. "Whatever's bothering her."

"You're finished are you?" he asked.

She eyed him. He eyed her back.

When she had started teaching, he used to make her laugh in that embarrassed way that excited him even more. "If your students could see you now..." but then after a while she had asked him to stop saying it.

"I'm finished all right. In more ways than one."

"Go to bed why don't you."

"Would I actually be sleeping?"

He was confused again. A sly smile about to break out on her face, or a put-off?

"Whatever the lady wants," he said.

"What this lady wants, can't be got."

"Never hurts to try."

"Okay. Aisling's teething to be magically disappeared, for starters. The iijits in my History class, the one they dumped on me, to know how to spell and to write a sentence, an original sentence. Less marking would be next. Less of a control freak for a principal."

"How about: it to be the day before the summer holidays."

"That goes without saying."

"Do you remember the desert?" he asked. "The Painted Desert place?"

She yawned, and nodded, and yawned again.

"Be nice to do that again."

"With Aisling?"

"Why not?"

"What would she do while we chalk up hundreds of miles in New Mexico, or whatever?"

"There are kids in the States, you know."

"Oh, a commune?"

"Come on. It'd be good for her. Remember we always wanted to keep going, not just turn into 'the parents.'"

She pulled over another paper.

"Christ," she said quietly. "Monastric. He actually wrote that. Monks doing tricks? Gastric, monastic. Spastic. Hello? Spell check, anyone?"

She pushed it away, looked up at him, and smiled.

"I got an email from Lizzie. Things are heating up."

Lizzie, he thought. The downer sister-in-law, the one without an ounce of talent, doggedly spending years trying to "break into acting." Her latest diversion was dating a director who had showed promise with a surreal cartoon about Dublin night-life.

"Well good for her. Is she up to it?"

"More to the point, is he? He's fiftysomething."

"I saw his name in credits going back to St. Patrick: "Director – Joe Rattigan.""

"Well he's still a biggish wheel."

"All those wankers. 'I could pass your name on to Colm Breen, Colm and I go back a long way.'"

"Age hasn't dimmed your kind regard, I see."

"I'm talking about when I was a kid, even. Well, a teenager."

"Lizzie says the separation from his wife made a teenager out of him. Spare me the details, I told her."

He knew there were bottles of Heineken left from the weekend, but they were in the cupboard. Still, he'd drink one.

"She says he's not the way people think. 'Joseph' he likes to be called."

Fanning walked slowly to the doorway and leaned against it. Bríd sighed and sat up and opened the paper again.

"Why are you telling me this," he said.

She seemed surprised.

"Lizzie happens to be my sister. Anyway. It's just talk."

"Networking, are we?"

"Maybe. What of it?"

"Leave me out of it."

"Did I say you were in it? In what, anyway?"

"You know. 'Putting in a good word for good old Dermot Fanning.'"

"Is that what you're thinking? Really?"

"Some of it, yes. It's not like, well, you know."

"'It's like it's all about me'?"

"Give me a break, Bríd. Christ's sake."

"I will if you let me take you out for a pint with Lizzie and him."

"A pint," he said, "with Joe Rattigan. I'd sooner kick myself in the head."

"Well there you go. True to form, anyway."

"That was a setup."

"You mean self-sabotage. That's what I'm hearing. Again."

"Don't we have a deal, that we never use crap words like that? Like the shite you have every day in school? Empowerment, facilitate – all that bullshit?"

Bríd stared at him.

"Why are you raising your voice?"

"Because, because I'm annoyed. Is that still allowed?"

She blinked several times and then abruptly returned to her marking. He watched her but she did not look over. Soon she was absorbed in what she was reading. He took two bottles from the cupboard.

"I'll do an hour or two," he said, "at the desk."

The desk was a family heirloom passed on from his great-grandaunt, a teacher all her life in Waterford. The desk had become his magic carpet, his portal. He'd even drilled a hole to bring the laptop's cable into the drawer.

He slowed as he passed her. She dropped her pen and reached out around his waist.

"Just let me do it," she murmured, "Joe knows your work. Lizzie already asked him about you."

It was almost more than he could muster to wait with her and to caress her hair. He knew early on there'd be no chance tonight anyway. The desire had left him quite suddenly, and in its place was the familiar, dense unease.

Things used to be different, was all he could think.

Chapter 20

THE SITE PHOTOS HAD BEEN ARRANGED on two notice boards, with more slotted into a binder. A third notice board – the back of a mobile whiteboard, actually – contained the timeline for Tadeusz Krystof Klos' last hours. The last entry of 22:30/23:00 was followed by three question marks. Minogue saw an entry for a shop, with "Marlboro" written next to the entry; an Internet kiosk, again with notes that Klos had been there before. "Slovenian" was written after a name, Peter somebody.

On the far wall was a large-scale Ordinance Survey of Dublin, with dates written on the coloured disks spotted about the map. Textbook setup, Minogue saw: effective, accessible, clear. He did not see a key to those colours yet. Wait – of course: green for reliable placing/witness. How could he have forgotten?

"The black ones are...?"

"Street-crime with violence. There's only five years on the map. The black you can guess."

"Three murders in five years?"

"Surprising, maybe."

"I remember only one," Minogue said. "It was one of the last we dealt with directly. On the Squad, I mean. The nurse?"

"It is. Another one was a brawl from a pub. But there was an execution one there from two years ago. That one on the right, the body in the car one, was the fella missing from

Newry. Paramilitary thing. Both of them are open. I have the files up on them if you want them.

Minogue turned to him.

"Nothing to take to the bank yet on our Polish man, is there Kevin?"

"That's about the size of it," said Wall after a moment. "So far, we see him as an ordinary punter wandering in there. Is he trying to score something, is he lost, expecting to meet someone, has some arrangement...?"

"Well," said Minogue, and took off his coat. "That's what we're paid for, I suppose."

He flipped open the file and glanced at the copies of the statements. On top was one Marion Mullen, employee of a cleaning company. Ms. Mullen had been coming off shift in the financial centre.

"Before you get dug in now," said Wall. "It looks like we might have some give. Coming in just now. Mossie is working on something."

"Linked to the case?"

Wall nodded.

"From a phone-in earlier on this afternoon. It's not printed out yet but I know it's entered on the database."

Minogue watched Wall hanging his jacket on a wooden hanger, flicking at the lapels and shoulders to make sure it sat straight. His shirt had been carefully ironed. Minogue wondered why he had not noticed the long unfashionable tweed tie already.

"Apparently a woman, the mother of a girl over in Whitehall, was eyeing what the young one was doing on the computer."

"A chat thing."

"Yep. Twittering, or MSNing or something. Her young one was over and back to someone, a pal. The mother got a bit suspicious. She doesn't like the other young one. 'Bad influence.'"

"Always the other one," said Minogue.

"Well. The daughter was in this to-and-fro. Very secretive. Got into a set-to with the mother. A row ensued, and the

mother got her dander up. The last straw, etc. Daughter ends up
in tears. The mother says the girls were talking about doing an
anonymous call or something."

"Anonymous, like to the tip line?"

"Didn't say. 'Whatever else you can say about that daughter of mine,' says the mother, 'at least she has a conscience.'"

Wall examined his tie then, as though consulting notes.

"Yep," he said and he looked up. "There was talk of some
prank that she pulled on someone. 'Some foreigner,' says the
mother. Gave him wrong directions."

"How old are the girls?"

"Fourteen. The friend is thirteen."

Minogue knew that Wall was waiting for a reaction. He
turned a page that had a thick bookmark.

"Where's it at now?"

"Mossie went out about half an hour ago. The mother is
picking up the kid from school, taking her back home to talk to
Mossie. He'll be phoning me – us – here."

Minogue looked down the page at a mobile phone number.

"The mother found it in the girl's room."

"Recent calls?"

"They're working on it," said Wall. "There were no calls
to Ireland anyhow."

Minogue looked at the email addresses.

"Phone shops, Kevin, what's the story on them?"

Wall used his ring finger to scratch his crown.

"City Centre has been done, and they have his photo.
Nothing yet. Some staff they haven't reached, and that's going
to stay leaking until we find them. Holidays, two – wait – three
of them. One quit, hasn't been back. Dublin fella. Likely nothing to it."

Minogue sank back slowly in his chair, and resumed scanning the pages. Soon enough, his eyes slipped out of focus and
they came to rest somewhere near the broad margins of the
page, or the desktop beneath. He heard Wall at the keyboard,
and looked over. Wall had put on glasses.

Something stirred in Minogue again. Several moments

passed before he realized that he had been remembering how she too had looked over her glasses every now and then yesterday. Maybe Danute Juraksaitis' glasses stood out in his mind because of the absence of things he had expected – earrings, makeup, necklace. She had worn a white blouse, that could equally have been a man's shirt.

Wall was going through the file log on the screen.

"Someone must have suggested Ireland to him," Minogue said to him. "As a destination."

Wall craned his neck.

"If he did, we haven't a sign of him yet – or her."

"And the police over there?"

"Four years ago, he showed up, but nothing since. He was a passenger in a stolen car. There was public drunkenness, name taken and cautioned."

"He'd fit right in here, you might think. But did he have any reason to leave there in a hurry?"

"Not according to the coppers there anyway."

Minogue narrowed his eyes.

"Payback, Kevin? Someone collecting, revenge?"

Wall folded his arms, and seemed to consider it. Minogue saw how the folds from the ironing remained sharp.

"If he did put something over on one of his cronies beyond in Poland, and then he flew the coop, there's no sign yet. Might be worth asking them again, of course."

Wall might have been going to say something, but the phone went. Minogue returned to Mrs. Klos' statement, but kept an ear open to eavesdrop on Wall's conversation. The statement been sent over today – this morning – translated. The footer gave the email address of Danute Juraksaitis.

The phrases were empty, but hard to read now. "A fresh beginning." "Maybe to study there." "To improve his English and also try for the U.S." "To get out into fresh country side." "He always liked the sea on our family holidays." Later: "to make new friends." "To get away from other people who were not helping his life."

"Helping his life?"

There was no mention of his past, or his troubles, in her statement. It was a list of her ruined hopes she had had for her son, and reciting them had been like her prayer, her eulogy.

He heard Wall say his name into the phone, repeat it, and then hang up.

"Mossie's coming up," Wall said. "It's a go."

"Grand. Is it something we can move on right away?"

"It looks like it. The girl has admitted she met him, Klos. She was with her pals."

Wall was waiting for a reaction, Minogue realized. He nodded approvingly.

"She's no daw, this kid, says Mossie. A bit of an operator. Wised-up, like."

"Covering for her pals no doubt," said Minogue. "The usual."

"Well yes and no. Gangs are big here, I suppose you know?"

Minogue hoped his surprise didn't show. How could he not have thought about that?

"First mention of gangs in this case anyway," he said. "I have to say."

"We sort of take it as a given up here."

Minogue detected no one-upmanship in Wall's voice. He remembered the Apache Country routine from Ward and Callinan.

"She told Mossie he gave them a bit of a fright. Asking about 'the river.' The Liffey like, down by the quays. We'll see what her pal says, the other one who–"

As though on cue, the door opened, and led by a long beak of a nose that preceded a tightly cut frizz of wiry, rust-coloured hair over a pale face, Detective Garda Mossie Duggan arrived. Minogue rose and shook hands with this too-tall, bony-shouldered man with an Adam's apple half hanging over his collar.

"Kev brought you up to speed here?"

"So far, so good," said Minogue. "I think."

"Well your timing is good," said Duggan. "This young one I talked to, she was with her friend – and their boyfriends. Four of them."

"Now there's a picture," said Wall. "Give me names, will you."

Duggan flipped open his incident book. Minogue began to copy the names that Wall transcribed on the board. Tara Lynch (14); Alison ("Ali") Rogers (13); Aidan Matthews (?); Justin Twomey (?).

"Thirteen-year-old girl," Wall said. "What does that say. Skangers, is what."

"Have you run the boys' names yet?" Minogue asked.

"Not yet," said Duggan. "But I could take bets before I do."

He walked to the end of the boards, and tapped at the timeline with his knuckles.

"This Tara Lynch puts Klos there at about half-eleven," he said. "'We just happened to be going that way, it was a shortcut to catch the last bus.' My nose isn't the only one twitching, is it?"

"Did she say how he looked?" Minogue asked.

"'Scary.'"

"Drink? Soliciting? Lost?"

"She thinks he might have had a few, but not falling-down drunk or anything. Said she couldn't understand him. 'The river I go, the side,' she thinks he said."

"The hostel," said Wall. "He was trying to get back to base."

"So they sent him up toward East Wall," said Duggan. "And off he went."

"She saw him walk off, she says?" Wall asked.

"Didn't get to that," said Duggan. "That's when the father walks in. The mother was grand with me asking a few questions, but then in comes your man. Very het-up, very belligerent. Starts telling me the law."

Duggan paused to set up his mimic.

"'That child of mine is an effin minor, I'll have you know!'"

"'I know my rights!'" said Wall. "The usual rigamarole?"

"'No effing way is she going to be dragged down to any effing Garda station!'" said Duggan. He dispensed with the fake Dublin accent then.

"And all the rest of it," Duggan resumed. "Big row with the wife, right in front of me. Not the first time, I imagine. She was grand with the chat we were having, but in he barges, minor this and minor that."

"Was she still minor," Wall asked, with neither amusement nor rancour that Minogue could spot, "when she was traipsing around at that hour of the night?"

"Well don't get started on that one, Kev," said Duggan. "But it got better than I thought it would. I wished I'd taped it, in actual fact."

"The parents having a row?"

"What she said to him, the wife," said Duggan. "Remember, she's the one who made that phone call. 'My child knows right from wrong,' et cetera. So she laid into him after he gave me the heave-ho. It was funny: there I was in the hall, him yelling at me. I'm ready to walk out the door, go back to the station here, start me paper work to get an interview with this kid, the whole letter-of-the-law routine. But out she comes, tells me not to budge. Stay right here, says she to me. 'I'm the child's mother! I come first, so I do!'"

"Standing up for her kid," Wall said. "Maybe a history of abuse there."

"Maybe," said Duggan. "I don't think she was scared of him. She was just fed up. Flaming row, but then. ... He backs down. Strangest thing. I thought I'd have to call in some lads, get the thing under control. Oh but if you could have heard it: 'I'm not having her grow up like I done! She's not going to end up like me!' Hell of a thing to say in front of him. But it worked. Bottom line: parents consent to us interviewing her at the family home, a proper interview. Parents attending, of course."

Duggan looked from Wall to Minogue and back.

"It gets even better," he said. "They were with two fellas that night. Boyfriends, surprise, surprise. You ask me, I think the mother knows what happened, had a heart-to-heart with the daughter."

"And wants to be first in the door," said Wall, nodding, "before the others."

"Hard not to think that, isn't it," said Duggan, and looked down at his nails.

Minogue realized that this was Duggan's way of showing he was excited – calmly excited. He glanced at Wall, and received a slow nod in return. The momentum would only pick up from here.

"Go ahead, Kevin," he said to him. "It's your call. I'm only window-dressing here, to be honest."

Wall made a brief smile, and lapsed back into thought.

"Could always start with the tough route," said Duggan. "Set them up here in the station, the four of them, and play the game. You know: he says, she says – and then wait. Throw a few shapes if things bog down: accessory, withholding, obstruction?"

Wall tugged gently at his tie again.

"Ah what would Hughsie do?" Duggen asked with a pained expression after a few moments.

"All right, all right," said Wall, his slight smile soon pulled back. "We'd better get started. Bring in the others – and uniforms and squad cars to do it. But fair's fair. We'll interview this girl at her house. But the minute it turns scrappy?"

Chapter 21

MURPHY ANSWERED HIS MOBILE on the second ring: but it wasn't Murphy.

"He's busy," said the man who answered. Fanning recognized the accent right away.

"I'll phone him later on then."

"No need. Where are you?"

"It's Murph I need to talk to."

"You said that already."

"So tell him I'll give him a ring later on."

"He told me you'd ring. He said for me to meet you. Help things along."

Fanning listened for any sounds in the background. That nowhere accent still confused him, often starting as a Dublin accent but getting lost quickly, only to roll back into it for certain words.

"Are you there? Did you hear me?"

A dropped h: East Enders. Fanning held his thumb over the button.

"Murph doesn't want to work on the project anymore."

"He didn't say a word to me about that."

"I know. That's how he is but, isn't he."

"He gave you his phone?"

"He loaned it to me. Mine fell and broke."

"Look, he and I have an arrangement."

"Right. That's why I'm here. Now I don't want to spread rumours now, do I. But you must know by now. Like I was saying to you back in that pub. I mean you can figure things out."

"What things?"

"Come on. You've got to admit, he's not the most reliable bloke."

"Well I wouldn't be discussing that here–"

"You know he's got a habit. I told you that, right?"

"I doubt Murph is too busy, especially for me."

"You mean his business. He was getting burned out, did he tell you?"

"No, he didn't tell me he was getting burned out."

"Sad to say, but there's problems in his family, mental things. He didn't tell you? It's a manic thing. He goes off the deep end every once in a while. Very rough I hear."

Fanning's thumb was getting a cramp.

"I'll meet you, and explain it all. Then you'll see."

"No, that's not going to work."

Fanning heard a "when" just as he hung up.

He placed the mobile on the table next to his saucer. His coffee was finished. It had found its way to someplace in his stomach where it now ate away, acidly. The two men at the next table were speaking Spanish. Georges Street looked grey, and traffic had come to a standstill. He looked down at the yellow stickies and the notes he had started. There'd be no way any director would put in a real dog fight.

He started when the phone vibrated. It was Murph's number. A hollow, airy feeling returned to his chest. He pushed the Power Off button, and held it. He thought about more coffee, and then the guilt of spending three Euro that were really Bríd's earnings wrung out of the brats that she taught.

He turned to the notes he had written about the sound of gunshot that had killed the dog:

– took/punched the air out of the room
– screaming silence in its wake

– shockwaves hammering the air

Not bad. He switched the phone on again, and watched it search for a signal. The tink of a notification came within seconds. There had been a mistake, according to Murph, but it had all been settled now. Phone him back.

Fanning picked up his pencil and drew an exclamation mark on the paper. Murph, scammer and schemer extraordinaire. So he had a habit, so he was a liar. Big surprise there. This carry-on was part of the package.

He didn't much care if Murph took him for a gobshite. After all, he had gone into this with his eyes open, and he had paid four hundred something Euro to Murph so far – then a hundred fifty for yesterday. That was what he had to do. Price comparisons hardly applied in this business. Whatever Murph charged was the going rate.

He made a quick inventory of what he could recall that Murph's "tours" had brought him so far. Characters he had met, sure – that family in Walkinstown who fenced anything, with the sister in on it too, as tough or tougher than the three brothers who made the deals. Less colourful, and much more malevolent was One-or-Two Tony, also Tony Bony, a slight and unassuming man whom Murph had pointed out in a pub. Tony was an enforcer who kept a selection of pieces of old plumbing pipe for breaking arms and legs. According to Murph, he gave some victims a cruel choice, usually their pick of which two limbs he'd break.

Yes, he now knew, and had documented expressions these lowlifes used. Their taste in clothes, and what their choices meant. Cars they had, or liked to rob, or aspired to. Sexual tastes, if that's what you could call them: more like a mixture of porn and animal husbandry. Murph had even given him a description of how you should walk, if you wanted to signal you were serious.

He now knew where some criminals Murph said he knew liked to go on holidays, and how they made their connections there. He had notes on Murph's stories and gossip about their petty fights and their drinking. Their troubles with wives and girlfriends, and kids. Epic family fights, at least two he remembered involved brawls, knives, hospital and prison time.

Murph had relished relating incidents of biblical cruelty by criminals who wanted revenge for stupid, childish things. Embellished or not, Murph's stories of cordless Black and Deckers into kneecaps, floor crucifixions, and rape of a rival's kid were now lodged in Fanning's mind, probably forever. His script would make damned good use of the shrewdness and native intelligence that some of them had, faculties so often sabotaged by their greed or their addictions, by bad genes, by mental illness.

But in the final analysis, Fanning had to admit that what he had learned on their excursions was often not because of Murph, but in spite of him. Like Cully had said – he talks, and he talks. His chatter ruined Fanning's observations, drawing people's attention, when all Fanning wanted to do was blend in. And the crowning irony: Murph continually telling him to say nothing, and to follow his lead always, while he, Murph, revved up the bluster and the bullshit himself.

That was not to say their time together had been wasted. Not at all. Parsing Murph's ramblings and boasts, and his self-staged dramatics had given Fanning a clear character for the script. Would Murph recognize himself in the film as that blundering, not-so-bright, petty criminal, with a grandiosity and a stupidity that would be his – and others' – undoing?

Fanning let his pencil run along the page and he watched the circles and the lines that his hand was drawing intersect, and then continue. His own private Ouija Board he called it, when people asked him what he was doing. It was to help him think, or rather to still whatever part of him was stopping him thinking clearly.

Soon he put down the pencil, and he examined the lines and shapes he had made. There were no shapes or patterns he could discern. His thoughts went back to the phone call, to Murph. Loyalty...? Hardly: Murph would screw him as quick as he'd screw anyone.

But to be fair, Murph had peeled the lid back enough to

give Dermot Fanning some inkling of what it meant to be born into crime, to live it. Never to have had a job – to scorn any job, actually – to go from day to day, taking what you could, or what you liked, what you could get away with. No waiting, and all guilt-free. No lost sleep over global warming, or the direction of the Euro or house prices, or the meaning of life. To see the world as something to prey on, to resent not having what others seemed to have and to feel entitled to grab it, to steal it just to show you could, to use it and to break it if it disappointed you, to discard it. Murph and the rest of them would never need the services of a shrink to help them unravel their neuroses, would they.

His pencil suddenly stopped doing its tricks between his fingers. He looked at it, as though it had a life of its own, and then he felt the creeping presence of doubt. The question was never far off, and here it was back, sitting right in front of him yet again: where was the story in all this?

It pained him to consider that Breen might have been right the other day. Had he missed Breen's thoughtful way of offering him a soft landing, with the mention of a documentary? For all she scorned Breen, Bríd had always maintained that he basically meant well. You just had to find his wavelength, she maintained, his buzzwords. Then he should use some of them – discreetly, of course – in conversation. And, she had told him, with much enthusiasm, he should even learn to mirror little gestures that Breen made. Let the subconscious do the work.

Fanning could hear her now: Why was he so cynical about Colm Breen? And when had that started? Hadn't they been friends? When had Colm Breen ever done him a bad turn? If Bríd picked up signs of his aversion during these exchanges, she could put an edge to her suggestions: Why was he so allergic to advice anyway? What exactly was wrong with networking? Then the buzzwords from the staffroom would surface, and he'd let a few go by before calling her on them – collaborate, share, build relationships. Well at least it didn't happen often, he thought then.

A familiar weariness was dulling his thoughts now, and he

was adult enough to admit he knew why. It was because the things that Bríd said were – for the most part anyway – probably true. If anyone would know about getting funding for a documentary, especially with social issues, and crime and what-have-you in the headlines every day, it would be the same Breen. A decent documentary might lead to more gigs, commissions even. It'd add to his portfolio at the very least, keep him in the game.

Game? His mind raced back to the dog fight, and again he saw the shouting mob, their faces twisted in contempt, and excitement, and blood lust. How was that not medieval? How was that not a thousand times more real than any documentary? Shouldn't it be Breen, or even Bríd, who should have to defend why they thought that fiction, real fiction now, couldn't match a documentary? Yes, he thought, he should use the old caveman example about the power of story–

He started when his mobile went off again. He held it in his palm and between rings he listened to the sudden thumping of blood in his ears. It was Murph's phone again.

Chapter 22

MINOGUE WAITED IN THE HALLWAY, content to pace slowly and let his thoughts ramble a bit. He made way for several arrivals, uniforms and detectives both, returning any greeting that was offered. He paused by the door again in passing. There was barely a sound. In the interview room with the wire-haired Detective Duggan was one Maureen O'Brien, a Garda from the station who had a good rep for interviewing kids. The girl had been crying a lot, Minogue knew. Apparently the mother was beginning to balk.

Someone descended the stairs at the end of the hall, whistling. Minogue turned and resumed his stroll. The door opened. Duggan closed it quietly behind him.

"The mother's had it," he murmured. "She's taking her young one home."

"Maureen can't persuade...?"

"Nope. The young one put on quite the performance. You should hear her. She's bawling her eyes out. Hyperventilating, pretty well. The mother has her back-up now, big-time."

"Well," said Minogue, "we don't want wigs on the green, do we."

Duggan tugged at his frizzy hair behind his ear.

"We don't want to arrest the girl," said Minogue. "But if Maureen's getting nowhere?"

"Well do you want to give it a try?"

Messy, Minogue thought with some foreboding, so very messy, with kids. He said it several times in his head while he eyed the door, visualizing an angry mother and her distraught daughter barging out, knocking him and Duggan sideways en route. The seconds hung in the air.

But in he went. The room was warm, and the air was filled with a mix of sweat and worn-out, pseudoherbal perfume that Minogue loathed. He pushed back mentally at the claustrophobia that fell on him by glancing from face to face. The mother's face was red, almost purple under the fluorescent light. She blinked angrily and uncertainly at the new arrival. Minogue had already put on his most avuncular expression. He introduced himself, sat down, and proceeded to say nothing for as long as the atmosphere would allow.

The girl was overweight, with those arms that reminded him of uncooked sausages. Her clothes did her no favours at all. Of course, everything was too small these days. With her wet, swollen face darkened by mascara or makeup gone astray, the girl looked like the usual mini-tornado of hormones, provocation, defiance.

O'Brien seemed resigned to the interview going south too.

Minogue tried again to make eye contact with the girl. She pushed her hair away long enough for Minogue to see she had some, but then she dropped her head again. She slid further down the chair, heaving every few moments to draw in breaths.

"I was hoping we could continue this chat, Mrs. Lynch," he said.

She pointed at Duggan who was closing the door behind him.

"He said, that one said, that he was going to see about Legal Aid."

"Why do you think you need Legal Aid?"

"Oh listen to you! I know what a leading question is. No more run-around. Come on Tara, we stayed long enough in this place."

She reached out and grabbed her daughter's upper arm as she rose.

"Here we are, trying to do what's right," she muttered hoarsely. "And this is what happens. I know my rights, and my daughter does too. She's only a child, so she is."

Minogue decided to maintain his oblique line.

"My expertise is in murder investigations," he said.

She turned to him and frowned.

"This is a disgrace, you saying that. By Jesus I'm going to report you, the lot of yous. Disgraceful!"

"Disgrace," Minogue said. "Why so?"

"Oh listen, I didn't come up to Dublin on the last bus! That's tactics, is what it is– 'I'm an expert in murder.' Intimidation, that's what you're trying to do."

"The Murder Squad, have you heard of it?"

She let go of her daughter and slowly stood upright.

"This has nothing to do with Tara, or me, or why we're here. If you think for one minute that we're going to stay here."

"I've been called in to work on it. This is a murder case, Mrs. Lynch."

Minogue glanced at the daughter again. Her breathing had become less panicked and though her head remained resolutely down, she was now very still.

"Detective Duggan and I think that your daughter has vital information in this murder case."

The mother's eyes narrowed.

"Those are reasonable grounds. Have you heard that expression?"

She shook her head.

"I'm saying 'reasonable grounds' because that's what comes up. It comes up when a Guard has to arrest someone."

"You can't arrest a little girl, a juvenile, I mean."

"It wouldn't sit right with a Guard to do it, but I can. And I will."

"Show me some identification," she said. Minogue saw Garda O'Brien roll her eyes.

Minogue took out his photo card.

"Where does it say Murder Squad?"

"It doesn't."

"Well then..."

Mrs. Lynch seemed to have discarded what she had planned to say.

"Well go and get the other ones then," she blurted. "They're the ones you should be talking to. My Tara is, she's just, you know, she's a follower, that's all."

"What, I mean who, are these people you're talking about?"

"The girl – that little bitch. God forgive me, but I don't care anymore. That Rogers one. Alison, Ali, whatever she calls herself. I'm after telling this fella here, this other Guard, and the woman here, all we know. And I'm sorry now I ever had that Guard talk me in the bloody door of this place – I'm sorry I even lifted the bloody phone to talk to a Guard!"

"'Ones,' you said," Minogue said.

"That one, Ali Rogers. She's the one. She got my Tara in on her – what's the word? She trapped – she enticed – my young one here, that's it. And she got her smoking and carrying on all hours of the night. That one has no-one at home to put manners on her, her parents out on the town themselves and they never should have..."

"Boyfriends? That's what you mean, I take it."

Mrs. Lynch started a little, and almost spluttered. Then she looked from Minogue to Duggan and back again.

"We can clear it up and have you on your way in short order, I'm thinking," Minogue tried.

Mrs. Lynch kept her eyes on him, as she sunk slowly back into the chair.

"Tara is upset," he said. "That goes without saying. It shows she has a conscience, I say. Well reared. And we're very grateful for you stepping forward. For making that phone call. But we can't let this be run by you, or your daughter. With all due respects."

He tried to form a sympathetic smile for her but found instead that he was concentrating on her changing expression. She seemed to be staring right back at him but her eyes remained out of focus. Minogue lowered his voice.

"It would be a terrible thing to be filling out an arrest for this young lady."

Mrs. Lynch's eyes returned to focus. Her lips began to move but she said nothing. She turned to her daughter again, and she nudged her.

"Tara."

The "no" was more of a moan.

"You have to, Tara. Sit up."

The girl's breathing became deeper again.

"I just want to go home."

Her mother pushed hard.

"Ow, Ma! Let me just go home! That's all I'm asking."

"I wish you'd thought of that the night you went out with that f… with that Rogers girl, so I do. Now sit up!"

"But I didn't do anything."

"We'll see what her and her cronies say to that! Haven't I told you a thousand times, that crowd would leave you in the lurch! Haven't I?"

The girl drew her arms in even tighter. Minogue was aware of Duggan's eyes on him, waiting to exchange a signal: "crowd."

"Tara?"

"Listen to him, Tara," said the mother.

"Tara, do you know what accessory means? Have you heard that word before?"

The mother glared at Minogue.

"It's not makeup, or earrings."

"Ha ha," said the girl. "I'm not retarded, you know."

"So Tara, it doesn't matter if you intended to commit a crime."

"But I didn't do anything!"

Minogue waited for her to collapse back into her slump.

"Were you there, Tara?"

When she didn't answer, her mother nodded at Minogue.

"We need to get this out in the open," Minogue murmured. "It wasn't just you and your friend there, was it?"

"It was," she said.

"All the time? You and Ali?"

She raised her head. Her swollen, running eyes reminded Minogue of someone who had been tear-gassed. He wondered if her eyelids could open at all now.

"They already know," her mother said, her jaw set hard. "I told them. I told them what I saw you writing there on the computer, didn't I? I had to. What else could I do? Stupid Internet, I should never have gotten it! It was for school, Tara, for school, remember? So's you could get good marks and go places and not... not be like me or your da! You stupid, stupid girl, what are you after doing to us all?"

Chapter 23

FANNING FELT LIKE HIS BRAIN was actually tingling. Not a single one of the hundreds of people milling about here on Parnell Street knew that the man beside him was carrying a gun. It was eerie, stupendous. It reminded him of being stoned, when he had felt privy to matchless thoughts and insights, with every detail around him sharply known to him alone. This should be terrifying, he thought again. Maybe later on he'd be able to figure out why it was not.

Murph had left the restaurant first. Fanning had watched him during the so-called meeting there, Murph trying to hide his agitation but betraying himself again and again with his eyes blinking like mad, and the flame of his lighter trembling when he had tried lighting a cigarette. He was only briefly ashamed to have enjoyed Murph's distress. Murph's twitchy earnestness rushing to shake hands with Cully on parting had kindled a contempt in Fanning that had repelled as much as it had satisfied him.

A quick glace across the traffic told Fanning that Cully's sidekick was still tagging along on the far side of the street. "West Ham" – it was too much, really. When Cully had introduced him back at the restaurant, there had been no sign that he regarded that name as anything unusual or funny. But from this West Ham character, Fanning had heard not a word. He had merely sat at the next table, never once making eye contact, but

spinning a scratched mobile phone between his thumb and forefinger.

Cully himself didn't project anything that Fanning could
pin down either. He showed no apparent interest in the goings-
on around him on the street, or the crowds through which he
and Fanning now made their way.

Cully stopped and looked down Parnell Street.

"You're not familiar with this area here?" Fanning asked.

Cully made no reply. Fanning looked back to the corner.

"Your friend there is keeping up with us anyway."

"My friend?"

"Over there. You didn't know?"

"West Ham? Is he really?"

"As if you didn't know."

"Are you worried?"

"Well I don't know. Should I? Murph wasn't his usual self
back there."

Cully looked up at the sky.

"'The rain in Spain...,'" he said. He glanced over at
Fanning then. "Is actually non-existent most of the time.
Drought. You believe this global warming thing?"

"I do, I suppose. Yes. Why?"

"You can get the sun in Spain. That's vitamin D, did you
know that?"

Fanning was sure now that Cully was filling in time waiting for something.

"I heard that, yes."

"You need it, especially in this country. Do you take a
tan?"

He looked over at Fanning.

"No, you'd burn. Been to sunny Spain, have you?"

Fanning shook his head.

"You could always go to those salons though, I suppose."

"Tanning salons? Tanning beds?"

"Right, right."

Cully found a step up by a shop door. Balancing there on

one foot, he looked over the crowd.

"I think," said Fanning, waiting for Cully to step down again. "I think we should decide what's going on."

"What's going on? Okay. You're doing your research, is what's going on."

"I mean why am I walking around with you, and him."

"You heard Murph. Explaining why...?"

"I hear what he said, yes. But that told me nothing."

"Really. Well Murph wanted out. The shape he's in. Pretty obvious."

"That wasn't clear to me, actually."

"Even though he said so?"

Fanning stood his ground.

"Murph doesn't even know you."

"Sure he does," said Cully. "He just forgot, that's all."

"He didn't know who you were there at that thing yesterday. The dogs."

Cully shrugged.

"Guys who have a habit, their memories aren't the best. Sad but true."

"How do you know he was an addict?"

"'Was?'" said Cully. "'Is,' you mean. You knew too, come on. Look, we were talking about tanning, so look."

He pointed toward the second-floor windows above a Chinese restaurant.

"See that one up there, the sign? See it? Tell you what. Stand here awhile any day. Afternoons are better. Count the number of people coming and going there, and keep track of who has the tan. You can't miss it, that orange look. You know?"

"I know. What about it?"

"Well, let's just say it's not about the tan. Can you put that in the script?"

"Look, I've got to think about this."

"Think about what," Cully said, returning to his survey of the street.

"This business about Murph, and where I am now."

"That's easy. Murph stepped out of the picture. And good riddance, you should say."

"He didn't bow out voluntarily."

"I did you a favour. He'd get himself into trouble. Drag you in too."

"I don't remember being asked about any of this, consulted...?"

"You'll see, don't worry. I'll show you stuff, believe me."

Fanning bit back what he'd planned to say. He looked at the passing faces, so many of them here clearly not Irish. Across the street, West Ham was resting against a lamp post, his mobile pressed to his ear.

"Murph knows Dublin," Fanning said to Cully then. "That's what I hired him for. Obviously."

Cully made a non-committal nod.

"So I need to find someone else from Dublin, I suppose," Fanning added.

"I know Dublin," said Cully.

"You sure don't sound like it."

"What do I sound like then?"

"Irish sometimes. Then English. Some of this, some of that."

Cully's jaw set in a way that Fanning read as irony, or some private joke.

"Your mate's not Irish, for sure."

"Too true. I could accuse him of being a lot of things, but not Irish. Let's say he's honorary Irish."

"Whatever that might mean."

"Oh don't think I'm slagging it off," said Cully, with a haste that surprised Fanning. "It means a lot to say that. Means a lot to him too, believe me."

"'West Ham,'" said Fanning. "I mean what's that about, anyway."

"Likes football, doesn't he."

Cully held up his hand. Fanning followed his gaze across to West Ham, who seemed to have awakened. He too had raised his hand, and now he nodded his head several times, his mobile pressed hard against his ear.

Cully looked at his watch, and then to Fanning.

"What were we talking about?"

"I was saying how I wasn't consulted on this, what you want to call it."

To Fanning, Cully finally seemed to get the idea.

"Okay. Yes. You want talk or something, I suppose."

West Ham crossed through the traffic now, and gained the footpath behind them. Cully seemed to take his arrival as a signal to hurry up.

"How long have you lived in London?" Fanning asked.

"London? Why do you say that?"

"Your accent," said Fanning.

"That much?" Cully said, with little interest.

"It's noticeable, to say the least."

"Well okay. That's your job, isn't it. Noticing, and stuff."

West Ham had caught up to them.

"London's all right," said Cully. "Most of it."

"How long were you there?"

Cully pretended he hadn't heard him.

"Lot of very strange people there this past while," he said. "Nasty types. Here too, I'm sure."

Fanning's frustration rose again, and it met with the steady current of excitement that had been running in him. He felt jumpily alert to everything on the street. His mind raced with questions that he knew would have to wait.

"Here we are," said Cully.

He slowed and then he stopped.

"A pub?" Fanning asked. "Now?"

"You have your phone? Keep it handy now."

West Ham was pretending to examine a billboard for holiday flights.

"Wait here," said Cully. "Back in a minute."

Fanning stepped over to West Ham.

"You're mates with him?" he asked him.

West Ham looked up and down the street. Fanning's mind scrambled for features and details he could commit to his notebook: didn't need to shave every day, sort of runny eyes – allergies? Lip hanging makes him look not smart. Twenty, twenty-one or -two? Did he have the West Ham team pyjamas too?

"Saw you at the thing yesterday," Fanning said.

"Look," West Ham said. He didn't look at Fanning. "You're his idea. Me, I don't want to talk to you. And I don't want you talking to me neither. So stay out of my way. And push off."

Fanning waited for eye contact. Then he noticed West Ham's stare coming back at him from the reflections on the plate glass of the pub window. Not much point to this, was there. He ambled the ten or so steps to the head of the lane, and he leaned against the brickwork there. He studied the dense razor-wire and wondered what it would do to someone's hands. The graffiti was layers deep on the walls. A minute passed. He considered just jotting down notes. So what if Cully or West Ham saw him. This was not his part of town, but still he eyed the people flowing down the street, half-hoping he'd recognize faces. He began to try guessing at nationalities. You couldn't go by skin colour of course. He had no clue what language two slight men were speaking when they passed, but he'd leave it at Slavic something or other. Polish, probably – or statistically likely.

West Ham hadn't moved. He was looking up and down the street with a slow, lazy stare. Someone, or something, was being set up, Fanning decided. Maybe him. Just as he had decided to walk away, he saw West Ham turn. Then a man came out the door of the pub in a hurry, attached to another man: Cully.

Cully had bunched some of the man's jacket in his fist, and he pushed and then pulled and turned the man left down the lane. West Ham was already on the move. He stopped at the door to the pub, and stood there.

Cully was keeping one hand in his pocket. The man he was holding and dragging stumbled, and he shouted as his arms waved for balance. Fanning felt his own hand closing on his phone. He made another step toward the edge of the footpath.

Nobody walking by seemed to care what was going on.

Two girls stopped in the street to avoid Fanning. He apologized and then slowly traced his steps back toward the laneway. He heard someone shouting what sounded like "police." Cully let go of the man's jacket and kicked him hard in the small of his back sending him sprawling and rolling out of sight of the street.

West Ham shot Fanning an angry glance just as the door of the pub was pushed open. Whoever had come out started to shout, but West Ham had his hand on the man's chest in an instant. He put his forearm on the man's neck and pushed him hard against the wall. He stared at the man he had pinned, and punched him hard in the belly. The man's feet actually came off the ground, Fanning saw.

West Ham let him go and he doubled up, and began to back away. West Ham shepherded him to the laneway and flicked his head toward Cully and the other man.

Fanning looked up and down the street. The traffic passed, the pedestrians walked. Nothing changed. He heard someone shouting his name, and he looked down the lane again. It was Cully.

"What are you waiting for?" Cully shouted.

"No," Fanning said. "No, I'm out of this."

Then West Ham was in front of him. A different man entirely, Fanning thought, taking the sight of his flattened nostrils and a sharp intensity in his eyes, nothing of the sloucher who had hung around in the margins.

"Don't piss about," West Ham said. "Go!"

Fear slammed into Fanning.

"I don't want this," he said. "This is wrong."

"Give it to me then. Your bleeding phone."

With that, West Ham grabbed his arm and pulled it up. Fanning didn't resist. One of the men was speaking now.

"Your pockets," Cully said to him. "Empty your pockets."

"Policia?" said the man. "Policia?"

"Yeah we're Policia. Now empty your pockets."

"How do you work this stupid thing?" West Ham asked.

The man that West Ham punched was straightening up. He eyed West Ham and then Fanning himself.

"How?" West Ham said louder.

"The menu, the main menu. Scroll down a bit."

"Do you know what pockets are?" Cully said, his voice rising. "Pockets, yes. Empty, now. Yes. Now, you're deaf as well as stupid?"

Fanning saw the man's hand go to his coat pocket. He stayed in a crouch and glanced back to the other.

"Video?" West Ham said. "Yeah, yeah. Okay, I did it, yeah."

He held up Fanning's phone.

"There we go," said West Ham. "Smile, thicko. You're going to be a star."

The other man with Cully was protesting now.

"Papieri, policia? Papieri?"

"No papieri. Empty your pockets."

"No speak English good."

West Ham turned, the phone held out.

"Now it's working. You take it."

The man glanced at Fanning and then he launched himself at West Ham.

"Got a knife," Cully called out.

West Ham let go of the phone, and Fanning followed its fall, watching it hop sideways and come to rest. His phone, he thought, wrecked: a man with a knife not twenty feet from him, another who had a gun.

The man with the knife hesitated, his free hand over his stomach still. He shouted a name, Andrey.

Cully's man had stopped talking, and was now staring at him.

"No Policia," the man with the knife shouted. "No."

"Do him," Cully said to West Ham. "Do him, now."

West Ham stepped forward, and his hand came from his back with a pistol. The man with the knife shouted, and spread his hands.

"Put down the knife," Cully said. "Put it down. Down?"

Fanning felt the brickwork against his back. He couldn't remember getting to the side of the laneway. His phone was still flipped open, and there were no broken pieces around it that he could see. He looked back toward the street. Where were the Guards, here in the middle of Dublin? The man with the knife seemed to be pleading.

"Down!" yelled Cully. "Put it down."

Still, Fanning did not dare look over. He heard something clatter on the cement. The two men were almost shouting now. Cully told them to shut up.

He risked a glance over, saw West Ham stoop to pick up a knife. The two men had backed closer, and Cully had stepped away from them.

"No," Fanning said. "Don't, for Christ's sake!"

"Shut up you," said West Ham, and shoved the pistol into the back of his jeans.

"You can't do this," Fanning said. "You can't."

West Ham's impassive face twisted suddenly into a grimace as he ran at the knife man.

He brushed aside a feeble arm and gave him a hard kick, and then kicked again as he went over. He said nothing as he kicked, and he darted in and out from the flailing man, dancing almost, and landing kicks. The man tried to cover his head, but West Ham landed a kick under the man's chin. The man yelped and turned on his side, and Fanning saw spots of blood on his lips. West Ham jumped in again, and a flurry of kicks followed. The man curled up, squirmed, and tried to roll away.

West Ham paused, his wheezy breath coming fast. Then he darted in with a kick to the side of his head. Something small had fallen on the pavement and Fanning saw pink and white. Now West Ham was whispering something into the man's ear, and he dragged him upright, grabbing his arm and turning it behind his back. Without warning West Ham shouted, jerked the arm hard with a grunt.

Fanning himself yelled now, jammed his eyes shut and pushed his palms hard onto his ears. Still he heard the bone break. He opened his eyes for a moment, saw the man's contorted face as he tried to shout something. The man went suddenly limp. West Ham let him go and he fell heavily to the cement.

West Ham strolled toward Cully. The other man had backed to the wall. His face had gone white; his jaw moved but he said nothing. He watched Cully go through the unconscious man's pockets, scattering bills and ripping open a packet of cigarettes. Cully lifted out a set of brass knuckles from a pocket and turned to West Ham and made a sly smile. Then he picked up the wallet and pulled out cards.

"Andrey," he said. "Andrey sombody I can't pronounce."

West Ham stood staring at the other man.

"Who do you work for?"

"I no," said the other man. "I no know nothing, nothing. Family. A poor man. Nothing."

"You don't look too poor to me. Who are you with? You and him. Who's your boss?"

"No boss, no. Roma, many bad people, no like Roma."

Cully held up a small bag of pills.

"Who gave you these?"

"Nothing, is not."

"Ecstasy? X?"

"No, nothing. A man. He give to me. He say 'sell, I give you money.'"

"What man? Who?"

"I don't know man."

"Irish? Ireland?"

He would not look back at West Ham's stare. But suddenly his eyes left the ground and darted toward the alleyway.

"Oi oi," said Cully.

A middleaged man with a shopping bag was now standing there, frowning, his mobile half-open in his hand.

"Is that man hurt?" he called out.

Cully stepped forward, picking up Fanning's phone as he did. He stuffed it in his pocket and lifted up the man's wallet again.

"Drug Squad," he said. "Garda Drug Squad. You need to

stay back now, there's a squad car on the way. Thank you."

"Drug Squad? Is that man hurt?"

"An overdose," said Cully, "the ambulance will be here any moment."

The man looked at West Ham, and headed back down the street.

Cully turned back. Fanning saw the man start as Cully stepped in closer to him.

"Go," said Cully and flicked his head toward the street. The man was trembling now; he nodded at the man on the ground.

"No," said Cully. "Go, or..."

He drew his finger across his throat.

West Ham made a feint in the man's direction as he passed, and the man stumbled, falling into Fanning. His stomach heaving and chest ready to burst, Fanning pushed him off. He had the clammy foretaste of puke in his throat.

"Yeah," said West Ham, and began picking up banknotes. He crammed the wallet in to his pocket.

The man on the ground moaned but he did not open his eyes. Fanning looked at his mouth and saw the blood was still draining down his chin. Cully was talking to him.

"You go through the pub, there's another door out, do you hear me."

Fanning stood rooted to the ground, watching the other man skip rapidly down the street.

"Gary, take him with you."

Fanning felt exhausted, and the cold, sweaty calm that came before vomiting had enveloped him. Somewhere in the nausea and reeling thoughts, it registered with him that now he at least knew this lunatic's real name.

Chapter 24

Minogue was almost finished making his own notes from the Effects list. Hughes himself had compiled it from the room at the hostel. Passport, Polish government documents: social welfare card, bankcard. No driver's licence for a twenty-two year old? No address in Ireland for contacts, for friends. Former friends even?

"We have one of the boys in here now," said Wall. "Mr. Aidan Matthews."

"Arrest, or for questioning?"

"Straight arrest," said Wall, with a strong hint of satisfaction.

"And what class of humour is he in?"

"No real fireworks," Wall replied. "But he's a Dub, isn't he. A bit belligerent when we put the word on him. Bit of effing and the like, but no actual resistance. He said we'd be sorry. Promises to sue us."

"And you told him to take his place in the queue?"

"I will if he says it again, I suppose."

"Well what does Mr. Matthews do when he's not litigating?"

"He sells phones at a place down there on Henry Street."

Minogue sat back.

"Any giveaways yet from him?"

"Nothing so far. He's not in the system at all, no form on him.

Lives at home. Doesn't admit to being her fella. Says he hasn't a clue what she's talking about. Thinks she's trying to get back at him for something. She's being a bitch, quote unquote, and he has no idea why, et cetera."

Minogue checked his watch.

"Let him cool his heels awhile," he said to Wall. "Do you think?"

"Can't hurt."

"And when the other fellow's coming in, what's his name?"

"Justin Twomey."

"Nineteen as well?"

"Eighteen actually."

"We can audition them both then."

Minogue sat up again and turned the page of his new notebook back.

"Can you bring me up to date on a few things?" he asked Wall.

"Fire away."

"Online stuff. Email, chat stuff. Messaging."

Wall tugged at his cuffs and suppressed a frown. Minogue had no trouble reading his puzzlement. In Wall's mind, that one phone call from the girl's mother, and the kid's admission, was money in the bank.

"Just so I'm caught up," Minogue said. "And I don't make an iijit of myself."

Wall shrugged and walked to the table in front of one of the boards. He pushed aside a stained plastic tray with teacups haphazardly abandoned amid granules of sugar.

"Klos phoned his mother twice to tell her he was okay, landed, etc. She said she heard other people talking so she thinks he was at a phone booth or one of those calling shops. He left his mobile back in his apartment in Poland remember. Nothing from the Internet cafes or phone shops, as of yesterday. City centre ones."

"No texting? Anyone in Poland? "

"Unless someone let him use their phone, say someone in the hostel."

Something in Wall's tone alerted Minogue, and he gave Wall a friendly, questioning look. Wall had large ears he realized and tried not to look at them. Was it the light here? A shadow?

"These two fellas," Wall said, uncertainly, "sad to say, and all that. But..."

"You think this one's capable, do you? The demeanour?"

"I do. Especially the denial she's his girlfriend. Lots to hide, I say."

"Girlfriend, my eye" said Minogue. "That age difference."

Wall wrinkled his nose.

"True for you," he said. "But we know how it is these days. Anything goes."

Minogue sat back again. How often he had heard these two simple words over the years, and how much it said of the person who uttered them.

"Around our neck of the woods here anyway," Wall added.

Minogue underlined the men's names.

"Well," he said, "I'd be a bit more excited if these two fellas had some form on them."

Wall seemed not to have heard him.

"Property crime of course," Wall said. "But sure that you could almost understand. It's the disrespect for life, I meant. I mean, it's all over the papers even. Killing a man is nothing these days, is it."

Minogue did not want to agree.

"Rap, films, what have you," said Wall. "Only skimming the surface."

Minogue let the quiet speak for him.

"Kids yourself?" Wall asked.

"Grown up. Well, for the most part. Yourself, Ciaran?"

"Five," said Wall with a quiet pride. Minogue tried not to react. He suspected now that Wall had steered this topic onto many people.

"I know, I know," said Wall, and tugged at his tie again. "You don't see that much anymore. I was one of eleven. 'The Irish Family' is gone, but, isn't it."

Should have known, Minogue scolded himself. The tweed tie, the grooming.

"Yep," said Wall. "When that goes, well anything goes."

He turned to Minogue with a kindly smile.

"Take God out of the situation like we're doing in Ireland, and you can expect things to slide. Common sense."

Minogue's irritation snowballed. He eyed the kettle and the Mikado biscuits next to the printer. A peace offering was his way out.

"My turn I think, Ciaran," he said rising.

He filled the kettle slowly from the tap in the tiny lunch room, and plodded back to the caseroom. Wall was on the phone.

"The Twomey lad's on his way up," he said to Minogue. "Mossie's taking him in."

There was a spark from the plug of the kettle as he pushed it into the socket. Unused Styrofoam cups stood stacked in a corner. He'd forgotten the milk from the fridge. He might as well have washed the damn mugs – and that manky-looking tray along with it. He'd better call Kathleen and tell her the case had started to move. His mobile signal was down to half strength in the lunchroom. She answered halfway through the first ring.

"Back on board the time machine," she said after his explanation.

"Short-handed," he said. "But it's no hardship on me. Is it on you?"

"What's that sound? Don't tell me you're in the toilet."

"I put it on speaker phone. Multitasking, with dishes."

"Can other people hear our conversation then?"

"No. I'm in a cubbyhole here in Fitzgibbon Street station."

"And you're enjoying yourself. Go on admit it."

"I admit I am enjoying myself. Somewhat. Not overdoing it, of course."

"'Happy days are here again...' Go on, you might as well say it."

"It wouldn't be true. Totally."

"Ah," she said with gentle scorn. "But if you-know-who was there with you it'd be perfect entirely."

"You're determined not to believe me."

"Guilty as charged," she said. He could tell that she was smiling.

The printer came to life beside him, drawing a paper in with a lisp. He watched it issue out.

"I have a question for you now," Kathleen said. "About you-know-who. A certain person phoned me, and she asked for advice – listen, are you sure no-one can hear you there?"

"Are we referring to the same you-know-who we were referring to a minute ago?"

"Oh come on. It was Maura Kilmartin phoned."

"Do I need to know what ye were gostering about?"

"Don't be like that. Listen to me. This could be the start of something. Are you ready? She said that Jim put out an over-ture to her."

"Fortissimo?"

"Stop that, I said. Through a friend of hers. An overture, you understand."

"It's a tin ear you're talking to, pet. I don't do overtures."

"Don't act the iijit with me now. Give me your take on it. That's all I'm asking."

"All right. What harm could it do. That's my considered take."

"Go on."

"That's all. Look, I have to go."

"So you'll do it then?"

"Do what?"

"She says she'd feel secure if we were there, an outing or something."

"You're having me on."

"And Jim will feel more secure too."

"Jim would, I suppose. If that were ever to happen."

"What evening will we do it?"

"I'm not in the marriage counselling business."

"Who asked you to be? All you have to do is sit there,

have a pint, and smile every once in a while. Do you think you could do that?"

The conversation was soon over. Minogue squeezed the power button as hard as he could.

He brought the cups back to the caseroom. Wall had made the tea. Its aroma calmed Minogue.

Wall sugared his after it had been drawn, and he put in a bit of milk to colour it.

"I'll take mine in with me," he said. "Okay with that?"

"To be sure. Now, the interview room's set up for recording, I take it."

"It is that. The controls are in the top drawer of the desk. A digital recorder there too; you can take the data home on a stick."

Data, a stick going home? Minogue was lost for several moments. Then he remembered USB sticks, and the circulars on their use and abuse that had been repeated several times over the past few months. He tucked his clipboard under his arm and he headed downstairs after Wall.

A corridor leading out from the main office led to a short hall that was chicaned by a photocopier and a newish vertical file folder. Wall's small tics seemed to be more apparent as he walked: straightening his jacket, gently tugging his shirt collar, spreading his fingers over the knot of his tie. The communications room door was open and Minogue got a glimpse of a uniformed Guard with his headset, stretching. Somebody had farted here recently. Wall pulled the communications room door closed and he approached the first of three doors. He turned and nodded at Minogue and then opened the door.

Minogue waited until the uniform left the room, and then he entered.

Twomey's face was pale and he frowned so much it looked like a permanent grimace. He kept eye contact with Wall as the detective moved two chairs.

"You've decided to help us with our inquiries then," said Wall.

"Are you bleeding joking me?"

"No, I'm not. Merely inquiring."

"Those two cops, the two Guards, at the house said I was under arrest. That's against my rights. No bleeding way am I here voluntarily, I can tell you."

Dublin accent, Minogue reflected, but not one that would scrape your eardrums. He was already storing impressions: acne; sweat by his hair; a smoker; trying to look confident and much put upon; fidgety. Scared.

He wondered if he were looking at the man who had killed Tadeusz Klos.

"What size of a shoe do you wear," he said, staring at Twomey.

"Shoe? What are you talking about shoes for? Jases. Shoes?"

There had been no give, Minogue realized.

"Eleven, I'm guessing."

"Who are you, exactly?"

"I'm a Garda detective," said Minogue.

"That's nice. But how do I know? I need to see some ID, don't I?"

Minogue downed the tea and then the clipboard and pulled out his wallet.

"You look different than your picture."

"Better or worse, would you say?"

"I'm not going after that one. As a matter of fact I'm not saying nothing to neither of yous. Talk to my lawyer."

"Your counsel."

"Lawyer, whatever."

"What's your counsel's name?"

"Legal Aid, whatever. Whoever. When I make my phone call."

"What phone call?"

"Don't try that one. Everyone gets a phone call. Basic democratic rights."

Minogue wrote the date on his clipboard. He opened the drawer and took out the microphones and placed them within arm's reach. Stretching his arm, his sleeve slid up, and he saw four o'clock on his infallible wedding anniversary watch.

Minogue ejected the tape, looked it over, and slid it back in again. He closed the lid on it and cued it, and then he hit Record and Pause.

"You're wasting your time with that," said Twomey, "I've nothing to say."

"So you were saying."

Minogue looked up to the corner of the ceiling where the Plexiglas covered the camera.

"You know what that is up there?"

"Of course I do. But you won't be needing it."

"It's to help safeguard your rights, Mr. Twomey."

"I want my phone call."

"Detective Wall and I have some questions for you. Detective Wall will start, I believe."

Twomey folded his arms, slouched deeper in the seat, and looked away.

"We have a sworn statement from a person who was with you on the night of the fourteenth of this month," said Wall, "so be aware that we already have information concerning your actions that evening."

Both detectives waited for a reaction. Minogue sipped at his tea and glanced down at the tape travelling through the spools.

"You were on Amiens Street, at eleven p.m. or thereabouts in the company of three other parties – people. Do you dispute that or can you confirm that for me?"

Minogue held the mug close to his mouth and watched Twomey's face.

"Do you dispute the statement that says you were in possession of cannabis resin that evening? Furthermore, that you were trafficking in same?"

"Lawyer," said Twomey.

"You're aware of the penalties for drug trafficking, Mr. Twomey?"

"Lawyer," he said, "phone call."

"And you're aware that a search warrant has been executed on your home, your family home, looking for evidence of this and further crimes?"

Twomey pursed his lips, drew in a deep breath and let it out noisily through his nose. Then he crossed his legs at the ankle and started studying his shoes.

"You may want to consider what forensic science can learn from even the most minute items," said Wall.

"My nute?" Twomey asked.

"Small," said Wall. "Tiny."

Wall exchanged a glance with Minogue.

"These drug charges are a start," he said to Twomey then. "We'll move on to child exploitation. Do you know what the age of consent is?"

"Lawyer," said Twomey and sighed, "phone call."

Minogue shifted in his seat. Wall took the hint and he sat back. Minogue let the quiet last. Twomey looked up after a count of twelve.

"So can I go now?"

"You can stop the performance," said Minogue, "if that's what you mean."

"Good cop, bad cop? I get it."

"You got your caution when you were arrested," Minogue said. "Fine and well if you want to play the sound citizen. You'll get your counsel. But as for 'my phone call' you'll only get that on the telly."

"I can sue you for this."

"Sue all you like. You have that on tape too. You'll have plenty of time on your hands to start your career as a hob lawyer."

"Are you threatening me?"

"Me," Minogue said. "I'm going to talk some more. You can listen or not."

"I don't need to be here to listen to you talking. So let me go."

"You're under arrest, Mr. Twomey."

"If I'm under arrest I want a phone call. Not to listen to you talk, or threaten me."

"What I'm giving you is information. Your paranoia's your own business."

"You have nothing, you're just trying to–"

"–First thing is, we're not in a play here. Nobody's acting here, except you. Nobody's trying to cod you, or put one over on you."

"Will Santy Claus be coming soon? With toys…?"

"We have plenty to do instead of listening to you, whinging about your rights. My job here is – was for many years – murder investigations. That's why I'm here. I think you need to know that."

Minogue mentally checked off a few signals from Twomey: the gaze stayed up to a corner of the ceiling, the forced attempt to stillness, the swallow.

"I'm assuming that you're listening and understanding. Will Detective Wall confirm that?"

Wall sat up a little and turned toward one of the microphones.

"Mr. Twomey is alert and can hear my colleagues' words."

"You need to know that this is about you going to jail for drug offences and exploitation of a minor. There won't be bail. Your pals are going to drop you like lightning. You're going to get slagged something fierce for going out with a fourteen-year-old child. There are people who really despise that to the point they'd want to show you in no uncertain terms. You might meet these people. You might hope and pray that the likes of me are there to protect you."

"Child," muttered Twomey, "what do you know about 'child'? Christ."

"Who cares what I know? What does the law say? We interviewed your girlfriend today. Two hours ago."

"And you believe what she says?"

"Let the court decide. To me, it's evidence."

"Not if you treated her like you're treating me. Refusing me my rights here. That'd be thrown out."

"Well now," said Minogue and sat back, "you're just full of bad ideas here."

"It's the company I'm keeping," said Twomey, with a sniff.

"You're determined to be your own worst enemy with your lawyer. I'll let you in on a few details then."

"Very big of you. But what's this story got to do with me? Nothing, that's what. Nothing. No thing."

Minogue waited a few moments.

"This girl was in the company of her mother when she was interviewed. Being as you're one for contesting the law, you might already know how it works, a minor giving an interview through the care and consent of her parent or guardian. Have you come across that in your law studies?"

"That's bullshit. You're making it up."

"You hope I am. But I doubt you're thick enough to believe your own propaganda here."

"Charge me. Let's see who's bullshitting now. Charge me, or let me go."

Minogue pushed his mug to the side of the table and he slid his clipboard near. He didn't look at Twomey when he spoke.

"You were arrested on a charge of possession of illegal drugs, cannabis resin to be correct. I'm expecting the search would yield further evidence to that crime and other charges. You are also being investigated for child exploitation. You are being the least cooperative when you should be the most. We haven't even gotten to the one that will surely have you really roaring and shouting for your counsel. Small blame to you, I'll be thinking too, because that's what I would be doing too. Yes, Mr. Twomey, there'll be wigs on the green shortly."

"Wigs on the green? My granny used to say that."

"This is the end of my peroration, you'll be glad to know. After these few words you'll be getting your phone call and your list of Legal Aid counsel. We are shortly going to charge you with murder."

"You're mad," said Twomey. "Totally off-the-wall, raving bonkers."

"You're not alone in your predicament," said Minogue.

"What does that mean? I'm not alone?"

"You know who. He was there that night too. He's in the same boat."

"What? This is just absolutely ridiculous, stupid. I don't believe this. I mean, you two are completely full of– Why are you doing this?"

Wall stood up slowly.

"Take a while to think things over," said Minogue. "Let me go downstairs and get that list of counsel. Then the system takes over."

"Wait 'til the papers hear about this," Twomey said. "The television, everything. This is crazy, unbelievable."

"Was it worth it?" Wall asked.

Twomey glared at him.

"Like what did he have on him? Twenty Euro maybe? Thirty?"

Twomey said something under his breath, shook his head, and turned away.

"Inspector Minogue is leaving the room."

Minogue held the door for the Guard.

"Garda O Keefe entering," he heard Wall say in the room behind him. "Interview concluded at 4:17 p.m. Garda O Keefe remaining in the room."

Chapter 25

ANNING CAUGHT THE 11A on O Connell Street. Reflexively, he stayed on the lower level of the bus, and headed down the aisle toward the back seats. Sitting down, he had the sensation that he was actually falling in upon himself, even collapsing. It was as though his frame had been unhooked and he was now tumbling into a collection of limbs and aching joints. The ache in his neck and his shoulders was like a big bruise.

How often he had sat into a bus, all his life practically, and let the familiar streets and buildings go by the windows. There was a different quality to what he saw now, some strangeness about things that unsettled him. A fever, he thought. Food poisoning, the flu? Images flared insistently in his mind insistently – the fear in that man's face, the way that West Ham calmly and savagely went about his business.

He distracted himself by checked his mobile. There was nothing. Again he considered phoning the Guards. They could track mobile though, couldn't they? He wished he knew more about that technical stuff.

He felt the phone slide from his fingers and knew he couldn't catch it. It slid down his lap and stopped on the seat. He wiped his palms and his fingertips on his trouser leg. The bus lurched and righted itself, the traffic slowed. His hands were sweaty again. He took out his notebook, but before he opened it, he tried to settle his mind by planning the evening ahead. That was the only way to get through this.

He had the fish thawing out in the fridge, yes. Broccoli – yes again! – and mash the spuds from yesterday. Milk? Had it – oh: yogurt for Aisling, the raspberry. She'd have her noodles as usual, and then he'd bring her out in the buggy. Bríd could decompress, have a bath, a cup of tea on her own – whatever she wanted.

Three women got on just as the driver was about to close the doors and drive off. They were breathless and smiling after their dash, and like sailors in rough seas, the three made their way down the passageway. The one with the headscarf didn't look Arab at all. She looked more, well, white, he supposed. The other two had frizzy hair and glowing, muddy-coloured skin. They giggled and sat, and they began speaking in French. Fanning decided they were North Africans, and words cart-wheeled gently through his thoughts: Sahel, Berber, Toureg. ... One laughed, revealed gums over snow white teeth before she covered her mouth with her hand.

O'Connell Bridge wasn't crowded. Maybe it was a bit early in the season for the hawkers to be selling their Celtic bead-work and jewellery shite. A lone, middleaged duo dressed in the fawn and khaki colours that Fanning pegged as German was taking pictures. The Liffey was at full tide, and its dull, coral green swill did nothing to awaken the colours about, or the seamless grey sky settled over the city.

He tried to imagine himself in a market, in Morocco say, where these women must have come from. Shadows cut on the high stone walls by a sun in a cloudless sky, stalls, awnings, fruit, coffee and cigarette smoke, and roasting lamb, donkeys waiting in the shadows. A land of simple, harsh choices, stark in its beauty, with burning sands leading south to the empty Sahara. This was where the world outside the city was medieval. Or so he had read in National Geographic probably. At least the tightness in his chest was easing now.

He began to make up a story then. Leaving their country would have changed these women utterly. Then, when they went back to visit, to a cousin's wedding, say, there'd be the clash with the old world… a marriage arranged by their families, an instruction to come home… a former boyfriend who…?

He took the pencil from the spine of his notebook. Scanning the notes he had from yesterday, he realized that he barely recognized his own writing. Shot: like a door slam? Like heavy books falling on a floor? Blood: lines, gouts? Wet fur, maroon. Smell: B.O., raw meat, cigarettes. Whiskey? Dust, oil? Disinfectant?

A long, deep yawn overtook him, and he gave into it. The tension was ebbing then, and the adrenaline gone. He could almost fall asleep here on the bus. His eyes slid out of focus, and he leaned his head against the window. Outside the glass, Westmoreland Street teemed with traffic and people. Three cranes stood out against the sky of the railings at Trinity College. The bus staggered and braked, wallowed and jerked as the driver fought to get into the lane around College Green. Fanning's gaze slid over the faces gathered by the bus stops and at the traffic lights. They looked expectant, listless, distracted. He had done this since the time he started university, grabbing images and scenes from the city and dropping them as words in his notebook. Which reminded him.

His fumbled with the notebook and it slid away from him. Dropping everything today, he was. He caught it before it went over the edge of the seat. The sudden movement had caught the eye of one of the three women, the one who sat sideways in her seat, fingering a small earring as she listened to her friends. She seemed so happy, he thought, so at ease with herself. Caramel skin: he must write that down too, caramel. Was caramel from Africa originally?

The closest he had ever gotten to Africa was Spain, that winter with Bríd. They taught English in Barcelona before it was a big deal, and then headed for the coast and Majorca – Robert Graves territory. Then in the new year they'd moved to the south of France, and later down to Siena. Returning to plain contradictable Dublin had been a strange pleasure. Unemployment, pasty-faced people, begrudgers and whingers galore, and a shocking lack of colour.

The writing really started after that. Glory years soon followed as Irish film became known. Soon there were film production companies springing up everywhere. Some serious money showed up. The script for Jack of Diamonds took him ten days, and put him in touch with Breen for the first time. He thought of moving to L.A. Bríd persuaded him that Ireland was the place to be. She was right, but it became the place to be for financial types and computer scientists – not self-taught scriptwriters.

Things went a bit sideways then, into writing articles on film for a weekend paper. He took it seriously. He wrote about Die Hard and Werner Herzog, Rambo 2 and Buñuel. He and Bríd kept at it, Bohemian-style, she teaching English at the institute on Westmoreland Street, he doing his articles and writing on the side. They lived in a flat on the second floor of a house near Beggar's Bush.

Things had crept up on them somehow. It was a new Dublin, a new Ireland, roaring and heaving all around them. The house they rented was sold, they had to leave. They tried to keep to the city centre but it was hard to find places now. Bríd's friends were starting families. She herself became pregnant when she was studying for her H Dip. She told him only when three months had gone by. He tried to push the gig he had at the paper but he had no leverage. After all, there were plenty of people who could turn a phrase in Dublin. He was glad when his half-hearted plans there came to nothing.

They staggered through six months after Aisling was born until the Blow Up. One night there wasn't any milk. It had nothing to do with the baby, but it was for a cup of tea and the breakfast in the morning. Hard things were said over a lack of milk. It passed. Things changed a bit. He did some columns for the suburban papers on green spaces and traffic. Bríd's aunt, a Holy Faith nun, got Bríd a start at a school the far side of Bray. They needed a car then...

The bus was stopped for more than a minute now. He leaned out into the passageway and saw that traffic as far as the Canal Bridge ahead was stationary. The three women had lapsed into silence, only putting out a word or a phrase occasionally. Those words brought a wry smile, a nod, even a yawn, but seldom replies. They were tired. He imagined them working in restaurant kitchens or McDonald's, wearily going through the motions, all the while thinking of their village on a stony hillside flattened by the sunlight of North Africa. A bit much, he knew.

But how could they ever make a go of it in Dublin on those wages? Had these women asked to be born poor, to be second-class citizens in some stupid religion they'd probably defend to their dying breaths? To be refugees here, to be homesick, barely getting by? There was no fairness, no justice

"You don't get rich from working."

It was Tony Morrissey who had told him that a few years ago, when he had bumped into him after a film. But then Tony, who had left Political Science in second year and had gone to Economics, climbed into a Beemer – this after nodding and smiling his way through the five-minute walk they shared heading back to Pearse Street. Fanning had thought about that evening a lot afterward, and over time it revealed things to him. Tony and so many more like him were in exactly the right place at the right time. They got on board when the boom started and they surfed it. They seemed to know the ropes, how to get on.

Yes, Tony had said how much he enjoyed reading his reviews, and he had made a little joke too about knowing someone famous like Fanning. Fanning was sure it had been a genuine compliment. If Tony knew how little Mr. Film Reviewer was paid, how precarious this little gig was, how close he was to losing it because he was not twenty-three or twenty-four anymore, how the column only drained him too often of a will to write anything worthwhile. Ideas were nothing. "Creative" meant nothing.

A Garda car went by in a hurry. Fanning thought about getting off and legging it. Forty-five minutes would do it if he moved smartly. But he still felt jaded, spent. He couldn't decide. He opened his notebook again. The bus began to move.

One of the women had been dozing. Fanning watched her

eyelids flutter, and then she frowned. What was it like, he wondered to be shaken awake to find you're in some strange country? Hardly the promised... That would be the title, and he must write it down: The Promised Land.

She drew her fingers across her eyes, rubbing them slowly. She yawned. Fanning imagined her face on the pillow next to him, her nipples dark against her skin. She let her eyes open slowly. Yes, he said within, you had a dream, but you are still here in this bus, in this strange city.

Her eyes met his. He nodded and made a small smile that he hoped conveyed understanding that she, like he, was tired. Her gaze stayed on him longer than he expected, and it sent a small current around his chest. Maybe she was wondering if she was really awake. Cheer up, he thought. She might have it bad waking up so far from home, but he was continually waking up in this strange place too.

She looked away. The others were craning their necks now to see what the flashing blue lights ahead could mean. Fanning looked down at the car next to the bus. A woman was driving – or rather not driving: she was on her mobile. In the back seat he saw a child with one of those Nintendos. An ambulance passed on the wrong side of the road.

This Promised Land idea could turn into the kind of thing that Breen expended clichés on: quirky, fresh, heart-felt. There'd be plenty of comedy available in the wings, of course, with Ireland meets the Maghreb. Maybe one of the three would fall for an Irish fella, and the other two would try to persuade her to go back and marry whoever had been picked for her...?

The women were talking again. He stopped writing and looked over. The one who had been dozing was murmuring something to the others. One of the two began to turn her head, but she stopped. When he looked down at the notebook again he was sure that he was now being watched. The dozy one laughed and the others joined her.

Embarrassment flared up in him. So they were amused at him being curious about them. They might even think he was giving them the eye. It was a major crime where they come from, no doubt. He turned back to his notebook and pretended to read what he had written.

One rose slowly and pressed the bell. The others got to their feet then, and followed her to the door. Fanning watched them shifting their grip from the bars overhead to the upright ones by the door, and back. The bus driver braked hard, and the doors hissed open even before the bus came to a full stop. The trio detached themselves from the railings and from one another after their stumbles. One giggled a bit. They stepped gingerly onto the footpath, and then began to walk back alongside the bus. Fanning pretended to be intent on his notebook.

The woman who had been dozing in the bus seemed fresh and energetic now. She cast him a quick glance, a mischievous one, he was certain, in passing. He abandoned his ruse with the notebook, caught her eye and smiled. She tried hard not to laugh outright and skipped ahead followed by the others. Something else began to leak into his thoughts now.

The bus moved off and he turned to look out the back window. They were having a great time of it now, staggering with laughter. They did not bother to hide their glances.

He turned back and closed his notebook. It wasn't embarrassment now, it was more like a draining feeling.

It was a while before the traffic finally moved again.

Chapter 26

LEGAL AID WAS A MAN IN HIS THIRTIES. He had a knapsack for a briefcase. Minogue almost heard Kilmartin's dry, sneering murmur: "Oh, so we're dealing with one of those, are we now." The abundance of lustrous, chestnut-coloured hair gathered in his ponytail struck Minogue as an affectation.

"Cormac Mahon," he said. He seemed to know that handshakes were out of the question.

The Garda who had let Mahon in made sure that Minogue and Wall witnessed his Mona Lisa smile.

"Your client had a cup of tea and a ham roll," Minogue said. "And a visit to the toilet, into the bargain."

Mahon unslung his knapsack.

"I've been in touch with his parents. His mother is on her way."

Minogue began to clean up the crumbs from his ham roll. The indigestion was already announcing itself just below his ribs.

"He wasn't brought for questioning first?"

"No," said Minogue. He tried not to notice how Mahon flicked his ponytail.

"You went straight for an arrest."

"Just so."

"Serious concerns?"

Asked so innocuously, Minogue was nearly caught flat-footed. He decided he had to kick for touch, while he pondered how to deal with any subliminal advantage this ponytail had allowed its owner.

"Ipso facto," he said.

"Pardon?"

"A sine qua non really," Minogue added.

"An arrest without a warrant?"

"Yes," said Minogue, "Section Two."

"Of the...?"

"Drug Trafficking Act, 1996."

"The time of arrest?"

"An hour and a half ago."

"Objections to release?"

"We'll burn that bridge when we get to it, Mr. Mahon. There'll be other charges in due course."

"There's someone else involved?"

"Let's have a wee chat after you see your client."

Mahon stopped taking a folder out of his bag to give Minogue a skeptical look.

"I get it," he said.

"I didn't mean to sound unhelpful. But we go one step at a time."

Mahon nodded as if he now understood something vital. He took his jacket off and laid it over the back of the chair.

"Goretex?" Minogue asked.

"I'll disclose that during our information exchange," said Mahon.

"Good one. I'm only asking because I'm destroyed half the time with the gorse. Savage growth this year again. It must be global warming."

"In Wicklow?" Mahon asked.

"All over, in actual fact. I'm nearly ready to stay home."

Mahon sat down and looked from Minogue to Wall and back.

"What are the other charges you're considering here?"

"We have several in mind."

"They would be?"

"Trafficking in drugs. Sexual exploitation."

"That's to keep him. What's the one you want to put on him?"

"I'm thinking Mr. Twomey would have confided that in his phone call?"

Mahon didn't give any sign he was miffed.

"But in the heel of the reel," Minogue added then, "it'll be murder."

Mahon bit his lip and looked down at his shoes for several moments.

"Well," he said, "it'll be a long evening."

Minogue smiled.

"It doesn't need to be," he said.

"You badly want him remanded, don't you?"

"I certainly do," said Minogue. "A man was kicked to death. A visitor to our country of Saints and Scholars. Looking for a better life apparently, a wee share of our Irish good fortune."

"A tragedy," said Mahon. "You'll know then that there are plenty of Irish people, people in certain Dublin neighbourhoods especially, looking for the same thing."

Minogue couldn't disagree.

"True for you," he said. "But I don't see that explaining away a murder."

"A fairly big leap there," said Mahon. "From Garda to prosecutor."

"Drugs involved," Minogue went on. "Exploitation of a minor: technically rape. Aggravated assault, robbery. Such a person needs to be off the streets."

There was still no sign of annoyance on Mahon's face.

"And have you said as much to my soon-to-be client?"

"I have."

Mahon put his hands on the armrests of the chair.

"All right so," he said, "I'm going to be working under the assumption that you are serious. These charges you're telling me you're going to take to the judge."

"Why would you imagine that we might not be serious?"

Mahon stood slowly.

"I'd like to know what evidence you have could back up this... barrage of charges. It's like fishing with sticks of dynamite."

"A bit early now for seeking disclosure, I'm thinking," said Minogue.

Mahon shrugged and left.

Minogue watched Wall's stretch.

"A substantial bee in his bonnet," said Wall.

"Substantial bonnet."

"There's women would kill for a head of hair like that."

"Figuratively, Kevin. Remember what we're working at?"

Wall conceded a smile.

"They're all like that," he said. "Not the hair. The attitude."

"Solicitors?"

Wall nodded.

"The law and justice parted company some time back," he said. "Don't mind justice: it's morality that went south. And here we are, with the results."

Minogue was a little surprised. He had to make an effort not to parse Wall's words or tune any further into stereotypes.

"As my mother, God rest her, would say, 'Man proposes, God disposes.'"

The awkward silence lasted several seconds. It ended with Wall clapping his palms on his knees.

"Well I wonder how Mossie's getting on with the other one," he said

"Sit in on it, why don't you," said Minogue. "I'll call you, if and when we get our interview with Twomey proper. After he consults with his esteemed counsel."

Wall closed the door behind him. Alone now, Minogue felt weary. He should be preparing a Charge Sheet to take to the Circuit Court in the morning. He should not care then that Cormac Mahon had tagged him as an overbearing cop, a tough nut trying to browbeat a suspect. He wondered what advice the same Cormac Mahon was giving his new client now. Start preparing alibis? Get off his high horse and realize that the Guards could hang a drug charge on him if that's what it took to keep him? Ask him straight out if he'd had sex with this kid Tara?

Minogue put his feet up on the table and slid back in the chair until his neck met the top. Against his own grudging efforts, he now let caution to the wind, and fell to imagining that this might be done in a few hours. It'd be up and down the hall between the rooms, playing Matthews off against the Twomey fellow. Then one would run out of nerve. Again he considered putting this Tara kid on the spot. Bring her in this very evening, see if she'd spill the beans now that she'd had a bit of time to see her situation.

But did kids – adolescents – actually feel guilt? The furthest she'd gone was admitting she'd taken Klos' money. By the time she had conceded this, she'd been almost hyperventilating, beyond hysterics. He'd heard that plaintive wail before, from his own Iseult, at that age. The martyrdom routine: "It's true, I swear! Why doesn't anyone believe me?"

Well, then.

All these dramatics had wearied him. The floods of tears and the wrenching sobs had gotten her what she wanted more or less: back into the custody of her parents, and home. He closed his eyes and listened to the faint background hum of the heating. He thought of Kilmartin looking furtively through the Self-Help or New Age shite in the bookshops, fighting off the gloom, waiting for a verdict. Waiting – something that James Aloysious Kilmartin had never been good at.

He shifted, tugged his jacket down, and closed his eyes again. He let himself wander again, and his mind took him straight to Graz and its lanes, where he had strolled with an Austrian copper and a French expert in counterfeit documents at a conference last year. Cobblestones, smells of ground coffee and sausage, violins on the street, trams and pedestrians in fine harmony, his own bewilderment that anything bad could have ever happened in such a beautiful city–

Footsteps outside the door: the door opened, cautiously; a

shaved head, a moustache, huge frog eyes.

"Ah, Matt?"

Minogue sat back again. He hoped it didn't show on his face that he believed this detective looked more like a pirate than a Guard.

"I was listening to Twomey lying in fifty-two different ways, and I realized, Jesus, I hadn't introduced myself."

"Good man."

"A complete pain in the hole, I'm telling you."

"Twomey, you mean, I take it."

Duggan had a manic smile. A bit of the Mr. Bean about him, thought Minogue, but with longer arms and a looser way of moving about.

"Hughsie is on the mend, I hear," Minogue said.

"Worse luck, the fecker," said Duggan. "A slave driver."

"Really?"

"Ah no. I'm only slagging."

Minogue returned the smile.

"Me and Hughsie go back these years. A fierce hard goer, Hughsie. But he forgot to take care of himself, I told him."

Minogue watched Duggan untwine his arms and begin to rotate his head and neck. He seemed so loosely put together that an extremity might fall off.

"This Twomey is cut from the same cloth as the Matthews lad. A bollocks, a complete fu–"

Minogue watched a mischievous expression come over Duggan's face.

"Stoney wouldn't appreciate that language," Duggan said then. "You know?"

"'Stoney'?"

"Stone wall...? He has a way of sticking to his "guns, like. But not in a bollicky way now. Very, how would I say, very decent."

"Good-living, you're saying."

"Doesn't wear it on his sleeve now," said Duggan. "No Holy Joe stuff."

"Good. I like that in a man."

"Don't get me wrong. It's just that you don't meet many, er. These days."

"Actual Catholics?"

"Oh more than that. Real believers, I mean, I suppose. No offence now. Are you, er, yourself, er..?"

Minogue shook his head.

"Oh, Church of Ireland?"

"No, Mossie. Pagan. Merely pagan."

Minogue felt sorry for Duggan's sudden awkwardness.

"But I'm well disposed," he said. "In general, like."

Duggan's face eased again.

Minogue let it go with a non-committal shrug.

"So," said Duggan. He looked at his watch. "No let up, no release?"

"And no bail," said Minogue. He decided to try a Kilmartinism. "We hang tough, I say."

"Fine by me. But Twomey's counsel is digging in his heels. That's why I left for a while – get away from it."

"That's the way I'd play it. Let him sit and think, argue with his counsel."

"Saves me going ape on him, I suppose. Giving him a clout."

"You'd be tempted," Minogue allowed. "Wouldn't you."

Duggan stopped unwinding himself, and sagged into his chair, his arms now resting on his lap. His knuckles almost reached his knees.

"Well, your timing was spot-on," he said to Minogue. "We were wondering, you know, but then comes that phone call. The girl's mother."

"The way of the world," said Minogue.

Duggan asked him about the Murder Squad, and how long he had worked to solve a case. Minogue answered with calcu-lated vagueness. Duggan got the hint. Soon desultory, the talk wandered briefly through the credit crisis, and somehow to free-range eggs, before it eventually lapsed. Minogue wondered if he'd find a second wind soon. Matthews and Twomey could go on as long as they liked being bastards. It'd likely be those two girls who'd be the key in the lock eventually. What lay behind the door was another matter.

He had a minute of mind wandering before Wall showed up. There was a fragment of food in the corner of his mouth.

"On the last lap, lads?" he said. "Think we'll have charges tonight?"

Minogue shrugged.

"Twomey's doing his shut-up routine," said Duggan.

"Asking about his mate down the hall yet?"

"Not yet," said Duggan. "He knows he's in a mind game with us. Left him simmering there a few minutes ago. As per plan."

Minogue, who didn't work by plan, didn't take the remark as a dig. He watched Wall looking for something in a drawer. Duggan unravelled his arms yet again and began pulling back the cuticles on his nails. He held his arm out every now and then, hands bent at the wrist, his head moving from side to side like a painter checking his canvas.

A Guard tapped at the door and entered.

"The solicitor in room fourteen says they're ready."

Wall was up out of his chair first.

"Come on with us," Minogue said to Duggan. "Give yourself something to raise the temperature on Twomey."

Mahon met them in the hallway. He was holding a package of Major, tapping it softly. A smoker? Minogue was stunned

"Has to be outside with the smokes," he said to Mahon. "Sorry."

Mahon pocketed the cigarettes. He looked at his watch.

"Do we have something to work with now?" Minogue asked.

Mahon looked from Wall to Duggan.

"Do you plan on laying charges tonight?" he asked.

"Undecided as of this moment," Minogue said, "We badly need your client's help to sort things out."

"Help?" Mahon said with a smile.

"He should clear his conscience. If he has any sense at all he knows we're almost there."

Mahon eyed Minogue.

"You'll be offering considerations," he said.

"Cooperation is always welcome. He knows we have Matthews down the hall here."

Mahon's jaw set. His gaze had turned into a steady stare.

"'The prisoner's dilemma.'"

"Did you explain to your client that even sexual exploitation of a minor is a five-year sentence? And drug dealing on top of that? There'll be no concurrent."

"We're having a very odd conversation," said Mahon.

"Only you know how bad a spot your client is in."

A flicker of irritation now crossed Mahon's face. He looked down at his shoes again and moved his toes.

"Are you one of those Guards," he said to his toes before raising his gaze, "who says that – hypothetically – a person passing a joint to another person is a dealer?"

"We go by the law as it is interpreted for us."

"He'll give a statement and expects to be released," said Mahon, evenly.

"Your client will be held over until noon tomorrow for District Court."

"The charges again?"

"We'll start with the cannabis, and move to sexual exploitation."

"You're fishing. The judge will know right away."

"Well would it help if we could get proper testimony from these two children – sorry, young ladies – to go right to a murder charge?"

Mahon took a breath and dug his hands deep into his pockets. Someone was cracking their knuckles. Minogue looked over at Duggan. The noise stopped.

"A word with you in private," Mahon said.

"I'll be telling my colleagues one way or another," said Minogue.

Mahon waited. Minogue was aware that Duggan had folded his spider arms and was staring at Mahon.

It was Wall who intervened finally.

"Go out for a smoke, why don't ye," he said.

Minogue led the way. He was a little taken aback yet from realizing that Wall had pegged him as a smoker without ever having seen him actually smoke. They went out the door by the evidence room to the yard. A squad car was just pulling out. Mahon held out his package of cigarettes.

Minogue took one. He had matches ready.

"Pretty irregular this," said Mahon after a long exhalation of smoke. "A big no-no, I'm sure."

"Well I'm fairly sure I can quit again," said Minogue.

"Not the cigarettes. I meant us talking like this."

"Well you're a bit of a non-conformist." Minogue queried, "What does non-conformist mean to you then?"

"You keep on poking," said Mahon. "Who do you have it in for the most, the accused, or his counsel?"

Minogue was momentarily spinny from the first drag of the cigarette. He looked at the tip. His second drag on the cigarette was more satisfying.

"A bit harsh there, aren't you," he said.

Tires squealed somewhere in the streets around the station.

"We're not doing so well," said Mahon. "Are we?"

Minogue shifted his feet. It was chillier than he'd expected.

"It'll work out," he said.

"You're trained to expect murder. That's a factor here."

"Who told you that?"

"Word gets around."

"Tell me what you want to tell me," said Minogue.

"Okay. Show me your 'reasonable grounds.' I'll work from there. My client may wish to cooperate then."

"It's indecently early for pleas. Let's finish our smokes, head back inside, and not be wasting our time here."

Mahon sighed.

"Fix this in your mind though," said Minogue, "about your new client and his mate. We believe that they know who took that man's life, plain and simple. When this man was most lost, and most vulnerable, he was lured. And then, he was murdered."

"So that's the scenario playing in your mind."

"Your client should come up with the truth and get in early, as they say. The bus will be leaving on time."

"I can tell you don't have evidence. Not even testimony, the way you're pumping it."

Minogue flicked the cigarette against the wall just to see the sparks.

Chapter 27

BRÍD PUT ON HER TRACKPANTS after Aisling finally knocked off.

"I have to," she murmured. "It's nearly a week."

He watched her take out her earrings.

"Good going," he said.

She pulled off her sweater. He counted two, then three rolls under her brassiere when she bent down to tie her runners. He returned to the dishes, and splayed his fingers over the plates that lay just below the surface of the luke-warm water.

There was no way you could just stage dog fights for a film.

Bríd stood then.

"How are you feeling now?"

"I'm grand."

"Must have been one of those bugs. That twenty-four-hour bug going around."

He came up with a smile.

"You looked pretty wiped, I have to say," she said.

He concentrated on scraping off some of the dried sauce. Bríd didn't move off yet. He looked back at her. She was smiling at him, tenderly.

"You're very good," she said. "I sometimes forget to tell you."

He knew that she meant it. He tried to show he appreciated it.

"You're on a roll I think," she said. "You've got that look about you, that faraway look. A portrait of the artist."

"Are you coming on to me?"

"What if I am? Remember the Bois?"

He feigned shock.

"If your students could hear you."

"Actually," she whispered, "thinking about that makes it even better. But you know that. Come on. You always go for the edge, the danger. Don't you?"

"Yeah, well," he said.

She watched him wash Aisling's plate. He wondered if his irritation showed now.

"'What do women want?'" he said.

When she said nothing, he stopped.

"No one believes Freud anymore," he tried. "A joke?"

She reached up suddenly and drew back a strand of hair from his forehead.

"It won't always be this way, Dermot."

"I know."

"You'll get the recognition you deserve. Really. The work you need."

Again he tried to smile.

"I always believed in you," she said.

"Thank you."

"You're a good father."

It was almost as much as he could manage. He looked down at the water.

"So tell me," she said, her voice gone soft again. "Is this new one the one?"

For the moment he didn't understand.

"Underworld, etc.?"

"I think so," he said. "Yes."

"Just don't be getting a crush on one of their molls now."

"As if."

She pulled on her Belfast Marathon T-shirt, and zipped up

the windbreaker.

"Where did I put the Yellow Peril, Der?"

"It's on the back of the door in the toilet."

She came back wearing the reflective vest. She closed the door softly behind her.

He had some forks left at the bottom of the sink and that would be that. He wiped the counter. Moving the germs around, really. He reached down into the lukewarm water and pulled the stopper. He'd seen people washing utensils with sand, on the BBC documentary about the... Touareg – that was the name of Tony's car, a Touareg. Those three women on the bus could hardly be Touaregs. No way.

The phone rang softly. He remembered Bríd setting it that way so Aisling wouldn't be woken up. His fingers were slippery on the plastic.

"So how's the script then?"

"Who is this?"

"How soon you forget. The script, are you going to use the bit with those two at the pub earlier?"

"You're...?"

"Come on. Has it been that long?"

Fanning clutched the phone harder.

"That's over. I told you. That's too far for me."

"Really? Could have been worse I say."

"Look, come on. I'm not involved in this. This kind of thing I mean. I told you, it's not for me."

"We didn't do it for you, did we. Let's do more of that research tonight. It won't take long. Small matter, but you'd be glad you came."

Fanning looked around the kitchen.

"I can't. I can't."

"You can't? No obligation now. Nobody's saying you're 'involved' kind of involved you know?"

It was that accent again, with the unexpected sidesteps from Dublin to London.

"No charge."

"I'm sorry but look, it's over. It's not what I want. It's just, well I'm not going to do the thing. I'm going to move on to another project."

"Another project? That mind of yours is just going, going, going. I wish I was like that. You know, able to make things up, just like that."

Fanning's grip on the phone tightened. He held his breath before speaking.

"For every project that gets done, there's ten others you throw out."

"What waste. Tell you what – one last go, one last, what do you call it – audition."

"Let me think about it."

"I can wait. Just you and me. No funny stuff."

"No West Ham."

"Naw. He was just over for a holiday, you know. Temple Bar. Rah, rah, rah."

"No crime. No people getting–"

"Of course not."

"Okay. I'll get in touch then, if I want to go ahead."

"Really? How will you do that?"

Fanning realized with a shock that Cully had been ready for this.

"Murph," he said quickly. "I'll get in touch through Murph. Only so's I can get in touch with you."

"Okay. Like I said, I can wait."

An ambulance siren grew louder outside and began to lessen as it passed. When it had passed, Fanning took his palm from his ear. In his earpiece he heard it peak and begin to fade again.

"How about an hour?" Cully said. "How about that?"

"An hour? No, there's no way this evening. I'll get in touch when–"

"–What?" said Cully, but with neither impatience nor anger that Fanning could detect. "She's going to run a marathon or something?"

Shock ran down from Fanning's head and erupted in his chest. He found himself walking backward as his knees gave out.

Chapter 28

By NINE O'CLOCK, Minogue and Wall had Aidan Matthews parcelled on a timeline for the night of the murder. Matthews had turned out to be the smarter of the pair. Where Twomey sweated and argued, Matthews turned inward, his voice often so low that they had to ask him to repeat what he had said. He seemed to want to lose his words, his voice even, in the small goatee – or whatever they called those preposterous half-beard experiments they went for so much now, Minogue reflected sourly – that he kept fingering. A shorter as well as a smarter man than his friend Twomey, Matthews had gotten Minogue's antennae quivering early on. As subdued as he looked here, this off-again on-again sheet-metal apprentice might well conceal an explosive temper.

The same Matthews was gone very pale now. His bottom lip had gone dry and he made the error of picking at it until it bled. Even when he spoke he spent a lot of time staring at the tabletop.

Minogue was in familiar territory now, and it wasn't his favourite. He had felt the dip coming, when his belief that these two were the warp on the murder began to slide. It surprised him a little, because he could not recall why he had begun to think this, or rather, to feel this. It left him dispirited but also grimly satisfied that his unease at what looked like good fortune and timing could now have its way.

As the hours went on, and the time was closing on the legal rights of the two men to be left sleep, he wondered now if he'd be taking home his secret with him tonight, that neither Aidan Matthews nor the others had killed Klos. Neither Wall nor Duggan need know his intuition until they too had faced up to the unease they were surely beginning to feel now too. It would take them longer, that was all. More importantly, Minogue could be dead wrong about the two men, and Duggan and Wall should be left to run their minds freely without the undertow of Minogue's skepticism.

Still, Minogue continued to press Matthews on the times. Twice he had left with Wall and they had had a confab with Duggan in the hall. Duggan was exasperated, but kept good self-control in the interviews. He had roped in a Garda in civvies, a keener, to fill out the interview room, and to do the silent glare routine.

"Okay," said Wall. Matthews glanced up.

"Let's run it again. Eight o'clock, you and the two girls and Twomey are down in this car park place, the steps. Is that so?"

"That's what I told you."

"Tell me the time you were there with Twomey."

"Around eight."

"You were there before the girls."

"Yep."

"Nobody else around."

Matthews sighed.

"No."

"But you said people knew about this hidey hole."

"Yeah. But it's not crowded like. I mean it's cold at night. The summer, there'd be more people."

"So you and Twomey are down there and you have your paraphernalia."

"It's not paraphernalia."

"Drugs."

"A joint? That's not 'Drugs.'"

"You and Twomey are there for how long?"

"I don't know, I told you."

"Was it ten minutes, quarter of an hour?"

"I don't know."

Minogue drew a line through eight-ten and wrote eight-fifteen beside it.

"You're already high though," Wall said.

"A buzz. Not high."

"You smoked up there while you were waiting."

"No."

He raised his head to look at Wall.

"That's what I'm saying. Two joints is all we had. So how is that dealing? Dope is nothing."

"You left the hard stuff at home, did you?"

"What hard stuff? There's nothing, I'm telling you."

"So the search of your house, of your bedroom, is going to show up?"

"It'll show up nothing, that's what."

Wall looked at his watch.

"Well we should know in a little while," he said.

"What? Now? Don't you need, like, a search warrant."

"Of course we do," Wall said, "but murder investigations tend to be at the top of the list here."

Matthews shook his head and breathed out hard. He rubbed his face with his right hand and he resumed his slump.

"Twomey is saying that you're number one," said Wall.

"You said that already. But I still don't know what that means."

"It means you're the one with the goods, with the contacts. You're the supplier. Right?"

"That's rubbish."

"Well at least you know he's ready to say anything to get out of this."

"I never heard him say anything, did I."

"He's the kind of fella who is more of a follower. The kind who caves in sooner than later. I think you know that. Don't you?"

Matthews said nothing. Wall waited and then exchanged a look with Minogue. The inspector nodded toward the clock.

"Okay, it's half eight," Wall said.

"Pardon?"

"It's half eight – that evening I mean. The two girls have showed up. You're sitting there on those steps. Right?"

Matthews nodded.

"Answer that question there," Minogue said.

"Yes, I – we are sitting on the steps."

"And you're...?"

"You know already," said Matthews. "I told you twice.

"What are you doing there on the steps?" Minogue asked sharply.

"I am smoking a joint," said Matthews.

"I?" said Wall.

"We are smoking a joint."

"That you provided."

"That I provided. Sharing. Sharing a joint."

"And this is ten minutes after the two girls met Mr. Klos."

"Ten? I don't know. Like I said, it had just happened. They said, Tara said. It was a laugh, see? This bloke wandering the streets."

"That's when you formed a plan then. To go after this man."

"No way. No."

"Twomey says you did," said Wall.

"No he didn't. That's because nobody made any plan."

"The four of you went down the street. You saw him there, he's lost. It's dark. There's no one around."

Wall paused then and watched Matthews shaking his head in slow, steady motions. Like a fiddle-player following a tune, Minogue thought.

"You know he's not Dublin," said Wall. "He's not even Irish. So: easy mark."

"You're making everything up."

"It's not hard to figure this out. He probably has money. You don't. You want to go to a hotel. You and your girlfriends."

"That is so off the wall. Why am I even listening any-more."

"Or were you at it in the stairwell? You and your mate. A foursome?"

Minogue watched Wall walk slowly up and down, taking each step as though balancing on a curb.

"You want to go all the way," Wall persisted. "You're frustrated. You're angry. Who was it said it first? Was it you?"

Matthews rested his elbows on his knees and looked at the tiles on the floor. Suddenly he looked up, and found Minogue.

"Is he always like this?" he asked. "This fantasy stuff. He should be in the film business. Lord of –"

"Just answer the questions," Minogue snapped.

"Or did he stumble on you," Wall said, "you and Tara having a wear? Or are you getting it on with a thirteen-year-old child, you and..."

"Would you shut up about that?"

Even Minogue started. Wall had stopped his walk and unfolded his arms. Minogue saw that Matthews' head was trembling slightly with the effort of staying still as he glared up. His tone was subdued again when he spoke, however.

"You're all the same. Guards! Yous haven't a clue. You think you have, but you haven't. Not a clue."

His face wrinkled in disgust, and he looked away quickly.

"Tell us then," said Minogue.

"You don't care. You won't believe me. I want my lawyer."

"Your counsel."

"Yeah I want him."

"Tomorrow," said Minogue. "You've had your legal rights respected."

"Tomorrow? I've done nothing. Nothing."

"You've sexually assaulted or exploited a–"

"Shut up, will you?! That is such a load...!"

Temper, temper, Minogue thought.

"Well you tell us then," said Wall. "What don't we know?"

"Life. Being young. The scene, you know? Bit of fun? Good times?"

"Tell us about the scene then," said Minogue.

Matthews slid down further in the chair but then drew himself back up suddenly. He breathed out slowly.

"Girls, they go to you and say anything and yous take that as gospel."

"What are we talking about?" Wall asked.

"About what you don't know. Girls. They're always innocent, it's the fella who's always guilty. You can't imagine a girl doing anything serious. You know?"

"'Serious' like a crime?"

"Well, yeah, a crime."

"What did they do then? What did Tara do?"

"I meant girls in general. You're not listening to me."

"You and Twomey got them to lure this man down there, didn't you?"

"That's so stupid I won't even think of answering."

"It was their idea?" Wall said. "Is that what you're trying to tell me?"

"I am not. You're putting words in my mouth. You're trying to set me up. Now I see it. Yous haven't a clue who did that fella in, so you just want anyone. Those two lied to you I bet and you gobbled it up like idiots."

"The girl lied? Tara?"

"I don't know, do I? I don't know what they told you, but whatever it is, it's wrong."

He grimaced then, and felt for the corner of his mouth where the skin had cracked.

"So it's all lies. I'm not going to say another word. Yous are taking away my rights."

"What reason would Tara or her friend have to lie?" Wall asked. "Aren't you and Tara a couple and all that?"

Matthews said something under his breath.

Minogue got up. He picked up his clipboard and headed for the door, closing it quietly behind him. The uniform, an older veteran with a grey moustache and a smell of cigar smoke, was reading the evening paper.

"Thanks," said Minogue, "we need a bit of time here."

The Guard folded his paper and grasped the door handle.

"Troublesome?" he asked.

"No," said Minogue, "no more than usual."

Wall came out of the interview room stroking his chin thoughtfully.

"Let's get Mossie here too. We need to shuffle the deck a bit."

Wall nodded. To Minogue he seemed as fresh and alert as when they first met this afternoon.

"I think we need to talk to those girls again tonight. Shake them up. Minors or not. We need to figure them out better."

Wall said nothing. Neither man moved. Then Wall tugged at his nose.

"Do you wonder maybe?" he asked Minogue.

"Two girls?" said Minogue.

"Yep. I know Matthews is pushing the line, without actually saying it."

"Each of them trying to sell the other one up the river," Minogue said.

"But forensic gives us 'shoes.' Leather-soled, hard edges."

"That's what they call stomped, isn't it?" said Wall.

"Big shoes, big heels? Small shoes, small heels?"

Wall lowered his head and looked up under his eyebrows at Minogue.

"Fair enough," said Minogue, "I'm getting delirious. Let's check with Mossie. We can all go delirious together."

Chapter 29

FANNING'S EYES WERE ITCHING from staring at the screen. Reflexively, his fingers tapped the Apple – S combination. Then he did a Save As to his memory stick before closing the file. He returned to Google Maps, and zoomed in on the lane where he had gone with Cully and West Ham. No, the image hadn't changed. What did he expect, that a satellite had passed, taken a photo and it was on the server already? Complete with the five of them in the lane behind the pub? Magical thinking indeed. But that guy with the broken arm must have gone to some hospital or clinic: he'd be traceable.

He began to compose an email to Breen. Subject: Real Crime Story. While the cursor pulsed on, awaiting his words, he imagined Breen reading this cryptic email that he was about to start. But did Breen junk his email? Did he even check his email? For several moments, Fanning imagined Breen opening the email, but then rolling his eyes and deleting it. Fanning trying to generate some buzz. Fanning trying to show off. Fanning deluding himself.

Tomorrow for the email, he decided then.

He closed the lid of the laptop and waited for the sleep light to begin. Then he stood and stretched. He felt no real easing in the tightness at the small of his back, so he moved the chair to get to the rug. It smelled of food and mustiness when he tipped it with his nose, and did his first push-up. He tried to focus on his breathing and to ignore the yammering thoughts. That ache at the bottom of his chest was an adrenaline hang-over. He still could not decide if this was from fear or excitement. He rested for a minute, staring up the table legs to the underside of the table, and the ceiling beyond. This Cully character didn't just beat up people for kicks. And the guy with him...?

Fanning's back was still tight. He rolled up and stood slowly, and he poised himself to do a bit of yoga. He focused on his breathing and started into a Greeting to the Sun, breathing loudly to try to still his mind better. It took him a minute or so to complete the routine, and he was soon back on the rug, as flat and still as he could. He listened to his blood coursing by, his own breath whistling slower in his nose. Calm settled on him then, and he could almost see in his mind's eye the truth coming to rest like a leaf on a sunlit path. Cully was mocking him. He was also daring him. It was a test, Fanning saw, and that made it easy to decide.

Aisling groaned in her sleep. Fanning got up slowly and tiptoed to her room. She was inert, splayed out, with her mouth open. She swallowed and she frowned and she turned over. He lifted the edge of the blanket to her shoulder and watched her settle again. He parted the curtains on his way back to the kitchen. The white BMW was still there, far enough from the street lamp for its interior to remain dark. The hall door opened, and a key was pulled out of the lock. He stepped quickly out of Aisling's room, glad to hear the familiar sound of Velcro being teased apart. Bríd was panting. She pulled the safety vest over her head and sat heavily into a kitchen chair.

"God almighty," she said, half-whispering. "I'm huffing and puffing tonight like an oul wan. Brutal."

"It's hard getting back into it."

She glanced at him before she leaned down to get at her laces. Jogging was not his thing, never had been, he thought of saying.

"Well that's it for me. A bath and bed. Feck marking for tonight."

"Good. I want to borrow your phone."

"Where's yours?"

"Oh I have it but it might be on the blink. Just in case."

She straightened up slowly.

With her flush cheeks and bright eyes, years had come off her.

"You're going out?"

"Just for a while. A chance to meet with some people, research."

"Fieldwork," she said.

She was holding back, he knew. He felt bold.

"I'll wake you up when I come home," he said.

She raised her eyebrows, and seemed to weigh his words.

"Oh will you now," she murmured.

He was able to hold her gaze, and even add a brazen touch to his own. She smiled cryptically.

"Only if I'm asleep," she said.

He hadn't expected that.

Murphy's BMW smelled like an ashtray. Actually, it smelled more like the ashbin from years ago, the one Fanning's grandmother had used. A hint of long used car-freshener only made things worse.

Cully waited for Fanning to pull the door closed.

"Okay," he said. "We'll go for a little drive then, won't we."

"How about Murph?"

"Loaned it to me, he did."

"So, it's just us?"

"Isn't that enough?"

"Not until I get some answers from you."

Cully lowered his hand from the key in the ignition and he looked over.

"Let's start with how you found my house," Fanning asked.

"You're pissed off, aren't you."

"I don't like you talking about my family. About my wife.

That's out of order. Big time."

"Big time?"

"I'm serious. That can't happen again."

"Or?"

Fanning stared into the reflections of the street lamps in Cully's eyes. His heart pounded harder.

"Leave my family out of this. Don't hang around my place."

Cully's voice seemed tighter when he spoke now.

"Talking tough, are you. For a bookish type."

"Where did that come from, 'bookish type'?"

"You practising dialogue or something? Rehearsals already?"

"We need to be on the level here," said Fanning. "This isn't a game."

Cully's face creased in a grin. He rubbed his nose as he looked away.

"'This isn't a game,' he tells me. Tells me."

He turned back to Fanning.

"Are you the same fella I was with earlier on?"

"I'm not the one asked for your, whatever, services, am I?"

Cully didn't answer. He turned the ignition instead, and gave the engine two short revs.

"How'd you know my place?"

"Whose car is this?" Cully asked.

"Murph? He told you?"

"It's not hard to figure out. Phone directory? The Internet?"

He waited.

"Look," he said to Fanning then. "We going or not?"

Fanning took a few moments before he put on his seat belt.

"Left, left again, then right for the Dundrum Road?"

"That's it. Where are we going?"

"A sort of tour."

"Where is 'a sort of tour'?"

"Social, that's all. Relaxing. R and R. No-one gets hurt."

"R and R, why do you say that? I heard you say it before."

"Just an expression, isn't it."

"Are you English? British?"

Cully smiled and he rubbed at his chin.

"This an interview?"

"Background."

"Oh, I'm going to be a character in your thing?"

"You sound like a Dub but then you go Cockney a lot of the time."

"Do I really? Do I?"

It was a perfect East End accent, Fanning had to admit.

"Watched too much Austin Powers," said Cully. "Probably. Mis-spent youth and all that."

"'Youff,'" said Fanning. "That sort of thing."

"You making fun of me?"

"What else did you do?"

"Cocky fella tonight, aren't you. What are you on?"

"You don't like questions, do you?"

"I don't mind actually," said Cully.

"So, what else did you do?"

"This and that."

"What does that mean?"

"Means what I said. Here, let me give you a little tip on etiquette here. Save your questions, save them for later. Just er, observe. Is that the correct term?"

Fanning couldn't tell how much was sarcasm now. Cully shifted to third but misjudged the clutch, and the car staggered.

"Shitbox," he said with little feeling. "Give me Jap any day."

"Nondescript," said Fanning. "Is that a clue?"

"Non – de...?"

"Ordinary."

"That sounds about right," said Cully. "Nothing wrong with being ordinary, is there. I mean it's okay to stand out, don't get me wrong, but for a good cause, see? Princess Di, Bono – that sort of thing."

"Princess Di? You actually believe that, what you just

said?"

"No."

Cully made the light at Milltown Road. Fanning took out his notebook.

"Notebook?" Cully asked. "Like a reporter?"

"It's too easy to forget stuff."

Cully nodded as if in appreciation of the idea.

"Keep it on you all the time, do you?"

"Pretty well."

"Just one?"

"One at a time."

"I should do that," said Cully. "Don't trust all the online stuff, I have to say. But does your stuff, your job, have a lot of detail? Appointments, all that?"

"Maybe not as much as yours," said Fanning.

"Nice," said Cully. "Nice way of asking."

The excitement in Fanning's chest had settled. He had expected Cully's evasions. He wasn't an iijit.

He began to jot down some notes, scribbling intentionally:

     – no bling

     – takes care (driving, appearance, etc.)

     – not defensive.

He couldn't imagine Cully sitting around a pub with a bunch of thugs. What could he have instead of Tony Soprano's restaurant and bakery routine?

"What does a fella do for entertainment?" he asked Cully.

Cully turned to him with a half-amused expression. In the oncoming lights Fanning caught sight of a line of shiny skin that ran under Cully's eyebrow.

"Not too shy about your questions tonight, are you."

Fanning took this as praise.

"Part of the job," he said to Cully. "If you want to tell me things, you will. If you don't, well you won't."

"It's a free country and all that, right?"

"So they say."

"It's free if you've got money," said Cully. "I mean look at this place. Rathgar. One mill, two mill, for a house here? But not too free when you're not on the winning side."

"You mean poor?"

"You use that word, do you? I've only been hearing dictionary words myself, like, well – you probably know them better. Underprivileged?"

"Marginalized."

"That's one. First time I heard it I thought margarine. Is that what poor people have to eat? What's so bad about that?"

Fanning scribbled the word "margarine" in his notebook.

"Are you going to use that? I don't want to look stupid."

"No. It's just a remark, for atmosphere. Ambiance."

"See, you left me right there, with words like that. That's something I could never do, I could never remember all those words."

"Was it hard-going for you at school, when you were a kid?"

"That's a weird question. Did you ask Murph questions like that too?"

"Sure, I did."

"And what did he come up with?"

"Not much, to be honest."

"What a surprise there. Anything he did tell you was fantasy. Whatever he thought he could get away with. You know?"

"Possibly."

"Oh, I guarantee it. Yes, I do."

Cully geared down for a light in the middle of Rathgar. He looked around at the parked cars, the pubs, and the restaurants.

"Lambo," he murmured, "over there. Lamborghini, a Diablo. AMG Mercedes a few down, see by that gate? Uh-oh a yellow Porsche. The killer one. Let me see if I can spot one ordinary car around here."

"You know a lot about cars?"

"I like them, is all."

"Are those ones easy to boost?"

Cully made a long blink and he looked over.

"'To boost?'"

"To rob. To steal."

"Well, listen to you," said Cully. "Cheeky."

"Well? Are they hard to steal?"

"How would I know that?"

Cully drove through the green light onto Terenure Road.

"Where are we going?" Fanning asked. "You said on the phone that you'd be stopping off at a few places."

"Do you know Kimmage at all?"

"Not much. Do you?"

This time, Fanning sensed annoyance in Cully's glance. Several seconds passed. It was long enough for Fanning's glow of pride at surprising Cully to subside.

"Cashel Road," said Cully then. "A road off that. I have to meet a man. Give him a message, collect something."

"Is it anything like the message you gave those two this afternoon?"

"Those two drug dealers? The pair from Siberia?"

"Siberia?"

"Well how do I know?"

"Eastern Europe?"

"Something like that I suppose."

"Were you paid to do what you did?"

"I do what I have to do," he said.

To Fanning, it was as though Cully had expected the question sooner.

He seemed to know the area well enough, steering the BMW with ease by the bends and the parked cars.

"This is Murph's playground here," he said in an almost cheerful voice then. "Kimmage. Did you know that?"

"Well, he grew up here."

"So he'd be wised up, you could say."

"I suppose."

"So he wised you up then. Not to shower people with questions."

"He did mention to mind my manners. Words to that effect."

"Too bad he doesn't practise what he preaches himself."

He drove on, each turn of the wheel and gearstick fluid and expert now, it seemed. His eyes went to all the mirrors often, expertly, easily. He coasted to the lights at Fortfield Road, and put on his indicator. It was a long traffic light.

"What did you mean about Murph?" Fanning said.

"'Practise what you preach' stuff? Or about him and his rubbish ideas?"

"Both. Either."

Cully looked over.

"Bet you're wondering about Murph, aren't you."

"Sort of."

"You know he was a complete spoof, right?"

"I let him just run with it. Took some of what he said with a grain of salt."

"Okay. I mean how could you check on anything he told you anyway, right?"

"That's about it."

"I mean can you see yourself sitting across the table from some cop?"

"Why would I do that?"

"I'm not saying you would. But it's common sense, isn't it? How would you know what Murphy said is true, any of it?"

"Well it's fiction I'm aiming for."

"Right, of course."

Fanning wasn't sure if Cully was baiting him again.

"Either way, you'll get nothing good off of him," Cully said. He accelerated quickly to get through the junction ahead of an oncoming van.

"Murph's out of this line of work. My suggestion."

"But he loaned you his car."

"Yes he did."

"And his phone."

"Yup."

"Very generous of him. I didn't think he loaned out his car."

"Well he did the right thing. I mean, he's not a complete prat. A person needs to make amends, you know."

"Amends for...?"

"It's a few things. Carelessness."

"For talking to me as well?"

Cully paused between gear shifts.

"Was that frowned on, him talking to me?" Fanning asked.

"Could be."

"Whatever that means. 'Could be.'"

"Let's just say certain people thought Murph was out of order. Okay, we're coming up to this place."

Chapter 30

CULLY PULLED IN BEHIND a parked van and he shut off the engine. He left the keys in the ignition and placed his hands on the rim of the steering wheel, his fingers stretched out. A bus passed, almost empty. Cully seemed to be concentrating on something.

"Okay," he said and tapped his fingers on the wheel. "What were we talking about again? Murph?"

"Yes we were."

"All right. Murph's in Marbella. That's the deal."

"Marbella?"

"Ever been?"

"No."

"Good for you. It's full of crims and blackguards, and their fat, tarty wives lying around on the beach, like bloody whales."

"'Blackguards? My grandmother used to use that word."

"Really. Well write it down. Blags, blackguards. Thieves and suchlike."

"That's English."

"That's what we're speaking, isn't it."

"You're telling me Murph's in Spain."

"Right. It's a good enough place to do some thinking, some penance for his sins, clean up his act, get advice."

"It wasn't the visit from Mr. Black-and-Decker then?"

For several moments Fanning thought he had gone too far.

"Where did you hear that kind of talk?" Cully asked quietly. "Murphy?"

"He said–"

"–there's an example of what I'm talking about. Hasn't a clue."

"Well he said they used nail guns to kneecap those two fellas before Christmas, in Skerries."

Cully shook his head and sighed.

"Let's change the subject. You're doing research. So you want background."

"Right."

"And you want it real, you say. Gritty. Okay, tonight's your night. I set something up for you."

"I'm not getting involved in stuff. I'm just observing."

"That's right. Here's how it goes. Ever wondered how easy it is to get ahold of a gun here in Dublin?"

"Sometimes. A lot of it goes on, they say. 'Rent a gun'?"

"You're on the ball, I see. So you think anyone can just do it?"

"I have no idea," said Fanning.

"You have to be in the know. Obviously. Have someone vouch for you. Like 'Johnny told me to get in touch.' Johnny being known to the bloke."

"Johnny who?"

"That's not funny. Johnny is the comeback if anything goes sideways. Insurance, in a way."

"Johnny knows everything then. The go-to."

"A phone call has been made, a certain person phoned and said there'd be a visitor who wanted something. This is where it gets done. Do you get it?"

"I think so."

"The goods have been sent out to an address, with a person who will actually do the business, arm's length, they say, don't they?"

Fanning nodded.

"Make sense?"

"I suppose," said Fanning. "Is it an organized thing, or just people doing their own thing?"

"Bit of both."

"Does it go wrong?"

"I haven't heard of it. People know people. So unless your client's going to run away and hide in a hole in the ground for the rest of his life, there's no point in dirtying the deal."

"So you're going to pick up a gun here."

"I beg your pardon?"

The change in tone was slight enough that Fanning was immediately alert. Cully's eyes lingered on Fanning before drifting back to the windscreen.

"Have you ever handled a gun before?" he asked.

"No. Props, I have. And a starter pistol once or twice."

"It's not the same. When you have a gun in your hand everything is different. Not just different, I mean you don't forget it. You remember how it felt, the weight of it. Thinking what it can do."

"Even if you never use it," said Fanning after a pause.

"Even if you never use it," said Cully. "If you have to actually use it, then you screwed up."

"Even as a last resort?"

"Well you shouldn't be in that situation, should you. Like I said to you, it's not a film where fellas go about waving guns and shooting everything. Talk to a copper who never has to draw a pistol in his whole career – that's a smart cop."

"Have they told you that?"

"As a matter of fact, yes. One told me that."

"Here in Dublin?"

Cully turned on the ignition and he read the gauges and the clock.

"At least Murphy should have told you to pick your questions. Did he tell you how not to get people's backs up?"

Fanning said nothing. Again he wondered how this confidence had come to him, how he could calmly carry on here in the car with this man. One part of him knew he was sitting beside a man who inspired fear in the likes of Murphy, but some other part of his mind was given over to some kind of calm audacity.

Cully switched off the ignition.

"Okay then," he said. "I'm going to make a quick call."

Fanning noticed that he dialled from memory. He wasn't waiting long.

"Yep," he said. "We're here."

He listened for a few moments.

"The shop?" he said then. "What kind again?"

Fanning made a smoking gesture. Cully nodded.

"Okay," he said and hung up.

"Some kind of French cigarettes?" he said to Fanning. "He'll be in the shop and he'll hear you asking for the smokes. If they have them, go ahead and buy them. If not, go back outside anyway. He'll follow you. That's it."

"What are you talking about?"

"The bloke, the goods," said Cully and turned the ignition. "That's how it's done."

"You said I was going to do it? Me?"

"What are we doing here? I don't want the package, do I? It's not me doing research, is it?"

"Who said anything about me doing stuff like this?"

Cully returned his stare calmy. Fanning caught himself then.

"It's an exercise," said Cully. "That's all. So you know what you're going to do in your story."

"You're not joking are you."

"No I'm not. Look. I have stuff here for you will make it easier. A minute on, a minute off we call it."

"I can't go renting a gun, for Christ's sake. End up in jail for ten years?"

Cully drew a plastic bag from under the seat.

"This is the real thing," he said. "Film stuff, professional stuff. Moustache, the comb-in grey – look I even bought fake pimples."

He dropped it in Fanning's lap.

"Glasses in the glove compartment here," he said. "Put on a scarf there from the back seat. Jean jacket there too."

"What are you doing?" Fanning was able to say.

"Details," said Cully briskly. "That's all they are. People are stupid, what they remember. They don't get height properly, or even a voice, but they end up holding on to stuff that's useless. 'He wears glasses.' 'He had bad skin.' 'He had a moustache.' 'He had a Chelsea scarf.'"

"You really think I'm going in there, and doing this?"

Cully turned his head to look at the dashboard, then back to Fanning. He spoke in a quiet voice.

"You're not up to it."

"Up to what? Up to insane?"

Cully shrugged.

"How are you going to get it right if you haven't been there?"

"This has nothing to do with it."

"Are you sure about that?"

"Yes I'm sure."

"I don't know," said Cully. "I don't know about that. I see a bloke who's always on the lookout, who notices things. A bloke with a notebook. Someone who has an eye for detail. I mean look at you, taking notes all the time."

"Maybe I've gone about this all the wrong way," said Fanning. "Have you as a consultant when I want to get it right on the set. But not to get me involved, actually committing crimes here."

"Interesting," Cully said. He took his hand off the gearstick and slowly rubbed his chin. "Very interesting."

"You're surprised?"

"Well I'd have thought, I'd have assumed like, that because you got started with Murphy and his, quote, research, that you'd be the fella for this. Not having a hairy, like. That you'd have a bit of bottle. Like you'd have a go at things."

"This is a different thing, totally different."

"Too real maybe?"

"That's not it."

"How can you make up stuff, believable stuff, if you've never stepped across that line?"

"Oh come on. There's a whole ton of stuff wrapped up in that remark."

"Like what? And why?"

"It'd take forever, no. Like what's experience, or authentic. Appropriation of voice – tons of stuff. A mess. I don't want to get into it."

"Me neither. But isn't that what makes a story good? Like people reading it, or watching it will know it's the real thing?"

"There's real, and there's real stupid."

Cully tapped on the gearshift slowly.

"I thought you were just trying to show me a few things," Fanning continued. "A few examples. Places. Stories."

"Oh I don't do that," said Cully. "Just facts. That's it."

"If I knew more about how you get to where you are, and what you do, that'd be really helpful."

"There's nothing worth talking about."

"How can that be? You just take it for granted, that's all. Not to me, though."

"It's the past. Who cares about the past, I say."

"But you know the big people here. The families? I saw you at that thing, that fight, the dogs. They seem to know you. Murphy sure does. Loans you his car, yes sir, no sir."

"Let me say something to you now," said Cully.

Fanning focused on keeping his breath steady and quiet. He had already felt out the door release.

"This is no big deal," Cully began. "This business here. Think about it. What could be easier? This bloke in the shop doesn't know or care who you are. He's got his guarantees, his insurance. And you won't even be yourself for this. Slap on the stuff I brought, and go to the shop, follow him out and that's it. He hands you some skin magazines in a plastic bag, and that's that."

Fanning watched an older couple come out of the shop and light up cigarettes, then they began a slow amble down the footpath toward the pub.

"If I don't do it," Fanning said, "then that's it for the research? I have to find someone else I suppose, start all over again?"

Cully stopped tapping on the gearstick.

"Not necessarily," he said.

"You mean I can say forget it, this thing here, and we just carry on?"

"Not that," said Cully. "My advice to you would be to leave the entire matter and go find other things to do. Other stories or something."

The quiet tone jarred with the message.

"You know something," Fanning said. "I just realized earlier on. I never made any arrangement here, like what kind of fee you expect for this."

Cully nodded.

"Right," he said.

"Like what's your role in this."

"Role? Like my part?"

"No. I mean why you took over from Murph. We never talked about that."

"We can get to that later."

"I don't know anything about you. A name? Cully, Cullen?"

Cigarette smoke billowed and hung in the damp air.

"Where else could we go?" Fanning said after a moment.

"Back the way we came," said Cully and reached for the ignition.

"That's it then?"

"That's it."

"Can't we skip this thing and just go on whatever?"

"That's not on," said Cully. "Now if you'd rather walk home from here, just tell me."

Cully backed the car into the forecourt of a small garage, and turned the BMW back toward Churchtown. Fanning couldn't detect any anger in him at all.

"Better all around," Cully murmured. "You do your thing. Nice setup you seem to have there. The whole family thing. Education, all that. Stick with that. That would be my inclination. A lot of people would like to have what you have. You've no bother coming up with ideas now."

"This one I'm working on is pretty good. It's worth sticking with."

"It's a free country, but people need to realize that people don't like getting their toes stepped on."

"Have I done that?"

Cully made a noncommittal gesture.

"Look," he said. "Someone must have told you at some point in your life that it's not good to piss off people?"

"Tell me who I'm pissing off."

"There's stories, and then there's the real world. They don't mix."

"But fiction shows reality better than facts, so-called."

"You really believe that?"

"As a matter of fact I do. It informs everything I do."

"And others too," said Cully. The quickness took Fanning aback a little. Deceptive, he'd have to add in his notes.

"I mean, everyone likes a good story," Cully went on. "But if I'm hearing you right, this thing of yours be leaving a trail for other people."

"Others, like...?"

"You've got it figured out, I'd say. Bloke like you, your talents?"

Every traffic light was red, it seemed. Cully was humming a tune very low while he waited. In the deserted bus shelter across from where they sat, the ad for gum rolled up to reveal one for Top Ten Talent, the lame new reality show.

His thoughts cleared.

"Pull in here."

"Crap night for a walk. And a long walk too."

"No. Turn around, I mean."

"Come on. It's a bit late for that one."

"Really," said Fanning. "I'm not joking. Really."

Chapter 31

ARDA MOSSIE DUGGAN'S ACCENT seemed ideal for his technique. That Monaghan drone reminded Minogue of bogs and lakes, and the long roads that always seemed to end in some secret place amongst the low hills or the drumlins of Duggan's native county.

Minogue had left Garda Wall with Matthews, and he was now sitting in on the Twomey interview. Yes, Detective Garda Duggan from Ballybay, County Monaghan, was a plotter. It was all under the radar, slyly effective, with a momentum that kept the talk going. Minogue began to conclude it was all about pacing, and that some kind of mild hypnosis was going on. Duggan would occasionally pounce on something Twomey had said, and he'd go into fast-forward, peppering Twomey with questions in a kindly, interested voice as though bubbling with a shared enthusiasm.

The effect was to make Twomey blurt out answers. It often ended with Twomey sitting back, arms crossed, refusing to say more. At those times Duggan backed off completely. Bashfully – almost apologetically – he gave off an air of regret, or embarrassment, at having apparently derailed things. But almost always it was Twomey who would put an end to the brittle quiet by trying to qualify, to explicate what he'd said in that rapid-fire flurry and back. Like boxing, Minogue reflected, if he'd understood Malone's explanation.

Minogue gave it a few more minutes, and then he gave Duggan the nod for a break. While he waited for them, he put the kettle on and he phoned Malone. Waiting for the call to connect, he heard the raised voices from the public office downstairs. Though he couldn't make out the words, he recognized the indignant tones and ragged voice of someone drunk. The evening's grim entertainment for this Garda station was started, then.

Had Malone been having a snooze?

"Tommy, am I phoning you at a bad time?"

"No. You're all right."

He had been asleep, Minogue decided.

"Just checking," he said.

"Checking what?"

"Well I don't want to be annoying you."

"Well you are annoying me, what – oh, now I remember. But I told you I'd phone you when I got hold of the bastard."

"Starts with an M? We're talking about the same fella?"

"Look," said Malone, an irritable tone coming to his voice now. "When I have something, you'll be the first to know."

"Thank you. I do appreciate your efforts in the matter, Thomas."

"Oh my jases, will you listen to that. I'll keep trying – but remember, he's not top of my list right now. You know?"

"Fair enough. Whatever you can do. Any break in the weather there?"

Malone didn't get it for a few moments, Minogue decided.

"Ah, hard to say. It's mad really. There's double the response teams out now, so…"

Minogue imagined the dozen and more unmarked cars, each with two detectives armed to the teeth.

"But you wouldn't believe the things we're hearing. For your ears only now."

"To be sure."

"I'm only telling you, so you'll get an idea of what the hell it's like these days here with us, and because it's a fella you know."

"Who?"

"Igoe, your boss."

"What about him?"

"Well listen to this, and I'll tell you. But it's only me and you, remember? This bit is top level here."

Secrecy, he meant, Minogue realized. Malone's expressions that he used at work hadn't all stayed in his head.

"Your fella has this meeting here with two of ours, yeah, the top two. Igoe brings it personally to talk to our fellas. That's how important. Got to do with a call from London, and I hear it came through HQ too. Not even the Met, but some other outfit that got the Met to pass it on to us. One of the shady boys' outfits they have now."

Wall came in the door, followed by the yawning Duggan. Minogue turned away and held his hand cupped over the receiver.

"There's a bunch of freelancers that do jobs all over the place," Malone said. "Work for anyone. Do anything. And here's the thing – it was the Brits that gave them the training and all."

"I don't get it."

"Okay, look I can't be talking here. But here's the gist of it, and it's pretty wild, I'm telling you. If it's true, like. The Met said that some of these fellas seem to be gone abroad, and they think to – guess where?"

"Here?"

"D-U-B-L-I-N-O, Signor. Yeah. The cops there like to keep tabs on them. They're a security firm, but not your basic gobshite at the door of the shop. They worked all over – in Iraq, for jases sake, even. They used to be soldiers. Isn't that something? Ever hear the like?"

"Never did," said Minogue.

"Remember that tough-guy speech some soldier boy gave over there a few years back? Actually an Irish fella, Collins or somebody. About what to do in Iraq when they went in? Royal Irish regiment, I found out. And half of them are Irish, did you know that? Google it and see. But remember there was trouble, some fellas got done for shooting and things? Court martials and that?"

"Can't say I remember that, no."

"All hushed up, but there was fellas turfed over the matter. All on the QT. But some of them made up their own security thing. And they went back into Iraq or someplace there a few times, made piles of money – a damn sight more than any soldier does. Might have even gotten themselves turfed on purpose, so's they could go back as private fellas. But they messed up, and got the heave-ho. Never to return, etc. So guess what they might be up to now?"

"Well what do you think of that," was all Minogue could think to say.

"I don't," said Malone. "It's too mad. Look, I'm off – don't be phoning me."

Minogue made sure he had killed the call. He shook his head.

"Everything all right there, er?"

"Matt. It is, thanks. I just have to digest some things I hear very slowly."

"Ah, the married man's lot," said Duggan.

Garda Wall was concluding a phone call to his wife. Things would run late and she was not to wait up. He called her "pet," something Minogue almost sniggered over. He had heard it used sincerely many years ago, but it had been mockery for decades now.

After Wall hung up he gazed at the phone for a few moments. Minogue imagined that he was saying a prayer.

"A chinwag," said Duggan. "Compare notes?"

Wall sat on the table. Minogue kicked off the conversation.

"All right," he said, "what's the word. Mossie?"

"For starters then, Twomey's a pain. He's got the mindset. Not one ounce would he give a Guard. I put it to him, I says, this is the only time in the history of crime in the whole universe that someone else assaulted and killed a person, and then left the spoils for you? Pull the other one, says he to me. A bollocks of the first order."

"He's not alone," said Minogue. "Do you want to swap then?"

"I dunno," said Duggan. "I dunno. He'll budge, I think."

"Well they had plenty of time to rehearse," said Wall.

"You think they're just reciting? Either of you now?"

"No," said Wall, "I'd have to say. There's not a drop of pity in Twomey. I gave him a picture of the man's mother, you know. In bits. Having to bring her lad home from a foreign country, only to bury him. How would your mother like that, I ask him, etc."

"And?"

"Says he, I'm not in a foreign country, am I. And I don't want to go to a foreign country. And then he says to me, maybe he should have stayed in his own country, shouldn't he?"

Minogue heard the kettle beginning to get up to steam now.

"Matthews is cut from the same cloth so," said Wall.

"Or they could be telling the truth," said Minogue, "much as it pains me to mention it. Well at least we have admissions they were there, at the scene. Are we not getting e're a bit of traction out of the sexual interference with a minor? Or trafficking?"

"Ah they're still laughing about trafficking," said Wall.

"Twomey's not impressed," said Mossie. "Or he's a great actor entirely. He wants me to charge him or let him go."

"Wannabes, the pair of them are," said Wall. "My fella doing this 'yo yo yo' thing with the fingers like a rap star. Pulling on his trousers, and his willy even. He must think he's on MTV."

"Yo yo yo," said Duggan, and struck a pose.

"My homeys in the hood," said Wall.

"New string, same yo-yo," said Duggan.

Any second now the kettle would pop.

"Swap over I'm thinking," said Minogue.

"More pressure?" Duggan asked. "Are we ready?"

"Fair enough," said Minogue. "Time to put a bit of torque into it."

"We go the sexual exploitation route now?" Wall asked. "The young ones?"

Minogue nodded.

"Tell them the girls are back in for their second interviews," he added.

"Ah," said Mossie. "So it'll all come out tomorrow."

"No," said Minogue. "Tonight. I'm after calling the girls' parents."

Wall looked at his watch.

"We need to," said Minogue. "So just out with the goods, tell this pair. And tell them they're out of time. They need to straighten their heads now and tell us what we need to know."

"Push on," Duggan said.

Minogue nodded. The kettle popped. Minogue got up slowly.

"I'll be moderately keen to find out how that Tara Lynch's mother, how she'll react," he said, "when it gets to her daughter having sex with Matthews."

"Begob," said Duggan. "Blood and snots flying. See wuzzup then, homey."

Minogue poked about for anything beyond tea. Though the room was warm enough, he shivered as he looked through the cupboard. There was granulated coffee, cup-o-soup stuff, sugar. He ended up making a pot of tea. Duggan was explaining to Wall that hip-hop was a lifestyle, but rap was only music actually, when the phone rang.

Minogue didn't try to eavesdrop. His guess was accurate enough. Soon enough Duggan put down the phone. Slowly, thoughtfully, and a little wryly, he eyed Wall.

"The other girl is downstairs now," he said.

"Good," Minogue said. "I'll do it."

"Her, ah, father is with her this time too," Duggan said.

"Grand."

"Maybe not. He's on the boil apparently. Big fella. One of the heavy equipment lads who dug the Port of Dublin tunnel. Dec Ahearne below says he might start throwing shapes any minute."

"Vexed?" Minogue said. "Great. We'll add that to the pot."

"You mean tell the boys inside?"

Minogue nodded.

"Watery, or real tea?" he asked.

"All the way," said Duggan. "Him too."

Minogue dropped in three bags and put the lid on the pot. He studied the stains on the table.

"Whose girlfriend was the Tara one again?" Wall asked.

"Matthews'," said Minogue. "The other one, Ali what's-her-name. She won't be fourteen until the end of the month, I found out."

"Thirteen years of age," said Wall and shook his head. "What are we coming to in this country?"

With that, the room fell quiet. Even the wail of an ambulance nearby seemed to leave the stillness intact. Lost in thought, Wall stroked his neck. Praying, Minogue wondered. Praying for the souls of Ireland. Duggan had his feet stretched out, almost pulling him down from the chair where he slumped, his elbows crossed jammed on the armrests. His hands joined at the fingertips only. This time the phone was painfully shrill. Wall was closest.

"Thanks," he said after a few moments and put back the receiver.

"The Lynch clan," he said. "The mother and the daughter only. Floods of tears apparently."

"I've an idea," said Duggan, grimacing as he hauled himself upright in the chair.

"We put the two girls' families in a room with those two fellas. Let them do the work for us. How about that?"

He stood up slowly and stretched.

"Jesus," he said with little feeling. "Oops, sorry there, em, Stoney."

Wall issued a tired grin.

"Slips out," said Duggan quietly.

"As my mother used to say," said Wall, "God is patient."

Duggan shot a brief, rueful look Minogue's way.

"How long can they keep this up," he murmured, "before

even they cop on they're going nowhere?"

Minogue took three Styrofoam cups off the pile.

"'We only found him there, we didn't do it!'" Duggan went on, in a poor version of a Dublin accent. "'We thought it was a hit and run!'"

Minogue held the lid on the teapot and he poured.

"Thanks," said Duggan.

"Who's good downstairs at interviews?" Minogue asked.

"Dec," said Wall. "Declan Ahearne I told you about. I know he's on evenings. Fin Flaherty's good too. Plainclothes."

"I saw Fin earlier on," said Wall.

"Big hefty fella, Finbar Flaherty," said Duggan. "Very intimidating but he's as mild as milk."

"Have they any doings with this case yet?"

"They do," said Duggan. "They were door-to-door for a few days, and they did some city-centre work with the notices and the photo circulation. They're on call for this when we need them."

"Can yous get them up to speed then," Minogue asked, "on the situation with Matthews and Twomey? Ten-minute chat say?"

He looked up in time to see the two detectives exchange a glance.

"They'd be taking over then?" Duggan asked.

"Not a bit of it," said Minogue. "We're just going to shift the goalposts a bit. Let's bring them in as specialists."

Duggan's eyebrows went up under his bedraggled hair.

"Specialists in what?"

"Sex crimes, let's say," said Minogue. "That ought to do it."

"Well now," Duggan said slowly. "I like it."

Wall lowered his head a little and looked at his colleague before turning to Minogue.

"Wouldn't last long on remand up on Mountjoy," he said. "Would they?"

Minogue looked in the next cupboard for hidden biscuits.

"That might be of some concern to the pair of them," he

said.

"Jesus," said Duggan quietly. "Ah sorry, Stoney. Sorry about that."

"Jesus what," Minogue said, suddenly exasperated with the enforced piety. "We have two fellas stonewalling us."

He tried not to read any reproach into the pause that followed. Still, he felt a silent reproach from Wall for his use of the Holy Name.

"What about consent?" Duggan asked then. "These young ones are fierce... you know? These days?"

"A bit wild maybe," Minogue agreed. "But I don't see a thirteen-year-old girl consenting to sex, do you? I doubt her father would either."

Neither detective said anything.

"Will you doctor your own tea lads?" said Minogue. "There's only that lousy whitener stuff apparently."

"Thanking you," said Wall.

Minogue saw that Duggan was still thinking about it.

"They might be able to laugh off a trafficking charge," he said to Duggan. "But if either one of them has a titter of wit about them, they'll know it's time to deliver."

Duggan's face took on a fixed expression.

"I like it," he murmured. "Yes I do. I like it."

Chapter 32

"I don't see him" said Fanning. "He didn't come out of the house."

Cully was looking through the menus on his mobile.

"Take it easy," he said. "He'll show."

Fanning was sure that Cully sensed that he was on the edge of panic. He tried to breathe through his mouth calmly. The rubber tang from the stick-ons was making him nauseous.

"He's late," Fanning said. "Call it off."

Cully looked over.

"You need to be patient," he said. "It'll be fine."

"This makeup stuff is the worst, I feel like puking from the smell."

"Ain't you been around that stuff though? Your books thing, films?"

Fanning ran his fingers around his cheekbones and his forehead again. The stuff felt like scabs.

"I wouldn't know you now," said Cully. "I swear."

"That's ironic."

"Ironic?"

"Coming from you, I mean. I don't know you, do I?"

"That's funny," said Cully. "I like that, yes. Funny."

There was that English accent slipping in again, Fanning noted. He pulled the mirror open at the back of the visor. The interior light of the car was yellow.

"See?" said Cully. "You're a natural. It's aged you ten, twenty years."

Fanning tilted his head to see if the grey had streaked or gathered in one spot. Cully reached between the seats and pulled a jean jacket from the floor.

"Look, enough," Fanning said. "This is not working out."

"No worries I said. He'll be there."

"Is he watching us? Does he know we're parked here on his road?"

"No he doesn't," said Cully. "You have to change into these boots – and you're using a hat, right?"

"And if he doesn't show up?"

"He'll show up. He does what he's told."

"Who's telling him?"

"We'll talk about that later. Use this."

He dropped a watchman's hat on the console.

"Do the boots outside, then we'll go into the shop. Wear the glasses."

"I don't want to wear glasses."

"These glasses have a tint to them. It shifts your eye colour a bit."

"'Shifts?'"

"I don't know. Just wear them. Every little bit helps."

Fanning closed the mirror and pushed the visor back. He watched the headlights on the cars passing up the road. When the roads were dry, the reflection of their lights flooded the surface of the tarmac with a dull shine.

"Is this a setup?" he asked Cully after a while.

"What?"

"I said, is this a setup."

He couldn't tell if Cully was angry or amused.

"A setup?"

"Right. Are you a Guard? Like some undercover type?"

Cully shook his head.

"And I'm some kind of bait?"

Cully eyed him.

"You want to call it off then," he said in a flat voice. "Right?"

Fanning imagined himself stepping out into the damp night air, walking by the houses, their windows flaring and glowing with the televisions, and crossing the road to the shop.

"What does this guy look like?" he asked Cully.

"No idea," said Cully. The abrupt shift to an almost pensive tone caught Fanning offguard.

"Young bloke I imagine. His dad's in the business, or was."

"Was?"

"He's doing time somewhere. Why do you need to know? Oh, right. 'Background?'"

"You've never seen this guy?"

"The dad?"

"No, the one who's supposed to be at the shop."

"No. Why would I. None of my business really, is it. I just made the call. Got told where to go. That's how things work."

"All to show me how I can get ahold of a gun in Dublin."

"Right. How easy it is."

Cully opened the door and left it slightly ajar. Fanning waited for him to look over.

"I'd feel a lot better about this," he said to Cully, "or at least, I could get it straight in my head, if I knew what was in it for you."

"What, for me?"

"Yes, for you."

Cully seemed ready to smile.

"Well you're going to pay me right? Like Murph. Whatever the going rate for him is."

Shadows cast on Cully's face, but the overhead light hit off his eyes.

"Something tells me that you mightn't be in it just for the money."

Cully leaned back against the door. Fanning was surprised to see a smile broke out on his face.

"Well I have to say this film business thing interests me a little."

"I'm only doing research."

"Have to start somewhere, right? But what I'm saying is, I was always interested in films."

"Who isn't," said Fanning. "Pirates of the Caribbean, right?"

"War films actually."

"Of course."

"Why 'of course'? Are they not good enough? Ever see The Thin Red Line?"

"Okay, so you want to be Colin Farrell. Fine."

Cully let the quiet last.

"You've got stagefright," he said at last. "That's what. Blathering away there. Trust me, you're safe as a house. He's not going to make you. And you don't even have to say a word, do you. Just buy those fags, and let him hear you. Pay for them – we're not doing robberies, remember. Then you meet him outside, you take the bag – and then it's pip-pip, over and out."

"If he wants to talk, or ask me questions?"

"He won't."

"Or asks me for money now?"

"Won't happen."

The draft of night air flowing into the car carried a faint smell of coal smoke.

"And yes," said Cully. "I'll be parked here. Where we said. Promise."

"Well at least you're enjoying yourself. Easy for you to sit here."

Cully spoke in a quiet voice.

"Look. It's no big thing. Just relax."

"That's Murph's script too: just relax."

"Really. Well let me tell you something. If Murph said 'relax,' then that's when you should worry. Now when I say it, I mean it. You're in good hands."

"How do I know?"

"Murph would have dragged you into a lot of situations. I'm telling you."

Fanning elected for silence. He tried to ignore the pungent

244

scent of the glue working its way into his nostrils again for another assault on his patience.

"And the thing is," Cully murmured, "you wouldn't have known, would you. Until it was too late."

Chapter 33

ALI ROGERS HAD THE REGULATION TIGHT clothes and half-on blouse over a tank top, and the too-small jeans. She sat hunched over; spoke only in whispers; never looked up; continued to pick at her hair. The kewpie-doll hank of hair tied up on the right side of her head disturbed Minogue. Child or vamp, was the message he was receiving from it.

Her father had a glazed look in his eye, and was breathing hard right from the start. He was often given to staring at her, sometimes breaking his stare to look up at the ceiling and then allowing his gaze to settle back on to the bloated, blotchy face of his daughter.

Mrs. Rogers, Margaret, was intense, and held herself away from the chair back. She was half her husband's size. She wore the same type of leather jacket as he did. Minogue tried to remember if she were thirty-five or thirty-six. He didn't know if it was makeup or a sun-bed tan she had.

Another Garda, Maeve Dwyer, had come in for the interview. She stayed in her civvies. The quiet in the room soon became oppressive.

"Tell the man, Ali," said her father.

The mother glared at him.

"Was it Aidan's idea?" Minogue asked.

She shook her head.

"Justin's?"

Again she shook her head.

"Yours? Tara's?"

This time she made no movement but stayed hunched in her chair.

"Come on love," said her mother.

The girl's voice was a little hoarse.

"I said, already."

"You said nothing," said the father. His jacket creaked as he re-crossed his legs.

Garda Dwyer gave Minogue a glance. For a moment he wondered if Women's Aid training courses for the likes of Garda Dwyer had included how she should be taking down very large, irate Dublin men like Rogers.

"Ali," said Minogue. "Can you see where we're coming from? A man was beaten up, and now he's dead. Why would he be beaten up and all his valuables just left there, the way you're trying to tell us?"

"He was," she said.

Her lips were almost sticking together now with a line of dried saliva.

"He was...? He was dead, are you saying?"

"I suppose, I don't know."

"Why did you think he was dead?"

"He wasn't moving," she whispered.

"Was he breathing?"

"I don't know. There was blood."

She nodded and she opened up her hand to let out a balled-up tissue.

"Because Aidan–"

"No! Stop saying that!"

The father leaned in suddenly with an ominous creak of leather.

"Didn't I tell you? Stop trying to protect those two fu–"

Minogue raised his hand. The girl's father stopped and looked down at his wife's hand with an expression of disgust.

"Leave her, Paddy. Just leave her."

"I'm not going to sit here and watch her digging her own grave, am I!"

"She's not," said the mother, with her effort at patience clear in how she was holding her breath. "Just leave her. We're here to do what's right."

"This is only helping those bastards!"

Minogue wasn't sure who he had meant. He kept his eyes on the girl. Her eyes moved from side to side but her face remained slack. The red streak and the highlights in her hair kept reminding Minogue of some exotic bird.

"This is a farce," the father snapped. "A farce entirely."

"Would you shut up," said the mother. "Excuse me, but would you just for once? What good are you doing with the carry on of yours?"

"I know what I'd like to do," he retorted. "That's one thing I do know. And by Jesus, if it comes to that, no better man."

The mother rolled her eyes. Minogue saw her chin quiver.

"Mr. Rogers."

Narrowed eyes turned to Minogue.

"This can't work if you carry on like that."

"Carry on? The pot calling the kettle black here, I'd say. I'm not the one dragged a little girl into a police station near midnight, to question her. Am I?"

Minogue saw that Garda Dwyer had taken a step closer to Rogers.

"Yous are the ones screwing things up," said Rogers. "I know what I'd do with those two, those two... scumbags. They'd be telling me what I needed to know. Right quick they would too, oh yes."

"We're obliged to protect everyone's rights in this, Mr. Rogers."

Rogers opened his eyes wide, sat back, and gathered the ends of his jacket on his lap. Minogue had no difficulty recognizing the Dublinman's sign of contempt.

"Rights?" said Rogers. "Now there's a good one. A funny thing, those 'rights' of yours. You ever notice that the only time you hear that word is for other people? It's never for ordinary people like us. Always for the what-do-you-call-ems, the asylum

types, and the refugees and all, always for foreigners. Oh yes –
it's all about their rights, the Muslim crowd and their school, or
getting a house for someone from fecking I-don't-know-where in
Africa..."

"This has nothing to do with why we're here," said
Minogue.

"Like hell it hasn't. What's he doing here, that fella who
got us all into this mess? Have you thought about that, have
you?"

Minogue tried to absorb what he had heard. He saw a
pained look spread across Rogers' face, a man at the outer limits
of reasoning, already sensing that he could not ever convince
the people around him.

"I mean to say," he said, almost in a whisper, "what's a
fella from Poland doing down those streets that time of night?"

Mrs. Rogers' gaze had settled on the tabletop, but her chest
was heaving. Minogue knew her peripheral vision was scanning
the situation. He looked back at her daughter. Shoulders turned
in, ragged parting in her hair revealing a white scalp. Fourteen; a
hormone hurricane; cub of the Celtic Tiger.

"Mr. Rogers," he said. "I'm going to ask you to leave the
room."

"No."

"I'll be leaving too," said Minogue.

"Do what you like. I'm her father."

Minogue gave it a few moments until he felt the tension
was sufficient.

"Her mother will stay, as will Garda Dwyer here. Garda
Dwyer is–"

"–the law is the law."

"Garda Dwyer is trained in working with youth, and
women."

Rogers' jacket made a squeak as he shot forward from the
chair.

"What? What's this? What are you getting at?"

"I'll explain to you outside."

"You won't."

"All right. I won't."

"If it's what I think it is, that's why I'm here. I'm her father, I told yous."

"I do get it," said Minogue.

"This is my daughter we're talking about! My daughter!"

Minogue eyed the jabbing finger, the reddening face, and then he looked over to Rogers' wife. She hadn't budged. He took his cue from her and took his own turn examining the tabletop. He'd give it a count of five. While he waited, he replayed Rogers' angry outburst. Daw-thar, muy, daw-thar. There was a sure sign of alarm, and panic, in Rogers' outburst.

The count was up. Minogue sat back and put his hands on the chair rest. He looked directly at Rogers.

"I know what you're trying to do," said Rogers.

"I'm trying to get you to have a cup of tea is what I'm trying to do."

"I'll kill him," said Rogers. "Them, predators they are."

The signals from Garda Dwyer were steady now. For a moment, he imagined her flooring Rogers with some super-specialized karate kick. Unlikely. "You're under a lot of stress, Mr. Rogers," he said. "But that remark you made is on tape."

"I don't care. I don't."

Minogue stood and stepped around to the back of his chair. Casting a wary glance at Rogers, he was almost surprised to see that Rogers' eyes were brimming with tears. He was indifferent to it, however. He saw that fourteen-year-old Ali Rogers was now a lot less slumped, and that she was even looking through a fringe of hair out at her father.

Rogers sobbed only once. He held his forefinger under his nose. He stumbled on the chair leg as he left the room. Neither mother nor daughter said a word.

Minogue heard Garda Dwyer begin her talk just as he pulled the interview room door closed.

Rogers leaned against the wall and closed his eyes.

"It's tough," Minogue said. "Very tough."

Rogers nodded. He wiped away tears with his forefinger and thumb.

"We'll do the best we can."

Rogers let out a deep breath and shook his head. Minogue imagined Rogers at work on that massive tunnel under Dublin Port. Some huge piece of equipment wielded effortlessly no doubt, hell-for-leather and proud of the new Ireland he was building too, probably. Had he been there at the face of the tunnel, Minogue wondered, and cheered as the last of the rocks and clay crumbled and the other crew's faces appeared? He'd made good money on the job, a man of Rogers' skills. A good provider, Minogue would bet. A little pity leaked into him now.

"Donegal Rogers?" he asked.

"What? I mean, pardon?"

"It's a Donegal name you have. The Rosses, Gweedore?"

Rogers' face eased a little.

"No, no," he murmured and he sniffed. "Sort of wish I was though. My da's da was Donegal. Annagary. But that's a long time ago."

"Donegal is still there," said Minogue. "I checked last September in person. Sure enough, there it was."

"It was, was it."

"Bloody Foreand, Glenties. All that, and more. God's country."

Rogers let out another long, deep breath and he settled his head more against the wall. He looked at the ceiling tiles.

"I wish to Christ I was there, yes. I haven't been in years."

Minogue nodded.

"They had nothing, my grandfather's people," Rogers went on in a low voice. "Nothing. It might as well have been the eighteen hundreds he used to say."

"Come over here," said Minogue. "I'll inflict a cup of Garda tea on you."

He half-turned to make sure Rogers wasn't still leaning against the wall.

"As long as you promise not to kill anyone," he added.

Wall was waiting for the all clear signal. Minogue nodded.

"It's so hard not to get angry, you know," he heard Rogers say behind him. "These days."

Minogue turned and motioned to the seat.

"You're going to have to control yourself," he said to Rogers. "This is a murder investigation."

Rogers blinked.

"If you get stroppy again it'll be the hard option for us," Minogue said.

"Is that the best you can offer?"

Then he sat heavily into the chair and he sighed.

"Hard times is right," he sighed.

"Pardon?"

"Hard times I said. You got me thinking of my grandfather again. How they had nothing, them times. But he done all right, the family, and all. All reared, all healthy, thank God. And I'm not saying we had it easy now – before the boom, I'm saying. But how quickly we forget, don't we?"

For a moment, Minogue recalled his days walking the fields and the Burren headlands while he tried to keep the sea in sight, walking through the hazel thickets that had grown over a dozen abandoned villages.

"I mean I worked in England so I did," Rogers was saying. "But I always wanted to come home here. And I did. We're doing all right now, doing very well, I don't mind telling you – until now, anyway."

He seemed to have noticed Minogue was waiting for him to finish.

"We have everything now," he murmured. "Don't we? Our kids anyway."

"In a manner of speaking, I suppose," Minogue conceded.

"Oh we have it all, there's no doubt. But the crazy thing is, you know what I'm thinking this past while now? Do you?"

"I don't. Tell me, why don't you."

"Them hard times?" He nodded his head for emphasis. "They're back. But like, in the opposite way. Aren't they?"

Chapter 34

"**Y**OU'RE NOT GOING TO FALL ASLEEP THERE," said Cully, "are you?"

Fanning didn't answer, but kept his eyes on the road ahead, where the farther reach of the headlights met the darkness. They drove under the Western Bypass and took the steep parts of the Edmonstown Road with ease.

"You're looking a bit too relaxed there," Cully said.

Fanning was undecided yet on Cully's tone. It was probably the sly mockery he suspected.

"I'm fine," he said, and scratched at his face again where some of the rubber glue had been hard to get off.

"Wasn't so hard, was it. The shop? Nice little acting job there?"

Fanning wouldn't tell him it was more embarrassing than nerve-wracking. That it had felt like some stupid dress-up, with a kinky undertow to the whole thing. They weren't porno mags in the bag either, just crap celebrity stuff. It was when he took the full weight of the plastic bag on his fingers that it turned nerve-wracking: a handgun weighed a lot.

He pressed his window up. The night air had a bite to it up here.

A signpost glowed in the lights: Cruagh. That was a mountain road too, he remembered dimly, leading up through the forested state lands of the Dublin Mountains. Cully steered left. The car began to make its way through steep, wooded hills looming close to the road. Fanning felt the uneven tarmacadam patches and the half-repaired potholes thump at the BMW's tires. He searched for any patch of sky ahead to give shape to the darkness.

He looked across the dashboard again at the glow from the panel. Cully's hand, rather his wrist, rested on the gearshift between them. He steered with his right hand only. The car shuddered once on a deeper pothole and Fanning heard a hiss of water sprayed from a puddle along with pebbles scattering.

"How far?"

"Not far," said Cully.

"You know a good spot?"

"A good spot for what?"

It was a wot, more than the Dublin whah, Fanning registered.

"For what you said."

Cully looked over. Fanning refused to take his eyes off the windscreen ahead.

"For the...?" Cully said.

"You know."

"Definitely, feeling quite at home, I have to say. Aren't you?"

"What do you mean?" Fanning asked.

"Snappy comments. Much more, what'll we say, assertive?"

"Is that bad?"

"Who said anything about it being bad."

"Okay. I'm just trying to get some information."

"Research," said Cully and made a quick jerk of the wheel to steer around a long puddle.

"Right."

"Good."

"Nothing to worry about then, is there."

Fanning hesitated. He wondered if Cully was inviting some kind of bluntness. Maybe it was a test of some kind.

"Sure there is. There's a hell of a lot to worry about. There's a loaded gun in here."

"A pistol – call it a pistol. A gun can be anything. Or call it a firearm."

"There's a loaded gun under my seat. A ticket to a ten-year stay in Portlaoise Maximum Security."

"Well you're not going to advertise the fact it's there, are you?"

"What do you think."

"Well no worries then. Right?"

Fanning said nothing.

"Oh wait," said Cully after a few moments. He shifted in his seat and half-turned to him. "I get it."

"You get...?"

"You're thinking, this a one-way trip. Aren't you?"

Fanning examined the beads of muddy water that had been flung up from the puddles on to his window.

"Of course you are," Cully said. "You're not an idiot. You've weighed it up right?"

Fanning shrugged.

"And I'm not an idiot either. You told people where you went, didn't you?"

"Do I even know where I'm going here?"

"Too bloody right you did. I would too."

Fanning looked over at him.

"We're adults, remember," Cully said. "What we're doing is getting established. Just getting to know the ground. Sussing things out."

"A recce, like."

Cully glanced over.

"You used the word before," Fanning said.

"You have a good memory then."

"Just don't say 'relationship,' or 'win win.'"

"Why?"

"It's a joke. PowerPoint talk. You know what PowerPoint is, right?"

"Of course I do."

Fanning didn't try to hide his skepticism.

"You didn't expect that, did you."

"Actually no," Fanning allowed. "Do you give seminars or something with PowerPoint?"

Cully seemed to consider a response.

"As a matter of fact," he began, but then shrugged away the rest of what he was about to say.

"Go on."

Cully shook his head

"Some other time, maybe."

The road through the pine forest crossed the river that ran along the valley floor dividing Two Rock Mountain, whose coastal side was part of the skyline of Dublin city, from Djouce, the first of the mountains that backed higher into Wicklow.

The car began to sway and even wallow as the roadway cut its way around the side of the valley. Fanning was visited by brief, scattered memories now of picnics when he was small, of the rock-strewn stream in the darkness alongside.

The headlights tunnelled in to the night, revealing the clumps of died-back grasses that the winter had bleached. Fanning inclined closer to his window and again looked up to the sky. There was only the faintest lightening high up where the slope met the night sky over Dublin City.

Cully was humming.

"Creepy isn't it," he said. Innit, Fanning heard.

"Be different now in the summer," he added.

"You know the place here?"

"Well, I did. Some time back."

Then, when Fanning didn't follow up with questions, Cully added, "Boy Scout stuff? Didn't get out of the city much then."

"Dublin, like? Growing up?"

Cully nodded, and resumed humming. There was no break in the flat darkness of the mountains to Cully's side.

"Expecting someone?"

"No."

He thought he heard Cully snort faintly. Then he slowed

and scrutinized the roadway ahead.

"Around here. The road."

"A forestry road?"

"I suppose, yes."

"It's just a track then."

Cully nodded.

"Just about… there."

He braked hard enough to scatter the gravel from the edges of the road.

"Here?"

"Yep, this is it."

The BMW's bonnet leaned and then dropped as it descended, lopsided, through the long puddle, the lights scouring across the undergrowth, then bobbing up to the conifers.

"There'll be a gate," said Fanning. "You wouldn't want to try going up in a car anyway."

The yellow gateposts caught the headlights.

"We're in luck," said Cully.

Fanning put his hand on the armrest to moderate the slow bucking of the car. He heard a metallic thump as Cully drove over a rut that turned into a low embankment.

"Won't be much left of Murph's car at this rate," he said.

Cully opened the window, and cold air scented with pine needles and sodden earth filled the car. Fanning heard a swish from the front wheels as Cully steered through another puddle. The rear wheels sizzled, spinning for a few moments, spraying water and mud hard on the underside panels of the car. Cully eased off the accelerator and sat forward as if to coax the car through.

The wheels found grip then and the BMW shot out of the slough. They were in the woods now. The track took on the dull khaki colour of the needles. The trees seemed to be moving in slow procession with passage of the headlights.

"How loud does it get?" Fanning asked.

"Louder than you think."

Cully switched off the engine.

"What about a silencer thing?"

"A suppressor, it's called. You're not going to get one of those."

"Why not?"

"Let me explain something. Even if that dickhead had one to fit the piece of junk he gave you, he wouldn't give it to you. You know why?"

"Because, I don't know, I'd wreck it?"

"Because you'd be renting the gun to use it."

"So...?"

"You don't get it. That's bad for business. If you use it, it's dirty. I don't mean dirt, I mean it's tainted."

"Traceable?"

"Right. So if you're asking for something with your 'silencer' thrown in..."

"I get it," said Fanning.

He listened to the ticks of the engine cooling. Staring into the darkness he could soon distinguish gaps of less dark sky. Cully released his belt and let it slide quietly into place. He yawned and pulled back the sleeve of his jacket to see his watch. He made no move to get out of the car.

"Are we going to...?"

"Soon."

"What are we waiting for?"

Cully rubbed at his eyes pinching the bridge of his nose and then stretched.

"We are waiting," he said slowly in a stagy voice, "we are waiting, for the right time. That's what we are waiting for."

Chapter 35

MINOGUE STRETCHED AGAIN. A familiar sourness came to his nostrils – the stale smell of late hours in the same shirt and jacket, of early morning hours spent sitting in interview rooms, or slouched in cars.

Duggan had moved his chair back to the wall so he could lean his head and shoulders against it. Wall looked as fresh as ever somehow. Minogue wondered how, but then decided that Wall's strong faith probably had an inner glow of freshness and cleanliness, signs of everlasting life conferred on the chosen, perhaps. Like the clean cut Mormons.

Minogue eyed the pictures again. He settled on the one of Tadeusz Klos' bloodied face, his teeth bloodied and broken, the swollen lips, the terrible sneer of death.

Duggan opened his eyes slowly.

"I had this brilliant dream," he murmured.

"It was perfect," he added, swallowing dryly.

"That Amy Winehouse one again?" Wall asked.

The unexpected humour heartened Minogue. Maybe Wall wasn't all piety. Maybe he actually had a bit of give in him.

Duggan shook his head.

"Long gone," he said. "That tramp deserted me, so she did."

"Is it too late to start a support group?" Minogue asked.

"Ah, no – but thanks anyway. I'll suffer in silence. Wait,

no: I'll blog it."

"That's Monaghan men for you," Minogue said. "'Stony grey hills...'"

The puzzled expression that was Duggan's response brought a little dismay to Minogue. Did nobody read Patrick Kavanagh's poetry anymore?

"Well, in anyway," said Duggan, gathering himself. "This one was about tonight, or this morning, whatever you want to call it. Set right here in this room."

Minogue looked over.

"Yeah," said Duggan. "All the yo-yos in there walked in the door here, along with their counsel, and confessed."

"Wild out entirely," said Minogue.

"It was brilliant," said Duggan. He rubbed at his ginger stubble.

"'Sorry to have kept you up so late,' said one of them, what's his face, the long stringy fellow, Twomey."

"Come on now," Wall said. "Hardly Twomey. He's a complete idiot. The way he's talking and posing? I swear he thinks he starred in some video or something. Did you hear what he said to his counsel after she showed up?"

"I know, I know," said Duggan and yawned.

"'Get out of here,' says he. 'You're working for The Man!'"

"Well it was grand while it lasted, that dream."

"Is that all?"

Duggan took his hands down from wiping his eyes.

"Actually, it wasn't. I think we all shook hands. And off we went."

"Off where?"

"We went to a pub to celebrate. Now did you ever hear anything like it?

"I never did," said Wall. "But I'll bet you they hear it all the time up in Portrane."

It took a moment for Minogue's tired mind to place the jibe: Portrane was for the criminally insane, right. A lull followed. The clock's hands had only moved five minutes since last time. Wall turned another page.

Duggan's yawn ended in a long groan.

"God almighty," he said and he levered himself robotically out of the chair. "Something's got to give here now, or there'll be no bed for anyone."

Minogue checked the time on his watch.

"Isn't it kind of sexist," said Duggan, "to be trying to get the girls out, and not the two head-cases?"

"No," said Wall, "it's about adults and children. The girls are supposed to be the children. Those two fellas are supposed to be the adults."

"As the law sees it, at least," Duggan grunted.

"Are her parents still in there?" he asked Minogue.

Minogue nodded.

"The father will turn Turk if she's held over," said Duggan.

"Well we'll deal with that," said Minogue.

"Begob, but it's raining. Drizzle. I–"

The knock on the door was a split second before the Guard off the midnight shift opened it.

"There's a solicitor wants to see ye, one of ye."

Mahon now reminded Minogue of a Goya painting. His cheeks flattened and even sunken in a way he hadn't expected, the dark rings around his eyes.

"A request," he said to Minogue.

"I'll be happy to oblige. If I can, of course. What's on offer now?"

Mahon shook his head.

"My client is very frightened," Mahon said.

"Is this the same Mr. Twomey we spoke with earlier on?"

"He's beginning to understand the position he might be in here."

"Okay. That's good for all of us."

"He's very apprehensive at the thought of, you know."

"Staying in a cell overnight?"

"Well, yes."

"Well if he'd stop holding out on us..."

"He's not."

"You say, that he says, that he's not."

"I didn't come down in the last shower."

"Fair enough. But I'm here since The Flood, and I don't buy that."

Mahon drew a long breath.

"Your grounds for wanting him remanded are not clear."

"Have I not shown you the site pictures? That is to say the photos from this scene, of Mr. Klos? Savage treatment. Brutal, sadistic, unrelenting. Now that's unacceptable."

"Grandstanding isn't allowed in court either, I think you know."

"Mr. Klos choked on his own blood."

"My client admits to taking items off the body – with the others."

"A body, or a live man? Unconscious and dying, and needing help?"

"Am I being cross-examined now?"

"One phone call from any of this foursome could've saved the man's life."

"He'll be no use if he can't get a night's sleep."

"Mr. Mahon. I'm not the one getting in the way of Twomey's shut-eye. You're the one made the request to keep this long consultation going so long. I mean, I admire your staying power tonight. Any other solicitor would be gone hours ago."

"Your mind is made up?"

"It is."

"Let me phrase it a different way. What is it exactly you are expecting from him tonight?"

"That he tells us what really happened. I'm more than content to wait until tomorrow and argue the same thing in the Circuit Court."

Mahon rubbed at his eyebrows, and then looked over Minogue's shoulder at the open door.

"You're here because this is a high-profile case. A lot of pressure too?"

"That's immaterial and irreverent," Minogue replied with a shrug.

"I know you have the girls here too. And you're playing everyone off against the other."

"The world isn't flat, Mr. Mahon. It hasn't been flat for quite a long time."

"Questionable process there. Juveniles, questioning at this hour of the night?"

"Phone a judge," said Minogue. "Have a go. No hard feelings, whatever happens. Or doesn't happen."

"Kids that age will say anything."

Minogue gave him the eye.

"Your client already said so. Several times, if I remember. No one is saying either one of these two girls is sugar and spice."

"I'm glad to hear you say that."

"Which always means the opposite, in my experience. You're driving at..."

"That people have blind spots. All people."

"Specifically?"

To his credit, Mahon wasn't flinching.

"That girls wouldn't be capable of doing it. That maybe the men here – boys really, or at least my client, I regard him as a boy really – have a misguided loyalty."

Minogue raised an eyebrow. Mahon raised one back.

"Mr Mahon, let me tell you something. I'd want you on my side, I really would. To be sure, people do the right thing for the wrong reason, and all the rest of it. I don't for a minute doubt what young ones – girls – can do, what they come up with."

Minogue took a step back toward the doorway.

"So, on account of my admiration for what you're doing here tonight – and I am not joking one bit, now – here's what had been going through my mind. The two young ones set Mr. Klos up and then they told the two lads when they showed up. All part of a plan. Who's to say the two girls didn't even lend a hand? Or a boot, should I say. But that doesn't diminish what your client did. What I allege he did. Why I oppose bail."

"You have forensic evidence to back all of this."

It was unworthy of Mahon, Minogue believed, but he was tired and frustrated too, no doubt.

Mahon cast a glance again at the doorway.

"We'll have to leave it at that," Minogue said.

Chapter 36

THE CAR CREAKED AS CULLY STRETCHED AGAIN. He sat back and closed his eyes.

"Well can I get out? Or open the window a bit?"

Cully looked at his watch.

"Wait a minute and I'll get out with you."

Cully reached under his seat and pulled out the shopping bag that held the pistol. He unwrapped the nylon pouch, releasing an oily smell into the car, and he lifted out the pistol.

"Here you go," he said. "Tell me what you're going to do first."

"I'm going to put gloves on."

"No, you're going to ask me to check it's safe. Safe is, it's empty, no rounds in it."

"Okay."

Cully remained still. Fanning knew he was staring at him.

"Can you do that then?" he asked Cully. "Please?"

Cully nodded slowly.

"Raring to go, aren't you?"

"Just want to get it done and get out of here," said Fanning.

"Cully pulled the ammunition clip from the bag.

"Clip is out, okay? But you always assume there's one in the chamber. Ever see that?"

"On television."

"Pull back the slide, empty. Here."

"You want me to...?"

"Sure. You've got to see what it's like. Heavy, isn't it?"

Fanning held it on his palm and lowered it to his lap.

"Hold it, go on. The grip there."

"The grip."

"The handle you call it. Yeah, hold it."

"Finger inside here?"

"Outside the guard."

Fanning heard his own breath escaping through his nose.

"Breathe," said Cully. "I'm not joking."

Fanning let out his breath in small, controlled breaths through his mouth.

"So what do you think?"

"I don't know."

"Sure you do. You just don't want to say it."

"Okay. Whatever."

"It's power," said Cully, "right?"

"I suppose."

"You suppose? You have one, the other guy doesn't. That's power. No one can hurt you. You can say what you like can't you? Pretty well do what you like. It's all up to you. Right?"

Fanning nodded. His heart rate wasn't slowing.

"Keep your head, show self-control and you're going to be able to do things. You see? But if you're an idiot, what you're holding there is only going to speed things up, until you crack. You have the gun, the gun doesn't have you. You know what that means?"

"I think so, yes."

"Okay then. We're going out there to take a bit of a stroll. Not far. I'll bring the clip."

Cold night air from the forest washed over Fanning's face. He felt his heels sink into the needles and he closed the car door. There was no door light in the car. It had probably been Cully's doing. He waited for Cully's dark form to come around the boot of the car.

"Christ," said Cully, "dark enough."

"I can't see anything out here."

"Anything?"

"I can see a few patches of light in the sky there."

Cully tapped the trunk with his knuckles before he made his way around.

"What is this thing anyway," Fanning said. "What make is it, like, what type?"

"That's a good one," said Cully. "Now's as good a time as any to tell you, I suppose. What you are holding is a replica."

"You're joking."

Cully was beside him now. He took something from his trouser pocket. A narrow beam of bluish light poked about the forest floor by their shoes.

"No, I'm not joking."

"What's the point then, what are we doing here?"

"It's a replica that's been converted."

"So it's real?"

"It's a real replica of a proper gun."

"It's safe then?"

"If it was done right."

"How will we know it was done right?"

"If you still have all your fingers when you fire off a round."

"This is ridiculous."

"No," said Cully. "It's research, isn't it."

"The innits were coming thick and fast now, Fanning reflected.

"Why didn't you say when you looked in the bag back then?"

"I knew already."

"Why didn't you…?"

"Ah that'd spoil it," Cully said. "There you were, your heart going bang bang with the adrenaline ready to break open your ribcage, you're all done up pro with a disguise – and I should have wrecked that experience for you? I don't think so."

"But you've got bullets there. That clip of ammunition."

"They're compressed air."

"Air."

"Here, I'll show you. Give me the gun."

The flashlight beam gleamed dully on the blackened metal.

"See? See that nail there. That's the maker. There in England. Lots and lots of these around, and coppers really don't like them. They're trying to get a ban on them."

"There's no way I'm paying a hundred and fifty Euro for twelve hours with this piece of crap."

"You wouldn't have known if I hadn't told you."

"But you let it happen anyway."

"It's not a big deal. Think about it."

"I have. It sucks. It's stupid."

"What do you know about the likes of this? It feels the same. It sounds the same. It will get you what you want most of the time. You stick this in someone's face, are they going to say hold on a minute let me check if that's the real thing?"

"So the guy knew back there in the shop, the guy who gave it to me."

"He did, he didn't. I don't know. He just hands things over. He's like a go-for. The one who runs the show, he's not out delivering is he."

"But it's just a colossal rip-off."

"Are you going to do this or not?" Cully asked.

The beam from the flashlight carried far but was narrow. Fanning's eye followed it over pine needles glistening with raindrops and down the trunks where roots showed from the carpet of dead needles. The ground was soft and springy, and the sharp twigs and branches Fanning had expected would block their path through the trees had been cleared. The ground sloped and dipped, revealing the odd boulder.

Cully was whistling quietly under his tongue and moving the flashlight beam up from their feet to the darkness ahead in a routine arc.

"Here is good," he said.

He slowed to let the light play on the tree trunks ahead.

He stopped when he found the plastic shopping bag attached to a tree. He took the clip from his jacket and held out his hand for the pistol.

"There's banks here that will catch the noise. Hold my torch will you."

"We're going to fire the thing here?"

"Yes," said Cully. "Here. Better here than O'Connell Bridge, I say."

Fanning tried to hold the light steady on Cully's hands but it kept wavering. A small glint came back up to him from the edge of the light spilling out onto the undergrowth. Cully shoved the clip home with a sharp click, followed by another.

"There are footprints here," said Fanning. "They're new."

"Are they."

"See how the heels are dug in, the little pools of water from the rain? They're recent."

"Could be, I suppose."

"You don't care?"

"No," said Cully. "Now, you're ready. Give me the torch, I want to show you something. The details on this are spot on, they have a working safety switch here. See it? Watch my thumb."

"Do I have to fire the thing?"

Cully stopped.

"We're all the way up here, on a crappy wct night and you're backing out?"

"What's the point, I'm thinking. It's not a proper gun. It's just a waste of time."

"You get everything except the lead flying."

"Well you go ahead then."

"Me? I don't need to. I don't want to."

"Really."

"I'll fire one off then you. Okay?"

When he got no reply from Fanning, Cully walked over to where the bag had been pinned to the trunk. He yanked it and tore it open and unfolded a piece of paper.

"Orienteering," he said. "Some club. Geo caching. Ever hear of it?"

"No. Maybe."

"GPS?"

"Yes."

"Okay, I'm gonna put this bag over here. Watch. I'm gonna aim at it and shoot. Take my word for it. It's easy at ten feet. You shine the light on it. It won't budge. Air. See? But it will make the same bang. Ready?"

"Okay."

Fanning let the torch play on the tree trunk. Cully spread the bag against the trunk and he stepped back.

"Two hands," he said. "Shine it on me for a second. Look. You see? One over the other, fingers like this. It'll pull up if you don't and you'll miss."

"Miss what? There's nothing coming out, you told me."

"If it was a real one, I'm saying. You ready?"

This pistol bucked immediately. Fanning felt like he had been smacked with a newspaper on both ears. He could almost see the shockwaves of air around him. The beam jerked but he could see that the plastic bag hadn't moved.

"Loud, isn't it?"

"That's for damn sure. Let's go."

"Give it one. Come on. It's your turn."

Fanning watched as Cully readied the pistol, moving the safety forward and back twice. He handed over the torch.

The grip was warm. The weight of the pistol seemed to pull it forward and down.

"No," he heard Cully say as his heart sped up again. "Really grab hold of it. The left over the right. Straighten your arms. Keep it pointing down there."

"I can't see anything out there."

"Too right you can't. Not until I see you're set up. You can feel the catch there by your thumb, the safety."

"Yes."

"Pull it toward you. Got it?"

"I think so."

"It's not going to fire unless you do. Be sure."

"Okay I have it."

"Okay. I'm going to put the light on where you shoot, okay? See it? Two hands, remember. Bend your knees like you're going to spring. Where's your forefinger now?"

"My first finger?"

"What you're going to shoot with."

Fanning steadied himself for the noise and the recoil. He stared intently at the bag lit by the torch. Somehow, his forefinger wouldn't squeeze. He tightened it more. Just when he committed, he heard a noise.

"Listen," he said to Cully.

"Listen to what."

"Somebody's out there."

Cully said nothing, but he stood still listening.

"Maybe somebody's trying to get into the car," Fanning whispered.

"A long way to come to rob a car."

He switched off the torch and began walking. He paused once or twice as though to get his direction.

Fanning followed him, trying to separate the sounds of their footsteps from any others. Cully stopped and listened again.

"They must have heard us again," Fanning whispered. "The shot."

He thought he saw Cully nod. Then Cully took a breath, and he whistled. Fanning froze. Cully waited and whistled again.

"What the hell are you doing?" he hissed.

Cully ignored him and whistled a third time. Almost immediately then there was an answering whistle followed a few seconds by another.

"Come on," he said to Fanning.

Fanning's heart was ready to burst. He took in fast deep breaths as quickly as he could. He heard more than saw Cully begin to walk again. He imagined himself racing through the trees, vaulting over undergrowth. Down the mountainside he'd go, and sprint through the scattered fields and then the houses into the suburbs, and home. Anything to put distance between himself and this place.

Chapter 37

"WAIT!" HE CALLED OUT and stumbled after Cully. "Who's there?"

"Don't worry."

"Tell me. This is freaking me out."

"You're okay. Just come this way."

Fanning grabbed Cully's shoulder. Cully turned and faced him.

"Don't do that," he said. "Don't."

"What's going on? Explain! There's someone here isn't there? You expected it. Planned it."

"I said don't worry. And don't grab me again."

"But I don't get it—"

"There's nothing to get. It's just the way it is."

"What does that mean? What are you going to do?"

"I'm a busy man," said Cully. "I can't just be doing the tour guide thing here without keeping up with my work. Multitasking."

"Who's here? Who are you looking for?"

"Who who," said Cully and turned to walk down the path again. "You sound like an owl."

Fanning's legs felt too weak to keep him standing, much less move. He tried to peer through the darkness again, half-hoping to find where best to disappear into the woods.

Somehow his feet drew him along in Cully's footsteps.

"Really don't like this," he called out.

Cully kept going.

"Who's out there?" Fanning asked.

Two flashes pulsed in the middle distance. Fanning stopped immediately. His chest surged like an electrical shock ran through it.

"Oi oi," said Cully and turned on his torch again.

"Ready," said the other voice.

Cully stepped forward. His second step snapping a dried twig.

"Two of you?" the voice said. It was English with that throaty inflection.

"Two and a half," said Cully. The torch beam found Cully's feet and lower torso and ran alongside him.

"Where's Guy Ritchie then?"

Cully stopped. The light darted and jumped from place to place in the darkness before finding Fanning's legs. Cully's flashlight settled on his face. Fanning held his hand up to his face to block the glare.

"Come on," Cully said. "Show's over." The light left his face and played on the ground ahead of him.

"Is that West Ham?" said Fanning with a croak.

"Best supporting actor," said Cully.

Now Fanning wanted to curse. He felt relief trickling in, but as he walked toward the light the fear still locked his chest hard, and the weakness in his legs wasn't letting up.

"Where's your wheels?" Cully called out.

"With one inch out of the ditch," said West Ham. "What were you thinking?"

"What, you can't drive anymore? I got the Beemer up here no problem."

"One way? Great, you're a hero. You never said it was going to be jungle here, what are we, ten miles out? Dark side of the bloody moon up here."

Fanning took in long gulps of air. There was a new smell, but he couldn't identify it clearly.

"Follow him there," said Cully. "I'll bring up the rear."

They were nearly on the car before Fanning realized it. The smell was from West Ham: some kind of booze on his breath. He searched around the back of the BMW with the light, stopping at two red plastic petrol containers.

Fanning stopped and took a step back.

"What's he doing," he muttered to Cully. "Are we out of petrol or something?"

"No. We're just going to top it up."

"But why did he come up here to meet us?"

"Many hands make light work," said Cully. "Didn't your mum ever say that to you?"

He took out his flashlight and shone it on his keys. He chose one and opened the trunk of the BMW.

West Ham put his own flashlight in his mouth and picked up one of the petrol containers. Over West Ham's wheezy breath, Fanning heard the petrol swish as West Ham tilted it to get a grip on the cap. Cully was opening the other one.

"Open the car doors," he called out to Fanning.

"What are we doing?"

West Ham said something that Fanning didn't hear properly. The flashlight still held in his mouth.

"We," said Cully and paused. "We are doing our home-work. Come on, open up the doors."

West Ham had pocketed his torch, and was swishing petrol into the boot.

"Christ," he said and wrinkled his nose.

Fanning opened the passenger door first.

"You're a sloppy bastard," West Ham muttered. "Er, sir."

"The back door too," said Cully to Fanning.

He turned toward the back of the car.

"Like do I need advice from you," he said to West Ham.

"Matter of fact you do," said West Ham, "you stupid Mick."

West Ham continued pouring the petrol into the boot.

"You guys are friends?" Fanning said to Cully.

Cully put his knee on the passenger seat, and he leaned

into the car's interior. Fanning heard the petrol swish and gulp as Cully began to empty it on the seats and the floor. Then he backed out, poured some on the seat, and closed the door.

"Are you?"

"Am I what?"

"Friends," said Fanning. "The way you talk to one another?"

Cully nudged him out of the way. He stepped around the rear door and began working on the back seat.

West Ham was standing by the open trunk. He looked in, frowned, and shook his head. Then he stepped away.

"What have you got then," Cully said.

"An Opel."

"Did you save some petrol."

"You mean, am I a moron?"

Matches rattled against the box as West Ham reached out.

"You're going to set fire to it?" he asked him.

Cully ran the flashlight over the bodywork of the car. A sheen of kaleidoscopic light glowed where the petrol had soaked the dashboard.

"That's Murph's car," Fanning said. "You're going to set it on fire?"

"It's an eyesore," Cully said.

"So's Murph," said West Ham.

"Shut it," said Cully, "and take him down to the car."

"Are we getting a little agitated here, boss?" West Ham asked.

"I'm doing nothing until I hear that car of yours actually start."

"What's Murphy done?" Fanning asked.

"Nothing," said Cully. "Everything. Now get going."

The tang of petrol filled Fanning's nostrils.

"Was there a falling out?" he asked.

"Go," Cully repeated, standing by the trunk.

"I didn't sign on for this," said Fanning.

"It's part of the package," said Cully evenly. "A freebie. Now get going."

"Come on," West Ham shouted. "You heard the man."

Fanning started at the noise. He thought about shouting back, but instead found himself following West Ham up the bank toward the Opel.

"Do you live here?" Fanning asked him. "In Dublin?"

West Ham said nothing.

"You're not Irish," Fanning went on. "I can tell. Did you move here?"

"Get in the back seat," West Ham said.

The car's interior was still warm. Fanning sat back.

The Opel smelled of old air freshener, mildew, and tired vinyl. Under the steering wheel the cover had been taken off and wires hung out.

"Hold this," said West Ham. "Shine it on the wheel here."

Up close, West Ham's breath was overwhelming. There was something sour and rotten breathing through the sugary leftovers of the alcohol. West Ham snorted softly as he worked. The wires sparked twice and the engine caught.

"Switch off the light," West Ham grunted. He pushed the horn once, put the car in first, and let it inch forward.

For a moment, Fanning saw himself from overhead, like a long pull-back shot, here in the forest, so near and so distant from the city. The fear that had seized him back in the woods had left him now. Now he took in every detail around him, the words racing through his head like a shoal of fish suddenly scattered: a wet glistening road, a stolen car, a strange odour from West Ham. He looked behind but they were still in the darkness.

"He's really going to do it?"

West Ham looked away.

"Why's he doing it? I mean what's Murph done?"

"None of your business," said West Ham quietly now. "None of mine either. Ask Cully if you want."

West Ham began tapping the steering wheel, but kept his eyes on the mirror.

"Been in Dublin before?"

The tapping slowed, and then resumed.

"Staying with friends?"

West Ham's head whirled around.

"Didn't I tell you to shut it? You're nothing to me. Got that? This is Cully's thing, so just–"

The flare of yellow light made them both turn.

Half-obscured by the boughs, the flames erupting from the back of the BMW showed a figure half-running toward them, skipping, sidestepping.

"Jesus," said Fanning.

"Wait til it gets to the seats," West Ham murmured, his anger suddenly vanished. "The windows closed, quick ignition – it will blow, and set the petrol tank off..."

Fanning stole a glance at him. He seemed both rapt and sleepy, the firelight shining on his eyes.

"A minute or two," he murmured, "and kaboom."

Cully was at the door. He pulled it closed behind him and sat in. The tires buzzed on the wet roadway and then bit. West Ham was changing in to second gear before Cully had the door shut.

"Take your bloody time," Cully said, breathing hard.

He busied himself wrapping the pistol he had taken from Fanning.

"Murph will be wanting new wheels I suppose," said Fanning.

West Ham took a bend faster than he should have. The three rocked back when he corrected.

"Well he should have thought of that," said Cully. "Shouldn't he."

"What has he done, Murph, he deserves this?"

Neither man answered.

"It's not like I'm going to tell anyone, am I," Fanning went on.

"Shut him up," said West Ham. "He's driving me mental."

"Well you'd know about mental," said Fanning.

"Now now," said Cully. "I can't leave you two alone for a minute, can I."

"Very funny," said Fanning. "Very funny, I'm sure."

West Ham muttered something under his breath. Cully

flicked his arm hard with his fingers.

"Drop it, Westie. Enough. Fun's over."

"Call this fun, do you? This has to be the stupidest thing you ever came up with, I tell you."

"Enough, I bloody said!"

The shout seemed to echo in the car, in Fanning's head even. The car seemed suddenly quiet. Something prompted Fanning to keep at it.

"Why does a guy get his car burned?"

"And you stay out of it," said Cully.

"We're here for research, remember? Research means questions?"

"Told you," said West Ham. "Now you see: bloke's a prick."

Cully leaned around the headrest.

"A few minutes ago it was knees knocking and teeth like castanets with you," he said. "Back up in the woods there."

"If you'd told me what was going to happen, it would have helped."

"And now you're getting into it here?"

"If you'd explained things..."

"Explained," said Cully. "What explained? This isn't school."

He turned back in his seat, and he rapped West Ham in the arm again.

"Oh come on. Back on track there, gunner."

"You know what I think," said West Ham.

"Cheer up, for Christ's sake."

"Don't push it no more. This is different."

"Mutiny in the ranks?"

Cully's mockery didn't draw any more response. They gained the entrance to the valley and turned down toward the city. West Ham drove carefully now.

"Give me some of that," said Cully. "Don't be a wally."

"What? What have I got?"

"Wot? Wot?" said Cully. "You know bloody 'wot.' Some of that jungle rum you got. That's wot."

Chapter 38

WEST HAM LEFT THE CAR RUNNING outside the chipper. He slammed the door, still grinning at something that Cully had muttered. He seemed to be unsteady on his feet as he walked, rolling his shoulders and shaking his head. Cully offered Fanning the rum again.

"No," said Fanning. "Thanks."

Cully sucked on his teeth after a swig, and he screwed the top back on.

Fanning sat back against the seat again and he watched the reaction of the girl behind the counter to West Ham's order. A couple of teenagers were eating fish and chips at a seat next to the window.

"He's a pretty good friend of yours, isn't he?"

Cully turned.

"Westie? Why are you asking?"

"You let him say what he wants to. Calling you a Paddy?"

"That stuff doesn't matter," said Cully.

"In England, it matters, I'd say."

Cully hesitated.

"Well we're not in England, are we. We're here in Dublin for a bit of a lark. It's me showing him about, isn't it."

"Doesn't look that thrilled to be here."

"Leave West Ham out of it, this thing."

Fanning could still smell petrol. Maybe it was on his

clothes, or on the seat.

West Ham was counting out exact change. The girl at the cash register looked quickly up to his face from his money, and then back. He said something to her as he handed over the money. She smiled nervously and began counting. Three teenaged boys came down the footpath by the clothes shops and entered the chipper.

"You don't mind sitting in a stolen car here," Fanning said. "Do you?"

"I've never done it before."

"Look," said Cully, "the cops don't care. They've got enough to do. Why should they put themselves out over it? Insurance covers it. Nobody cares, believe me."

"Murph will care."

West Ham had the same shambling gait on his way out of the chipper.

"I don't know about that," said Cully. "Be interesting to find out, I suppose."

"You don't sound like you care much."

"'The rain in Spain falls mainly down the drain.'"

"On the Plain. It falls on the Plain."

"What Plane?" West Ham asked as he opened the door. "Are we going back?"

The greasy heat from the fish and chips came out as vapour.

"It's nothing," said Cully.

West Ham sampled some of the chips, holding them between his teeth and breathing on them. He made no move to offer them around. Fanning noticed the first drops of rain sliding down the window.

"You might as well just pour lard into your arteries," said Cully.

West Ham's eyes met Fanning's in the mirror.

"You stick to your carrot juice and tofu then."

Cully shifted in his seat.

"I'll drive," he said. "You can stuff yourself."

Fanning heard West Ham mumble something as they exchanged seats.

"What," said West Ham after swallowing a chip.

"I can drop you somewhere else," Cully said to him.

"Christ, now? Get a few drinks, see what's up."

"Later on, maybe," said Cully, and he pulled over.

West Ham grunted, but slid out of his seat and stepped out onto the footpath without complaint. Neither man said good-bye.

Cully crunched reverse twice before finding it.

There were few enough people walking along the foot-paths. Buses swished by in a haze of drizzle. An ambulance passed by slowly, followed by a Garda squad car. Fanning stole a glance at Cully. He seemed unconcerned.

"So, you like motoring about in a hot car," Cully said.

Fanning looked over for a moment.

"I'm not sure."

"That means you do," said Cully. He braked for the turn by the Rotunda Hospital, and turned onto Parnell Square.

"I'll tell you how I know that," he said pausing to avoid a taxi, "how I know you like it. You would have said so if you didn't like it. 'Not sure' means you do, but you don't want to admit it. It's a middle-class thing."

"Ah, psychology," said Fanning.

"Call it what you like. It's true."

"A weakness, you think, no doubt."

Cully shrugged

"I don't care," he said, "if it is or isn't."

Parnell Square was almost deserted.

"Where are we going?"

"We're getting rid of this thing. You can study that. Write about it. Anyway, it's not too far. Then, who knows."

"Why did you tell West Ham to go his own way?"

"Don't need him for this. Do I. Gets in the way some-times."

Fanning felt for the pencil through the fabric of his jacket pocket.

"Is it the way he talks?"

"What about the way he talks?" Cully asked.

"Well he says things."

"He says what things."

"What he said when you told him you'd be dropping him off in town here."

"He likes to bitch. Sometimes it's a laugh. Not tonight. But I'm used to it."

"No," said Fanning. "About the job, the work you do. How it was finished and couldn't you just go out for a few pints and that."

"Yeah well he likes to take it a bit too easy sometimes," Cully said. "Tough to keep an edge with that kind of attitude."

"I mean something else he said. Something like 'op's over.'"

Cully watched the traffic lights and pushed the gearshift from side to side.

"Who knows what he'd say. It's just talk."

"Military-style talk."

"Really."

"It sure sounds like that to me," said Fanning.

Cully stopped pushing the gearshift to and fro and looked over.

"And what would you know about that?"

"I'm just saying. I know what 'fall out' means too. Even if he was being sarcastic."

"Well good for you," said Cully. He spun the tires in first gear before easing off the pedal. He came around the north side of the square and found his way through the heavier traffic car by car, turning abruptly back onto Parnell Street.

"What about the gun?" Fanning said.

"The pistol you mean. I'll take care of it."

"Are you going tell them?"

"Tell them...?"

"That it's a rip-off?"

"Maybe I will."

"You don't care."

"Not much. No."

Fanning gave up on his effort to draw Cully out for now.

Cully took the turn down Gardiner Street. With the new three-level apartments drifting by to either side of the car, Fanning thought back to his days as a student. Coming up here for pints was considered daring. It was still Corporation flats, tenements, and vacant lots, with pubs full of people who started drinking at half-ten in the morning and were still there at closing time. Bohemian, he had thought, proletarian: real.

Through the wipers and the bleary glass he saw the Custom House just above the railway bridge and Beresford Place.

"Leave me off here at the Custom House," he said to Cully.

"Don't you want to see how to dump a hot car? It's only a five-minute walk from the bridge."

"So close to the city centre?"

"What did you think? We're going to go to some cliff somewhere?"

"I don't know."

"How would we get back if we did that?"

"Well maybe West Ham will appear with another car."

"That's funny," said Cully. "But not too funny. He's in no shape to do that now. That's what I'm saying to you. You can't count on him a hundred percent."

"I don't want to be too late getting home."

"The missus waiting up for you?"

"No. But she's a worrier."

"Can't relax these days, can you. Trying to keep things going right? The breadwinner thing. Is that what they call it?"

Fanning wasn't sure if it was a dig or not. He pretended to study the pattern on the shutters of a shop. Cully braked gently and curbed the car. He shut off the ignition and watched a couple walk by under an umbrella.

"Okay," said Fanning.

Cully took something from a pocket inside his jacket. An envelope that had been folded twice. He unfolded it, held it level, and began rummaging for something else.

"Hold that a sec," he said.

The envelope was light but there was something other than paper in it.

"Is that what I think it is?"

Cully took out a phone card from his jacket pocket.

"What do you think it is?"

Fanning felt suddenly vulnerable again. The city outside had been washed away by the rain running down the windows. Cully sighed as he leaned to his right and lifted the corner of the floor mat.

"I'm out of here," said Fanning. "I don't want anything to do with this,"

"Open the glove compartment there. There's a lid of a plastic box, give it to me."

Fanning pulled on the door release.

"Don't," snapped Cully. "You'll blow it all over the place."

"Look, I've got to go."

"Bail out you mean. Reality too much for you?"

"It's not that."

"You have no clue, do you."

Fanning watched Cully put the envelope on his knee just above where he had placed the plastic lid for the sandwich container. Cully continued to unfold the paper with one hand.

"It's research I'm doing, not getting involved in crime."

"You don't say. Ever done this? Coke?"

"A few times. It was ages ago."

He watched as Cully angled the paper up. Small grains of powder fell out. And then clumps. Cully tipped the paper back up, folded it, and put it back in its envelope.

"So what did you use then?"

"It was ages ago, I forget."

"A straw? Smoke it? In your arm?"

"Not in my arm, Christ, no. I was drunk. I don't remember."

"You have an answer for everything."

Cully had already began separating the powder into four separate clumps, and then into lines.

"I didn't say I was proud of it," said Fanning.

Cully tipped the phone card and handed the plastic lid to Fanning.

"Careful, okay? And close the door properly. It takes a minute. Can you spare the time?"

Fanning said nothing. The car rocked on its springs as Cully reached in to his trouser pocket. Some coins spilled between the door and the seat and he drew out a roll of bills. He peeled one off and dropped it into his lap, and replaced the roll. He rolled the banknote, tugged it tight at both ends, and then rolled it again.

"Okay," said Cully. "Are you ready?"

"No thanks. I'll stick with the self-preservation bit."

Cully looked sideways at him. His face seemed to crawl with the shadows from the rain-strewn windows.

"There you go again," he said. "Philosophy or whatever. Let me tell you something. Self-preservation takes brains. And for a bloke with a big brain, you're doing pretty crap."

A chill descended on Fanning. He fought to keep his arm from wavering.

"Yeah, well you should be nervous," Cully went on. "I don't think you realize it. You are lucky you went to that fight with Murphy. That's what I'm saying. It was luck, not brains."

Cully went back to tightening the rolled-up bill.

"Murphy was doing you no favours. He was playing you."

Fanning didn't care now if his anger showed.

"No he wasn't."

"Sure he was. You just didn't know it."

"Look, whatever it is about you and Murph–"

Cully made a sudden, short laugh.

"Me and Murph? What are you talking about?"

"All I'm hearing is 'you haven't a clue,' or 'this is reality,' or… 'you don't get it.' Like you guys are geniuses, and I'm a moron."

"That's you thinking," said Cully, suddenly serious.

"And for another thing, I didn't expect favours anyways. I pay Murph– I employ him!"

"Really? Well then. Tell me why you were paying a bloke who has fifty ways to skin you out of your money?"

"But that's just you saying that, isn't it."

Alarm alternated with pride in Fanning's mind in the quiet that followed. Light flickered off Cully's eyes as he glanced down at the lid.

"I know what you're saying," said Cully thoughtfully. He looked over the lines of powder. "But..."

"I know: 'But you don't get it.' I know."

"Shut up a minute and listen to me."

Said in the same calm tone, Cully's words had no sting to them now.

"Murph, your bosom pal there," Cully went on. "Now he's nothing but trouble, isn't he."

"You must have said that a dozen times the past day or two."

"That's how long it's taking to persuade you then, isn't it. Struts about, cock of the walk. But what's he got? Nuffink."

"Nuffink. That's more like it."

"Thought that'd get your attention. Look, he owes all over. Can't even cover his habit, can he. The only way he got in was his uncle, kind of adopted him I heard. You don't know this. His uncle was big, even inside. Inside, like...?"

"Jail?"

"Prison, you can call it. Right. Fifteen years they gave him -- not here, over in England. Just another Paddy on the game there. He was greedy, to be honest. And lazy. Thought he knew everything. Didn't do his homework on silent alarms."

"What is his name, the uncle?"

"I'm not telling you, am I. But what I am saying is, everybody knows everybody. Here, there. People aren't stupid, are they. But his uncle isn't around anymore. He got the big C there last year, in the lungs. So last year, he goes to meet his maker. R.I.P."

"I think I read something about it, wasn't he–"

"–it doesn't matter, I said."

Cully placed the fat end of the rolled-up bill in his nostril.

"I'd like to hear Murph's version of this sometime."

"Oi," said Cully. "Can't you see I'm busy here?"

Chapter 39

FANNING TRIED TO SEE THROUGH the teeming windows.

With his index finger over the other nostril, Cully snorted one line, and then a second. He sat back and shook his head, and he began to slowly squeeze his nostrils between his thumb and his forefinger.

"Once in a blue moon," he said then. "I only accept donations."

He drew in his breath, closed his eyes and let it out again. His eyes popped open.

"Go ahead," he said," it's proper order, it is, yes."

He held out the rolled-up note.

"Now we're talking," he said. "Cock-a-doodle-doo."

Before he knew it, Fanning was taking the lid from Cully.

"Just a sampler," Cully said.

Fanning's arm rested on the door again, his hand already anticipating the feel of the door release. Cully licked his lips and smiled. Fanning realized it was the first time he'd ever seen him smile.

"See," he said. "Puts you back in the game."

"You're used to it."

Cully's eyes opened wide and then almost shut.

"Oh, I get it. I get it now. You're sure you're going to be a junkie now. Poof! One go and you're doomed, right?"

"I don't want to get into it."

"Of course you don't. You're Mister Respectable. You're going to do what you're told. Follow the rules and all that. No wonder you want to make up stuff about criminals and all that."

When Cully held out the lid, Fanning's hands moved reflexively. Cully said something about holding it this way. The anger roiled in him. The end of the roll felt like a roach. Raising it with his left hand, he poked his nose with it, twice. Then it was pushing against his nostril, inside. His hands worked on. The lid was close enough to his nose for a strong scent from the plastic. He couldn't remember having decided anything.

He let his head back. He felt the urge to sneeze, but it passed quickly. It was followed immediately by a dull burn that reminded him of a head cold. The warmth spread under his eyes.

"Nothing," he said to Cully. "It did nothing."

Cully hawked, rolled down the window and spat out. He rolled the window back up slowly, as though listening for something. Fanning's heart began to speed up.

"All I hear is 'you don't know this' and 'you're clued out.'"

"You said that already."

"You were actually listening to me? You know how hard writing is?"

"Pencil and paper. It can't be that hard."

"It's damned hard. It's the hardest thing. Nobody knows that."

"Nobody...?"

"And I'm sick to death of people who..."

Fanning stopped. He glanced at Cully and saw that he seemed to be concentrating on something.

"I'm talking a lot, aren't I."

Cully nodded. Whatever he was interested in seemed to be in front of the speedometer.

"You do understand that, right? What I said about writing, being a writer?"

"What did you say about it?"

"I'm saying it's tougher than anything. It takes it out of you like you wouldn't believe. No-one gets it. No-one."

Cully looked over.

"Yeah they do."

"No they don't," Fanning said. "No way. No how."

"Shut up," said Cully.

"Oh, it's a one-way street, is it? You say whatever you want – nothing most of the time, for Christ's sake and I get told to shut up?"

"You're yelling," said Cully. "And I don't like it. The yelling. So I'm telling you again, shut it."

"'Shut it.' Who says 'shut it' here in Dublin, in Ireland? You're English, you're Irish. You're this, you're that. But you tell me nothing. What the hell use is that?"

Cully was staring at him.

"You're losing it," he said. "Calm down."

"How often do you do this, snorting–"

"None of your business. And shut up."

"You're undercover," Fanning said. "That's it. Now I get it. You're trying to entrap me. That's what's going on."

"Listen to yourself," said Cully. "Do you know how paranoid you sound?"

"Admit it, come on."

Cully shook his head. He began feeling around in his pocket for something.

"See," said Fanning. "Don't think I'm blind, right? Or stupid. Treating me like some kind of child, like an iijit. You don't know me – nobody knows me, what I do. What I can do."

"Really."

"There you go again!"

"What?"

"Discounting, that's what."

"Discount?"

"Fobbing me off. Like…"

"Who?"

"A guy called Breen."

"I don't know any Breen."

Fanning realized that he was beginning to sweat. Things were getting stranger, like when he'd had the flu or a fever. He felt almost painfully alert to everything now. He could feel the blood going around in his body. He could hear the sound of Cully rubbing his eyelids.

He stared at the islands of light in the deserted street ahead. Flashes of images came to him, a satellite image zooming down to nighttime Dublin, hovering over the black Liffey waters nearby, over the flat where his wife and child were turning over in their sleep.

"You're off your trolley," Cully said. "Look at you, listen to you."

Fanning felt his chest was rising up through his throat. He had to go, had to. He imagined himself sprinting away along the wet pavements all the way to Hope or some place and then back.

Cully was turning a lighter over in his hand. He lifted a joint to his lips then and lighted it. The end of the paper sparked as he drew hard once, paused, and drew again.

"You smoke dope too?"

Cully ignored him, taking two more long pulls. Then he held his breath and passed the joint over.

"This will calm you down, Superman."

"I am calm."

Cully coughed but kept scanning the mirrors.

"So what's next?" Fanning asked.

"What's next?"

"Yeah, what's next?"

"We're ditching this car is what."

"But what then?"

"So far as I know you're going home to your missus," Cully murmured. "And I'm off about my business."

"That's it?"

"Was that you a minute ago, saying you had to go home right now?"

"I know. But I've got my second wind."

He passed the joint back to Cully and watched the eddies of smoke that he released every few moments rising and then sliding toward the window.

"How long does it last?"

"What last?"

"The coke."

Fanning reached out, his sleeve held by his fingers, to wipe condensation from the windscreen. The rain had stopped, for now, at least.

"You get your fifteen minutes of being God," said Cully. "That enough for you?"

Fanning saw a moving shadow down the street. Somebody walking.

"And you crash afterwards. Right?"

"Not right away."

The person walking was a man. He was carrying a pack-sack on his shoulder. Fanning looked over at Cully. There was something disappointing in seeing Cully trying to get the last toke, taking short stabs at it.

The man walking sidestepped the brimming puddles, but then he missed one. Fanning sniggered.

"What's so funny?"

"Nothing. I was just thinking."

"Better that then yelling your head off," said Cully, rolling down the window and blowing out a volley of smoke.

The man stopped and drew out a map. He angled it, held it up, turned to the light to read it. Fanning knew by Cully's still-ness that Cully too was watching him.

The man lowered the map and turned to face the end of the street. Then he turned back and resumed walking.

"Talking to himself," Fanning murmured. "Must be local."

Within a few steps the man had noticed them. His gait slowed slightly and he pulled the pack tighter on his shoulder. How amazing to be able to read a person's mind by how they walk Fanning thought. How easy it was now.

Every minute movement was apparent to Fanning now: steps taking him away from the curb toward the wall the closer he got to the car. The hand now holding the strap of the pack-sack tighter, the head apparently turned away but the lateral vision locked on the car. He heard the footsteps now, saw the white lines on his runners against the wet, glistening pavement.

The man slowed and readjusted the strap.

"What the hell," Cully murmured.

The man was almost stopped now, uncertain.

Fanning tried to see into the shadows on the man's face. The man sniffed the air and nodded appreciatively.

"Good," he said. "Is good."

Fanning's mind teemed with detail: a foreign accent, twenty or twenty-one; pale with an excuse for a goatee; a smell of saturated clothes, cigarettes.

"Ah, you can maybe give...?"

The man mimicked a quick pull on a joint.

"No much," he added. "Just one, man?"

"Where are you from?"

"From Poland."

"Poland."

"Yeah man. Is like Ireland, you know? The people, nice. Cool, you know?"

"You're from Poland, and you're looking for...?"

"Fun, man. Good times. This I hear, Dublin is good times. People they are fun."

"Fun? You're looking for fun?"

The man made a self-deprecatory smile.

"No much English. Fun is, cool, you know? Good times."

Again he raised his two fingers to his lips.

"How do you know we're not the Guards?"

"The Guards? I don't understand."

"Guards. Police. Politzei?"

"Ah. Politzei is German. Yes. I go Germany but no like. Some Germans people cool, nice, but not all. No, no."

"Pretty high standards you have, haven't you?"

The smell of the man's breath seemed to be everywhere now.

"Uh-uh, no understand. Sorry? Is big problem, this English,

I am–"

"So you come here and you wander around the place look-ing to score?"

"Shut up," said Cully, "just leave him."

He turned the key. The engine didn't catch at first.

The man shrugged, and made another cautious smile and he nodded. Now the engine caught. Fanning's chest felt like it was ready to explode. He tugged hard on the door release.

"What the hell are you doing," Cully said. "Shut the door."

"Did you hear him? Did you?"

"You're freaking out over nothing. Close the goddamned door."

"Like I'm some kind of dealer? Hey! I live here, you under-stand? This is my city? Irish? Dublin? You getting any of what I'm saying here?"

The man had stepped back from the curb. Fanning got out slowly. He left the door ajar, felt the slight give of the wet curb-stone underfoot. The night air worked around his neck and his chest.

The man was walking away sideways, back to the wall. He was about to run. Fanning rummaged in his pocket.

"Here," he said. "Wait, I've got some. Here."

Watching the hesitation showing on the man's face, Fanning began to marvel at how clear everything had become. Small beads of rain on the car bumper, the scuffing of the man's runners as he made a tentative step toward him, the dank oily stink of the Liffey nearby. Cully's leaning and stretching across the passenger seat to pull the door closed again. The sickly yellow light.

"You're on your own," Cully called out before tugging the door closed.

"Is problem?" said the Polish man.

The hand out already, Fanning registered, the fingers almost twitching in anticipation of a joint.

"No," said Fanning. "No problem. No problem in the wide world."

He took his hand out of his pocket and held it out, still clenched. He watched the man's changing expression, how he looked back from the fist to Fanning's face. Fanning opened his hand and spread his fingers and he smiled.

"There's your fun," he said. "Do you like it?"

The young man said something in Polish, and he glared at him.

"You too," said Fanning. He began to laugh. It felt like he hadn't laughed for years.

"Is joke?"

Fanning nodded. He felt twice his normal height. The laughter seemed to have let all the pressure out of his chest. He eyed the Opel's exhaust hanging in the air.

"Asshole," Fanning heard from the young man as he ran.

Then he was standing back, watching the Pole hobbling on and trying to flex his knee where Fanning's kick had landed. Again it astonished Fanning how clear and sharp and predictable everything was. He could not remember running after the Pole, much less kicking him.

"Is that cool now? Man?"

The Pole stopped and glanced at the lights of the Opel getting smaller. He made a feint in that direction and then he ran.

Fanning watched and smiled. Then he turned to watch the car's progress away into the distance. Even from here he could hear every detail of the car's tread as it rolled and hissed over the pavement. Amazing.

"Fack you! Facking Irish asshole!"

The Pole had slowed. He was massaging his knee now as he walked, his packsack sliding awkwardly off his shoulder.

Fanning pretended to make a dash toward him and as soon as the Pole saw him on the move he let go of his knee and began to move.

Fanning slowed to a walk. He looked at his watch. Ten minutes to get the last bus. He heard the sound of the runner tripping and looked up to see the Pole crashing hard on the footpath. He even heard the breath go out of him, the scratching of fabric and shoes as the Pole skidded along the flagstones.

"Idiot," he muttered. "Serves you right."

Chapter 40

THE MAN WAS BREATHING HARD and pushing himself up when Fanning caught up to him.

"That feel cool? Good times now?"

Panting, the man got one knee on the pavement under himself. He grimaced and muttered as he tried to examine the torn flesh on his hand.

"Did you like that, did you?"

The Pole grabbed awkwardly at his packsack. He wouldn't look up at Fanning.

Fanning's kick landed under the side of the man's ribs.

"Who told you that you could go around calling people names?"

"No," the man wheezed.

"Liar! I heard you calling me names. You know what a liar is, do you?"

The man was trying to get up now, scuttling sideways toward the wall. Fanning stepped around him and the packsack came up.

Fanning's kick hit something hard in the packsack.

"Who's an asshole now?"

The Pole reached the wall. He placed his back against it, but stayed in a crouch.

"No, man," he said. "Is no problem! No say nothing. Is

okay! Okay? Okay, man?"

Fanning grabbed the packsack and yanked on it. The Pole spun until he was sitting on the pavement. Fanning jerked it harder and soon the man was sprawled and scudding across the pavement.

Fanning let go. His next kick reached under the armpit. The man let go of the bag and pulled up his knees. His feet kept moving, trying to get traction to spin him away.

"It's not okay," said Fanning, and he stood back and watched the Pole get to a sitting position. "Got that message? You don't come here, to my country, insulting people. You get that? Have you?"

Then Fanning felt suddenly weary. Something was dropping out of him, and he slouched. The Pole was watching him through clenched eyelids, drawing in harsh breaths through his teeth. Fanning nodded at him.

"Now," said Fanning. "It's okay now."

He took a step toward him. The Polish man curled himself up tighter and put his head down between his knees.

It was no use, Fanning decided. He could never explain to this guy that he wasn't really mad at him. But he wasn't pretending either, was he. This guy deserved a bit of a hiding. So what if he was a foreigner, or just plain thick in the head. A doper, an addict even, with a circus going on in his head.

"You're lucky it's me," he said. "I'm telling you. But you had this coming to you. You learned your lesson and you go back home. Poland."

"Polska," said the man, quietly.

"Irish people," said Fanning. "We're nice, you know. But you don't want to insult them. Us I mean."

The Pole tilted his head up and nodded.

"Right? You understand?"

"Yes. Nice. Irish peoples nice. I say sorry, yes? Okay?"

"Sorry is good. Good, you're getting the idea."

"Okay, good."

"Stop saying okay, for Christ's sake."

"Okay, yes. Peoples nice."

Fanning looked up and down the street. The hum and the whisper of the city around him was barely audible. Not a trace of Cully and his stolen car. The whole centre of the city, emptied by the rain: deserted. A wave of despondency washed over him.

The sounds of the packsack being dragged across the pavement brought Fanning back. The Pole stayed in his crouch still watching him wearily. Slowly he put the strap over his shoulder.

"Don't forget now," said Fanning.

"Is good, yes. Peoples nice. Okay?"

Fanning rolled his eyes. This heaviness wasn't going away. He closed his eyes. He could hear the blood coursing around his head.

Running footsteps made him open his eyes again.

"Irish Fack," the Pole shouted. "Fack Irish, asshole. Fack."

Fanning watched as the man slowed and turned.

"Fack you!"

So Polish people use the middle finger, Fanning reflected.

"Facking Irish asshole!"

And the Italian arm. Interesting. No, not interesting.

Fanning made a lunge, and pretended to run after him. The shouting stopped and the Pole began to run again. Fanning slowed after a couple of steps. The Polish guy wasn't hobbling now, was he? It had all been an act.

But wasn't he acting too?

That thought struck him with great force, its clarity roaring in through him: he had been acting. Acting for...? For Cully, to show he knew a thing or two about how to act on the street? Or that he wasn't just a feeble voyeur trying to write about things he knew nothing about?

He'd miss the last bus if he didn't get a move on.

He began walking again, and soon broke into a slow jog. Ahead of him the Pole looked over his shoulder. Fanning waited for a yell, but instead saw the packsack go up as his leg went out from under him. The Polish man fell sideways as his. There was a shout or a yelp and then he was on the roadway. A dark sprawling mass clear against the sheen of the street lamp.

"Christ," said Fanning. "Not again. What a complete idiot you are."

He didn't slow his jog, but he kept his eyes on the Pole. This time there were no limbs coming out slowly for the man to pick himself up. Fanning passed a drain, his ears filling for a few moments with the sound of distant underground gurgling. So this is coke, he thought. You notice everything, you've got no obstacles, everything is clear, and everything fits. Fits?! Here he was actually jogging, something he hadn't done for years. Maybe he could even jog home.

"Get up," he called out as he closed on the Pole. "Get up you gobshite, and buy yourself some new shoes."

The stillness of the figure on the pavement, his splayed legs seeming to draw light from the street lamps.

"Here I come, you better get up, you iijit."

Fanning slowed to a walk, his breath steaming now after this short run. He saw the eyelids flutter and a frown come to the man on the ground.

"Get up and go home," he said. "You're too stupid to be out, you can barely stay on your feet. And buy yourself some shoes, you thick, so you don't be falling over."

It was Polish words he was hearing now, groaning and then tense whispers.

"You hit your head on the road. Get up. And go home."

The man's arm moved and he leaned on one elbow and felt at his face with his hand.

Fanning put out his hand.

"Come up," he said. "You're such an idiot."

But the man flinched. He gave Fanning a look of loathing and bewilderment and then continued to examine his hand.

"Go home and wash that," Fanning said. "That's what you have to do, do you understand me? Wash?"

The man reached awkwardly into his jacket, sighing. Fanning listened to the city around him again, the wet murmur of the traffic and the empty dripping hush of the rain. Anyone with brains was at home in bed or in front of a television.

He glanced down again.

"Look, if it's any consolation, I'm soaked too. Now are you happy?"

The man's movements were slow and he was breathing hard. He muttered as he fumbled. Fanning looked up into the night sky bronzed by the city lights. He felt neutral now, not ashamed of what he had done. This surprised him a little. He and this fellow were here: circumstances were the way they were; it rained on everyone equally, just like Beckett wrote in that poem. He tried to see individual raindrops coming down through the light.

"You haven't a clue what I'm saying, have you," he said to the Pole.

He caught only a hint of the sudden movement below. The Pole grunted and said something as he lashed out. Fanning was late stepping back. Whatever it was, it was hard, and it had run across his shin. Then he saw the reflected light on the knife as the man lunged again.

"You bastard," Fanning said quietly.

He kicked at the arm and connected, drawing a muffled yell. There was a burning pain in his calf now. He didn't want to think about what it might be. His second kick got under the man's arm and hit something solid. The man drew his legs up and tried to put his arms over his face. He shuttered as Fanning kicked him again but he said nothing.

Fanning's breath came out in fast, separate clouds as he panted and cursed. He paused, stepped back, and looked down at his feet. Turning his leg toward the lamplight he saw the stain and the cut across the denim.

"Look what you did," he said. "You lousy bastard. Look it!"

He wondered why it didn't hurt more, but he didn't want to lift the end of his trousers to look. The headlights that turned onto the street drew his gaze up. His whole chest felt unbearably tight and hot, his throat too tight to breathe or to talk. The car cruised down slowly toward him, too slowly. He shielded his eyes and squinted through the glare. There was no Garda sign on the roof anyway. He looked back down at the Pole, who was now propping himself up on one elbow and rubbing at his mouth.

The Pole said something thickly and he spat, and groaned softly and began touching his mouth.

The car had stopped. The driver stepped out slowly, left the door open, and began to make his way over.

Fanning began to walk away, ignoring the feeling in his leg but he knew the voice calling out.

Cully stood next to the man on the ground.

"He took out a knife. A knife?"

"What? On you?"

"My leg, I've got to go."

"Wait– he knifed you, this bloke?"

A gloomy disgust had swept out of nowhere and taken hold of him. He was exhausted.

"You're serious?" he heard Cully say. "Talk to me. He knifed you?"

Fanning nodded. Before he turned away he saw Cully kick out sideways. The Pole's head jerked back and he rolled once. The sound came to Fanning late, and it sickened him. Cully had leaned over and was feeling around on the pavement for something. He kicked something metallic on the wet roadway until it stopped in a pool of water.

"Leave him," Fanning shouted.

Cully raised his arms and he began kicking again, alternating his feet.

"He's not moving," Fanning yelled. "Leave him alone."

His whole body ached, as he made his way back.

"Stop," he said. "Enough, this is just stupid."

Cully was stomping with his heel now. Slowly and selectively. Fanning hesitated, pushing his fingers further into his ears.

"Stop it!" he yelled.

Cully lowered his arms and he stepped back.

"I'm getting out of here," Fanning said. "You should too."

"Why are you covering your bloody ears?"

"There's no need for this, I gave him a going-over."

"A going-over? You?"

"We should never have come down here."

Cully's face twisted up. He stepped over to Fanning quickly.

"He knifes you, and you're apologizing?"

"There's no need to do any more."

"You're shaky, aren't you?"

"It's the coke."

"Shaking like a leaf, you are," said Cully and looked down at the Pole.

"I'm going to phone for an ambulance," Fanning said.

"An ambulance? You can walk, can't you? As far as the car?"

"For him, he's not–"

"He's not supposed to bloody move," Cully said. "What do you think this is?"

"He's unconscious, he's hurt."

"I should bloody hope so! A bloke tries to do for you, some foreigner here, and you want to tuck the bastard into bed or something?"

Cully took a deep breath and tugged at his jacket. Fanning felt the chill now. And his face and eyes were getting the feeling he remembered from when being a child with that fainting thing. There was something pasty and sour at the back of his throat. The lights of the car swelled and receded. It seemed that Cully was speaking from a long way away.

"You're going to pass out," he heard Cully say from a long way away.

He did not want to look again at the strange wetness around the man's head. It gave off a dull gleam that was different from the rain.

"I've got to go home," he said.

Said it? Or thought it?

He was aware of moving, of awkward steps, and the sound of soles scuffing and scraping under him.

"Come back," he heard Cully shout. "Don't be stupid, get

back here! I'll drive you."

No: he was jogging now, and it was effortless and smooth. He heard Cully shouting again, and the sound of tires and revving.

But how fast he could run, and how easily. He turned onto the quays. Traffic, sounds, and even a few people. He stopped and looked back for headlights coming around after him. Everything was still amplified, sharp, engrossing. A flurry of footsteps erupted nearby, and he pressed into a doorway. The racket was two girls half-running and half-staggering, their heels dragging and clattering on the roadway, their boyfriends pulling on their arms, coaxing them on.

The normality of it flooded him with relief.

He waited a few moments, and then made his way toward the lights and crowds of the city centre.

Chapter 41

FOR A MOMENT, Fanning didn't know if he was still in the dream. It was he himself who had shouted.

"God almighty!"

That was Bríd's voice.

"What was that? Was it you, Dermot?"

He couldn't straighten up. He was stiff everywhere. He heard Bríd's slippers sliding on the floor.

"Jesus," she whispered. "That was you yelling?"

"Sorry."

His arm was asleep. The chair back had dug into his shoulder and lodged there.

"What are you doing out here?"

"I must have fallen asleep. I got home late – don't. No, no light. Please."

She stood in front of him, waiting. He began to rub at his face.

"You're in a fierce state. Did you go overboard on the drink?"

The reproach and suspicion in her voice didn't bother him now.

"I'm just exhausted. I got home, sat down for a think, and..."

"Well there's a can of something there by the side of your chair."

He raised his back slowly from the chair.

"Beer," he said. "Right. I didn't even get to it then."

"And your phone," she said, stooping. She picked it up with two fingers and held it out. "It's soaked."

"It'll be okay in the morning."

He knew she was holding back questions. The pins and needles were like fire down his arm.

"There's a smell of something. Petrol. Do you smell it?"

"Right, yes. Well, I helped a fella push his car off the road there. Broken down."

Her tone changed again.

"You got soaked, I bet."

He shook his head. He was pretty certain now that the knot in his shoulders would morph into a headache.

"Dermot. Dermot?"

"I'm here."

"Are you okay?"

"I'm half asleep. That's all."

"But is everything okay? That's what I mean."

"Everything's okay," he said. "Yes."

"Whyn't you come to bed when you got home?"

"Ah, you know."

"Do I? I thought I was getting the come-hither earlier on."

"I know you need your sleep," he tried. "I didn't want to wake you. Was Aisling wandering around in the night?"

"No. Not yet. If she slept through that, she'll stay asleep. Jesus, Dermot. I only heard you like that once, remember after the accident?"

"Sorry," he said.

She took a step toward the chest of drawers and leaned against it. He could still feel her battle between annoyance and worry.

"Did anyone phone?" he asked.

"What, in the middle of the night, you mean?"

"After I left."

"Who were you expecting?"

"No-one, actually."

"Colm Breen, maybe?"

"Not funny, Bríd. Not this hour of the night."

"Or that Guard you were supposed to talk to?"

He started in the chair.

"What Guard?"

She folded her arms.

"Oh whatever his name is. How would I remember? You said you were going to get a meeting with him. The research thing. Oh, what's his name! Molloy? No – Malone. You pointed out his name in the paper last month. Him."

He sat back slowly.

"That never panned out," he said. "No."

He straightened his back, and then arched it as far as it would go, and sat forward in the chair.

"Jesus, Dermot! Your trousers! What happened?"

"I know."

"They're wrecked, so they are! And the dirt? My God."

The light hurt his eyes.

"That's not just muck and dirt, Dermot. Tell me what happened?"

His throat felt blocked. A sharp pain ran down the middle of his chest.

"Stupid stuff," he managed to say. "I was out in some fields. Barbed wire. Dark of course, and didn't see it. Stupid. Embarrassing."

She knelt by his leg.

"Don't mind embarrassing," she said, her voice now thick with concern. "Think tetanus."

"It's not that bad."

"Well what the hell were you doing out in some field in the middle of the night, and it pouring rain, do you mind me asking?"

"You don't have to believe me," he said. "It's okay."

"Oh don't try that on me," she said. "Let me see it, you have a cut there."

He drew back in the chair.

"I'll take care of it," he said evenly. "It's okay. Thanks."

She looked up sharply.

"How could it be okay? It's more than a scrape. What on earth were you at?"

"Nothing, Bríd. Nothing."

Her expression was all too familiar to him now, coming from a place between exasperation and fright.

"If I wasn't so knackered coming home, I'd have changed, and you wouldn't be giving me the third degree. I didn't plan to fall asleep, did I?"

"Can't you accept that I am worried? What's so hard about that?"

He was almost glad that his anger had made him alert now.

"Bríd. For the love of… Give over a minute, will you? We're adults, okay?"

"What does that mean? Or should I ask?"

"It means you know the score. I know the score. When did you start to be my mother, or something?"

"Christ, that's rich. Your mother?"

"Remember? Remember what we were?"

"You're still drunk. Or something."

He grasped her forearm, and began to massage it.

"Remember what we said, what we swore to one another? How we wouldn't end up like, well, my parents? The whole married thing? We'll live the way we want, not in some prison full of clichés and stupid habits and all that?"

"Dermot. Listen. This is basic."

"That's what I'm saying! We don't give up who we are. We do our thing– you do yours, I do mine. We don't, you know, do surveillance on one another."

"This is beginning to sound like 'open marriage' stuff, and you know what I think about that. I'm half-expecting to hear 'bourgeois' next. Or 'repressive' or the like."

"Really," he said, and he felt his mood lurch abruptly. Something stung his eyes. He remembered the humiliations of childhood, the sharp resentments that so easily went to tears.

"It's fine and well to talk about it," Bríd murmured.

"But come on – things change."

"I know," he hissed. "I know, love! If anyone knows, I do. Trust me, okay?"

She looked down to where he had stopped massaging. When she spoke again, her voice was barely more than a whisper.

"Jesus, Dermot, I mean…"

She was close to tears herself, he saw.

"Jesus Dermot what?"

"I can't believe," she began, pausing to catch a breath. "I can't believe we're sitting here this hour of the night – of the morning."

She looked up at him. He saw the trouble he had caused. He coaxed her toward him and he drew back strands of her hair from in front of her eyes.

"It's okay," he said. "Really. We're fine. We are."

The nape of her neck was sweaty.

"You're programmed to worry," he said to her. "You have to stop sometime."

"You've got so much, Dermot," she said, and snuggled in tighter. "So much already."

He said nothing.

"But you can't be doing this," she went on, with a soft urgency. "It's dangerous."

She paused, and he sensed she was going to lay a big one on him now.

"Dermot? You're thirty-eight. It matters."

Before he could say anything, she wiggled and began in a stronger voice.

"Listen, love – remember the one you were going to do, the children of The Rising? 1916?"

He nodded.

"That would be so good," she whispered. "I've been thinking about it more and more. So good. Anyone I talk to thinks it's brilliant."

He winced. By anyone, she meant fellow teachers. The kiss of death.

"Can you get that going again?" she asked.

"I suppose," he said. He was certain that he had told her there was zero money for children's film. Zero.

"And you could leave this crime thing."

He stopped stroking her neck. She turned to him.

"Dermot?"

"I'm right here."

"I hate to see you frustrated, love. I just hate it. All that talent, running up against a brick wall. But this crime thing, it can't be good. I mean...?"

Her words trailed off. She rested against him again.

"I'm not trying to upset you," she said then. "I swear. There's no-one like you, no-one in Dublin – in Ireland – no-one who knows things like you do. The gifts you have. The insight."

The weariness had come over him in a matter of moments, pressing him deeper into the chair. He felt his thoughts sink too, under some other gravity he knew he couldn't resist.

"It's for someone else now, Dermot. Someone else's racket, this crime stuff. This gang stuff."

"It's what people want," he said.

"Oh," she said. "That's not like you one bit, for God's sake. Remember, 'don't follow the herd'? And all the killing and the dugs, and all, I mean why make it worse?"

"Make it worse?"

"You know. Come on. Make it look cool. Gangsta rap."

"Dublin," he said. "Dublin, Bríd."

"But Dublin's gone," she said. "You said so yourself, how everything's gone inside out. How it could be anyplace now."

She shook him gently once.

"It's true, love. Unfortunately."

Fanning kept his gaze on the base of the lampshade by the door. This was one of those moments, he knew, but he cared nothing about it. All he knew was that something was coming loose, and that he felt things falling away.

He heard Bríd say something that included Breen's name.

"It's no trouble," she said. "I would actually like to talk to him. I mean, he knows me."

"What," said Fanning. "You're not serious, are you."

"Breen?" she retorted. "What's it to him? If he can't do it, he knows people who can. It should be no big deal for him to do that."

"No," he said.

"If you put your foot down with him, he'll respect that, Dermot."

Cully kicking down with his heel, like a grotesque Riverdance move, again and again. The Polish guy unmoving. That scraping sound as his scalp was ground and dragged along the cement of the footpath with each kick. And Cully shifting his stance to stamp again, like he was trying to put out a fire.

Bríd sat up, turned, looked at him. She reached out awkwardly for his chest.

"I can hear your heart hammering," she said. "All the way down to your knees!"

She inclined her face closer to his, as though to break his gaze on the lamp.

There was a spike in his throat, swelling fast.

She grabbed his shoulders.

"God," she said. Without looking, he knew there was panic in her face now.

"Are you going to be sick again?"

Chapter 42

MINOGUE LOOKED AT HIS WATCH again, and then glanced across at Wall. Even Wall was fading. Downstairs in the station, there was still plenty of activity. He wondered if the place ever grew quiet.

He sat back, and let his eyes wander up to the clock. Ten minutes off, its hands were almost 180 degrees now: 1:40 a.m.

"What a night," Wall murmured, and sat back too, stretching his fingers over the keyboard.

"Go on, Ciaran. I'll finish up."

"You're not going to do it all tonight, are you."

Minogue closed the folder on copies of the preliminary charges for Twomey and Matthews, and he slid it under the one holding the statements from the girls. Twomey, the more belligerent one, had been crying when they brought him down. Matthews was a horse of a different colour, going off quietly enough, a mixture of resignation and disgust on his face.

"God no, Ciaran. Excuse me."

"Ah don't worry. Like I say, it's one way of praying."

Minogue was sourly proud of how he held his own against a surge of annoyance at Wall's condescension.

He saved his work and closed the database.

"There's no proper reason we can't go to our homes now," he said to Wall. "As long as we're let in at this hour, I suppose."

Wall smiled.

mobile, but decided quickly not to. If he knew Malone, this was another episode of a fiercely conscientious copper just slamming the door. It could take a few hours, or even days. Minogue remembered that Malone's C.O. was understanding. But walkouts like this were what could surface during the interviews for Sergeant, and Malone knew it.

"You know, Matt, I actually don't mind," said Wall. "I sort of let on."

Minogue turned to him again.

"Which now, Ciaran?"

"Well I'm not going to repeat it."

Minogue was beyond confused now. Wall's sympathetic smile returned.

"What you said there. Whatever you read there, it must have gotten your goat something wicked, is all I can say to that."

Had he been cursing out loud? He was more tired than he knew then.

"It's a sign, I suppose," he said to Wall. "Hit the hay."

Wall folded his arms.

"So we'll see what a night in custody does to their recall that night," he said. "And a search of their effects at home?"

"Exactly," said Minogue.

"And track any extra money they have, or had. No doubt it'd be spent already anyway."

Minogue nodded. He was finding the drawer for the folders ornery. Wall shuffled over.

"There's a trick to it," he said, and jiggled it. "A Hail Mary does it."

This only speeded up Minogue's departure. He had been thinking of the tin of Gosser beer in the fridge at home.

Wall was on the stairs behind him.

"I had been meaning to ask you about something," he said. "But of course, it'd probably be, you know. Off limits?"

"Give it a go anyway."

"Concerning a friend of yours, a colleague."

Minogue stopped on the landing.

"Jim Kilmartin," said Wall.

"Friend," said Minogue. "Both."

"Am I stepping on...?"

For a reason that made no sense, Minogue shook his head.

"Good. We've been putting out feelers to him. Now you'd hardly know that. But we have."

"Who has?"

"NightWatch. Have you heard of us?"

A small hint flared but disappeared into the pit of Minogue's tired brain.

"Started up there a couple of years ago. We decided to go formal. Out of the closet as they say."

"You're saying Jim is gay?"

Wall made a teacher's laugh.

"Oh no, no, no. That's a good one. I must remember that one."

Minogue's anger was rising.

"Ciaran, I have no clue what you're talking about here now. But you have me jittery. What gives?"

Wall turned serious. He gave Minogue a searching look.

"Jim's predicament," he said. "What happened that night."

Minogue gave him a hard look. Did every damned Guard in Ireland consider it his business to comment on Kilmartin's folly?

"NightWatch," he grunted. "Is that like Road Watch, the traffic reports and all?"

"In a sense, Matt, in a sense. It is to guide a traveller home safely."

"What roads would they be, I wonder."

Wall hesitated, but Minogue knew he was committed to his message.

"Heaven, basically. Same place we all want to end up."

Minogue examined Wall's face.

"The name is from Holy Week," said Wall. "Kind of good timing I suppose, there with Good Friday just behind us."

Minogue's thoughts went to Rachel Tynan. Had she waited until after Good Friday, to leave at Easter instead, a wish for her husband's future that he might bear her death better? But she was never a "religious" person, was she? He remembered the paintings around the church at Calary, the happy racket from the birds throughout the ceremony, the highland bogs and the skies. The right type of holiness, damn it all, the only type worth having.

"Remember Gethsemane?" Wall asked gently. "The apostles falling asleep, not one of them to keep watch with Him? That's what started it. Only Guards know what Guards go through, Matt. That's a given. Don't you think?"

Kilmartin and his Half Three Divils that kept him awake, haunting him with what could have been, should have been. The nights in the hospital, the long awkward frame of James Kilmartin asleep on cushions by his wife's bed.

"The dark night of the soul," Minogue muttered.

Wall's eyes lit up, and his smile returned.

"Exactly. I knew you'd be the sort of a man that'd get it."

Minogue watched a sleepy Garda pass them in the hall on the way to the toilet. He looked at Wall.

"We might have a word about it tomorrow then?" Wall whispered.

"It's tomorrow already, Ciaran," was all he could come up with.

Chapter 43

IT HAD BEEN SOME TIME since he had seen Bríd crying. He could not remember her crying from pain, ever, even when Aisling was born. He watched her head moving slowly from side to side, her fingers spread through her hair while she rested her elbows on her knees.

"Bríd," he tried again. Her arm shot out, the hand upraised, and then slowly returned to the side of her head. A coldness was coming through him.

"I'll fix it," he said. "I will."

This time she said nothing. The wheezes he had heard from her drawing her breath began to grow softer.

"It's finished," he said. "That's a promise. It's just..."

"Just what," she said, but did not raise her head. "It's always 'just this' and 'just that.'"

"You'll see it happen. You will."

She sniffed and rubbed at her nose, and threw her head back, pushing her hair out of her face. Her face was so different, he thought.

"It's too much," she whispered. "I can't do it. I can't."

"You know I wouldn't do anything to let you down, or Aisling down."

"Dermot," she said, gathering herself, and dabbing at her nostrils while she looked at the floor. "Dermot. It's three o'clock in the morning. It can't possibly make sense, this thing."

"You head back to bed," he said. "I'll kip here. That way I won't disturb you."

He shivered, and then grabbed his knee tight to guard against his hand trembling. Bríd seemed to be hypnotized by whatever she was staring at.

"A bit of daylight isn't going to fix this," she murmured.

"Everything looks weird at night," he said. "Come on, I'll get you to bed."

She shook her head.

"I can feel it, you know," she said. "What you don't tell me. It's like a big thing here now. Like a big shadow."

"Bríd. I have no secrets from you."

She nodded now, as though she agreed. In the seconds that passed, he began to sense she did not.

"You might believe that yourself," she said, quietly. "That's what I have to think."

She glanced up at him.

"Otherwise, where are we?"

He grasped his knee tighter.

"I have enough," he said. "Enough research, I mean. It's finished. No more. Tonight was the last of it."

She was very still, but he could hear her raspy breathing. She began to get up. The ringing shattered the quiet. He put his hand over the mobile.

Bríd frowned and sat back on her heels. He pushed at the power and held, but one more ring escaped.

"You're shaking," he heard her say.

"I didn't know I left it on. Sorry."

"Look at you, Dermot. What's going on?"

"It woke me up, gave me a fright, love. That's all, I wasn't expecting it."

She stepped back, and stared at him. A teacher move, he knew, and anger joined his panic.

"What," he said. "Will you stop with the, the nanny treatment here? Jesus, this isn't Abu Graib or somewhere, is it?"

"Something's wrong, I know it."

"I'm half-asleep, for Christ's sake, Bríd. Give me a bit of

space here, will you?"

"This weekend, Dermot. This weekend, we have to talk."

"What does that mean? We talk every day. We're talking now."

"Tell me what's gone wrong."

"Nothing! Nothing has gone wrong. Okay?"

She waited. He took in the silent reproach.

"Let's go somewhere," she said, "just the pair of us. I'll get Ma to take Aisling for the day."

From tears to cool practicality, Fanning thought, all in a matter of a minute.

"We'll go down to Dwyer's Cottage," she added. "The long way, over Sally Gap. Rain or shine."

She was waiting for him to answer.

"No talk about school," she said. "I promise. Unless it's slagging the system. How about that?"

He was holding his breath, and he wasn't even aware of it until the floaties showed up in his field of vision.

"Earth to Dermot? Are you receiving me?"

He nodded, and concentrated on his breathing.

"I promise not to nag too," she said. He tried to smile, but couldn't. Her eyes were big and clear now, he saw, and full of that teasing tenderness.

"Great," he said. "That'd be great."

Her eyes flickered with concern.

"We'll make it, Dermot. We always have."

The turmoil was actually hurting his chest.

"I know it's tough," she whispered. "Working away, trying to get things done. Reinventing yourself, and having to depend on yourself so much."

He had to do something tonight: that was all there was to it. Waiting wouldn't help.

"You're a good father," she said. "And you're a good husband. You keep it all together. There's not many can do that. Very few, in actual fact."

An image flashed into Fanning's mind of reaching out and slapping Bríd across the face. The shock of it stole his thoughts of Cully, and the puddled footpath where the Polish man lay. He rubbed hard at his eyes. Bríd's face was inches from his when he stopped.

"Give it to me here," she whispered, and he felt her hands on his thighs, reaching.

"Jesus, Bríd," he muttered, and saw her face take on its usual set. She sat back on her heels, and looked sideways at the table. Then she sighed, and got slowly up.

"Sorry," he said. "That didn't come out right, I know."

"It's okay," she said. She was in teacher mode, he could tell.

She was hesitating.

"You know Liam and Susan, how they were, back last year," she said.

Liam was his friend, he thought of reminding her. Had she forgotten?

"Good ideas, we should go out with them some night. Yes."

"I meant Liam, what he did. The time he, you know?"

Fanning knew immediately. When he was ten, he had seen an accident between a car and a cyclist, on the Clontarf Road. He remembered knowing it was going to happen a few seconds before it did. There was something about the way things were going that made it inevitable, he believed.

"Bríd, don't start that again. For Christ's sake."

She was not going to let it go.

"I'm just saying think about it. Please. I mean, you yourself saw what it's done for Liam, for the whole family. You said so yourself."

"I was joking–"

She stood very still, and he could see the anger turn her face impassive.

"It saved their marriage," she said. "That's nothing to laugh at, in my opinion."

Fanning was up out of the chair in one move. She frowned at him. It surprised him that he did not feel rage, so much as an unbearable impatience.

"You think a frigging counselling session is going to help the situation, do you? Like sharing feelings, and a good cry or two? Screw that. Not going to happen."

"Then I'll go myself," she snapped. "I'm the one needs it, and that's plain to see, isn't it?"

"Whatever that means."

"I'm the one who's the shock absorber in this family, Dermot Fanning. Or haven't you noticed? The one who has to bite their tongue. Hold back. Be a saint pretty well, when I feel far from it."

"You're not biting any tongue now, are you!"

"Oh freedom of speech is only for the creative types, is it? 'Cause they're the ones make the rules? Oh now I get it – but it has taken me a while, hasn't it. I'm a slow learner, I suppose. I don't have that, what'll we say, flair."

"You switch over from being me mother to a... well I'm not going to say it, but all I'll say is it was faster than I ever saw—"

"Well I have to be your mother half the time!"

The words seemed to bounce off the walls for several moments, reverberating in Fanning's mind. The room seemed very quiet now. He took in the folded arms, the hurt look, and anger.

"You're shouting," he said. "Did you know that, Bríd?"

"Screw you, and this 'you're shouting' crap!"

"You want to wake up Aisling. You want her to hear you ranting."

"I don't care if she hears it or not! Why would I worry? She already knows. Children know, you know. They're not like adults that way."

"Adults," he said.

"That's right: adults. Adults hide things, or try to. Or they hide, themselves. They avoid. They run away from things. From people."

He glanced at her, and then looked down the short hall, half-expecting to see Aisling there. He wondered if the people next door were listening. Of course they were.

The furniture looked dull and even ugly now. Even Aisling's art on the walls looked faded. The whole place looked pathetic, comforting, futile.

"People do that, Dermot. They let things go on too long."

"You mean us, do you?"

"Of course not. I mean taking care of things, of themselves."

"Who needs a shrink when we've got one in the house right here."

"Stop that!"

It was a shriek. Fanning counted to three before he heard a tapping on the walls.

"Because change is too scary," said Bríd, her voice ragged now.

It had never been this bad, ever, Fanning thought.

He looked around the room, and then picked up the can of beer and his mobile. He took his time walking to the sink, and he poured the can down the drain. The smell coming up from the sink reminded him of when he was ten again, going down to the pub to buy stout for his grandfather in the village near Bansha.

"Go ahead to your counsellor dude," he murmured. "And do what he tells you, like a good little girl, and behave yourself."

The words hung in the air. He wondered where they had come from, and how they had tumbled out of his mouth with so little effort. He heard the bubbles from the spilled lager still breaking on the stainless steel below. He didn't turn around.

"You fucking asshole, Dermot Fanning," he heard her say in a quiet voice. Then the footsteps, and the pyjama bottoms rubbing together as she made her way back to the bedroom.

He knew he had to do something now. He switched his mobile back on and waited for the Unlock prompt. He couldn't go back into the bedroom for a change of clothes. His shoulder bag was by the door, though. He opened the washer/dryer, and pulled the clothes out onto the floor. It didn't matter now. There was a T-shirt, and the white dress shirt, and knickers. It took him a few turnovers of the clotheslines to find a second sock.

His fingers didn't seem to be working so well. He thumbed his way slowly to the Recent Calls. There it was, Murph's number. Though he had expected it, the shock surged through his chest and down his limbs. He switched off the mobile again.

He looked in his wallet, and checked that he had the two tenners and the twenty that he had yesterday. Movement in the window brought his eye over. It was himself, his face shadowed by the flaring light coming up from the table lamp. The row had actually happened. Aisling might be awake right now, about to cry out.

He had no plan. It was a few hours yet before the city would come to life proper, and he could figure out what to do. He would wait until he had a spot somewhere in the city centre, and then phone Cully. So things had gotten out of hand, and someone had been hurt.

Cully's two arms up in the air, like a dancer, stomping.

He clenched his eyes as tight as he could. Colours came and went quickly. He opened his eyes, and tiptoed to the door. There were gloves and a folded-up umbrella in the shoulder bag. Fanning paused, and considered the laptop again. It would be an impediment. He folded the shirt as best he could, and slid it into the bag, along with the phone.

The door squeaked, he remembered, but only after it was about halfway opened. He squeezed the handle hard and opened the door, working his way around it before it had swung too wide. He turned the key before he pulled the door behind him.

Chapter 44

THE HALOES AROUND THE STREET LAMPS seemed to pulsate as Fanning walked through the muggy air. He heard no traffic, but there was a low, background hum to everything. A cat walked back into a driveway, pulling its shadow with it under a car. The car windscreens reflected any light in filigree; the tiny on-off lights of their burglar alarm lights put him in mind of dragonflies. A dull shine from the roadway kept pace with Fanning, fading and then strengthening as he went from light to light. The electricity transformer at the end of the avenue buzzed as it always had, from the first time he had noticed it when they had moved in.

He began to listen to his own footsteps, and the shoulder strap rubbing against his jacket. Soon, he felt a rhythm set in. The nausea had disappeared, but in its place was a numbness. He should be panicking, he knew. It both satisfied him and unnerved him that he was not. Other than to get away from the flat, and to head into the city centre, he could still not come up with any plan. He thought of Bus Áras, and the long-distance buses that'd be lined up there soon, idling as though raring to be on their way out of Dublin and headed for every corner of Ireland.

Aisling was actually fascinated by trains. She had been thrilled as much as scared when they had watched the DART rumble by at Merrion Gates. She had twisted around in the

buggy, he remembered, reaching frantically for him when the
level-crossing gates descended and the tracks began to tick and
hum with the weight of the approaching train. And then she
had surprised him by pushing him away. She had caught sight of
the train, and was captivated. Was that peculiar for a girl? It was
just sexist to think like that.

He wondered if she were awake now. He saw her in Bríd's
arms, and Bríd rubbing her back to console her. Was Bríd thinking what he was thinking now: what the hell had happened?
How had this come upon them so suddenly? And did she too
wonder if this was it, and that there was no going back? What
was said was said, and it had been brewing for a while? She'd be
right to say that, Fanning knew, and now a week ago – a day ago
even – seemed to him an impossible distance.

A small van sped by on Bird Avenue. He looked at his
watch: a quarter to four. There'd be some light by six, he hoped.
He passed the shops, glancing through the shutters at their dim,
yellowed interiors. This was the newsagent's with all the crap
that attracted Aisling, the one place he avoided when he had her
with him. Three or four sessions of tears were enough: she'd
want things he knew he'd have to refuse her – the sweets, the
cheap, crappy toys and baubles pouring in from China.

He was by the window when he sensed more than saw a
small flicker on the glass behind him. When he looked across
the road, there was only the bus shelter in its dome of light. He
moved on, but the panic had set his heart racing. He thought
about legging it over through the campus at Belfield. Between
the buildings and the acres of playing fields and trees, here'd be
no end of places to lie low until it got bright. One of the cafete-
rias might open early, even, and the coffee there would have to
be pretty vile for him not to buy it. With a bit of daylight and a
dose of caffeine, things would be clearer. But there'd be a hell of
a lot of phoning to be done to even get a start on sorting out this
mess.

Fanning swore quietly: his mobile had been losing its
charge.

He took it out of his jacket pocket and switched it on;

stopped after a few more paces, waited for the battery indicator to show up. There was only a quarter left. His thumb found the power button again, but he hesitated. If Bríd were trying to reach him, if she had realized what she was doing to him. ... He keyed in the password, and pocketed the phone again. A taxi passed on its way out of town.

He crossed the Goatstown Road and set his mind on the half-hour or so it was going to take him to get into town. Soon his stride returned, and a jittery alertness that had replaced the panic took over. Everyone, every married couple, had gone through this and worse, he decided. It was just that they didn't talk about it. The dark night of the soul, he could call it.

He felt the familiar reflexes returning to him then, the urge to make something of this disaster. A short film – not like Bergman stuff, that godawful Cries and Whispers – about a crisis between a man and a woman, and a child involved. The ground has been shifting under this couple. Because of that comfortable cowardice that sets in a marriage, neither acknowledges it. They have invested too much in it, they've made too many deals, and compromises. They have hacked off too much of the people they would have been. Somewhere deep in their minds each knows the truth: that though to want to walk away from one another, it would only remind them – unbearably – of what they have lost. Fault Lines – there was the working title right there. And, he could work in the newcomer-to-Ireland angle, the catalyst that gets it started: she works in an office where a new employee is a refugee, and she meets the woman's husband. She falls for him. But it's nobody's fault, it's just the humdrum pain of being alive, and there are no answers. Unflinching, that would be the word.

Breen would see it, and would jump at it.

This was crazy. He was doing his escapist thing again, like he had done since he was a kid.

He sped up. He felt the soft slap of his shoulder bag against the small of his back, a reminder of his student days. There was a light on upstairs in one of the houses coming up to the traffic lights, and a shadow passed against the blinds.

Hearing a baby yowl, he slowed to listen, and then resumed his stride.

He had some excuse for giving that idiot a few kicks, that Polish guy. The way he had been carrying on, the language out of him! And then, pulling a knife on him? Anyone with a brain would have high-tailed it out of there of course: called the Guards right away. But that was cocaine, he supposed, the belief that you could do pretty well anything. The guy was probably stoned already. How else would he have had the nerve to walk up to a parked car and ask for dope?

Fanning skipped across the road and gained the footpath on the far side. Another taxi drifted by. He thought to the hours ahead, and the dawn that would slink in so unspectacularly under all this cloud. There was nothing much heroic about this, was there. He thought of the narrow road with the hedges that met the main road, the nearest the bus would get to the farm. Aisling thought the sheep were pets they kept forever there, just like the farm cats.

He almost missed the short ping of a message. The strange compulsion that he mocked in others exerted its hold on Fanning too however, and he quickly found his way to the short, misspelled message: outisde ur place call me NOW.

Chapter 45

MINOGUE'S DREAM ABOUT A PHONE RINGING was interrupted by Kathleen. In a sleepy voice that gave way to alarm, she said: "That's our phone."

He was wide awake in a moment, up on his elbow. Ash-grey morning light. It was just gone six. He saw the fright on Kathleen's face, and he began to calculate what time it was with Daithi Minogue, resident of California, USA. Ten o'clock, was that a dangerous time over there?

He did not consider clothes, but made his way hurriedly to the stairs, steeling himself. Freeways full of impatient people, short-tempered people with guns, drugs, earthquakes, serial killers and drifters, and people going postal, and wildfires.

The answering machine had taken over, but had just started the announcement.

"Ignore that thing," he said into the receiver. "It'll be over in a few seconds. Stay on the line. I'm listening."

The other person hadn't hung up.

"Daithi? Cathy? Just wait for it to finish. I'm here."

"Jaysus," came the voice in a low, exasperated growl after the tone. "Bad enough I have to listen to you, but two of you – and at the same time? Too much. Too much, I'm telling you."

"Tommy. What the hell is this? It's six o'clock in the morning. I hit the sack at three. I'm far from happy about this."

"Have you heard of mobile phones?"

"They keep you at work twenty-four hours a day. Those things?"

"I was going to leave a message."

"Make it a good one, will you. I have a message ready for you here. But I'll wait until I hear yours."

"Take a powder there, boss," said Malone. "You had three hours that I didn't have. Here's what I do have: Murph, you know about. If it's Murph, that is. The bit of toast they found in the boot of his car up in the Pine Forest. So you won't be taking to Murph."

"Got that. Move on."

"Listen to you. I'm doing your work for you here. I expect a cut of that paycheque of yours, you know."

"Settle for a wedding present – but only if you lift the ban, and let me go to the wedding."

"That's another matter. Here's the goods then: I got this message from a woman the name of Bríd O Connor. It was waiting on me when I checked in the office late. Trying to get in touch with me yesterday, but had a bit of an issue tracking me down."

"I don't know the name."

"Wife of one Dermot Fanning. Now you know her?"

"Your ticket to stardom, okay. But what's this about?"

"Listen, I'm telling you. You know the routine in our place, about routing calls and that. If we're out on a job, stuff just has to wait its turn. No interruptions. There's a gatekeeper, Alec Dowling, a Sergeant. He handles stuff, decides if we get a contact. Anyway. That's why I only picked this up late, I should say early this morning. She's in a state. Husband did a bunk, and she can't get ahold of him."

"Okay. Look, Tommy, I haven't done a jigsaw puzzle since I was a child."

"Did they have them then?"

"Proceed. I'll save my bad words for when I meet you in person."

"She and the hubby had a big row the other night. Out he walks, and she hasn't seen him since."

"Unusual?"

"Yep. According to her. Oh sure, the artsy-fartsy lifestyle and all, but she's a teacher. Says she to me, 'We're a very normal couple, I want you to know.'"

"The point, Tommy, the point. I'm on a low battery here, man."

"Point is he's missing, and she says he had been doing some odd things before he, um, took his leave of her."

"Odd. Isn't that what filmy, artisty people do?"

"She says he came home with a cut on his leg, and he was manky, and out of it."

"Like I said about that crowd?"

"Will you stop hopping the ball on me for a minute there? Fanning was doing research on gangs here in Dublin. Hanging out with them."

"Got fond of it maybe?"

"She says she thinks he was stoned the other night. That that's the only way she can account for him losing his rag with her. Mild-mannered, wouldn't hurt a fly, says she."

Minogue broke his gaze on the rings of the new cooker.

"Okay," he said. "I'm getting it, sorry. It's Murph he was hanging out with."

"Good. You saved me shouting at you there. Now I haven't got to the real story here. She left a message, said that Fanning had tried to call her that night – that morning actually. But she didn't answer the phone. She knew it was him, she said, and she was mad at him. He leaves a message on their machine, but it gets cut off. She doesn't know why, but she remembers him talking about getting a new mobile, or something about a battery. So she thinks the phone died on him."

"Okay. But why am I here?"

Malone went on undeterred.

"What she tells me in this message is that he, Fanning that is to say, mentioned something about a thing that happened down the quays. That he wants to talk to her about it, but he has to think it over some more."

"The quays. That's all?"

"'The back of the Custom House Quay' she says. 'Something happened,' says he. 'Something I'm not proud of.'"

"Did she save the message?"

"I don't know, do I. But by Jesus, I am sitting here outside her house – I know from her phone call that they have a little one, and she was crying – and I'm going to knock on her door right now and find out."

"Where is this?"

"According to my GPS," said Malone, grandly, "5.3 kilometres from your place. Off Bird Avenue."

Chapter 46

THE CAR WAS A NEWISH Honda Civic, with a Dublin registration. It was a sensible, reliable safe car, Fanning thought wistfully, a real teacher's car. Cully had been watching him in the mirror from the time he had turned the corner. There was no sign of his sidekick. There were no lights on at the house, and the Golf hadn't moved. Fanning looked up at the window of Aisling's room – a box-room it should be called.

His legs were still rubbery. He wondered if his fear showed on his face. He wished he had that Swiss Army knife again, the one that had gone missing on him after Christmas. But what use would that be? He wasn't thinking straight at all.

Cully looked tired and drawn, with dark patches under his eyes. This surprised Fanning, and for a moment he felt some weird sympathy.

Cully rolled down his window.

"You didn't knock, did you?" Fanning asked. "Right?"

Cully shook his head.

"Let's go somewhere to talk," Fanning said. "Bríd might be awake. I don't want her seeing us."

Cully seemed in no humour to dispute anything.

"Get in," he murmured. He parked by the shops. He and Fanning waited until a long articulated lorry went by, and the road was empty again.

"Hanging up on people is bad manners," said Cully.

"I switched it off actually."

Cully looked up from his hands.

"You know, you're getting cheekier and cheekier. Talking back? Snappy answer for everything?"

"Just stating a fact, that's all."

Neither man said anything for several moments. Fanning did his best to swallow without making any sound.

"So," he said then. "What are we going to do?"

Cully stopped tapping his fingers on the wheel.

"You're asking me?"

"We should do something."

"Like...?"

"Work something out."

"What are you talking about here, 'work something out'?"

"An agreement, I suppose."

"Go on."

"To go our separate ways, I suppose."

Cully threw back his head and laughed.

"That a script you're writing? 'To go our separate ways.'"

"We decide on what to do, and stick to it."

"Oh, bossy now."

"You asked me for a suggestion. I'm giving it. Remember, I don't have any experience in this sort of stuff."

Cully glanced over, but resumed his slow tapping on the wheel.

"There's a lot you don't know," he said. "I'll grant you that."

"Look, you take over then. I'm in no fit mind right now probably."

"You mean it? I take over?"

"I'm not thinking straight. I'm tired."

"Oh. You like the 'up' part, but you're not so keen on the afterwards bit."

"I don't know what you mean."

"That little bit of white powder you took a liking to?"

"I didn't. And it didn't work for me, didn't work much anyway."

"Tell that to the bloke back there, the one you put the boots to."

"Me? You mean yourself. It wasn't me did that."

"Really. That's what you're going to say to them?"

A chill grabbed at Fanning.

"I'm not telling anyone. Didn't I say that?"

Cully shook his head.

"Well don't get that idea," said Fanning quickly. "There's no way I'd want to tell anyone about that, ever."

Cully said nothing.

"Ever," Cully added.

"Never, ever, ever," Cully murmured.

"Why would I want to do something so stupid as that? Like tell them to throw me in jail or something?"

"They wouldn't throw you in jail. They'd probably give you a medal."

Fanning stared at him, but Cully kept his gaze on the empty roadway.

"Or put you on the payroll," said Cully. "Like Murph."

"I have no idea what you're talking about. No idea."

"Oh but you're the ideas man, and you have no idea? You make it up as you go along. You said so yourself."

"That's about scripts, and story ideas. It's not about real life. Come on."

Cully looked over with the beginnings of a smile. Fanning realized that there was a plaintive tone to what he had said.

"I'm never going to talk to anyone about it. To tell you the truth, I'm appalled–"

"Appalled, are you."

"Ashamed. Shocked. The things I said, I can't believe it was me saying them. Racist, even. I can't believe it."

"He pulled a knife on you. Did you notice?"

"Of course I damned well noticed. I have a cut here on my leg, here I'll show it to you."

"No. Don't."

"I wouldn't tell anyone. Not even my wife."

"Well I know that."

"What do you mean? Why did you say that, like that...?"

"Well she told me where to go, didn't she."

"You spoke with her?"

"Can't say as I blame her either, can I."

"You talked to my wife. When? Tonight, I mean this morning."

Cully sighed and looked at his watch.

"Half an hour ago."

"Why did you speak to her?"

"Actually I didn't speak to her. She did the talking. Yelling, I should say–"

"What did you say to her?"

"...telling me I was the cause of this thing, you showing up all dirty, with that cut and so forth. To stay away from her husband. And so on."

"What did you tell her?"

"Nowt. Nothing. Nada. Couldn't get a word in, could I."

"You had no call to be phoning her, especially that hour."

"Whoa there," said Cully and he rubbed at his eyes. "This isn't Falluja or somewhere. It's not a crime to talk to a woman, is it?"

"Falluja? What's that about? It's four in the morning, I just told you, so why are you phoning my wife at four in the morning?"

"Which question do you want answered first?"

"You can't do that, it's not part of our arrangement. Our deal."

"Oh. We have a deal, do we? An arrangement?"

"You know what I mean. Leave her out of it. We settle this ourselves."

Cully seemed to consider it. Then he resumed tapping his fingers on the wheel.

"This is important," he said, "isn't it."

"Damned right it is."

"Well you shouldn't turn off your mobile then, should you."

"It died. Ran out of juice."

"Should I believe you?"

"I'll show you."

"No, no. Let's just move on. What were you saying?"

"Okay. Whatever turns up out of this thing, you know, that guy. ... We do nothing. Right?"

"Forget it ever happened?"

"Something like that."

"He takes his licks, and he – what do they say in the television things... 'he moves on with his life...'?"

Fanning felt the fear returning. Cully didn't do irony. He must know what he'd done to the man.

Cully let his hands drop from the wheel.

"You give me your word?" he asked.

"Absolutely, I do."

"Not a word, even to your missus."

"Not a word. As if she'd let me talk to her now anyway."

Cully's half-smile returned and then dissolved.

"You shouldn't be so hard on her there. You and her wouldn't be fighting if neither of you didn't care, would you."

"It's hard to remember that when you're in the middle of it."

Cully nodded, and yawned.

"So we're okay then," he said. "You and me."

"I think so, yes."

"Even after you read the papers, or whatever you writer people do every day."

"Right."

"Because, sooner or later, you'll come across something, and you'll wonder," Cully said. "Sooner, rather than later."

"There are a lot of those kinds of things in Dublin," said Fanning. "What happened there, with that guy. It probably won't make the papers."

"Well there'll be something," said Cully. "I'm pretty sure about that. Just want you think about that."

"I gave you my word."

"They have the car by now," said Cully. "Doesn't take much, obviously."

"The car. What car is that?"

"Murph's car."

"A lot of joyrides end up like that. I wouldn't worry."

"Leave it to Murph to worry, right?"

"I suppose."

"Well he's not worried."

"That's good," said Fanning. "I suppose?"

"It'll take them a couple of days though," said Cully. "On account of the petrol."

"Well I could phone him and tell him if you like," said Fanning.

"That's a good one. I like that. Nothing wrong with a sense of humour, is there. Sign of that creativity thing, isn't it. That's what they say."

They looked at a lone cyclist on a racing bike heading out toward the Scalp and Wicklow.

"Wants to get out before the rush hour," Cully murmured.

Fanning felt the weight begin to ease.

"So...?"

Cully looked over.

"I'll give you a lift then," he said. "You were making a run for it, weren't you?"

Fanning froze, but saw that Cully was putting him on.

"From the missus," he added.

"I was going to go into town, see if someplace was open, I could get a cup of something. Think things over – with her, I mean."

Cully started the engine.

"Okay," he said.

Fanning allowed himself a bit more room to stretch.

"Don't forget your belt there," said Cully. "Don't want a fine now."

He pulled out slowly onto the road.

"I've been meaning to ask you," said Fanning.

"Falluja," said Cully. "Let me guess. That's another story. But not now."

"No, I wasn't thinking that. More like, why you're inter-

ested in this stuff. What I'm doing, I mean. Scriptwriting is not
that exciting, you know."

"Oh I don't know about that. But to tell you the truth, I've
always been interested in films. I mean who hasn't."

He looked over at Fanning.

"Larger than life, and all that? Better than the real world,
and that's no joke. Right?"

Fanning was not in a mood to disagree.

"Money, of course. There's money in making films, isn't
there?"

"Not enough," said Fanning. "From my end anyway."

Cully had dropped something down between his seat and
the door. He stopped fumbling for it to change into third gear.

"Never quite realized the impact of a camera," said Cully,
and began fumbling again. "But, like I mentioned there, you see
things."

"What place is that?"

"Falluja. Actually not in the place itself."

"I thought it was an expression of yours, you know, I've
got a pain in the fallujia, or something? Like a cockney expression or something?"

"Cockney?"

Fanning saw that he had stopped fumbling.

"Just a guess," he said to Cully. "It's not important."

Cully looked over at him. His face had taken on the blank
expression that Fanning remembered from the dog fight.

"I'm Irish," said Cully. "People don't seem to think that's
proper, or something."

"No offence," said Fanning. "Really. Look, at this stage,
I'm just babbling, I'm so knackered. Just stupidity. I've been
saying stupid things all night. But I'm going to fix that. Starting
with Bríd. She's right, you know."

"They're always right," said Cully, absent-mindedly, and
returned his attention to the road. "Aren't they."

Fanning closed his eyes to yawn. Opening them, he saw
lights in the mirror, a car turning onto the road behind them.
An early shift, he thought; nurse maybe, bakery or the like.

Fanning had noticed it too.

"Much more practical," said Cully, glancing in the rearview mirror again. "Women. Wives."

Something was working its way into Fanning's mind now, and it suddenly loomed.

"They say that men are the facts people, but it's not true," Cully said. "They make things up more than the women, I tell you."

He turned in his seat to look at Fanning.

"They lie more too."

"Wait," Fanning said loudly, the terror already engulfing him.

He saw Cully's hand come up, and the flash that came at the same time as the explosion. The belt cut hard at his neck. There was another flash but he did not hear any sound this time.

Chapter 47

"JAAAY–ZZUS," said Malone, and pocketed his mobile. Minogue hadn't even tried to pretend he wasn't eavesdropping.

"They had a row, you say," Minogue said.

"They did all right."

"Over what he was doing, she said?"

"Or not doing," replied Malone. "But, man, she's upset now, I'll tell you."

Minogue spotted the Toyota coming around the bend at speed.

"Her mother, I think," said Malone. "I got her to phone them."

"Well it's father driving, I think."

Malone climbed slowly out of his car. Minogue half-listened to the hurried conversation with Bríd O Connor's parents. The mother had been crying. The father looked angry and frantic, drilling a stare into Malone as though to extract something from him.

Malone was patient for a man who had been up all night. Minogue heard him say something about all avenues. He hardly means the roads around here.

"Hard to know what to tell them," Malone muttered as he sat in again.

"You phoned him in officially, did you? Missing Persons?"

Malone nodded.

"She's beating herself up over it," he said. "Over why she waited. On account she was so mad at him. All in the past now, I can tell you."

Both detectives looked over at the house when they heard a shriek. Bríd O Connor clung tight to her mother. The door closed awkwardly.

"What do you want to do," Malone said.

Minogue shook his head. He thought of Matthews, and Twomey, the two girls. Proper little bitches, he remembered the desk Sergeant muttering yesterday evening.

"Climb back into that poofy new car of yours, and go back to bed?"

Minogue didn't bother replying.

"I actually don't want to think about this anymore," said Malone. "That woman in there. And the kid. Bad enough that I'm so wired already."

He shook his head slowly from side to side.

"I'd better do something," Minogue said. "Those two fellas are up in court at eleven, looking for bail. I have to get my stapler going on the bits and bobs of paper for that."

"What about the two young ones you were telling me about, the ones you decided to release last night?"

"Going to charge them," said Minogue. "No sexism here."

Malone sat up and frowned, and he gave Minogue a hard look.

"Why are you going around wrestling paper for this stuff? Aren't you case officer for this? Get some of your butties there to do the court appearance and all the rest of it."

"So I can do what instead?"

Malone waited a few moments.

"So you can see how we do real police work instead. Tracking down these two fellas that Fanning told her about."

Minogue thought about it.

"Nothing's going to happen without a bit of something to eat," he said. "A cup of something."

Malone knew his way around Rathmines. In spite of the

traffic, he and Minogue were seated in The Red Shoes, their fry ordered and coffee before them on the table. Malone had to go outside to take a call from his boss. He came back in just as the plates were put down on the table. He stood by the table, eyeing the scrambled egg and the two shiny sausages as though they held a secret for him.

"Sit down, you're making me nervous."

"We have a bit more from our friends in the quare place," he said quietly. "The Big Smoke."

London, he meant, Minogue realized.

"And it's beginning to look like we're dealing with the same people. Head-cases, I should be saying."

Minogue forked some of the egg onto a piece of toast, but much of it fell off when he lifted it.

Malone went on in a thoughtful tone.

"What he told the missus. 'English, probably, gangsters.'"

"Not all English people are gangsters."

"Didn't want her worrying, maybe," said Malone.

"A bit cryptic all the same."

"Whatever that means."

"Mysterious. Like he didn't make it clear."

Malone sighed and launched into his breakfast. His phone went again.

"Where?" he asked, and he sat up straight. He looked at Minogue.

"Two of them? How deep is it there?"

He listened, chewing on the sausage that he had picked up with his fingers.

"The sooner, the better," he said. "If they're asking my opinion."

"Two cars," Malone said after he had hung up. "In the water there, up by the Port of Dublin. Not far from the quays."

He gave Minogue a knowing look.

"They're starting on it in a while," Malone added.

Minogue was feeling full now. He concentrated on the coffee.

"Any more on the two men?" he asked Malone.

"One they think is a fella, Kilcullen. Great name for a soldier boy, I suppose."

"Irish, though?"

"Half and half. The mother is. The father, well he shagged off. Mother reared him herself."

"No family here?"

"No. There's a brother of hers, his uncle. But they're not on speaking terms. Plus, he's in the nick. Fancy that."

"But this Kilcullen, he's not a career criminal, according to them?"

"Huh," said Malone. "That's what they're telling us. But they'd hardly be admitting they get their recruits in jails. I mean, this isn't any oul regiment we're talking about."

"The Queen Mother's crowd, I seem to remember," said Minogue.

"I never thought there'd be Irish fellas in the British Army, I have to tell you. Shows how little I know."

"Well he wasn't in it that long, was he. Just long enough."

"That's a fact," said Malone, in a leaden tone. "Teach them how to use weapons, let them loose over there in Iraq. Big surprise they go haywire, isn't it. Well, some of them anyway."

Minogue tried to remember the name of the officer who had given that speech before the fighting started over there. An Irish name, maybe even born here somewhere. Some contro versy about him afterwards?

"Nothing on the second fella yet?"

"No. Could be anyone. They've contacted the regiment, and they're going through their records. Their list of nicknames, for all I know."

"West Ham. I don't follow the football."

"They're nothing much anymore. But the fans are another matter. 'The Hammers.' They have a name for going over the top."

Minogue looked down at the cooling smears of grease on his plate. There would definitely need to be more coffee. He switched on his mobile.

Kevin Wall was at his desk already. He gave no sign he was

at all annoyed about Minogue's rebuff last night. Minogue asked if he would do court, for Matthews and Twomey. No problem, was Wall's cheerful response, and Minogue believed there was no sarcasm involved. Mossie Duggan would prepare the charges for the two girls.

Minogue closed the phone and stifled a belch. He thought of phoning that Danute Juraksaitis woman from the consulate. And tell her what, exactly? That they had two iijits in custody, and two more being charged, but that they weren't willing to charge any of them with the death of Tadeusz Klos? Well he should phone the Assistant Comm then, and let him give the news to Barry, and whoever else was in the spin cycle on this.

Malone seemed to be mulling something over in his mind, eating distractedly and with little enthusiasm. Minogue decided that he would return to the house, take a shower, and pretend he could get a day's work done. He wondered how he'd last the afternoon. He remembered Malone's take on it – you're the case officer now, you say what goes – and wondered if he dared going down that road a little.

Malone pushed the plate away.

"They could be long gone," he said. "Nobody has said that out loud yet."

The second cup of coffee was not up to the mark. Minogue didn't want to argue about it with a waitress whose English was poor, who looked harried, and almost in tears.

"I'll take care of it," said Malone.

Malone rolled his eyes when his phone went off. Minogue watched the waitress try to juggle a tray while getting a bill to two brittle-looking fashion plates in their forties. To have to smile in the job was the worst of it, he remembered Iseult saying several times.

Malone hunched lower over the table, his finger is in his ear now.

"Right this very minute?" Minogue heard him say, and then, "Are you sure about this? Really? Well you better not be spoofing me."

He took his hand from his head and looked at Minogue.

"Are you ready for this? There's something after happening up at a place in Dorset Street, one of those hotels. There was shooting. Not five minutes ago."

He took away his hand, and turned aside from Minogue again.

"Who says?" he demanded. A frown settled on his forehead while he listened. Then he said a yeah and hung up.

"Are you coming?" he asked Minogue.

"Not my parish, Tommy, but thanks."

"I'm serious. Come on. Seeing is believing, they say."

"I'm not a fan of shootings. Go on yourself."

"You'll miss your chance. One of them is dead."

"One of who?"

"They think the West Ham one is the one is dead. The other fella is touch and go. If it is them, like."

Chapter 49

NO LESS THAN FIVE DETECTIVES, two openly displaying submachine guns, were marauding on both sides of the tape. The
uniforms milled about, many of them edgy with the show
of guns. One of the detectives yelled at Malone as he pulled up by
a squad car. As though to placate him, two uniformed Guards
skipped over.

"Move on there, you can't park here. Move on."

Minogue fumbled for his wallet. Malone was ahead of him.

There were brown faces in the small crowd gathering
across the street. What little traffic was abroad this hour of the
day had been stopped, and Minogue saw more tape going up
across the whole street by the traffic lights farther on.

"Oh look who shows when the time is right," said the
detective who had yelled. There was little sign of humour on
his face.

"Tell your sister me answer is still no," said Malone.
Minogue watched the detective's reaction.

There were plainclothes in the hallway, and more standing
on the stairway. The place smelled damp, and Minogue took an
instant dislike to the feel of the carpet, and the tacky mirrors,
the thoughts of how many lonely nights people had spent here.

"Too many heroes in the one place," said Malone to a red-
faced detective who seemed to be waiting on some answer from
his phone. The detective reached over to try to swat him on the

way by. Minogue had to wait until he stepped back.

He held up his card, and followed Malone upstairs. There was a burnt smell here on the stairs now. Malone took the stairs two at a time. Looking up, the man standing in a doorway looked familiar to Minogue but he could not fix on a name. Did nobody secure crime scenes anymore, he wondered. Well, now. Best he keep that question to himself until later.

The man said something to Malone, and shook hands, and he looked down at Minogue. He made his way over to the top of the stairs.

"Top of the morning to you," he said to Minogue, and extended a hand. "Brian McNamara, Serious Crimes. I'm the ringmaster here."

McNamara's face put Minogue in mind of an Easter Island statue. In his late thirties, Minogue guessed, an expert in controlling his impatience. For no clear reason, he wondered if McNamara didn't have a kind of a divorced look to him.

"There's people would pay money for such a mighty Clare name like that," he said to him.

McNamara had a neutral nod for Minogue, but no remarks that could be even mildly congenial.

"You have an interest in these fellas here, I was told."

"I think so," was all Minogue could think to say. "I hope so."

McNamara craned his neck to see what he could between the banisters leading to the upper floors. More armed detectives appeared, and then Minogue could see two fully kitted ERUs two floors up, the chins of their balaclavas pulled down under the helmet straps. They seemed to be taking their time.

"Every floor," said one of them.

The smell of cordite was stronger, but there was the beginnings of some kind of aftershave too. McNamara turned back to him.

"They took the live one," he said. "The other one can wait."

He seemed to have divined Minogue's unspoken question. "Mightn't make it," he added. "The way he left here."

An ambulance attendant came out of the room, carrying a bag. He was looking for someone. The someone seemed to be McNamara. He said something to McNamara about dressings. McNamara said they didn't want them.

McNamara filled his cheeks with a breath, held it for several seconds, and then let it out.

"It won't be textbook," he said in a voice little above a murmur. "Will it, now."

Minogue was tempted to let McNamara in on how many sites he had worked on, sites that had been trampled on too. But McNamara's remark took on its intended meaning before he said so, however. Collusion was being called for, if he and Malone were going to get anywhere. He wondered what favour Malone had called in to be allowed into the site before the Technicals showed up and began their painstaking prowls, like ghosts or Hallowe'en figures in their suits.

"If it was textbook forensics we did every time, we'd be in the ha'penny place," he said to McNamara.

McNamara looked at the splintered edge of the door. He seemed to weigh Minogue's words.

"A quick once-over then," he said, and reached into his jacket, "while the going is good. Very quick. But if the Scenes lads arrive, you're out that door in a flash. Nod's as good as a wink?"

"In a flash," said Minogue.

McNamara handed Minogue one, then another glove. Malone was already pulling on his own.

"What's that smell," Malone said. "That perfumey one. Do you smell it?"

"Maybe it's yourself you're smelling," said McNamara.

"If it was I'd be passed out on the floor. No, there's some pricey kind of smell. Men's stuff."

McNamara gave him the eye. Malone shrugged.

Minogue looked ahead before each footstep, stopping each time. The blood on the carpet was almost black already, and gave off no sheen.

"How's this for witnesses, Brian?"

"Zero. There's no night staff."

"Access, I wonder?"

"Child's play from the outside. Have a look at the delivery door out the back, on your way out. That'll tell you plenty."

Minogue looked back at the splintered doorframe, and the door, with its smashed edge sticking out like feathers.

"Classy joint," Malone said.

"They might have a nice honeymoon suite," McNamara murmured. "Tell herself, why don't you."

"That's it," said Malone. "You're off the guest list."

"Not that I was ever on it."

"Sonya only felt sorry for you," said Malone. "Thought she might be able to get you fixed up, you know."

McNamara had no smile, but in his voice Minogue now heard the dry restraint of the Claremen he had grown up around.

"If you mean getting me a date with some wall-eyed cousin from Hong Kong, yous were doing me no favours. It's Sonya or nobody for me. She's too good for the likes of you."

"You'll answer for that one in the ring. Mister Tough Guy."

Ah, Minogue realized, a cohort from the Garda Boxing Club.

McNamara took a plastic bag from his pocket, and held it in his palm, arranging its contents.

"UK driver's licence. Justin Anthony Kilcullen, the one carted to hospital."

Minogue squinted at the photo, the expected neutral expression. Dependably nondescript.

"Looks real enough," he said.

"Maybe so," said McNamara, quietly. "But he's a goner now. I don't know why they didn't put one in his brain, but."

McNamara let other cards slide into view.

"The fella on the floor is going by the name of Gary David Parker. Is. Was."

There was a spray of darkening blood on the wall by the window where the man's body lay. Most of the lines down ended after a few inches in the maroon beads that Minogue expected. Blood had pooled in his armpit, and freckles of it were under his jaw. A pistol lay eighteen inches from the man's knee.

"Is that gun taken care of," he asked.

"It is," said McNamara. "It was a full clip that came out. He didn't get one off at all. The other fella's was still under his pillow, if you can believe it."

"That fast," said Malone. "There had to be a few of them."

Minogue eyed the awkwardly turned leg and the one outstretched arm that ended in a bloody pulp where the palm used to be. Had he reached out to grab the gun?

The boxer shorts were saturated with blood, and his singlet had been pulled up in his last movements.

"'The Hammers'?" Minogue said. "What is that?"

"Don't you know that?" asked Malone. "I was going like the hammers in me new French car? Like the hammers of hell...?"

"Hardly, now."

"Do you have a thing called a telly vision in your house out there in wherever?" Malone asked. "And when you're finished milking the cows or whatever yous people do out there on the south side, do you look at the front of the telly vision, the glassy-looking bit? There does be a thing called soccer on there, a lot. A crap team called West Ham."

"Okay, I get it. I would have gotten it by myself eventually."

Malone gave him a skeptical look.

The smell of latex from the gloves was beginning to irritate Minogue's nostrils.

"Savages for fans," Malone added. "Looks like they have one less now."

"Any particular items you're looking for?" McNamara asked.

"Effects belonging to some people," Minogue said. "Any sign at all."

"Are you sure about that."

McNamara spoke with no hint of exasperation that

Minogue could detect. Still, he made sure of his footing, and his balance, and he half-turned to McNamara.

"I'm not being contrary," said Minogue. "I actually have no idea."

"Fair enough," said McNamara. "Now did Tommy here tell you anything? These pair aren't, weren't, shoplifter league."

McNamara pulled at his gloves over his knuckles and looked over at Malone.

"Tommy. Your outfit got the same bill of goods as we did, right?"

"What kind of a question is that," said Malone. "Of course we did. Even faster than yous."

"On your arse, you did," said McNamara. "You chancer."

He turned back to Minogue.

"Was he like this when you worked with him?"

"Worse. Infinitely."

"Doubt that," said McNamara. "So you know then that these two were serious business. Ex-army, dog-rough and all. They'd be getting well paid for their trip here. Well, whatever the going rate for hit men is, fancy ones. So housebreaking wouldn't be high on the agenda."

"It could be they were up to no other stuff," said Minogue. "Their own sidelines, as it were."

He returned to his study of the floor, a location that he had learned over many years was where gravity placed items that would be useful in his investigations. He eyed the folded pieces of silver paper by the half-empty bottle of vodka, and began to make his way over. No traces of powders that he could see.

Malone had made his way foot-over-foot to the toilet, where squatted, opened a pen-knife and used it to lever up the edge of a towel. He stood slowly, and leaned out to look into the shower stall. Minogue heard him lifting the lid on the toilet tank, and replacing it.

"So," said McNamara. "There was some expertise on show here, planning and carrying this out. That much we know."

Minogue continued his inventory of what he could see

from where he had stopped. Half-bottles of white rum, empty; a takeaway coffee cup, salt and vinegar crisps, a remote for the television. No cigarettes. Bits of paper – receipts they looked like – on top of the chest of drawers, next to coins. Jeans in a ball by the leg of a bed, T-shirt, one sock. Malone was looking behind the television now, balanced on one leg like a ballerina.

"A setup from the start, even," said McNamara. "What do you think there, Tommy? Are the Egans that underhanded?"

Malone merely snorted.

"Those bags," said Minogue, looking at the soft-sided bags by the door to the toilet again. "Could we…?"

McNamara sucked in his breath noisily, and shook his head.

"We're pushing it already. I have to close it down. Count to twenty and that's it, you're out of here."

There was a mobile phone by the leg of the bed.

"Can you get them to go through that phone first, Mister Sir?"

"Shag off, Tommy. The Bureau has its own thing. Like you didn't know."

"But you'll hassle them on my behalf, right?"

"I don't want a falling-out with them, do I, by mentioning your name."

"Why are you such a bollocks?"

"What else did your mother say to you?"

"The bags, come on. Nobody'll know. We're on the same team here, I think?"

McNamara didn't bother to answer this time. He gave Minogue a diversionary look, a signal of his forbearance. He must owe Malone a lot, Minogue thought, to go through this.

"Come on, lads," he said then. "I plan to keep me job. Let's go."

Minogue let his gaze travel along the carpet by the edge of the bed. The shadow there diverted around something. He got down carefully on his hunkers.

The notebook was one he had seen in a window in Wicklow Street, and almost admired it. Moleskin…? Hardly. He found his pen in his jacket pocket, and got its chewed end around the back of the notebook, and he gently drew on it. It took several stops-and-starts as it pivoted around the pen.

Malone had spotted what he was doing. McNamara too was watching.

The pen skipped on Minogue's first try of the cover, but he lodged it under the cover and pushed in when the cover began to lift.

"Well," said Malone. It occurred to Minogue that Malone had already decided on matters here.

"In my world," said McNamara, "hit men don't carry little notebooks. How about you two."

Minogue said nothing. The writing was often bunched together in small boxes, with the writing going in several directions, and there were drawings everywhere. Some of it was illegible, but still its author had underlined several parts. There were numbered lists, exclamation marks.

Minogue heard Malone stoop down beside him.

"That says Donneycarney," said Malone. "And there's Finglas. Ronanstown. Crumlin – and I know that place, by God, Captain's Road."

Minogue made out other words: innit, dunnit/dannit, roight, London?

"Well who owns it?" McNamara said.

Almost reluctantly, Minogue lifted his pen and let the pages fall back, stopping only when the inside of the front cover began to lift.

"'Reward offered,'" said Malone. "And there's a phone number."

He stood, and took out his mobile.

"That's Fanning's number," he said after a few moments. "His mobile."

"'These notes have no...'" McNamara said. "What's that?"

"'...monetary value,'" said Minogue, "'....but are of value to the owner. If found, please call...'"

"Where's his name then?"

Minogue looked up.

"Wanted to stay anonymous there," said McNamara. "So's anyone wouldn't think they could, you know, get a big whack of money out of him."

"Is he famous?" Minogue asked.

He received no answer. He poked his way back to random pages. There was a drawing of a street that seemed to be running with rain, with street lamps reflecting off the puddles.

"He's a good drawer," said Malone.

Minogue could now make out most of the words in a box that ran to the outer corner of the page. T falls for M's girl – she agrees M is psycho, wants out – M enters pub coked wants to get T.

"Plots," he said. "Ideas."

"That's not bad at all," said McNamara. "That drawing. Real Dublin type of scene there. Very not bad."

There were footsteps outside. McNamara stood up quickly, and strode to the door, where he intercepted a detective.

"Already?" Minogue heard him say. "Christ. Okay, go down and get them started, I suppose."

Minogue let go of the pen as he finished reading something about a shipment from the docks. The notebook seemed to fall in on itself.

"Time to split there," said McNamara. "You were never here, unless you hear me say you were, okay?"

"Thanks," said Minogue.

"Tommy?" asked McNamara.

"I'm a ghost then," said Malone. "See, I'm invisible. Him too."

"You're a ghost who owes me a big one then," McNamara said.

In the hall, Minogue peeled off the gloves with some difficulty. He pocketed them, and turned around in time to see the first of the Technical Bureau appear in the lobby.

"Done in for his notebook," Malone said. "That'd be a first."

"What did his wife say again, about down the quays, and the Polish man?"

"He said he couldn't tell her then and there, but if anything happened, to look in his notebooks."

"Notebooks? Not, notebook, singular?"

Malone shrugged, and began a long, slow yawn that seemed to cause him pain.

Chapter 50

KILMARTIN WAS FIDGETY, and he had a cowed, expectant look to him. The new clothes he had taken so much trouble to pick out just didn't work. The cut of the jacket, the pattern on the shirt, looked way too full of effort, and the shoes looked downright uncomfortable. He cleared his throat, and turned up toward the restaurant with Minogue.

"A stone cold killer they call them," he said. "The FBI."

Minogue had almost forgotten the course that Kilmartin had taken years ago in Virginia.

"They profile them, they dissect them – in a manner of speaking now – and they do a thousand interviews with them, but they're still a what you call it, a..."

"Enigma?"

"That's the word. Puzzle, we'll call it."

I heard they gave him four transfusions no less. Four. All those donations, just to keep him alive. And for what?"

The old Kilmartin was revving up, all right, Minogue noted.

"As for the other fella, well he wasn't as quick on his feet as he should have been, was he."

With eyes almost clenched shut, Minogue had taken a fleeting glance at the other man lying awkwardly between a chair and the table. The dark mass above his scalp was blood and something else Minogue didn't want to know about.

Kilmartin seemed to be walking slower on purpose. They came to Wicklow Street. The Chang's restaurant was within sight now. The deal was that Kathleen would bring Maura Kilmartin earlier.

"A shame about that poor divil though," Kilmartin said. "That Fanning fella that got mixed up with them. Never knew what hit him, I suppose."

Minogue was a little tempted to ask Kilmartin if he felt a bit sorry for the Murphy character, the one awaiting positive identification from the car.

"And then to just dump him, and the car of course – on top of a car he dumped earlier on. What kind of a man can do that, I say to myself. What kind of a human being. ... But why should I think that. God knows, we met enough of them over the years. Didn't we?"

Kilmartin had been talking non-stop since they had parked.

"And another thing," Kilmartin went on. "There's no way around this: it dehumanizes people. The army, I'm talking about. Any army. Put a man in a uniform, give him a gun, let him think he's better than the people he's looking at, and that's what you're going to get – oh, and keep him ignorant, of course, so he's sure of himself and doesn't be thinking too hard about what he's ordered to do."

Minogue did not want to dip his toes in that one.

"But who's responsible in the final analysis, I say."

"For what?"

"What that fella did, or those fellas did. Out there in Iraq, I'm saying. By the way, don't take this the wrong way, but your listening skills are not up to scratch."

Minogue gave him the eye.

"It's true," said Kilmartin. "You know it. Sorry to say, but."

Straight from the Self-Help section, Minogue wanted to retort. He began to make up titles for what Kilmartin had read, or consulted. Spousal Bliss Through Listening to Your Life Partner. Ears of Love. Tantric Listening.

"He should have turned in that other fella," Kilmartin said. "When he found he was dealing over there. 'West Ham' or whatever his name was."

"Parker. Gary Parker."

"No sense of right and wrong when you're in the army. And sure the world knows, you can't deal with a junkie. Not one inch can you trust one. But there he is, covering up for this fella over there in Iraq. That's not how to do things, is it."

"Hardly."

"The story I heard," Kilmartin said, his voice dropping. "I heard a rumour they were, em, gay."

"Em gay, or just gay?"

"There you go again. But did you hear that too?"

"I heard nothing."

"I thought gay fellas were supposed to be, you know?"

"So did I."

"I'm just saying that it's not the stereotype."

Minogue said nothing.

"So here's this fella, a corporal, and he's trying to shield the other fella. And then see what happens for his trouble – your man goes off the deep end one night, and that family there in Iraq winds up dead. Isn't that it? Tell me that's an accident now."

"Not in the record," said Minogue, the urge to mischief returning. He thought of Kathleen's injunction, and the promise she had extracted from him, to try to avoid rows tonight.

"Ah stop it, would you? The army brass got them out of there so fast, whitewashed the proceedings. Like they do everywhere, the British. Oh yes. Some people may forget, but the Irish don't."

"Don't forget what?"

"Are you going to tell me it's okay for some freelance hit men, trained and primed over in England, to be let loose here in Ireland?"

"Our gangsters hired them."

"And what does that prove?"

Minogue looked up and down Wicklow Street. It was still

one of his favourite steets of all in the city. The curve as it slid down toward Grafton Street beckoned him always, its trove of side streets like adventures of their own.

Kilmartin made a sour laugh then.

"Wonder who gave those other fellas the tip-off," he said. "I say it was Egan himself. The kind of thing the bastard would do. Save him having to pay them."

Minogue couldn't disagree. Malone had told him that the word was West Ham had gotten out of hand at an after-hours in Finglas, and blathered about what they did, and what they could do. He waited until Kilmartin took a pause.

"James. James?"

"What. What are you Jamesing me for?"

Minogue looked at his friend, took in the fierce eyebrow slant, the blinking.

"James. You're just blathering. It's too much. Okay?"

Kilmartin made to say something but held back. A look of desperation crossed his face for a moment, but was quickly gone.

"Easy for you," he said, quietly.

Minogue did not think so. Nor did he think he could ever tell his friend how much he had tried to dissuade Kathleen from doing this.

"Look," said Kilmartin, nudging his arm. "It's like I told Herlighy. That old goat, sure he's gone deaf, I'm sure. 'I want what I had,' I says to him when he asks me where I wanted to be when this was over. 'Well you won't have that,' he says. 'Nobody can have that.' Something about the same river twice?"

"Not as deaf as you think then, is he. Or as dumb."

"Whisht, will you. Says he, things are not just going to happen – what's the word he used? To ensue. Big word. You have to write the script, practise your role and then produce the film, says he. Or the play – I was going to say 'drama' but by Jesus, I don't want to use that word, do I."

Minogue nodded. The thought of the Szechuan noodles had cheered him a little.

"It's just a dinner," he said to Kilmartin.

"For you it is. For me, it's auditioning."

"Just keep it light, that's the trick."

"No mention of why she tried to kill herself then, I suppose."

Minogue stared at him. Too far gone? Maybe he had misjudged Kilmartin entirely. Maybe the silent bitterness ran deeper and longer than even Kilmartin himself knew.

"Well you got that out of your system at least," he said.

Kilmartin sighed and shuffled his coat.

"I don't know why I said that."

"You're nervous. But I'm going to kick you under the table if I think that class of a comment is on its way out of your mouth again."

Kilmartin examined the cement edges of the footpath. He let out a deep breath. He looked up then, his face easing a little.

"Did you say a kick, or a tap under the table?"

"A kick I said. I'll root you out of it, so I will."

Kilmartin nodded as though to agree.

"And you're certain she doesn't know?" he asked.

"Not unless you told her."

Almost against his wishes, a small smile of satisfaction crept over Kilmartin's features. He looked across at the restaurant window.

"I don't much like Chinese food," he said.

"Ask them for potatoes and cabbage instead, why don't you."

"I don't want any trouble from you. Kathleen I like, but you, you're work."

"You behave yourself in there. You Mayo bullock."

"Listen to you. A mucker from Clare. I'll have to show you how to use a knife and fork again, I suppose."